Plan: Chaos Rising

Plan: Chaos Rising

Book Two of The Joshua Chronicles

Steven Neil Moore

For my Lord and Savior, Jesus Christ
Without whom none of this would be possible.

For Sebastian,
The bravest boy I have ever known.

"So you take the world I love as recompense for your imagined slights? No, the Earth is under my protection."
- *Thor: The Avengers*

Contents

Prologue

The war.

It remains ... never ending.

A continuing conflict that has spanned ages before corporeal beings entered the mix. Mankind plods along about their mediocre lives, oblivious to the true reality around them; one where angels and demons *do* exist. Where a higher power is the driving force behind all subsistence. Where a notion that something other than their plane of being, is perceived by many, but very real for a select few. Where there is more to life than just a soy latte and a mortgage.

For millennia, humans have been guided in their thoughts and actions without so much as an inkling as to who is doing this and why. The untruths that have been ingrained in their history since time immemorial, started with but a single thought that turned into a massive rebellion.

Some are unwitting pawns in a much larger game where the stakes are higher than their minds can comprehend. While most live in this cloud of deception, there is a minority that understands the true nature of their permanence. Some fight for the forces of good, while others manipulate for the side of evil.

Those that work against the Light are called Familiars; servants to the enemy for a purpose founded on lies. The revolution against the Light continues today as it always has. Through fallacies, greed, duplicity, and lost hope, the world revolves around one's self and their achievements rather than serving a higher purpose of the greater good, the intended design for the collective, or simply just doing what is right.

Then there are those that fight against the Darkness. They are called Associates. Their understanding of their part in the ongoing campaign is simple: put the greater good ahead of themselves and keep the bad guys from winning. Easier said than done.

For centuries, light and darkness have been battling; angel against demon, human against human. Both sides gaining momentum for their cause, and losing the advantage time over time ... never moving forward, always in contrast.

Every so often, though, there is a champion. Someone chosen to provide an edge in the continual quest for dominion. Many have been selected over the years. They have filled key positions of influence within man's realm. Unlike the agents for evil, though, they have been given the greatest gift bestowed upon man ... the power of choice. The free will to determine their own destinies can be a blessing, as well as a burden. It is a virtue that some take for granted and most do not even recognize. Sometimes, greatness is thrust upon those whose potential to lead and enable change has been foretold since the beginning.

Occasionally, one will rise above the rest. For those elite few, the decisions they make come with a heavy price. The responsibility of tipping the balance in favor of the Light is never without cost. For many to be saved, some may be sacrificed. Not fair to the chosen one, but that's how life goes, sometimes it is just not fair.

If one were to keep count, the unfairness piled on by life would exceed the many chapters in the book of Joshua Arden. His endurance that started at a very young age, could be the subject matter for the Greek tragedies of ancient times, or various country music artists and their sad, tearful ballads.

His ability to overcome these obstacles has been orchestrated through a series of events influenced by both the Light and the Darkness. Of recent, his potential to fulfill his destiny has glimmered with a blinding brilliance for the power of good, much to the dismay of those that serve the enemy. Accepting this responsibility came of his own free will. The resources to execute this change, however, comes from a much greater power.

Of the many vehicles of change throughout time, the most influential in today's modern world is Jonah International. A global multi-conglomerate that does one thing first, help mankind. Humanity sees Jonah as a beacon of salvation that comes in many forms: financial lender, charitable donator, a disaster-relief provider, and so on. The illusion of their presence throughout the business world gives countenance to their façade in the marketplace. The mist that surrounds mankind's perception is intentional, as that is, and has been, the new contract birthed from the ultimate sacrifice. For only to those needed to maintain the balance and enforce the rules is this semblance waved.

The rest of mankind meanders about their religious affiliations, either born of new discovery, or as a family legacy passed from generation to generation. The mind can only accept so much before the erosion of the fine line between their comfort zone and sanity gives way.

Joshua has come to realize that the knowledge of the true reality can be of tremendous benefit for the power of good. It can also be a lightning rod for change against various inequality spread throughout the world by agents of the enemy.

Now, angels and humans work together to fight against a common adversary. The opposition's plots and conquest for power is far from over. In their minds, the battles are just beginning.

Part 4: The Theft

Taipei 101

The full moon was very clear tonight. The temperature a bit nippy for this time of year. Not that unusual, and mostly unremarkable to those that did not pay attention. A beautiful night for a moonlit stroll, or a romantic dinner along one of the numerous dining establishments in the Xinyi District. These were completely unfavorable conditions for a crime.

It was getting later in the evening, but still early enough that patrons, shoppers, and lovers were out and about. Commercial businesses started winding down. A waiter brought a check to a couple sitting at a table outside of a café. A few patrons were exiting a bookstore and computer retailer, while shift workers at a Starbucks were performing the final closing duties to their latte-producing machines. Traffic was minimal: a few taxis but mostly personal vehicles. There were no maintenance or delivery activities scheduled for tonight; therefore, no service vehicles were in the vicinity. This would cause a slight alteration in the plan. Not a big deal though ... this was not the first time Nigel and Victoria had worked under these conditions.

At this time of night, the police patrolling Sōngshòu and Shīfù Road were periodic with their rounds. This would make using the secondary exit a matter of timing. If the plan worked it would not be needed anyway, but a backup route was a standard protocol.

The plan, was a robbery.

An integral part of said plan was the Tsingtao Microplex Corporation. It was a moderate building of no significance. Five unremarkable floors that held the brain trust behind the latest innovation of a synthetic polymer that could withstand extreme temperatures, and reportedly had the tensile strength of maraging steel. Whether that was true or not was irrelevant; what was important is because of that unique discovery, Tsingtao garnered a private investment which allowed them to move into a building down the street from the monstrous Taipei 101; the actual target for tonight's after-hours activity.

The security inside the big building was a combination of technology and foot patrol. There were 14 night shift guards to cover the 101 floors; some specific to building security itself, while others were privately contracted by the building's tenants. Each guard had a specific routine that they regularly followed. It took some patience to amass their movements and plot a precise course to the target, so again, timing would be everything.

"Can you hear me?" Nigel said, testing his ear piece.

"Loud and clear," Victoria responded.

The two thieves had been doing reconnaissance for six weeks. They knew every facet of their target within Taipei 101, knew the routes of each guard on the floor, and the security protocols of the surveillance system, or so they thought.

The hardest part of planning this job was the cleaning staff. They were very unreliable in their movements; all over the building at any given time during the evening shift. If the target had been on the lower floors, it wouldn't have been as big of a consideration. In fact, the entire plan would have been easier.

Neither Nigel nor Victoria liked plotting around unknown variables. Of all the possible schedules, predictable and unpredictable patterns, and moving parts, none of their scenarios were optimal. The final decision for approach came down to using a path of least resistance. The money for this job was too good to pass up, so they would deal with the inconveniences.

They both had some debate during the exploration about who would take point and who would do operations. Her argument was that she was better at bypassing locks and security systems. The job would move more quickly if she went in. He, on the other hand, had done most the foot work and casing posed as an English financier. He knew the layout better. "You would stick out like a bloody thicket on a manicured lawn," he said. It was hard to argue that point with her bright-red hair and pale skin. Still, she thought she would be better on the inside.

During the recon, Nigel determined that it would be too difficult to enter 101 directly, as building passageways were guarded and monitored at all times. It didn't help that all persons were accounted for entering and exiting. It would be noticed if an Englishman went in but did not come out. A direct path into Taipei 101 seemed impossible. So, Victoria came up with an alternate entry using the utility tunnels beneath the city. Nigel had entered Tsingtao's building two hours before and stowed away in a cleaning cupboard waiting for her signal. Once given, he moved down to the sub levels.

An alarm went off on her wrist watch as she continued to view the video feeds from the traffic cameras, retail stores, restaurants, and the building lobby of 101. She turned to a separate terminal and began typing in commands. This brought up an array of the building's schematics, to include elevator controls and internal security surveillance feeds.

"The shift changes in 30 minutes. Are you in position?" she said.

"Working on the last weld to the access plate," he said. "Almost there."

Then the last solder on the edge gave way. He checked his map of the utility tunnel once more before he stowed it, and the torch, in the duffel and entered.

* * *

As the bus started to slow, Kevin Huang carefully marked his place, then put the macroeconomics textbook next to his backpack. He stretched his arms and yawned before reaching for his uniform jacket. After making sure that his tie and coat were in order, he gathered his things and stood on bus 669 as it came to a complete stop. Checking his watch as he stepped off, he thought if he hurried, he could get a cup of coffee before his shift. The bus was running about 5 to 7 minutes late tonight. His favorite shop might still be open. He hoped so; he needed the caffeine.

Kevin managed to make it just in time to get a Vente black just before they closed the gates. He took a sip and closed his eyes in anticipation of the resurgence the coffee would bring. As he walked toward the building, he hoped that his assignment was on the lower floors tonight. He needed to prepare for a probability exam tomorrow. Lower floors would make the break room more accessible for studying. He greeted a fellow security guard as they entered Taipei 101.

* * *

The tunnel was surprisingly clean. In truth, Nigel didn't know what to expect when he opened the access plate. He had visions of decay and waste from lack of maintenance and years of no use. A silly notion really, as that defeated the purpose, but such thoughts crossed his mind when he planned jobs. Backups to backups, redundant contingency plans, every conceivable scenario he could dream up; he was always thinking, never one to be unprepared for any situation.

Once Nigel was inside, he carefully noted his position and the direction in which he needed to go. He did not want to have to think about the trail back once he had the prize. Time would be of the essence. He had a natural ability for spatial relations to begin with. That, plus the map he paid a city engineer handsomely for, guaranteed a quick exit in his mind.

* * *

Kevin and his companion strolled into the break room with some of the other night shift guards. His demeanor immediately changed to match those of his colleagues; very serious with a sense of purpose and honor to his duties. Most of the pride in doing a good job came from his father's lineage, and wanting to continue the legacy of rectitude within the Huang family dynasty. The rest was ingrained with the responsibility of ensuring the safety of the building and its tenants. He shared that last one with his fellow workers. Sure, he felt like the rest of the people in 101 looked down upon his lowly position; ignored him as he passed them on the way out to their cars, but that was okay, at least with him. He knew that he wouldn't be working this job forever. He had a better plan for his life. It was a struggle currently with his school load and a full-time job, but he chalked it up to paying his dues forward to reap the rewards later.

He waited his turn to check the duty station roster for his assigned levels.

* * *

"Are you in position yet?" Victoria asked.

"Almost there, love," replied Nigel.

"That's what you said seven minutes ago. We are running out of time. The shifts are beginning to switch," she said bit snippy.

"Would you stop your bloody nagging and relax? We'll be just fine. I built in some extra time just in case."

He half-grinned as he worked on the sub-panel access door to Taipei 101. Victoria always got herself into a nit if things were slightly off schedule. Sometimes, there was a difference of opinion on whose timetable was more accurate. Regardless, she was always nervous during the execution.

Whether remaining time existed or not, Nigel worked with a quickness. He popped the panel and connected the relays to a high-tech switch box, then clipped the feed for the alarm. Once he was satisfied that it was bypassed, he punched in the access code for the door release. Some extra money for the engineer, but a pittance compared to what this job was paying.

He did a quick inventory of the supplies he would need, placed them inside a smaller, more manageable pack, then stowed all remaining items in his duffel. The black tactical coveralls and flak vest felt a bit tight; probably because of the business suit underneath. It might be hard to maneuver should there be any physical confrontations, but he would deal with that if, or when, the time came.

He looked at his watch. "Time?"

"18 minutes," she replied.

"I'm heading to the first security door, be ready."

"I've been ready," she quipped.

There was no response as he entered the sub level stairwell.

* * *

Disappointment is a common feeling of dissatisfaction with many different levels. It has a fine line that could tip the bearer one way or another, and set the tone of the mood for some time to come. Kevin's assignment was in the mids tonight. He remained stoic and determined to carry out his appointment. He found a free locker for his bag then checked the duty log for his floors in preparation to relieve his second shift counterpart.

* * *

Nigel made it to the first door on the main level in around 90 seconds.

"I've got you," she said looking at the cameras of the building's security monitoring system.

"Loop?" came the reply.

"Active. I can see you; they cannot," she said through a smile.

He smiled as well. He knew that Victoria was good at what she did. Both possessed unique talents that complemented the other. They had been working together for so long, sometimes speaking was not even necessary. Thought patterns synchronized in so many ways, it borderlined on creepy. There had been times on past jobs where the situation became precarious and the other could sense something was wrong. A connection like that was rare. To have a relationship on an almost empathic level, made what they did in some ways, easier. It was not necessary for him to ask, but he constantly did, and she unfailingly answered. Backups to backups.

"Right then, on your signal," he said.

"Standby," she said.

Thirty to 40 seconds passed as she watched the lobby monitors. Her fingers slid over the keys and punched in the access sequence for the maintenance door to facilities. The estimation was 3 to 5 seconds of exposure to any foot traffic between the doors. The last person rounded the South-east corner. "Go."

The door access from the stairwell changed from red to green then clicked a millisecond before he pulled it open. With the grace of a cat burglar and a ninja, he sprinted as fast as he could to the maintenance door. His trust in Victoria was absolute; there was no need to look around. She pressed the Enter key completing the sequence on the doorway as his hand touched the knob.

He silently closed the door behind him then listened for any traffic on the other side. When he was satisfied that he had made it, he noticed the camera in the upper corner and smiled. She smiled back.

* * *

He was flipping through the charts when his friend, Chen, sauntered over. "Hi Kevin, what is your duty station tonight?"

As he continued perusing the checkpoint status, he said, "Mid-levels, 50 through 57." He tried not to show his true feelings regarding the assignment. The job must come first. He would manage to get in the necessary studying when he could.

"I am in the high levels tonight. Maybe we can synchronize our breaks," his friend said.

"Umm, that sounds great, but I have a big test tomorrow that I need to study for. I should use my time wisely during the shift."

"Oh," said Chen with some sadness. The disappointment was not born of not being able to spend time with Kevin, but more so from his lack of doing anything different with his own life. He secretly admired Kevin's tenacity and willpower to continue pursuit of a degree. "That's okay, I understand." He half-smiled and walked away.

Kevin shook his head. He could see the disappointment in Chen's face and knew he just wanted to spend time with him. They had both been friends long before working together at Taipei 101. Lately, their friendship became distant due to Kevin's schedule. His schoolwork was important to him and what it meant for his future and family, but it he could not let it come between his friendships and other responsibilities. "Chen, wait! Maybe we can work something out and have our lunch together."

His friend turned around and smiled. Kevin grinned. "What does your floor shift schedule look like?" he asked.

Chen's smile stretched impossibly wider as he walked back over.

* * *

Nigel pulled out a penlight and quickly began to search the large facilities' room for markings. Even with the low-level after hours' illumination, the light was too small to see anything of significance, but might aid him with identification. As with the tunnels; everything was written in Mandarin.

"Per the schematics, it should be located 55 feet back on the Southeast wall, just behind the steam-works," she said into his ear.

He passed through and behind the piping scanning labels and signs he mostly didn't understand, then found it; a single door separating the rooms.

He read the label. It all looked like gibberish to him; it could have been hieroglyphics for all he knew. He quickly tried the door, but was not easily rewarded. Extracting a set of lock-picks he began to work—

He heard a faint beep and the click of the main entrance.

"Bloody hell!" she said.

He began to grind his teeth. "You are supposed to be watching the door."

"I was spooling up the elevator controls and preparing the bypass. I only took my eyes off the monitor for a—"

"Not now, love," he said, concentrating on the activity at hand.

* * *

The security guard pulled out his flashlight and slowly scanned the maintenance room.

"Anything?" came the voice over his radio.

"I don't see anything from here. Are you sure you registered a signal?" said the guard.

"B-126N, Main Tower entry popped about 60 seconds ago. No security card access, so it registered as unauthorized."

He continued shining his flashlight around the room. Sensing his hesitation, the voice said, "You'd better walk the room."

He was so close to getting off shift. He rolled his eyes thinking that an incident report on what was most likely a technical malfunction would need to be filed. That would be an additional 15 minutes of his life that he would not get back. He turned towards the door and flipped the breakers. The main lights shuttered and blinked to life. "Walking the room," he said in a monotone voice.

The guard moved about the machinery and equipment looking over, around, and under. He looped back up to the right and started for the steam-works. He shook his head thinking that this was a waste of time. Picking up his pace, he headed back for the hallway entrance. He slowed to a stop and then turned towards his right. He bent slightly and noticed an access door just behind the pipes. Shaking his head again, he said something that could be loosely translated into a Chinese curse word, and headed for the door. When he reached it, he stared at it with a deadpan expression. Putting his hand on the knob, he gave it a slight twist.

Nothing.

He pulled out his key ring and started searching for the right one to open it. As he inserted the key and began to twist, a feeling pulled him from his curiosity. He no longer needed to check behind the door. Not wanting to be there to begin with, he didn't question this newfound urge to withdraw.

He removed his key, turned off his flashlight, and headed for the main hallway. "It's all clear," he said into the radio, as he turned off the lights and exited.

* * *

The few minutes seemed like a lifetime. Victoria dare not try to contact him until she could confirm his situation. Upon seeing the guard exit facilities without Nigel in tow, she began to breathe. Albeit somewhat shallow, but breathe nonetheless. "Nigel, are you all right?" She said in almost a whisper.

A few seconds passed; more than she cared to be comfortable with. "Nigel!" She said with a bit more intensity.

A few more seconds. "They could be listening you know," came the reply.

"What!?"

"You broke the first rule. We're not supposed to use names," he said.

"Bugger all! You had me scared to death!" she said.

"I'm fine—"

"Answer me the next time I call you. You're in a dead zone now. I don't have visual. I thought I lost audio too," she said with worry in her tone.

"The poor chap was almost on me. Had he come through the door, it would have been tragic." He removed the Osprey suppressor from his Walther p22, and place them both in the quick release of his flak vest.

"Okay… Now, where were we?" he said with a casualness that was indicative of his sociopathic nature.

Anger replaced her worry. "This is not over."

"I wouldn't have it any other way, love," he said as he started assessing the different units.

Of all the places that he had been within the building over the course of reconnaissance, his cover and visitor access did not allow him near any of the maintenance rooms. Although the blueprints they procured were greatly detailed, environmental usage and containment units were very secretive. Taipei 101 was one of the Eco-friendliest modern structures in Taiwan. Everything was state-of-the-art and provided clean energy. Far be it from them to be left out of the Global Green Initiative.

Her fingers danced over the keyboard as she looked at the building schematics. "The elevator banks are directly behind the South wall. How many ventilation units do you see?"

Looking up and across the ceiling, he said, "Six; number one and number four have ducts directly above."

As he was speaking, Victoria was pulling up the elevator shaft designs. She executed a trace program that produced a direct line to the unit that would be needed. "Number four."

Nigel quickly scaled the unit in question and found the best position, then began cutting an opening with a small micro laser.

"The duct should curve two meters passed the ceiling. Another four and you should see the vent for the elevator shaft," she said as she continued to type. Victoria turned to the monitor with the elevator controls.

He breached the inside of the duct and began his climb. As his head crested the first turn, he saw his target just as Victoria said. "I see it," he said with the penlight in his mouth.

"You'll have to hurry. We'll need to time this perfectly with the rotation," she said.

He smiled. Always the worrier, she was. He started the horizontal crawl towards the shaft. "I'll be in position within a matter of minutes."

* * *

Kevin punched his card into the time clock. He was now on shift. No time to fret over what could have been; his duty assignment was clear.

Trin Yann was sitting at a side table shuffling papers rather roughly.

"You okay?" asked Kevin.

He cut his eyes up to Kevin. "Hey, yeah, I suppose..."

Kevin dipped his chin a bit to look Trin in the eyes. "It doesn't seem like it."

Frustration was apparent. With a very audible and exaggerated sigh, he said, "I've got to fill out this paperwork based on a stupid call to the maintenance room." He went on to explain to Kevin what happened.

"Well, that's the procedure when any of the alarms go off," said Kevin.

"Maybe so, but there was nothing there," said Trin still resentful.

Kevin knew that it didn't matter what he said, Trin was going to be in a bad mood regardless. "Look, would you like some help filling this out?"

Trin's eyes sparkled. "Really? You would be willing to help me?"

Kevin slightly smiled and nodded his head, "Sure."

"That would be great! I—" the security chief for Kevin's shift strolled up to Trin while flipping through papers on a clipboard.

"Hello, sir," said Kevin respectfully.

The security chief's eyes briefly cut to Kevin with a slight nod then he turned to Trin. "Mr. Yann, you missed a badging at your last security check point on 62."

Trin's eyes widened. "What! You're kidding?"

The security chief continued to look at the clipboard and shook his head slightly. "The computer printout for the ending shift statistics says otherwise."

If Trin was depressed before, his mood deepened even more now. First the maintenance room, now this? How could he have missed that? He had been anticipating his date with Tina for a week. Tonight, was going to be the night. He wanted to take a shower before meeting her at the theater. His focus was absent because all he could think about was getting home. It was quite possible that he was lost in thought as he completed his last round. He sat there for a few seconds with silent hope that the chief would overlook it and just walk away. He did not budge and looked at Trin expectantly.

"Sir, can you just this once–"

The chief was already shaking his head. "I need the checkpoint reconciled before I can sign off on the next shift's rotation."

Kevin stood there in silent observation. He felt bad for Trin. He knew he was in a hurry to get home. Although he was not jazzed, he had an idea.

Kevin held out his hand.

Trin looked at him with confusion. Kevin grinned with a slightly inpatient and exaggerated look. "I have things to do. I'm not going to wait forever. Give me your card."

Trin snapped with the realization. "No way! You would do this for me?"

"Finish your paperwork. By the time you are done, I will be back, and I will turn it in for you."

They both looked to the security chief for approval. He flipped the papers back down flat on his clipboard and said, "I don't care who does it; I just want it done," then turned and walked away.

Trin handed Kevin his security card. "Man, I owe you–"

"Yeah, yeah, …" said Kevin taking the card and turning towards the door.

* * *

The rivets from the inside of the air duct were harder than he anticipated. It was clear that no one, or thing was meant to come from the inside out. Nigel never would have admitted this, but he was running out of time. He was about to pull out his micro laser when he heard a familiar chirp.

"Elevator seven will be in position in twenty-seconds," she said.

No time for niceties. He quickly cut through the bolts as the elevator came to a stop just below the air duct.

With a little panic in her voice, she said, "Someone is waiting to enter number four. Are you ready?"

He shifted his body and started pounding the metal grate with his feet. After the fourth kick, it gave way and flew down with a crash to the top of the lift. He pulled himself out feet first and landed gracefully on the top. "In position," he said, trying to control his breath.

* * *

As the doors to the lift opened, Kevin heard an enormous clatter. It startled him like a gunshot. As he cowered down, looking inside and upward, he reflexively reached for his radio. "Dispatch, there appears to be something wrong with elevator H7. Can you verify any maintenance activity?"

A few seconds passed, "Negative. H7 is not in the cycle this month. Is something wrong?" came the response.

Kevin slowly entered and looked all around.

* * *

"Bloody hell! Was that you that made all that racket? What are you trying to do? Get us caught, and you captured or killed?" said Victoria all excited.

Oh, shut up, woman! Thought Nigel. *I can't hear a thing with all that yapping.*

He remained still, not moving an inch. He listened intently for any movement or sound below. He could barely make out a lone voice, but couldn't discern the words.

There!

He thought he heard a radio too.

Blast it!

If he had gotten to the bloody grate sooner, maybe two minutes, he would've been able to handle his entrance with a bit more finesse. If they shut this lift down, they are pinched. If that nagging siren were on top of her job, she would be able to tell him what was going on. He was becoming very uncomfortable with all the "If" thinking. Nigel's backups to backups did not include another way to the target.

* * *

The elevator doors closed as Kevin stood and looked around. The lift went nowhere as no commands were entered. He slowly walked around each side of the box, his hand grazing different points along the walls. He knew absolutely nothing about mechanical or structural engineering, but the perception of touch gave him more of a mental reassurance than anything else. After finishing his physical examination, he stood there for a moment and continued to look around. The indecision of riding this elevator versus waiting for another was his internal argument for the moment.

* * *

As if on an empathic queue, Victoria's hands began to, once again, dance across the keyboard. She was ensuring that she still had command override of the elevator controls, and could hack into the lift's video surveillance. "It looks like there's one guard. He's speaking into his radio, and moving about like a blind man feeling the walls."

Nigel reached up and clicked his microphone twice indicating the message was received.

As silence overtook them, they both thought similar things. If this bloke doesn't take this elevator, and has already reported a malfunction, it would look very suspect for it to move on its own. Had the guard not entered the picture at all, she could have simply sent the elevator up under the guise of being summoned by someone wanting to descend. Their best option was for the guard to take *this* elevator, and hope that his floor selection was close to the one they needed. They both knew full well that the elevators were monitored by security. Too many movements after hours would rouse suspicion.

* * *

By all indications, it looked like this elevator was okay. Kevin had no way of truly knowing if there was a problem or not. It was just a sound that he heard; he did not see anything. The elevator shafts are long, and funnel sound as well. It may not have been the lift at all; it could have come from somewhere else. Dispatch had nothing on record. If he hadn't been there at that precise moment, he would never have known the difference. "No, everything is fine. I thought I heard a sound, but it turned out to be nothing," he said into his radio.

"Copy that," squawked the voice at the other end.

Kevin reached for the keypad, punched floor 62, and swiped Trin's security badge. As he made that decision, he was completely unaware of another existence on top, or for that matter, *in* the elevator.

2

He Doesn't Belong

After the guard pushed the button, Victoria realized with a quickness, that elevator H7 bypassed the lower floors and serviced floors 50 through 65. "Listen to me! You need to hold on tight. This is an express! It will shoot straight up at an accelerated speed!"

No sooner had she finished her last sentence when the box took off and slammed him into the top; his penlight popping out of his mouth and clattering down the shaft. It turned out that Nigel didn't have to hold on at all as the pressure from the ascent pushed him down.

"Are you all right?" she asked.

"Fine," he managed to squeeze out with the velocity. The wind of the acceleration made it sound like he had his head hanging out of a car while traveling down the highway. "What floor is this going to?" He tried to say without screaming over the noise.

"Sixty-two. I'm going to slow the ascent so that you can get off at 56," she said as she started typing.

"No! Let it go. I don't want to raise any more questions or give them cause to shut this down," he shouted.

* * *

Kevin's head shot towards the ceiling. He thought that he heard a voice. First, the loud sound, and rattle as the elevator took off, and now a voice? The first two made sense if something were truly malfunctioning; this last one, not so much. Maybe he was imagining things. He had been studying an awful lot in preparation for these midterms. He was also suffering from lack of sleep; though this would be the first time since he took on this workload for his imagination to overwhelm his senses. Still, he should report this to dispatch and have this elevator placed on the maintenance rotation. At the very least, they could shut it off for his shift and label it as a safety concern.

The elevator slowed its ascent as it reached 62. The box announced its arrival in a lovely female voice. Kevin always enjoyed her voice. It was soothing to his ears and gave pause to his hurried life. He exited the elevator and made his way to Trin's missed check point.

* * *

Nigel started to feel nauseous from all the movement. It was funny how the perception of being outside the box could make him feel physically ill. He had ridden these lifts over the course of the last two months and never felt like this. Inside versus out; it would probably shake anyone's equilibrium.

Once he heard the elevator doors close, he clicked on his microphone. "How are things looking, love?"

She pulled up the security video feed for the lobby of his current floor. "The guard is entering the North-west corridor. As soon as he is out of range, I will lower you to 56."

"Okay," he said checking his supplies making sure nothing else was lost during his high-speed trip. He needed that penlight in this dark shaft. Nothing could be done about that now. He would just have to make do with the ambient lighting available.

"Standby, beginning to lower in three, two, one."

Nigel braced himself as the box began to descend.

* * *

Kevin walked nonchalantly towards his objective. His mind preoccupied with statistical figures and facts of probability. His awareness to his surroundings was mechanical in nature as many the floors' layouts were similar. He was a guard there for 18 months. He knew the building like the back of his hand. As numbers drifted in and out of his head, his senses were not in tune spiritually, and that was by design. He had no way of knowing that he was not alone. Suddenly, he remembered the elevator. He reached for his radio. "Dispatch, this is guard 264. Request deactivation of elevator H7. Unidentified sounds coming from the unit and the shaft. It could pose a safety issue."

"Copy that. Will deactivate H7 and notify facilities."

As Kevin replaced his radio, the presence that moved with him, lowered its hand from his shoulder.

* * *

The box began to slow its approach to 56. Victoria was monitoring all floor activity as well as the position of the guards. Everything still looked good.

She turned her attention to the objective of the job.

On a separate screen, she pulled up the security schematics for tenant 56D, Advanced IntelliCorp. Ventilation and crawlspaces were not an option as they were small. The laser grids with refracting mirrors was also a large deterrent; there were too many undetermined angles for an effective reroute. If a single beam were broken, it would automatically trigger internal defenses and initiate a lockdown. This company spared no expenses in their security. They even adopted the FIPS-201 standards developed by the Americans. This was most definitely a tough egg to crack. Probably, the main reason for the hefty 1.4 million payout. Luckily, biometrics was not something that this company invested in. Badging and access keys could pretty much get them anywhere, but that was not Victoria's major concern.

All video surveillance was tied to the security system itself. On a normal day of operation, facial recognition patterns were weighed against traffic in each room. As the system monitored access and entry, it also tracked movement based on proximity to security points while running video in parallel. The high-definition cameras could follow a single individual throughout the office floor. There was literally no place within Advanced IntelliCorp to hide. The system could be both admired and loathed at the same time.

While Nigel had been casing the building for the last six weeks, she had been busy preparing for this moment. There was no way they would be able to bypass, disable, or trick the system since all employees were tagged like cattle with RFID.

Instead, she simply chose to create a virtual employee.

She researched the hiring procedures of Advanced IntelliCorp. Finding the right candidate by searching and cross referencing census records, certificates of birth, and educational institutions, produced three qualified applicants. Background credentials could easily be forged. Once she identified the prime employee, she began the process of integrating him into the company.

As with all businesses lately, part of the standards to be GGI certified was to be predominantly paperless. This worked perfectly into her process. Victoria called the candidate masquerading as a representative from Advanced IntelliCorp regarding his interest in an open position within the company. She electronically arranged for an interview with actual company employees. After the technical phone screens and the customary in person, the company decided he was not a viable candidate. Again, this was perfect. As he was already in their system, she just changed his status to offer accepted, and created an artificial position. He was processed through Human Resources like any other employee. The company did all the work for her by creating security and access privileges.

It was only a matter of hiring a grifter to pose as the employee to gain complete access, key codes, and most importantly, the security badge. He got his money; she received her access. No questions asked.

This still did not address the issue of the video surveillance integration. She had an idea though.

* * *

The descent was not as rapid as there was only a difference of six floors, but his stomach still turned a bit from the motion. He was already popping the levers on the emergency hatch in the ceiling before it came to a complete stop. "The feed in the lift ready?"

"The stills are in place. You're invisible," she said.

He slipped through the ceiling into the box. As he landed, he heard the finishing wail of that annoying female announcement that he had arrived. He hated that voice. The endurance of casing this building over the last several weeks stretched his nerves to the limits every time he heard her caterwauling. He would not miss that in the slightest.

He dropped his pack and quickly began to shed his coveralls.

"I can keep the doors closed and hold the lift for 30 seconds before it registers with security," said Victoria rapidly.

"Plenty of time," said Nigel as he smoothed out his suit and adjusted his tie. He admired himself in the polished chrome finish of the doors. He bent down and rolled his coveralls into a tight spiral, then began to extract the supplies he needed, when the elevator started moving.

"What did you do?" He asked as he braced himself slightly. "Why am I moving?" A bit more sharply.

She was furiously typing and checking the controls. "I don't know!" She said in almost a shout. Then she saw it.

"Bloody security has recalled the lift. It's heading for the main lobby!"

"Well, stop it!" Nigel shouted. He glanced up at the floor numbers decreasing in a rapid succession. Once it hit 50, they were replaced with a double XX.

As her fingers manipulated the keys, the screens on the monitor specific to elevator controls shifted back and forth between each lift's position and a command prompt.

"Victoria," he said in a sing-song voice.

Now who's breaking protocol, she thought. "Almost there."

In the split second he had heard her reply; the elevator began to slow.

He let out a breath, "Cutting it kind of close, aren't you?"

It was her turn to be snarky. "That's not me, *love*. You have reached the main lobby."

In a panic, he grabbed his gear and maneuvered himself into the forward corner of the box. Nigel didn't want be in front of the doors when they opened. A stupid ruse as the entire box had chrome plating and acted as one gigantic three-dimensional mirror. There wasn't enough time for him to get through the top of the hatch; he had to do something. He wanted to call out to her to see if there was someone in the lobby waiting, wanted to know what she was doing, wanted to know how she could let something like this happen and didn't see it coming. So much for all those backups to backups.

The box came to a complete stop, and the doors did not open.

He waited a few more seconds thinking that it may take some time but they would eventually part. Then the box started moving upward again.

She did it.

He waited for her to say something, but her voice never came. As the double XX was replaced with 50 and moving higher, he said, "Victoria, I—"

"You're welcome. Get ready and act normal. From this point on you need to behave like you belong there."

She was very short and direct in her response, and it did not go unnoticed. He thought for a second and wondered why. What could she possibly be irritated about? He was the one that was trapped inside the box going in the wrong direction. He was about to throw the old girl a bone and simply apologize for being snappy, until she cut him off.

Being self-absorbed and master of his own universe, it didn't occur to him that it might not have been *what* he said, but rather *how* he said it. For supposedly being the dominant gender, sometimes men were not that smart; especially when it came to understanding women.

A glimmer of this inkling flashed through his mind but for a brief second as he bundled his belongings and pushed them through the lift's top hatch. Nigel supposed that he had treated her somewhat poorly, which would account for the abruptness. After this job, he would try to find a way to make it up to her. Maybe he could—

He shook his head as if something were on it. What was he doing? He needed to concentrate upon the task at hand. Distracting thoughts such as this would only complicate the flow of movement both physically and mentally. She will get over it. Her feelings were just going to have to wait.

The caterwauling returned, then the doors parted.

* * *

Trin finished up the last of his paperwork with a big smile. Even with mishaps and distractions, he would still have time to grab a quick shower before his date. The security chief eyed him warily as he handed over his report.

"Hey chief, something is going on with H7," said a voice behind him.

"What's the problem?" He said disinterested as he reviewed Trin's work.

"We got a broadcast that it was malfunctioning so we brought it back down to the main for lock down."

"And ... So?" Responded the chief still not caring.

"And it went back up on its own," responded the operator.

The chief was still reviewing Trin's report. "Where is it at now?"

"Fifty-six."

Still looking through the report. "Where did it come from?"

The operator swiveled his chair to face him. "Fifty-six."

The chief looked up. He turned and gave the operator a curious look.

The shift security chief was a no-nonsense guy. He rarely interacted with his subordinates, and it was well-known that he had absolutely no sense of humor. He was by the book on all departmental regulations; and took this job extremely seriously. All those who worked with him were not afraid, but understood the chain of command and held a certain amount of respect for the position, not necessarily the man who occupied it. Conversely, he knew that it would be in their best interest to ensure his happiness, so joking about *anything* was simply not a smart play.

He eyed Trin for a half a second with a mental, nonverbal look indicating he should stay put, then walked over to the operator's duty station. "Show me," was his only command.

The operator immediately swiveled to queue up the video surveillance of H7. The feed clearly displayed a vacant elevator. The command must be coming from the floor itself. "Let me see 56 common."

The video surveillance switched from inside the box to the lobby of floor 56. As the camera cut, they saw someone exiting the elevators; a gweilo in a business suit. The chief cocked his head slightly. "How many elevators are on 56?"

"Just H7," said the operator, a half a tick behind on understanding. Then it occurred to him just as the chief was walking to the duty roster.

The video showed no one inside the box.

The chief flipped through tonight's rotation assignments. Once he found what he was looking for, he keyed the microphone on his shoulder. "264, this is dispatch. What is your location?"

* * *

With a clearing of his throat, Nigel emerged from the elevator banks and casually went to the left passed a directory of the floor's tenants. Not wanting to outwardly appear as anxious as he felt inside, he walked with a clear purpose and meaning to his stride. It was as if he was coming from a meeting with thoughts of his daily schedule, or preparing for his next business venture. Never mind the fact that it was after business hours, or that the floor itself was practically deserted; employee tracking had previously confirmed that. The idea behind this was as Victoria stated; he had to *appear* as if he belonged. He was now an actor on stage, giving tonight's main performance. When everything was said, and done, video playback of the event would show an employee of Advanced IntelliCorp going about his business. Nothing remarkable for the cameras to catch, until it was too late.

He strode passed a cleaning cart that propped open a door to one of the floor's main restrooms. He did not break his cadence as he glided around it, but was keenly aware of the activity inside; carefully listening to the position of the noise to ensure there was no line of sight. That was going to be the tricky part from this point forward.

Nigel and Victoria practiced the fine art of casually moving throughout their environments for years. Being seen without being noticed; appearing to belong to blend. They changed the gait of their walk for each job that required a necessary public appearance on the off chance that a few looks would linger.

He knew every position of the cameras throughout the floor. He would continue to maneuver to the objective as the "belonged," but would never be discerned.

* * *

Kevin was practically to the missed security point when his radio buzzed. "Dispatch, 264 – I'm coming up on checkpoint F 62, over," he continued to walk as he waited for the response.

The chief had a quizzical expression as he looked around, then caught the goofy smile of Trin, who was thinking about his date. With slight exasperation and a roll of his eyes, he said, "When you have completed Mr. Yann's last responsibility, I need you on 56. We have a–," the chief suddenly stopped. He looked at the operator with realization and asked, "Who reported the malfunction with H7?"

Without hesitation, the operator replied, "It was Kevin."

This was becoming quite the puzzle. "264, was there anyone in the elevator with you when you reported the issue with H7?"

"No sir."

"Tell me what happened that caused a concern," said the chief.

Kevin stopped short of the missed checkpoint. "There was a loud bang as if something had been dropped on the elevator. After careful evaluation, I made the decision to proceed using H7. As the elevator started, I heard some minor metallic sounds, like something was coming loose. After reaching 62, I decided I should report the elevator irregularities just to be on the safe side."

Concern creased the chief's face. Eyes began to shift to him as the conversation proceeded. Looking at the operator, he said, "Show me the video of H7 beginning right before Kevin got on. I want to see what he saw." The operator began typing in the commands. The chief keyed his microphone. "Is that all that you heard? There was nothing else?"

Kevin thought as he stood there alone in the ambient lighting of the Northwest corridor. He wondered for a brief second why all these questions seemed so important about reporting the malfunction of an elevator. Then he remembered; the voice. There was no one in the elevator with him; there was no one there upon entry or exit. He could have sworn he heard someone though. He didn't want to appear foolish in front of the shift chief, but his questions seemed very direct. Suddenly, he felt obligated to tell the chief everything. "I heard a voice as the elevator took off. I thought it was nothing, but now you have questions that make me think otherwise."

"Chief," said the operator. The chief leaned down to watch the monitor. He saw Kevin enter the elevator from a camera shot in the lobby. The view switched to the inside of H7. The box was empty. None of this made any sense.

He keyed his microphone. "I need you to get down to 56. We just saw somebody come out of your elevator. We do not have a record of any other transports on that level now."

Kevin was a bit hesitant. "Chief, it may be an employee. We still have some late workers leaving the building."

"This person was entering the floor *from* the elevator; he was not leaving, and there was no originating movement from H7 prior to you. Internal cameras showed the elevator empty; even when you were using it."

Now Kevin became concerned. "Copy that sir, but I do not have the shift badge for my rotation. I will not be able to access that floor without it."

All eyes continued to watch the chief as he swore. He used much of the same words that Trin did when checking the facilities' maintenance room.

He thought for a moment. It could be something as simple as Kevin's theory. Some employees regularly worked after hours. Still... By the time he returned to pick up the badge and get back up there, the mystery man may be gone. That option would not be good enough; too much time would pass. He needed a man now for verification.

The chief turned around to looked for someone, anyone. Everyone knew what the chief wanted, especially Trin. As their eyes met, Trin looked down and away. Had he held the chief's gaze, he would have seen the disappointment that everyone else observed.

"I'll do it, sir," said Chen from the other side of the room. He had heard the exchange on his radio. He walked over and held out his hand waiting for the security badge.

The chief set his jaw. Looking to an attendant, he nodded towards Chen, who was quickly rewarded with the badge.

The security shift chief for Taipei 101 would never know how pivotal that moment, that choice would be, or how it would forever affect their lives. That one decision would cause a ripple of change for someone on his staff. For another, it would bring about an end.

As Chen turned towards the door, the chief said, "Find out who he works for and why he is here. He doesn't look like he belongs. If you sense any danger, you radio back. Do you understand?"

"Yes sir," said Chen, then he turned and headed out the door.

He was followed by a presence.

3

Do Not Engage

Nigel casually strolled up to the double doors of Advanced IntelliCorp. To the right was a keypad and badge swipe. Victoria hounded him at least once a day regarding his six-digit personnel identification number. He needed to commit that to memory for his performance to be completely authentic. Had this been during the day, he imagined holding a cup of coffee as he fumbled with the code and the badge. It would have been a nice touch to appear less than perfect, but impractical for the job at hand. *Do what must be done to blend,* he thought. He entered the sequence then swiped the badge as casually as dialing a phone or using a credit card.

Now came the part where he had to move about as the belonged. There would be no looking at codes, no stopping in corridors to see which way was next, no maps of objects in a room; he must be an employee. He memorized every single layout of each room through the camera taps. He watched employee access protocols, and studied mannerisms of specific resources to help him move freely about, but in such a way as it appeared normal, and kept his face off camera. It took a bit of concentration, but this was not, as they say, his first rodeo. It also helped to have his little bird in his ear.

"Down the hall, last door to the right. That is the anteroom before the vault," said Victoria as she monitored his progress.

He continued his casual cadence pretending to look down and away every so often when he came to a camera. She continued monitoring the in-house surveillance system to ensure that the security protocols did not kick in with facial recognition.

As she watched him, she glanced somewhat to the elevator controls, and did a double take causing her eyes to widening slightly. "Elevator nine is slowing to 56," she said trying to mask the concern in her voice. She quickly punched up the video feed for the moving lift. "It's a security guard. He's going to get off on your floor."

As he punched in the code for the outer room and entered, Nigel took advantage of a blind spot between cameras. "How much time?"

"Two minutes, maybe less."

Although he did not verbally utter them, a few of the finer English swear words floated through his mind. Once again, he felt like she dropped the ball. There would clearly have been more time for him to prepare had she been monitoring the security room entrance and lobby elevators. "Stall him."

"Are you daft?" She said in clear astonishment. "If they haven't already figured out something is going on, causing havoc with another elevator will surely confirm it."

She noticed that he had quickened his pace to the vault security entrance. "I'm afraid that it may be already too late for that, love. We'll have to go with exit strategy three. Lock the elevator down now."

"You need to slow your movements. Visual tracking will pick up anything erratic and alert security."

"Who is daft now? It's a good bet that they already know something is afoot. Do you have the manager's authorization code?" He was preparing to enter his into the chamber entry's access panel.

She monitored today's vault shift manager via the security cameras. She focused on the code that he used for technicians to access the exterior lock chamber of the vault. The lock chamber was a one-person cylinder that when properly authorized, would open on one side for someone to enter, then rotate around for the completion of passage to the other. Much like the new screening devices at airports.

An employee must enter his identification number followed by the shift manager to complete the authentication and entry. It was part of a two-person security protocol to ensure that a single person could not gain access alone. The manager's code was changed each day.

Victoria spewed the number as quickly and clearly as possible while attempting to shut the approaching elevator down.

* * *

Kevin stood in front of the missed checkpoint; deep in thought. The numbers and statistics were replaced with concern about the unidentified man. A man whom he did not see, but heard. How was that possible? It was after hours, and most employees had checked out. Part of the nightshift routine was to verify all personnel during the day. If someone swiped their badge into the building, but not out, they would appear on the nightly log printout; he wondered if the chief had checked that. His fatigue was a definite influence on his senses, but hearing the voice in the elevator was apparently not a figment of his imagination. The chief identified someone coming off the same elevator as him, a few minutes after Kevin exited. How did he get in there? Did it stop on another floor after Kevin? If so, it had to have been a floor between 62 and 56. Kevin was smart enough to know what companies had multiple offices on the various floors. By his recollection there where not any related businesses between those levels. Again, that didn't seem plausible as he heard the voice *before* he got off on his floor. He wondered about the time logs from the video cameras. Would the chief cross-check them to see the precise sequence of events? These questions circulated through Kevin's weary but active mind. He was so lost in thought, that he half heard the radio chatter. Something about being on 56. It was Chen's voice.

* * *

"What is the bin number?" Asked Nigel.

"C 26–5J," came her answer.

He began rushing through the aisles; they were in alphanumeric order.

A camera in the south-east corner came to life and focused in on Nigel.

"Security measures have been tripped. Facial recognition is commencing. I told you not to move too fast!" she said. It was Nigel's turn to make a mistake.

There were several criteria that would cause a sequence of actions should there be something classified as a break-in. With his erratic movement, coupled with the after-hours access, and to the technology vault, the very expensive security system activated the first passive stage. Although she was correct about the speed of his movements, that was not what set off the chain of events. Neither he nor Victoria counted on the system to know the difference between the two codes being entered by the same person. Unbeknown to both, the system had been watching and tracking since he entered the office. The code entry just cinched it.

Nigel was right.

They were caught before he entered the vault.

* * *

An operator in dispatch sat at his station a few chairs down from elevator controls. He, along with everyone else, was following the conversation around the unidentified intruder. He happened to look towards his monitor when he saw it. "Um, sir?"

"Yeah?" Said the security chief with the same disinterest shown as before.

The operator turned to his station and began typing protocol commands. "A silent alarm has been tripped on 56. The tenant's security system has detected an intruder. Passive measures are now active."

The chief looked up, then ran the few steps towards operator two's station. "Who?"

"It looks like it's Advanced IntelliCorp."

The chief bent down to look at the monitor; it displayed the details of the encroachment. The screen directly above flashed a red banner that simply read INTRUDER. It looked a lot like the red alerts seen in the newer Star Trek shows. "Taipei City Police have been notified. They are en route," said the operator.

Things were getting interesting now. This whole event played out like a car crash. Nobody could look away.

The chief stood up slowly; a trickle of sweat rolled down his face. What is going on? Who is this guy? Why is this happening? More importantly, why is it happening on his shift?

Out of these questions, the one that did not readily occur to him was why *this* tenant was being targeted? Once it did, it shifted his thought process from malicious trespassing to theft.

The chief continued to think about this as he acted. He turned and yelled to no one in particular. "What does Advanced IntelliCorp do? Does anybody know?"

"Sir, they do research and development on next-generation technology; enhancements to artificial intelligence, smart microchips, that sort of thing," said someone. All eyes turned towards the speaker and gawked like he had a growth sprouting from his neck. "What? I applied for an internship there last semester."

The chief's eyes darted back-and-forth as he processed this new information. Unknown intruder, silent alarm, after-hours access, high-tech company, city police en route ... his thoughts were interrupted by somebody else in the room.

"Sir, if this is a robbery in progress," he paused. "Chen is up there by himself."

"No," said the chief in a whisper. This new thought caused a nauseous feeling to bubble in his throat. He clicked on the microphone attached to his shoulder strap. "Chen! Come in!"

* * *

Chen smiled as he passed the cleaning lady near the restrooms. She smiled back as she emptied a dustbin. His thoughts were split between his task and educational pursuits. Prospects of Kevin and his accomplishments sparked a reawakening of interest in trying to better himself. He was formulating the areas of his interest and questions he could ask Kevin on their lunch break when his radio crackled.

It hissed with static, letting loose a garbled word here and there. It sounded like the chief. He slowed a bit and began to adjust the tuner. "Chief?" He kept saying between modifications. It sounded like he wanted Chen to abort something; he picked up the word "return" in the sequence of the static conversation. This was weird; the radios had never failed before.

He continued to play with the buttons and knobs, but nothing seemed to work. He thought for a moment. Was the chief calling *him*? It could be something else entirely. Chen tried one more time to contact Dispatch. After the failed attempt, he continued with his objective of identifying the stranger. He looked around as he moved through the hallways.

Advanced IntelliCorp was known for its cutting-edge technology. Not only did it develop artificial intelligence with the most progressive self-awareness capabilities to date, it was conducting research into biometric fusion; synthetic organic nano-tech that would revolutionize the medical industry. Those were two of the more lucrative areas of concentration for the company's development and market.

It would only stand to reason that they would employ some of their own technology in other matters such as security and surveillance.

As part of the passive measures, the artificial intelligence, that was the brain behind their surveillance, used its neural network to hypothesize numerous variables to account for the current situation. It determined that containment within the boundaries of the facility was not a prudent course of action, as the intruder or thief might damage property or pending research attempting to escape capture.

It was smart enough to know that one of the first rules of warfare was to cut communications. Unfortunately, this meant all microwave signals within a given radius and proximity.

That would account for the bad reception with Chen. His choice to continue with his instructions followed the protocols of his job responsibilities.

The presence that moved with him held a solemn face; for he knew all too well the consequence to the decision made.

* * *

Kevin held his radio close to his ear and listened intently to the conversation between the chief and Chen. More specifically, the chief; his friend's responses indicated that he was not picking up the chief's instructions at all. It wasn't until he heard him say he thought this was a break-in, and the intruder was most likely armed and dangerous, that Kevin broke into a run back toward the elevators. He was so preoccupied with his friend's safety, that he completely forgot the last security checkpoint. That was no longer a priority.

As Kevin was about to round the corner, and ethereal hand touched him on his shoulder.

Don't.

Clouded in the mist of the world, it came across as a feeling, a psychic premonition of sorts, a nudging.

Stop.

He suddenly stopped, and he didn't know why.

Turn away.

The presence that roamed with Kevin was hopeful that his charge would take heed of his suggestion. He was connected to his brethren, and aware of what was transpiring. His instructions were very clear. He needed to keep Kevin away for just a bit longer. If only for seconds, that would be enough.

Enough time for a life to be changed. Enough time for an act of desperation to unfold. Enough time to alter a reality that would affect countless lives in the new world.

As with most humans, Kevin would not yet be able to handle the truth that for so long had been hidden. This truth would be the guiding compass as the world he knew came to an end. Humanity would be awakened to it soon enough, and people like Kevin would need to embrace it to survive.

* * *

Time was not a measurement in which the Guardian Host existed, but was bound in; to serve as a protector of souls. If time *did* matter, countless centuries would pass in mere days.

Their existence was infinite. There was no living; just continuance. Created for an objective that can be defined in moments; points in a measurement that had meaning for the humans. Once upon a time, the Host existed for other purposes before humans were even a concept.

That purpose has long since passed.

Every division of the Host has since served in the protection and cultivation of mankind with a singular focus. One that most humans still do not understand, but is the most important aspect of their very being.

The Elodine realm had the most interaction with the humans. For millennia, the Guardians were set forth to protect their assigned charges with a function, a means to an end. Once the end of that fragile life came, they would be reassigned accordingly to fulfill yet another unknown purpose.

Airowyn watched Kevin intently as he struggled with his next move. Throughout Kevin's life, Airowyn unfailingly marveled at the boy, now man, and his desire to only be happy, or content. His father was always pushing him to do more, much to Kevin's chagrin, but he still managed to find happiness in all that he did. Throughout

Airowyn's existence, that was a trait he noticed within humans that was too few and far between.

As his hand rested on Kevin's shoulder, he thought of the pending events that were unfolding. As with most divisions of the Host, he knew only as much as was needed to fulfill his duty as a guardian. His was not to question, but simply obey. That elemental understanding failed some of his brethren long ago; this long-standing war the result.

The tide was now beginning to turn. More of the Host was being dispatched to fulfill their part of the plan. His duties would be shifting because of this very event. A moment devastating to the humans, but necessary to further the cause.

His head turned upward as he received his instructions. He then looked towards Kevin with compassion. He gazed once more upon the man, who was once a boy, with sadness; knowing that the innocence within, would be gone in moments. His hand fell from Kevin's shoulder, and he waited.

The fog in Kevin's mind cleared, and he hurried around the corner, only to skid to another stop with a realization. He did not have the security access card needed for floor 56. Mentally punching himself, he also realized that Chen probably took the key to help Kevin. If Chen was in danger, it was indirectly because Kevin was not doing his job. He briefly flashed to the thought that if Trin had done *his* correctly, Kevin would not be stuck without any way to get to his friend. Or for that matter, have a need to, as it would be *him* instead investigating the intruder.

A mental light bulb went off. He quickly raced through the main corridor searching. His breathing started to become labored; not because of the physical exertion, but the stress and worry over the situation and his friend.

There she is!

He raced towards a cleaning lady, who was startled by his fast approach. He quickly explained the situation and asked her for her master access card. It wouldn't get him into any offices like the security card, but would allow him on any floor. He thanked her politely as he snatched it out of her hand and began running back towards the elevator. He prayed that he would not be too late.

* * *

"Victoria!" He shouted again. There was some sort of static in his ear. He focused his anger on her and the failing technology. Nigel took a sideways glance at the security camera in the hopes that she would still be monitoring him visually. The glowing red indicator underneath the lens looked back angrily and motionless. He held the object out and away from him, while looking the other way, indicating that he had it, then turned to the lock chamber. His eyes darted up and down as his brain attempted to access the security manager's code. He punched in his bogus credentials, then the managers. The incorrect entry sparked a sharp warning tone, followed by a static red glow on the display. For the very first time during this job, Nigel started to sweat.

"Victoria, where are you?" Came his voice in barely a whisper. His anger towards her was dissipating; replaced slowly by fear and abandonment. If the system had not already done so, he knew that one more improper entry would seal his fate, and contact the police. He would need a miracle to get out of this now, especially without his trusted, and very much missed partner.

He closed his eyes and took a deep breath in the remembrance of her voice and the numbers for the manager's code. In a very calm motion, he opened his eyes and raised his hand to the keypad. Nigel punched in the numbers methodically. This time, he was rewarded with a green display light, and a hiss of the vacuum seal as the inner door of the lock chamber parted. He guffawed in a maniacal manner at the pleasure of his success, while also in the disbelief that it actually worked.

As with everything up to the point of his entry into Advanced IntelliCorp, Nigel did not know as much as he thought he did. The code that he punched in was again, incorrect, but the neural network of the artificial intelligence behind the security system released him anyway. When Nigel held up the object to the video camera, it was immediately identified, then a new set of protocols was enabled. Taiwanese Special Forces was contacted; so was the National-Security Bureau of China, Interpol, and the company's CEO.

Nigel had no idea what he had just taken.

After he had exited the technology vault, he ran through the corridor to the front lobby. With the object in one hand, he rotated his arms back and forth over his head. Nigel was clearly attempting to obscure his face from any of the memorized positions of the security cameras throughout the office. His feeble attempt was admirable, but wasted.

There was no reason to hide his face now. He all but gave them a high-resolution snapshot when he half-turned toward the camera inside the vault. The smart security system was already running facial recognition patterns. It would only be a matter of minutes before he was identified.

In his mind, he still thought he had a chance now that he had escaped the vault. He needed to get out of there fast before the cops showed up.

* * *

Chen stopped at the front lobby doors of Advanced IntelliCorp and peered through the full-length glass. Nothing seemed out of place as he looked around. He tried the handles; they were locked tight. He turned to the left and the right of the main halls and saw no one. As he glanced back towards the doors, he was startled when he saw a man suddenly appear behind the glass.

* * *

Victoria couldn't feel her heart beating. At least, that is what she thought. She did notice a hollowness in her breath as her lungs completely emptied, and a sharp thud as if she was punched in the chest when her communication with Nigel went dead. The office video feeds on her monitors went to static systematically; then an unbearable feedback echoed through her headset, causing her to rip it off violently. She desperately tried adjusting settings, switching frequencies, anything that she thought might work to establish some sort of connection, but to no avail. It occurred to her that maybe she should check the security cameras outside the office. She definitely felt her heartbeat when she saw a partial picture of a security guard outside the doors.

Then she saw Nigel.

* * *

He was just as surprised when he saw the security guard standing outside the doors. A bit unnerved by the experience of exiting the vault, coupled with the overwhelming desire to get out as quickly as possible, he rushed up to the doors as if being chased by a savage beast; most assuredly not in character, or fitting in as the belonged. By the shocked look on the young man's face, he was certain he was pinched.

A mental switch flipped in Nigel's head, as if on an automatic command, that allowed him to be deceptively smooth in his transition from a frenzied person, to a concerned and confused employee.

It would be a shame about this chap, though.

A nervous smile spread across Nigel's face. He waved slightly as he turned the door handle, but it didn't move. "Um, excuse me... I can't seem to get out."

Chen looked at him suspiciously for a moment, then cocked his head as if trying to understand what Nigel had just said.

Nigel very expertly, slid the burgled object into one of his pockets. As soon as his occupied hand was free, he used both to try the handles again. He shook them and looked confused; then a goofy expression creased his face as his hand came up and playfully smacked himself in the head. "I need to use my security key," he said, making a dramatic show for Chen's benefit.

Still a bit confused, Chen nodded slowly as he understood, then backed up a few steps from the glass.

The video feed was still a bit choppy with static, but Victoria had watched the exchange between the two.

As Nigel slid his badge through the reader, it glowed red and sounded the same disturbing warning tone as back in the vault. He played it off with the first swipe as he looked at Chen. "Must have done it wrong," shouted Nigel.

The presence that was with Chen approached and placed his hand upon his shoulder.

Beware, danger.

Chen's confused look became more worried and cautious. He placed his hand on his radio and spoke to Nigel. "Sir, I need you to show me your identification."

Nigel continued to swipe the badge and smile at Chen. He knew that the security guard had said something. He was going to maintain his character as long as he could. Upon realizing that the security guard was talking, Nigel's expression changed to one of compliance. He held his hand up to his ear and indicated that he could not hear what was said.

Chen's eyes widened with understanding that neither of them could hear each other. He nodded and then held up his own security badge while pointing to the card in Nigel's hand.

He playfully smiled and nodded goofily as he brought up his ID and placed it against the glass.

Chen grinned back and moved closer so he could get a better look at the picture and the name. He brought his radio up and began relaying the information. As his eyes were focused on Nigel's badge, the goofy smile and expression on Nigel's face disappeared. He had hoped that this could be contained with just the guard. It was obvious that he was trapped in the office. The police were most certainly on their way, and there was a stronger than average possibility that every exit was either locked down or in the process of being so.

Nigel did his research on the office and building architecture. He knew there were tempered points in the outside supports around the glass that could literally withstand missile shots, but there were always areas of weakness in every structured building façade. As with all the other knowledge accumulated, he had paid another city engineer for specifications on those exterior points and their floors within Taipei 101. All that knowledge did him absolutely no good if he were trapped within the office. He wondered if there were weaknesses in the doors before him.

* * *

"Dispatch, this is 264. I managed to get a security access key for 56 off one of the cleaning personnel. I'm heading down there now," said Kevin.

The chief clicked his microphone immediately in response. "Negative! I repeat, do not go down there. The city police are on their way."

Kevin tried to sound respectful, as much as he could under the circumstances. His senses and intuition were flying off the charts in response to his newly acquired feelings. "Sir, I heard your instructions and the concern in your voice. I'm not sure that Chen did. He tried to respond but you obviously did not hear. I *know* him; he will continue with his original orders as planned. If he is in danger, as you stated, I can't leave him there by himself."

All eyes were still watching the chief as this drama continued to unfold. The chief could feel the weighted responsibility of the situation, and desperately wanted to remove his people; to let the city police takeover. Why weren't they here yet?

It was funny how time seemed to stand still during intense and stressful situations. Funny is not necessarily the right word, but he didn't want to think about a negative connotation that might jinx or worsen an already tense moment. In the recesses of his mind, he was falling back on his training as a shift security manager, to secure and protect this building. Those procedures were being trampled by his military experience to protect his people at all cost. The tremendous burden of the situation was only compounded by the many eyes looking to him for instructions; simply waiting to be told what to do next.

He had to come up with a decision quick in the interim. Right now, Kevin was the closest to the situation.

He looked over to one of the operators. "Are any of the cameras working again?" Dispatch lost most of their communications and feeds near the tenant as well.

There were two people at the surveillance monitoring station desperately turning knobs and pushing buttons. "We managed to get a partial feed from one of the cameras outside of Advanced IntelliCorp. It's not the best, but we can see Chen." The chief, and as many people as possible, crowded around the tiny little monitor.

They saw bits and pieces of a shadowy outline creased with static. Suddenly, it crackled into view, and they could see Chen looking through the glass.

The chief's eyes widened as he saw the intruder on the other side.

He was now sweating like he had finished a workout. He reached for his microphone in a fluid motion. "I can see him; he is talking to the intruder. They are separated by the glass doors of Advanced IntelliCorp. Do you know where that is?"

"Yes sir," replied Kevin.

"It looks like the intruder is trapped inside," said the chief as he thought about the security measures. "You get there and pull Chen back to Dispatch as quickly as possible. You *will not* engage the intruder. Do *not* let Chen argue with you. You drag him back by force if you have to."

Kevin began to sweat now, "Y-Yes sir."

"I mean it Kevin. This is a dangerous situation. Do *not* engage," finished the chief as he brought his microphone down slowly, and continued to watch with the rest of the room's spectators.

Kevin stared off into nowhere as he similarly brought his radio down. He took a second to summon his courage before he started to move again. Airowyn stayed within 3 feet as he moved with Kevin towards the elevators.

4

There is Always a Choice

"Dispatch?" Chen said repeatedly. He relayed the information from Nigel's fake credentials, but kept hearing static in return. He adjusted the knobs a few more times, but no one responded.

Nigel continued to glare at him. As Chen's eyes were busy examining the fake badge and his radio, Nigel looked down at Chen's own security badge.

He had an idea.

* * *

Fausta remained by his charge's side. Placing his hand upon Chen again, he urged him to abandon this investigation and follow his instincts of danger. Chen looked up momentarily from the badge to Nigel, who immediately fell back into character. He smiled at Chen with curiosity. He knew that whatever interference was causing havoc with his earbud to Victoria, was most likely affecting the security guard's contact with his people too. This could work out well. He simply needed to convince the poor chap now. "Is everything all right?"

Chen began to back up slowly.

"Wait! Where are you going?" Nigel said in mock panic.

Chen shook his head slightly, as the red flags began to surface in the recesses of his mind. He could feel the danger on an internal level, but could not rationalize with his conscious mind; it was like he knew something was not right, but could not put his finger on it.

Nigel needed to make a play for it before this person left. He was his only ticket out of there. He changed his expression from goofy and carefree, to one of worry and frightened. "Listen, I know that you probably can't hear me," he shouted, "but, strange things are going on in here; alarms are signaling," as he pointed around his head and his ears, "and my badge is not working," he said waving his where Chen could see it. His look was one of pleading and desperation. "I don't know what is going on, but I am scared, and just want to go home."

He looked at Chen with some hope. After a few seconds, he slowly pointed to Chen's badge and directed his eyes towards the external keypad outside of the double doors. Chen looked in the direction that Nigel had pointed, and understood what he was being asked.

Fausta did not remove his hand from his charge. His influence was emanating as intended, but Chen's independence and freedom of choice must be allowed dominion. Fausta raised his head as he received his instructions, then sorrowfully removed his hand.

As Chen looked between Nigel and the reader, he weighed his options between his feelings and instincts, and his duty to protect as a guard. This man's credentials appeared to be authentic; just an employee working late. He looked to the left and right again, and saw no immediate danger, or the intruder that the chief identified. It didn't seem like this man trapped in the office was any threat. He was in a business suit and looked like he belonged. Wouldn't a dangerous person be dressed in something more appropriate to the task? He wished he had taken the opportunity to get a look at the intruder before he left Dispatch. It would make this decision less hard. He couldn't raise anyone in the security office to validate this man's identity. As he looked once more into Nigel's eyes, he saw someone that was genuinely afraid.

This man needed Chen's help.

The indecision that circled in his head cleared. He straightened up and grinned at the man with a professional nod, then moved towards the security badge reader.

For all the smart surveillance system's contingencies, building security could still access tenant offices as an override in case of emergencies.

Nigel didn't know this, but was hoping for the best.

Chen never saw him reach into his coat.

As if on cue, Fausta looked to his left and saw a Transition Emissary appear.

As the final beep and the green light on the badge reader completed, Chen walked back over, and politely opened the door for Nigel.

His smile gone, Nigel simply said, "Thank you," and brought his hand up in one swift motion.

"No!" Victoria screamed as she watched on the monitor.

"No," shouted the chief as he saw Chen's head snap back.

The gentle hiss of the radios was all that could be heard throughout Dispatch. All of those who witnessed just continued to stare at the monitor in disbelief.

Nigel stepped over Chen, and began running down the corridor.

He heard a crackling in his ear as he ran down the hallway. He brought his hand up instinctively. "Victoria? Are you back with me?"

"You fool!" She practically shouted through his head.

His response was immediate. "He had seen my face. I had no other choice. If I were nabbed, you would have been pinched as well."

"There is *always* a choice; he was prepared to let you go. Had you maintained your cover, you could have slipped away undetected," she said with venom in her voice. "As it stands now, our employer is not going to be pleased with this mess at all. A mess, mind you, that could have been completely avoidable had you just followed the plan!"

Nigel sprinted around the corner to the South-east side hallway. At the end was full-length glass from ceiling to floor, that offered a spacious view to the outside of Taipei 101. He came to a stop and peered out. He then began to rip out the inner lining of his suit jacket to reveal detcord filled with PETN (pentaerythritol tetranitrate). He unraveled about 3 feet or so, not needing more than that to breach the weaker point of the glass. The city engineer had told Nigel that the seal closer to the South wall would be his best option.

He began molding the shape charge into the corner as he spoke. "Look, *love*, we have both been doing this for a long time. Up until this point, we haven't had a job of this magnitude and payout. I am not going to let anyone detour its success simply because of being in the wrong place at the wrong time, or a difference in moral beliefs. That would include your opinion on how to handle this field op. *I* am in command; I always have been, always will be," he finished the cord placement. He turned back towards the entry hall.

"Are we perfectly clear?" He asked more as a statement than a question.

There was no response.

"I will take your silence as compliance," he said as he moved to a safe position.

* * *

The elevator doors parted, and Kevin stood there slightly shaking. He was understandably scared, but tried not to be completely paralyzed by his fear. He wasn't sure if it were fear of his own safety, or that of his friend.

Airowyn rested his hand on his shoulder for reassurance. He watched the innocence of not knowing what was to come; it was like a flame he knew that was about to be extinguished.

Kevin managed to muster his courage to exit the elevator. He cautiously approached the corner then leaned forward looking to the right. Satisfied there was no danger, he turned to the left, and gasped.

He saw Chen at the end of the hall; lying there, not moving. He broke out into a run towards his friend. Tears starting to form in his eyes. As he came up to his friend, he knelt slowly. He all but forgot about the intruder. He picked up Chen's head and cradled it in his lap; his sobs becoming more prevalent when he saw the vacant stare. Kevin began to scream in anguish as he held his friend.

Tears were building in the eyes of those who were watching through the security cameras. It became very poignant for all once they saw Kevin's reaction.

Victoria was surprised that a tear rolled down her cheek. This person meant nothing to her on an emotional level, but was she affected nonetheless. Nigel's blatant disregard for life made her sad. As the heartache gripped her, she held onto it tightly for she knew that was what made her human. She had no answer for what Nigel was, or had become. She only knew what his future held, and was saddened further.

* * *

Chen was slightly confused. He looked down at his friend holding someone, but did not recognize whom. He wondered why Kevin was so upset. As he began to ask, he noticed there was some other people standing there. "Hello," he said with a smile.

Airowyn and Fausta smiled back. The Transition Emissary approached. "Hello Chen, my name is Akelah. Will you please come with me?" He gestured to nowhere in particular.

Chen continued to smile, but then looked back down to his friend. "Why is Kevin so sad? Will he be okay?"

Fausta walked up to Chen and placed a hand on his arm. "Kevin will be fine. I will see to it," he said in reassurance.

The smile returned to Chen's face. "Okay," he said, completely satisfied with the answer. He walked to the emissary, who led him away.

Airowyn turned to Fausta. They gripped each other's forearms in a bonded greeting. "Are you okay, my brother?"

"It's always saddening to see the loss of a human life, and the grief that it brings about for their loved ones," said Fausta looking down to Chen's lifeless remains.

Airowyn turned and looked down. "Yes," he agreed. "The suffering that humans must endure is even more painful to those who deserve it less." He turned back to his friend. "There is a shift in the winds of change."

Fausta nodded knowingly.

They both raise their heads as they received their next instructions.

"I hereby relieve you of your charge," said Fausta.

"I stand relieved," said Airowyn with a courteous nod. He looked back towards Kevin, who was still sobbing uncontrollably. "Take care of him. He is a good man."

"Always," said Fausta with a nod.

With that, Airowyn's wings unfolded, and he took flight.

* * *

Nigel clicked the button on the remote detonator. The blast itself sounded like a firecracker, but the explosion of the glass panel and subsequent whoosh of air made it sound like the building was coming down. Nigel placed the detonator back in his pocket, then made sure that the object was secure. "I'm exiting on the South-east side. I'll bring it down as close as I can to Sōngzhi Road. Be ready."

He reached up between his back and his jacket and pulled a paracord line with each hand. This released panels on either side of his jacket and the top, allowing the back to become more open. Without looking back, he ran as fast as he could out of the window to clear the distance of the building. As soon as he was certain he was clear, he pulled the small lollipop handle on his chest releasing a hidden parachute. He started to smile thinking about how they had pulled this off.

Victoria had shut down all surveillance and video links from the van where she monitored the mission. She moved from her seat to the front and started it. She pulled out of the parking structure without as much as a look from any remaining patrons who happen to be out and about. Victoria heard the sirens from the approaching police as she went the opposite direction. As she drove to the rendezvous point, she thought about how sad and pointless their lives had become.

* * *

Airowyn saw the district Regent in the distance. He flew up to meet him as another of the Host was departing. "Greetings, Regent," he said.

"Airowyn," he said with a nod. "How are you faring, my brother?"

"Well." He looked back towards Kevin; other humans arrived and were tending to him and Chen's body. His gaze shifted to the left and saw souls traveling with their emissaries. Chen was smiling as he held Akelah's hand. Airowyn then looked back towards the building and down to the ground. He saw Nigel gathering his parachute as Victoria's vehicle pulled onto the side street. The Regent was watching as well.

"Have you ever wondered why humans choose the path of immorality?" Airowyn asked.

"Not all of them do," said the Regent.

"True enough," said Airowyn as he looked back to Kevin. "But they cause themselves great pain where none should exist had they only denied their basic impulses for evil."

The Regent nodded thoughtfully. "They are a perplexing species, but you must remember their destinies serve a much greater purpose, one of which can only be accomplished if they can freely discover the truth without the obstacles of those who wish to control them. It is our duty to shape those influences and provide clarity on all their choices. Whether we agree with them or not."

Of course, Regent," said Airowyn respectfully.

"It is shameful that the enemy misuses them for an ambition that cannot be fulfilled."

"That, Regent, is a discussion for another time," said Airowyn with a smile.

"True enough," he said returning the smile. "You are to report back to Elodine. You must inform Lucaous that it has begun." The Regent looked across the horizon throughout the globe and saw the increase in activity. The events were happening as foretold. He and his brethren, as well as the humans, would be assembling for the coming Eclipse.

"The time has come to prepare for the Harvest."

Part 5: The Plan

5

A Proper Cup of Tea

As the whistle on a teakettle sounded, a server was preparing an arrangement of pastries; the favorites were blueberry muffins and various assortments of Danishes. The kitchen staff had learned over time; those were the preferred and most popular menu items of the young master. Although his schedule sometimes did not permit each meal, when he was in residence, the staff was attentive to his likes. One thing remained constant no matter what time of day; he liked juice.

Reginald, the head of the residential staff, wanted something more special for the young master's last day. A proper English send off with an American flavor. A three-course breakfast to include all the American staples: meat products of bacon and sausage, various types of fruits, an assortment of juices, breads, and pastries, and eggs prepared in a variety of ways. More food than one person could possibly digest, but as with most mornings, the young master would most likely not be alone. There were always two or more of his executive staff waiting for him as he emerged from his private residence. Today would not be any different; however, the proper sendoff would be for not.

A staff representative delivered his itinerary for the final day, which called for a speedy exit this morning due to various stops before his flight back to the Americas.

Reginald would make sure though, that his last beverage in this house would be properly prepared cup of English tea.

As one server carried the pastry tray, another carefully balanced the tea pot, condiments and the cups, then began the walk towards the blue sitting room. The young master preferred as little pomp and circumstances as possible, so the smaller room suited his needs better than the main dining room.

He was very abashed when it came to making a fuss. He clearly did not like to be the center of attention. From what the staff had gathered during his stay, he desperately wanted to be as normal as possible. Given who he was, that was an impossibility. There were even times that he would just come into the kitchen and eat with the staff.

Being properly trained in the etiquette of serving and household management, Reginald found the informal mingling difficult at first, but grew to understand that this was a typical trait of this young fellow. But when the young master tried to make his own meals, that is where Reginald drew the line.

He had seen the press and knew of this young man far before he came into his service. He has watched him accomplish wondrous things in the benefit of humanitarian efforts. The thing that impressed him most, was that he never wanted anything in return. He was the nicest gentleman whom Reginald had ever known and served; and he would be very much missed by the staff.

Working for the young master was a boon for all their careers in domestic service. Over the last few years, they had hosted foreign dignitaries, celebrities of various industries, as well as, the prime minister himself. This young man garnered attention worldwide in any endeavor he undertook. The staff bent over backwards to serve with distinction.

As the servers walked through the house, there was a lot of activity in preparation for the move. Not so much personal effects or luggage, but mostly items of a corporate nature; computer terminals and workstations populated some of the more prominent areas of the house.

The employees of Jonah International tried to work in harmony with the household staff with respect to their job responsibilities. There were times that each appeared to be in the way of the other, but over the years, they had managed to work out a system for synonymous occupancy. Of course, it was made clear up front that Reginald was responsible for the house, and Jonah International employees took their direction from him. The young master had insisted that he and his staff were guests in their country and house, and would abide by their traditions and standards, as much as they could for their position. The security detachment, on the other hand, followed no one's rules except their own.

As the two servers approached the blue room, Reginald stopped them to give the trays a once over. After he was satisfied, he waved them forward.

In the time that it took to walk from the kitchen to the blue room, they passed four separate JPS agents. There was another two waiting at the entrance of the room. As they approached, one of the security personnel raised his hand and spoke into his sleeve. Like robots in perfect synchronicity, the other guard automatically opened the door for the servers to enter.

"Ah, good. Breakfast!" Kelan said, as he met them at the side table in the corner.

She momentarily stopped tapping on her keyboard; her eyes shifted towards the tray. "Don't take the ones with the cream cheese. He likes those."

Kelan frowned a bit, then grabbed a muffin.

She put her laptop aside and headed towards the breakfast table.

As she passed, the young master reached up and gently grabbed her arm; his eyes never leaving the newspaper. "Alice, you are no longer my assistant. You haven't been for a long time. Let them do their job," he said in a deadpan voice.

One of the servers half smiled as he prepared the tea and danishes.

She looked down at him. "Now, you don't know that I was going to get you something," she said with mild amusement.

Joshua looked at her and smiled. The server arrived and placed the tea and danish on the coffee table in front of the plush leather sofa.

Alice watched the process with a look of disapproval that confirmed his thought.

"Thank you," said Joshua politely.

"Yes, sir," said the server with a crisp English accent and a nod.

Joshua Arden had slowly come to terms with the station set before him. It was a difficult process at first. People revered him for his contributions, prominence, perceived power, and ridiculous celebrity status. All of which he came by honestly in his endeavors to make the world, as they say, a better place. All these years had passed, and he continued to think that he was just doing his job. He began to realize the changes he was making when he could see the economic impact from his efforts. It was also evident in the appreciation shown by the people it directly affected.

He never dreamed in all his life he would be where he is today. His position of influence had gone beyond anything imagined. It was all playing out as Lucas and Malcolm had foretold. The one thing that had not changed was his desire for this power.

He never wanted this responsibility.

Joshua Arden's destiny was planned since his birth. He would like to say he had been a victim in the events that led to now, but he realized that his own choices shaped his world just as much, if not more, than anything else. He often pondered how different things might be if he had not made certain decisions.

"I may not be your assistant, but we both know that your life runs much better when you do it my way," said Alice with a smile, then headed to the breakfast table.

The door opened, and in walked Langston. "Did you see this?" He said holding a newspaper.

Joshua held up his paper slightly and waved it in response. "It's not that big of a deal. He just likes to hear himself talk."

Kelan walked over and took a seat. "Senator *Blow-heart* spewing forth accusations again? Doesn't he have anything better to do with his time?"

"Apparently not," said Alice, as she sat.

As Langston sat down he began reading a quote from the article aloud. "It is fundamentally impossible for corporations like Jonah International to yield growing profits in the wake of the staggering market conditions resulting from this recession. Yet they seem to be doing it. We have strongly suspected for some time that there may be illegal activities surrounding certain business dealings with their direct involvement. My committee has been closely monitoring this disturbing trend over the last several years. It seems a bit coincidental that the shift in their profitability corresponds with the rapid rise of a very inexperienced young man. These types of gains are simply impossible." He tossed the paper onto the coffee table.

"Langston, it's okay. We will deal with this," said Joshua as he took a sip of his tea.

"He all but called you by name in this article. He's coming after you, Josh," he responded.

"Sure sounds like it," Joshua said calmly, as he took a bite of danish.

Kelan took a sip of his tea. "Sen. Artimus Joffe is a Familiar. I would be disappointed if he did anything less. From a tactical perspective, he will not get anywhere near you. All that other stuff—," he said with a knowing smile, "—that's all you."

"Surely he wouldn't be dumb enough to come after him physically," said Alice.

"These are elected positions. They don't necessarily have to be intelligent or take a test to get the job. They just have to fool the voters long enough to get sworn in," said Kelan.

Langston leaned forward. "We have to be smart about this. More Familiars are being brazened about their activities as of late. I'm afraid this is just the beginning," he said pointing to the paper.

"I agree," said Kelan. "I'll work with Tim on the threat-level scenarios. I think it's time we pop them up a notch." He looked at Joshua. "I know this is not what you want, but we have to be prepared."

Joshua had come to terms with his security arrangement long ago. After the last attempted attack at the London Eye, any illusion that he was under about living a normal life had vanished.

"If it hasn't already done so, this article will go viral internationally. I'll work up a response," said Alice.

"Good," said Langston. "We'll review the draft together prior to a release." He looked over to Joshua, who had just finished his tea. When he put the cup down, it was immediately replaced with another. As the server walked away, Langston chose his next words carefully. "It might be worthwhile to get an assessment from Lucas on other activities. A complete picture could not hurt."

Joshua glanced at his watch. "I'm actually expecting him any moment."

His three colleagues looked around the room.

Joshua half smiled as he leaned forward to retrieve his fresh cup of tea. "I'm pretty sure he'll come through the door," he said under his breath.

They kind of chuckled a bit at the silliness. The anticipation of seeing something remotely supernatural had always peaked their excitement. They had to be realistic about the times and places though.

For Joshua to become successful at his true mission, he felt it was important to share some of the truth with his inner circle.

All three were aware that Lucas was an angel.

They only knew as much as they needed to aid the cause. There were still some aspects that Joshua was to keep to himself. If, and when, the time was right, he would share more. Unknown to Joshua himself, that time was fast approaching.

Joshua furrowed his brow for a moment, then took a longer look at his watch. "Sentinel, where's my wife?"

"Just outside of the blue room, sir. She will be entering in 2.3 seconds," came the voice from nowhere.

Over the years, the remarkable artificial intelligence from Jonah International had been instrumental in Joshua's quest for fairness, equality, and simply doing the right thing. During that time, Joshua had also learned that it was much more than just a computer system. Though he was unaware of the magnitude of Sentinel's capabilities or true purpose; he still knew more than everyone else. Many of the top-level executives, as well as some mid-level management, knew of Sentinel and its amazing abilities that could well establish it as the most advanced computer system to ever exist. As with most everything else, they too knew only as much as they needed.

Joshua's first exposure all those years ago did not faze him as it would most people. He has handled all his encounters with the amazing intelligence as casually as sending an email or booking travel plans online; it's unrealized potential still hidden.

The smaller box of blue waving lights known as Excubiarum was Joshua's key to mobility when not in a Jonah environment. As Joshua's authority evolved, it no longer became necessary to have it on hand. The nucleus to its untapped power manifested as Joshua grew in his understanding of the truth. His words were now enough to engage and activate every facet of Sentinel, no matter where he was in the world. It was as if Sentinel was omnipresent.

To sashay would be the incorrect word, but when Professor Melina Arden walked through the open door, it was with a purpose. Trailing behind was her assistant who was furiously taking notes.

Joshua had looked up towards the door at the precise moment that Sentinel had calculated. Her expression was all business; a look he knew all too well.

They both smiled at each other as she bent down and gave him a kiss. She then sat down next to Joshua on the leather couch. One of the servers came over with a cup of tea, but she politely waved it away.

"What's going on?" asked Joshua.

Her expression changed to that of disappointment. "I have to go to Cambridge," she said.

Joshua's brow furrowed again. "Anything serious?"

"Dr. Albright is apparently sick. Midterm review sessions begin today and they can't find anyone else qualified to run the class."

"They are aware that you're scheduled to go back to the states today, correct?" He asked.

"Yes," she dipped her head reluctantly, "but these are my kids and no one knows them, or the exam qualifications better than I do."

Joshua did a rough calculation based on his knowledge of Melina's class schedule for that day. "You're going to be cutting it kind of close, aren't you?"

"The helicopter is on its way. It shouldn't take more than 20 minutes to get there." She grabbed his hand and gave it a gentle squeeze. "Please tell the Prince and Duchess I am so sorry I could not make lunch."

"You know; it's not every day that someone cancels on the future king of England," he kidded. Everyone there smiled.

Just then, an agent opened the door and crossed over. "Ma'am, the helicopter is here."

She looked back over to Joshua and smiled, leaned in and gave him another kiss. "I love you."

"I love *you*," he said as she stood up. He looked at Felicity, Melina's assistant. "You know what time the plane leaves, right?"

"Yes sir."

"Make sure she's on it," he said with a smile.

Melina just rolled her eyes. As she rounded the couch, she gave him a smack on the arm.

Her assistant smiled too. "Yes sir," and gave Joshua a nod.

As Melina approached the agent, he spoke into his sleeve. "Jargon is on the move." The door was then opened by the agent standing guard. The rest of Melina's detail was waiting for her on the other side. She passed Joshua's assistant, Jillian Arthur on her way in.

"Mr. Arden, there's a slight shift in the 1 o'clock with the prime minister," she said as she arrived.

"Doctor," said Alice.

Langston and Kelan started snickering.

As Jillian waited for Joshua to answer, she realized that Alice was talking to her. "Excuse me?"

Alice just gave her a sharp look and raised her eyebrows. The snickering got a little louder. Joshua gave Alice a look that said to let it go.

The realization then struck Jillian. "Oh! I am so sorry Dr. Arden, sir. Please forgive me–"

Joshua held up his hand. "Jillian, it's alright." He looked at Alice. "Was that necessary?"

Langston and Kelan were openly laughing now.

With a smile on her face, Alice said, "Now look, you've spent the last three and a half years working on your doctorate. The title also comes with the diploma. You need to start getting used to it."

As soon as Joshua blushed, all three were laughing. They knew he hated all the attention this position had given him. Having his doctorate in Applied Theology just pushed him further into an elevated status from which the unrequited reverence could only grow. It seemed the more that he wanted normalcy, the more distant it flitted away. He felt like he was on a make-shift raft in the middle of the ocean with solid land drifting further out of sight.

Everyone in Joshua's inner circle understood his feelings around this. Over the years, they became more sympathetic to his situation as they understood the burden of his position and the power that it carried. That still didn't keep them from laughing about it. They all knew that the humor was desperately needed to offset the responsibility. They also knew there were secrets that he carried.

Secrets for him alone.

Joshua came to place his trust, and his very life, in the hands of these three people. Deep down, he knew they would do anything for him, as he would for them.

"Okay, you know what?" He said in mock anger as he balled up his napkin and threw it at Kelan. This only made them laugh harder, and Joshua grinned. He turned back to Jillian.

"The prime minister has an unavoidable conflict at 1 o'clock. He was hoping he could push your meeting to 11 AM instead," she said.

Knowing that his day was packed prior to the flight, Joshua said, "Won't that make things a little tight for the luncheon?"

"Not at all. The prime minister has asked the prince if he minded hosting your meeting at the palace. He will then join you for the luncheon. Your 11 AM can be swapped for 1 PM."

Joshua raised his eyebrows. "That was convenient. If the prince is fine with hosting a state official, and—" he stopped. He looked at her with a raised eyebrow then glanced towards Alice. "You've already made the arrangements, haven't you?"

Jillian glanced towards Alice then they both smiled. Alice shrugged. "What can I say? She learned from the best."

Langston and Kelan were laughing again.

"Honestly, why do either of you come to me if you're just going to make all the decisions anyway?" Joshua said.

The door opened and Tim Marshall, the head of Joshua's detail, walked in. "Sir, we are ready to transport."

As the laughter faded, all stood up in preparation for departure. Servers began clearing dishes as Alice packed up her laptop. Once they were finished, the servers stayed where they stood as per protocol.

Joshua buttoned his suit coat and turned to Tim. "Did Lucas arrive yet?"

"Yes sir, he's waiting in the car," said Tim.

"I need to speak with him alone." As Tim relayed the information into his sleeve, Joshua turned to Langston, Kelan, and Alice, with a look they had seen before. They nodded their understanding.

"I'm going to stay behind. There are a few more arrangements to take care of," said Alice.

"Okay. See you back at the plane," said Joshua. He turned to Tim and gave him a nod.

Talking into his sleeve, Tim said, "Okay, everybody stay sharp, Paladin is on the move."

As Joshua and his detail weaved their way to the side entrance of the residence, he noticed that none of the household staff were anywhere to be seen. He had grown quite fond of them in the last few years and was hoping he could, at the very least, show his appreciation and say a proper good-bye; especially to Reginald. Upon reaching the outside door to the caravan of vehicles and security personnel, Joshua came to a halt, and just stared.

Lined up on both sides were the residence staff; silent and smiling at him. Humbled by the show of respect, he slowly made his way towards his vehicle as he acknowledged and shook hands with each one of them. At the very end of the line, was Reginald.

Joshua grabbed his hand and held it in both of his as he shook it warmly. "Reginald, I can't thank you enough for everything that you and your staff have done for my family. All of you–" gesturing to both sides, "–have made our stay in your lovely country, one of the best experiences that my wife and I have had in all our travels. It has truly been a pleasure to share our lives with yours."

"Sir, might I say on behalf of our staff, that you and Mrs. Arden have been the kindest and most generous employers whom any of us have had the pleasure to serve. The pedigree of dignitaries who have graced our employment records notwithstanding, yours will always be the highlight of our qualifications. That is not too bad for a couple of Americans," said Reginald with a slight smile.

Proper etiquette had always been the first rule of the residential head. Over the years of working for Joshua though, Reginald had come to understand that sometimes it was okay not to be wound so tight.

A big smile crossed Joshua's face. He reached up and gave him a couple of pats to the side of his shoulder. "I'm going to miss you, Reggie."

He couldn't help but to return a full smile. Reginald understood the sporadic need for informality with the young master. It wasn't due to a lack of respect for tradition, status, or station; it merely reflected his personality, and showed how he cared without creating an all too familiar ego that sometimes came with people of Joshua's position. The young master never acted better than anyone else. It took Reginald and his staff some time to come to that realization; as evidenced by some of his meals in the staff dining room.

Tim opened the back door for Joshua as he turned and waved once more before entering the car. As he looked back over the residence staff, he saw each of their auras emanate in various shades of green.

They were all Associates.

As the motorcade and security detail left the residence for the last time, the staff began filing back through the door. Reginald remained to watch the final car round the corner. Once it was gone, the smile faded to a feeling of absence. It was not specific to an unemployed head of the house, but more the loss of what some might call, a friendship.

He was met just inside the door by Alice. "Good morning, Miss Williams. May I assist you with something?"

She looked at him and smiled. "Reginald, how do you feel about New York?"

6

In Due Time

As Joshua entered the back of the car, he saw Lucas in the opposite seat. He gave Joshua a regal nod and waited. But it was only after Tim had entered the front passenger seat and gave the order to move, did Joshua speak. "Sentinel, seal it up."

The privacy partition slid up between the front and rear compartment. A slight wave of shimmering blue light then began at one point and enveloped the entire area around them; it came together at the other end, then faded as if nothing where there. They were now completely cloaked from human technology, and unwanted supernatural forces.

"The compartment is sealed, sir," came the voice.

Lucas and Joshua leaned forward at the same time and embraced each other's forearms.

"Joshua, my friend, it has been too long," said Lucas.

"Three weeks," said Joshua leaning back into his seat. "It's great to see you again. I assumed when you told me you had been called back that something heavy was brewing."

He was silent for a moment, and Joshua read it in his eyes.

"Come on, Lucas, I can see the activity across the globe. I've been monitoring the increase in transitions over the last couple of weeks. There has been a twenty percent jump in the number of Associates' deaths. Those are more active in the eastern part of the European and

Asian regions, and expanding westward at an alarming rate." He raised his hand in a fluid motion, moving it from left to right.

This produced hard-light imagery of the demographical and geographical references in midair. The images ranged from pie and bar charts, spreadsheet data, to a spinning map of the globe fluctuating in hues of red and green. As they both watched, they could see the variations in numbers and colors as they happened globally. It was like seeing stock market numbers in real time.

Joshua was very familiar with the data before them. It caused him many nights of restlessness. He only displayed it to make his point. After a few more seconds, he moved his hand in the opposite direction with the same fluid motion, and the visuals disappeared.

He then watched Lucas, and waited. All these years, Joshua had considered him one of his best friends. Angel or not, he coveted that friendship; much like he did with Harry.

Kelan, Langston, and Alice had a permanent place in his heart, but his feelings for them were unique. Melina was in a category all to herself. He didn't want to admit how much he needed her, their relationship. The reality was that he couldn't see past the next few seconds without her. To his enemies, that would be a weakness to exploit.

The loss of Harry was hard on Joshua. His friendship was a void that had never truly been filled, but if anything could have come close, it would have been Lucas. He couldn't explain it; he wasn't even sure that he understood it, but there was a connection, and Joshua felt that Lucas had it too. As much as that was possible for a being from the Host. He could be open and honest with him without the fear of being judged or used. That was now a rare commodity in his celebrity status.

"It's only a matter of time before this hits the States. Please tell me I'm wrong?" Joshua said.

"I am afraid we are in a similar position as before," referring to their first meeting all those years ago. "I am not at liberty to give any more details now other than yes, you are correct that there has been a rise in transitions. The realms are more concerned as to why," said Lucas.

Joshua was surprised. "While I'm sure it is not fair of me to say, I would've thought that your people would have more insight to things along that nature."

Lucas turned his head a bit with a raised eyebrow. "Whether I tend to agree or not, we are given only the information needed. Even *we* are not privy to all plans."

Joshua pondered that statement for a second. If the Host were in the dark like the humans, then something major was indeed on the horizon. Both would agree that not knowing was most unpleasant.

"Familiar activity is escalating," said Joshua. "My team is concerned about the physical threats increasing. Is this something that we should plan against? Not that I don't have enough protection, mind you, but..." he hesitated.

"It's not just *your* safety anymore," finished Lucas.

If the situation weren't serious, Joshua might have found the way Lucas could guess what he was thinking a bit uncanny. They had been together long enough that it was no longer surprising. In this case though, unsettling was the more appropriate term, as it confirmed that Joshua was justified. He never cared about *his* safety; that was covered. The people that were close to him though, that was another consideration entirely.

Lucas leaned forward. "Joshua, you know that if I had more information and permission, I would share it, but that time has not yet come."

Being frustrated at not knowing things and piecing together riddles was something in which he was well versed. Joshua tried not to take it out on the messenger. "What *can* you tell me?"

"There is a shift coming within the Host."

"What, like guardian assignments?"

"Yes, and not just in Elodine, but across all the Majaliant. The activity is the likes of which we have not experienced in many millennia."

Joshua thought for a moment and wondered how bad things were the *last* time they encountered this. He looked down with concern.

Lucas could see the worry during Joshua's deliberation. Whenever times like this surfaced, it was Lucas's place to provide reassurance.

From his present position, though, he did not know what to advise as he was left without clarity as well. Multitudes of angels across all the realms were repositioning, preparing for something, and he did not know what. Although his existence was to do without question, his thoughts were troubled of late as to why *he* did not have answers. With his assignment to Joshua, he thought it was paramount to be included.

Lucas found himself in an ironic predicament as this is what Joshua must have felt in the beginning. Now, both he and his charge were in the same entanglement. As he considered these different reflections, Joshua completed the cycle of thinking for both.

"We need more information if we are going to be ready. I can't be prepared, or fight something that don't know about or cannot see."

"On that, we are in complete agreement, my friend," said Lucas.

"The only one who has the answers..." he trailed off.

"Aye," said Lucas understanding.

The car made a turn as Joshua leaned forward. "I need you to go back to Elodine, Lucas, and persuade the Chairman to give us something. If angels and humans are going to work together, we must do it in the best interest of cooperation. Whatever is developing is going to affect both sides. We can't be expected to just sit here and wait for it to happen."

"What you are requesting is not that easy," replied Lucas.

"I know, and I would not ask this of you if it weren't important to our cause."

"This protocol does not necessarily fall within the Majaliant et praecepta. The last time the rules were not followed, things did not turn out well," he said with remembrance.

"The Chairman knows how difficult my job is. I'm also sure he's very aware that I do not want it, but since I have been *chosen*," Joshua said with finger quotes, "I need to have the information and the authority to exercise the position."

Unaware to both, that very statement did not go unnoticed. As Joshua finished, Lucas raised his head towards the sky. Joshua sat back with anticipation, for he knew that Lucas was receiving instructions. When he was finished, he looked down. The confidence of a plan was present in Lucas's steel blue eyes. He smiled at Joshua.

"What just happened?" he asked.

Lucas continued to look at him with a smile.

"You know something, now give," said Joshua anxiously.

"My friend, you should be mindful of that which you ask."

Joshua's eyes widen. "What does that mean? What did I ask?"

"You requested the need for information and the authority to exercise your position."

A few seconds passed. "Yeah? And..." He said waiting.

Lucas smiled even wider. "In due time."

Josh threw his hands up in the air. "Seriously!? That's all I'm going to get?"

"Joshua, you know how this works. Both sides will receive the information needed at the appropriate time."

"So even though we both have the same concerns, albeit from different perspectives, about the unfolding situation, you get some of your questions answered, and *I* don't?" He said exasperated.

"Apparently, yes," replied Lucas.

"Joshua, listen," he continued, "the responsibility of what yet is to come is tremendous. Your destiny as a leader is just beginning. I ask that you trust in the plan and let it unfold as intended. As always, I promise you will receive the answers in which you seek."

"Plan? What plan?"

"I am sorry; I must go now. Stand ready, for everything begins," said Lucas.

His guardian began to shimmer; Joshua said rapidly, "I don't understand! What begins? When?"

As Lucas faded, his angelic voice trailed, "Now."

* * *

The caravan stopped at the side entrance to the first meeting of the day. As Jonah Protective Services secured the area, Tim gave the signal for an agent to open the car door for Joshua.

He stepped out of the back, buttoned his suit coat, and glanced toward Tim, who noticed the all-to-familiar look; he had seen it many times before. As he walked to his position around Joshua, another agent waited for the second passenger to exit. After a few seconds, the agent peered in. Tim half-smiled at the reaction of confusion. A little caught off guard, the agent looked to Tim, who just waved him into formation. He was going to have to find a way to help him accept the unexplainable things that didn't make sense; otherwise the new guy would drive himself crazy. Tim learned that the hard way.

* * *

Alice sat in what was left of her office in the residence. What was once carefully arranged with stacks of papers, itineraries, and business projects, now held nothing more than a desk with a bare surface and a single chair. She scribbled some notes down on her legal pad, while balancing her cell phone between her shoulder and chin. She used her other hand to tap on her laptop keyboard.

She had always been efficient at her job; even when she was an executive assistant. Now serving as Joshua's Chief of Staff, her responsibilities weren't that much different, just on a larger scale. The position though, did afford her a staff of her own.

As the movers bustled about, one of her staffers walked up to the doorway. She had some papers in her hand, and dutifully waited until her boss was off the phone.

As Alice finished her conversation and put her cell phone down, she looked up. "Hey, Sally."

She crossed over and placed the papers on the desk in front of Alice. "Lisbon confirmed receipt of the shipment. The manifest has been signed and sealed per protocol," she said.

Alice picked up the papers and looked them over. This made Sally's attitude shift a bit. "Will there be anything else?" She said a tad snippy, and started for the door.

Alice stared at her with a surprised look. "Hey, hang on."

Sally turned as Alice waved her back and motioned for her to close the door.

Alice studied her for a moment. "What's going on?"

"With what?" She said coldly.

"With that, —" said Alice pointing to Sally, "–the attitude."

A few more moments passed where neither said anything.

"Look, we can talk about this as friends, or if you prefer, I can talk to you as your boss," said Alice.

Sally broke eye contact first; she looked down as her mood softened. "I'm sorry, Alice. This is my problem, not yours."

Now Alice's look changed to one of worry for her friend. "Sally, is there something going? You've been on edge for what seems like weeks now." Truth be told, Alice noticed something amiss with her best friend far longer, but thought that it was a personal matter and didn't want to pry. She got up and walked around to the front of her desk, then hopped up. She patted the spot right next to her.

A smallish smile appeared in the corner of Sally's mouth as she took the seat. If anyone were to walk in and see them, it might look like two schoolgirls sitting on a bench swinging their feet back-and-forth while talking about boys.

She stared with a sheepish look towards the floor. Alice waited patiently for a few more seconds, then leaned into her and bumped shoulders. When Sally looked up, Alice cracked a huge smile. It was infectious, and she couldn't help but smile back.

Alice's grin then faded somewhat as she went back to her question. "Sally, what's going on?"

"I'm not going anywhere," she said embarrassed.

Like a good friend, Alice tried hard to understand, but struggled with the words. Whatever it was; she didn't want to make it worse.

Sally could tell that Alice didn't get it. With a little exasperation, she took a big breath and finally relented. "I'm being left out. I'm not going anywhere in this position. I've been with Jonah for over 12 years, and look at where I am?"

Alice recoiled a bit in surprise. "Sally, you work for the most powerful man on the planet. That's not too shabby."

"No," she said shaking her head, "*you* work for the most powerful man. I work for you," she said somewhat pointedly.

"I don't really see it that way—"

"Well, I do. I'm not involved in anything. I was in a somewhat higher position than you when we both worked in international relief. Things got strange with Joshua when that whole artifact and him being targeted situation came about. But when he came to us for help, that's when it looked like things were turning around." She paused for a bit. "You know, I didn't always want to be an economics analyst, and his sudden rise up the corporate chain looked to be the ticket out. You can't really get anywhere without riding someone's coattails."

Alice listened to her friend and provided her a supportive look, but inside, she wondered if Sally was jealous. Granted, things worked out differently for Alice; more so than she could have imagined, but she had always felt that decisions had been made for a specific reason. When she was offered a position as chief of staff, she thought that Joshua had given it to her because of her experience as his assistant. She knew him; his likes and dislikes. She could anticipate his needs when sometimes *he* didn't even know. Her move made the most plausible sense, as Sally's experience was primarily in research development and economic analytics.

She didn't see it as Sally being left out on purpose, but more so, that there were other opportunities in which she would be more suited. On the other hand, if Alice had not brought her on as part of her own staff, would she still be working in international relief? Was she intentionally left out of the core team? When Joshua was the relief division lead, he interacted with Sally daily. Alice couldn't remember the last time that Joshua had even talked to Sally. His only connection to her now would be Tim. She wondered why Sally had not approached Joshua before to discuss this. "Have you thought about talking with Joshua?"

"Are you kidding? With his protection and a schedule that I am not privy to for security reasons, I wouldn't be able to get within 50 feet, let alone any private time to discuss a personal matter," said Sally. She looked back towards the floor with some sadness. "It's not like it used to be when I could just walk with him in the hall," she said softly.

"It's not like he has forgotten who you are, or that you can't–"

"Don't be so sure, Alice. If I was that important, I would be involved. I have been cut out on purpose."

"Look, you've known him just as long as I–"

"My point exactly."

Sally could see that she had placed some doubt in Alice's perspective of the situation.

Good.

She softened her look even more to make sure that Alice could still see the hurt. "Listen, I'm very sorry for giving you attitude about my poor pitiful situation. I shouldn't have taken the way I'm feeling out on you. I am very grateful that you have given me the chance to travel the world," she made a grand gesture with her hands, "and be a part of this fantastic movement. I'm sure, if the time is right, I will be recognized for my contributions and maybe move into a position with more trust."

Alice's eyes widened a bit at the last statement. "I don't think this has anything to do with trust."

Sally hopped off the desk and faced her best friend. "You don't think so?" She said with a slight mischievous grin. "Tell me Joshua's itinerary before he gets on the plane."

Alice's mouth popped open to the question. Sally couldn't tell if it were because she was going to divulge the information, or that she was genuinely shocked at the question itself.

"I know how this is going to sound, but–" began Alice.

"I know; it's because I do not have the security clearance." She gave her friend a hug. "It's okay, Alice. That's where I am right now." She opened the embrace resting her hands-on Alice's shoulders. "Sometimes, there's just not enough room for everybody at the top." She turned towards the door and slowly made her way across the office.

Wait for it.

"Sally, maybe I can talk to Joshua to see if there are any opportunities for advancement. I know that he would consider it."

Sally stopped; a quick smile spread across her face. She composed her sullen look and turned. "I don't want to put you into that position. This is my problem, not yours," she said again dutifully.

Alice hopped down and walked towards Sally. "Now you know that you could never do that. You are my best friend. I just wish you would've come to me sooner." She gave her another hug. As she pulled back, Alice looked at Sally confidently. "I will definitely pull him aside and discuss this. Remember though, there is a purpose to everything that he does. If you don't get access, there is a reason. Not that you will need it, but it can't hurt that your boyfriend is the head of his detail," she said with a grin.

Sally rolled her eyes and waved her hand. "That doesn't do me any good; he doesn't tell me anything either."

They both laughed. Alice walked back to her desk to gather her things. Sally waited for her at the door. "I don't mean to sound like your boss now, but we need to start working on the presidential brief. We can start assembling the information on the plane."

Sally smiled. "You forgot, didn't you?"

Alice turned back around with a quizzical look, then it dawned on her. "Oh, that's right; you're staying on a couple of extra days. You and Tim have big plans?"

Excitement filled Sally's eyes. "We are going to Rome! We're meeting some friends we made in Cabo last year. This is their first trip abroad."

"That sounds fun. I'll try not to bother you with any mundane requests," she said jokingly.

"I'll just send you to voicemail."

Sally walked Alice to the end of the hall next to the library and stopped. "I've got to pack up a few more things. I'll meet you at the car to see you off."

Alice smiled then continued walking. As Sally watched after her, all expression fell from her face; the stare was piercing like a dagger.

7

Rock Star Status

Other than the last-minute cancelation of the one o'clock, the day went without a hitch so far. Dr. Arden was with the prime minister and the prince in what would now be the last meeting of the day prior to leaving England. He had just made a joke, and both dignitaries were laughing.

Tim looked at his watch. "Roadshow status check," he said into his sleeve.

All the various units on the detail from agents to watchers and analysts checked in. Satisfied that the area was secure and everything was nominal; Tim walked over to another agent. "Heading to C2ISTAR." The agent nodded as Tim opened the door. Another agent immediately took his place inside the room.

As he walked through the palace towards the side entrance, he admired the priceless art and the magnificence of the rooms and passageways. He imagined how many years of history had walked through these very halls, how many state banquets and court ceremonies it had hosted, or the numerous bombings from World War II it had undergone. If this place could talk, it would be a historian's dream gig.

Upon exiting the palace, Tim surveyed the area for known points of observation. His tactical team and agents were exactly where they should be as the West entrance off Constitution Hill was canvassed with royal guards and JPS personnel.

Protective Services was, by far, one of the largest of the corporate entities under the umbrella of the many divisions within Jonah International. Since its inception a few years ago, it had grown to not only protect the most powerful man in the world, but other VIPs requiring more specialized handling due to their status. Over time, JPS had expanded its market of service offerings to include technology systems and surveillance. The expertise in all areas of security was immense. All JPS personnel were vetted with the highest clearance processes known to the intelligence community. It's training program was academy-level, and rivaled, or even surpassed many national agencies. It is, in effect, the largest privatized security force in the world.

The entire division was run by the Director of Defense for Technical Operations, Kelan Tindal.

Tim walked towards a cluster of semi-trucks and buses that served as the Command and Control for Intelligence, Surveillance, Target Acquisition, and Reconnaissance. JPS personnel were everywhere; some were on guard, while others moved between vehicles. He nodded towards one of the guards; they punched in the security code for the door and waited. As Tim stepped up, he placed his hand on a bio-pad to complete the security sequence. The pressurized door hissed as it popped open, then he entered. All the duty stations were manned by personnel covering everything from communications to satellite surveillance. At the far end of the compartment sat the DDTO himself. Tim sidled up and took a seat.

Kelan was reviewing some cost expenditures. His computer array was just like everyone else's; hard-light imagery. "Hey," he said glancing towards Tim. "Everything going okay?" He said referring to the meeting.

"Yep. I would expect it to wrap up within the next twenty."

Kelan finished his adjustments to the overall cost data then placed his palm on the hard-light screen. The imagery changed to a virtual version of a bio-pad. The scan ran once then changed to green. It beeped with a confirmation indicating acceptance of the approval. As soon as he removed his hand, all hard-light visuals disappeared. He turned his full attention to Tim now. "TAC teams ready for transport?"

"All units are standing by. Once Paladin is in the air, remaining ground support will tear down and prep for dust off. Estimate wheels up three hours from Paladin's departure."

"Escort?"

"Four F-22 Raptors out of Mildenhall. They will continue escort until we reach international waters."

Kelan leaned back in his seat. "Excellent. Once we are in the air, First Team will need to review threat-level measures."

Tim perked up a bit. "Is something going on?"

Kelan rubbed his forehead, then his hands drifted down to his eyes. He needed more sleep. With his voice lowered to where only Tim could hear, he said, "It looks like Familiar activity may escalate given some of the press and chatter we have been seeing lately. I'm concerned about his vulnerability. We need to tighten up security ... just to be on the safe side."

Tim nodded thoughtfully. "We should look at shift rotations on personnel. Maybe we could switch things up; reduce the hours and fatigue, keep them fresh."

Kelan nodded as he stifled a yawn. "That's a good idea."

"It looks like you could benefit from a schedule like that too," said Tim with a slight grin.

Kelan waved him off as the yawn passed. "This is just from last night. I was up early this morning in anticipation of the trip back. The readjustment to the states is going to be tough."

"It's only a six-hour difference," said Tim with some amusement.

"What can I say? I'm a lightweight."

"More like a marshmallow," he said with a laugh.

Tim and Kelan had developed a good relationship over the last few years. He trusted Tim, and for Kelan, that was a change.

As Kelan grew into his new life and role within Jonah, he began to see his style of management differently from his old life at Alastar-McGlocklin. He learned a lot about what not to do as a department head. Because of that, he didn't take the same motivation with him when Joshua offered him a job. His current boss saw something in Kelan that he, himself, didn't see or understand in the beginning.

He had faith in him.

That was a leap he was never given in his old life. Everything was different now. Because Kelan was doing the right things for the right reasons, his role was bigger than he could ever have imagined. The responsibilities were ridiculously high, but Joshua kept telling him that he would do fine. He guessed for someone who was supposed to save the world, his own workload was a smidgen in comparison. Since trust in his team was paramount to their mission, he went out of the way to cultivate a good rapport with his First Team.

Even though he reported directly to Kelan, Tim ran Joshua's detail his way, without any interference. Another thing that Kelan learned differently from his old job.

"No matter what we decide though, we need to keep it transparent," said Kelan.

"To the boss?" Tim said knowingly.

He raised one eyebrow. "Well, *yeah*," said Kelan with an obvious nod.

Tim had known Joshua longer than Kelan, but both were completely aware of the innate need for a normal life. Especially after he and Melina were married. Joshua was not naïve by any means, but that did not keep him from expecting his staff to honor his wishes as much as possible.

Joshua's importance grew exponentially with each endeavor he participated in. His popularity among all walks of life increased to well above rock star status. His face or an article was in every type of media imaginable at any given time. Just like any prominent official though, he had his fair share of enemies.

Kelan and Tim left nothing to chance. After the attempt in Kiev, security had been tightened up to that of presidential status. Joshua didn't like it, but understood it.

When he moved to England to pursue his doctorate, he and Melina had taken a weekend to tour London. One of the many stops was the London Eye.

That's where everything changed.

Kelan made it a priority to investigate the bombing. Forensic and criminology specialists were flown in to work with England's national intelligence agencies to piece together the exact sequence of events. The initial report said that it should have been much worse than it was; even to the point of destroying the London Eye itself. A lot of unknowns surfaced that day and the weeks following; questions went unanswered even still.

Joshua saw it all though.

As he and Melina approached the wheel, he saw them drop from the sky; angels under Lucas's command were converging on their location dressed in full battle armor. As Joshua followed their trajectory, he saw a hoard of demons guarding specific points on and around the wheel. The warriors attacked them in a methodical formation— some circled the explosives and spread their wings in a protective fashion. Lucas dropped down in front of Joshua and Melina wrapping his arms and wings around both. As he did, all of them fell to the ground. To Tim and the other agents, it looked like Joshua had seen an unknown threat, grabbed Melina instinctively and went down as he was trained. Each bomb went off in a carefully planned sequence, but the damage was minimal.

It was later discovered during the investigation that shape charges were precisely placed at strategic points; and that, had they gone off properly, would have killed anyone in a 100-meter radius.

Everyone knew that it was meant for Joshua. The investigators also knew that it would have taken time to set up that type of complexity.

The itinerary for the weekend tour was classified. Someone outside the trust circle knew.

Since that attack, JPS had close to 120 personnel protecting and watching Joshua 24 hours a day. And now, they were going to come up with more creative ways to increase the security once again.

Kelan could see that Tim was still thinking of other security possibilities. "Don't stress about it now. We have a six-hour plane ride to come up with contingencies."

"Roger that, —" the look on Tim's face changed to surprise then realization.

Kelan noticed. "What is it?"

He closed his eyes and slowly brought his head down to meet his hands. "Sally."

Kelan was only confused for a split second when he realized what he meant. "Tim, I'm sorry. I completely forgot."

"So did I," he said with his head still in his hands.

"Listen, you go on your vacation; we'll—"

"No, First-Team protocol comes first," said Tim matter-of-fact.

"Back in the old days when I was a tyrannical, dictatorial, all business boss, I would have agreed; things have changed, and so have I. We can work through this without you."

"With all due respect, no ... you can't," he said looking back up.

"I beg your pardon?" Kelan said with amusement.

"I control every facet of agent and detail assignments. That includes TAC team and shift rotations. The schedules have been planned weeks, and in some cases, months in advance with coordination from every single department. Any microcosm of a change requires reevaluation of all watcher and analyst assignments too. Dr. Arden's travel schedule will need to be considered with these contingencies, and we both know that all First Team must be involved and approve every change. As I said, First-Team protocol," finished Tim.

Kelan wanted to argue with him, but quickly realized his point.

"... and you don't know diddly about my process. You'll just mess it up," finished Tim with a grin.

"Fine. But I'm not going to take the heat with Sally on this one."

"No, not this time," said Tim.

A bell chimed in everyone's earpiece, followed by the voice of the watcher supervisor. "Roadshow departure in 10 minutes, confirm."

Tim raised his eyebrows and spoke into his sleeve. "Affirmative. Roadshow is a go for departure."

Everyone began preparation for Joshua's meeting to wrap up and his immediate exodus.

"Well," said Tim standing, "I better get back in there."

"Okay, see you back at the plane. Good luck," said Kelan with one last look.

"Yeah."

* * *

Thirty minutes later, all parties were on their way to a secluded hangar just outside of London's Heathrow Airport. Tim followed the standard protocol for travel like always. He had made sure that all routes were appropriately blocked, all communications with local law enforcement were active, and that the plane was prepped and ready for their arrival. This time, he was in the pace car that followed Paladin, Joshua's call sign. When satisfied that everything was on schedule and under control, it was only then that he allowed himself to relax and dread the inevitable.

He pulled out his cell phone and dialed. "Hey."

"Hi, honey," said Sally.

There was silence for a few seconds.

"Is everything okay?" She said.

"Listen, Sal..." started Tim.

She knew what was coming. It wasn't like this was the first time he had canceled on her. Still, she was going to make him say it.

"Something has come up," he said, then paused.

He stopped intentionally to gauge a reaction. He could hear her breathing, but nothing else. Tim knew that she had figured it out. He also knew that this one was going to cost him; big time. He waited a few more seconds to see if she was going to let him off the hook. When that didn't come, he rolled his eyes slightly as he prepared his speech.

He let out a slight sigh. "I'm not going to be able to go to Rome." He closed his eyes and waited for the wave of disappointment.

"Okay."

His eyes popped open from the simple reply. It can't be that easy. *Big time*, he thought.

"A situation has developed that requires all of First-Team."

"Honey, it's okay. I understand. This is your job and Joshua's safety comes first," she said calmly and casually.

This caught him off-guard. "You're really not upset?"

"Well, I *am* disappointed. The Martins are arriving later today. I'm not sure what I'm going to tell them, but I will think of something. I'm going to have to cancel the hotel and the dinner reservations though; that's going to be a pain. The plane tickets are non-refundable."

Plant the seed.

"Baby, I'm really sorry about this," he said. She was being extremely understanding about the situation. Not uncharacteristically so, but Tim knew how much Sally was counting on this weekend. He didn't want to deny her the holiday she deserved because his priorities had changed.

"Listen, you should still go. I know how much you were looking forward to it, and seeing the Martins again. We had such a good time with them in Mexico."

Sally smiled slightly. "Oh Tim, I couldn't do that. You deserve this vacation too; it wouldn't be fair for me to have fun while you're working."

Add some water to the seed.

"It is completely fair. My schedule is all over the place, and you should not have to suffer because of it."

"I don't know ..." she replied with mock concern.

Let the seed grow.

"Sally, I insist. Please go and have fun."

Bingo. Her smile spread.

The taxi had just pulled up. She looked around and saw no one else as the driver put her bags into the boot.

As they finished their call, her thoughts drifted to other things. She imagined two or three JPS agents escorting Alice to the plane. How different things were between the best friends. Sally was just enough on the outside of the exclusive group to know a few specifics, but not nearly enough. No matter. There were other ways. None of that would be of any significance if the plan was carried out correctly.

She looked up at the clouds; a raindrop hit her cheek and slid down her neck. The cabbie opened her door, and she entered.

It was very fortunate that the Martins had called two weeks earlier to cancel. That saved Sally the trouble of fabricating an excuse to them; and Tim, what a sweetheart. Providing a convenient way for them to be separated was more than she could have asked. It would be a shame about him though. She grew quite fond of him as of late.

* * *

Joshua stared through the window as the motorcade came out of the roundabout onto Hogarth Lane. His mind was swimming with thoughts and speculations regarding what Lucas had said about a plan. Before, when he felt helpless and in the dark, at least he had company in Lucas; he didn't know anything either, even after going back to Elodine. The saying *misery loves company* didn't exactly apply in this context, but in a small, morbid way, Joshua felt a little better about sharing the same discomfort with his protector, his friend. Now he didn't even have that.

Inwardly, he felt like a crybaby whining about a toy truck that some-one else was playing with. He knew his belief was stupid, that Lucas was right, and he would know the answers when it was time. It didn't make things any easier though; and quite frankly, he was sick of that rule. Joshua had learned long ago, though, that his timetable for those answers was anything but accurate. He was still trying to make sense of what it was that he "asked for" when Langston nudged him with his foot.

Joshua turned and looked as Langston motioned towards Jillian.

She held out a cell phone. "Sir, it's the president."

He pursed his lips as he took the phone. "Hello, Mr. President."

"Hello Joshua, or should I say Dr. Arden." quipped the voice on the other end.

"Please sir, just call me Joshua. Nothing has changed as far as I'm concerned."

Albert Masters was in the third year of his first term as President of the United States. His election to the office was due, in no small part, to the indirect support of Joshua and Jonah International.

Even though he no longer led the international relief division, Joshua was frequently involved in humanitarian efforts to help those who could not help themselves. On one of the more globally visible initiatives, Jonah International provided relief in the form of food sub-sidies to help alleviate widespread famine throughout Somalia. The United States, under then Sen. Masters' request, offered additional aid, with the brokerage of Joshua, to help ease the tension of the countries' relationship. It was on this platform that Masters had built his candidacy for president. He and Joshua had a friendship of mutual respect ever since.

"Well, when are you going to start calling me Albert?" The president said.

Joshua smiled. "Not anytime soon, sir."

Masters laughed. "In all seriousness, son, congratulations. Your accomplishment is well deserved."

Joshua blushed. "Thank you, sir."

"I'll get right to the point; I know that you're coming home to-day, and was hoping that you would drop by and see me within the next couple of weeks. There're a few things regarding the re-election I would like to discuss with you."

Joshua listened intently as the president outlined his agenda. There was an occasional response here and there, most of which consisted of "yes sir," while the remaining occupants of the car sat in silence and listened.

"Mr. President, it would be my honor and pleasure to meet with you next week." He caught Jillian's eye with a look as she began roaming through her smartphone and taking notes. "My assistant will be more than happy to work around your schedule."

"Joshua, I can't begin to express my thanks for your time on this. Please remember that this is of a sensitive nature, and I need your discretion. The opposition's party candidate has not yet been selected, but preliminary indications look like it's going to be Humboldt. If it is, then this country, our mission, and the fate of everything is going to shift," said the president.

Joshua could hear the concern in POTUS's voice. "Mr. President, you have my word that all of my resources will be available to support the election within the letter of the law," he said very carefully. He knew the phone lines were secure, but had no idea of who was listening at the White House. He had learned a lot over the years in crafting neutral phrasing.

"I know that, son, and you have my gratitude. Oh, and all of this business with Joffe, ..."

Joshua rolled his eyes slightly at the name.

"I hope that you know, that if I could, I would put a stop to this–"

"I know, Mr. President, and the thought of your willingness to step in is all the support that I need. Sen. Joffe is not a problem nor a threat. Believe me when I say that I *will* handle this."

Joshua's eyes widened after the realization that he had just cut off the President of the United States in mid-sentence.

"I know that you're more than capable of handling this. Even though I cannot comment publicly, off the record, my support has been and always will be with you," said the president.

Joshua smiled. Albert Masters was a good man. He was an Associate.

They finished their conversation then Joshua handed the phone back to Jillian. "When the White House calls, change my schedule to accommodate."

"Yes sir," she said nodding.

"Is everything okay?" Langston asked.

Joshua raised his eyebrows in a way that reflected his disappointment at the information he had just received. "Masters believes that Humboldt is going to get the party ticket."

Audible sighs and deflated looks hit both Langston and Kelan. They all knew a Familiar taking the office of the most powerful country in the world was inevitable at some point. The question was always when. Masters was a key element in the war. His position provided a strategic platform of widespread influence that could not be denied by the enemy. Should they assume this office, it would cripple the efforts to strengthen mankind's hope and their faith in each other. It may even undo some of the good that Joshua and Masters have accomplished in their careers.

The tide could change quickly with something as simple as one negative social media outbreak. Resources would have to be allocated to mitigate and repair the damage. Things like that fell into the category of rework. Joshua hated rework. In his mind, the best way to prevent rework was to do it correctly, quicker, and better than the enemy; a strategy that he has been successful in since his rise.

A Familiar taking over the White House would be a setback, but only a minor one in Joshua's opinion. That is but one political position in the United States government, albeit the most powerful, but just one of many. Associates were everywhere too; quite a few in key government functions. Familiars knew that, and didn't like it.

Joshua continued his gaze through the window. He felt a chill in his bones with thoughts of the unknown.

8

Kelly Granger

The motorcade arrived at the Southeast entrance to the secluded airstrip right off Heathrow. The gate was manned by JPS personnel, and opened as the caravan pulled up. As with everything else that day, the fluidity of motion by the Jonah personnel was amazing just based on the sheer number of resources involved. Coordinated efforts of so many people took a lot of planning, time, and patience; no easy feat by any stretch of the imagination. As Joshua's car passed through the gate, he watched the individuals performing their assigned tasks. Each had a specific activity such as relaying communications, securing the perimeter, and even opening the gate at the precise moment necessary to allow them to pass through.

He knew in the back of his mind that these people were doing their jobs, but it's still bothered him somewhat that it was all specifically to protect him. He wondered how it got to the point where a single individual rated that much attention. Especially when the individual was just him. The spotlight was the last thing that Joshua wanted, but as some would say, that ship had already sailed.

* * *

An agent had just received word that the motorcade was three minutes out. "Stay sharp. Paladin has arrived," he said into his sleeve.

He stood in the doorway overlooking the staircase to the outside. Although he couldn't see them all, he knew the tactical team was watching and waiting. He turned towards the interior of the plane and walked to the main cabin. It bustled with activity from Jonah's personnel and press correspondents. "Ladies and gentlemen, please take your seats. Dr. Arden will be arriving momentarily."

This was the adopted universal procedure for any dignitary's arrival to ensure minimal security risk as the VIP boarded the aircraft. Although aircraft personnel were not necessarily required to sit, they were to remain stationary until Dr. Arden was secured.

Kelly was just completing some last-minute stocking in the SPICE galley when the same announcement was relayed over the aircraft's intercom system. She hurried with the last cart, then secured it into place. She stood, straightened her uniform, then moved quickly around the corner to take her place with the rest of the flight attendants.

The captain had just come down the spiral staircase from the flight deck. He straightened his tie then tucked his hat under his arm. He caught Kelly's eye and smiled. Instinctively, she smiled back.

The cabin noise died down a bit. People were motionless for the few minutes that it took for Joshua and his entourage to board. As he came through the doorway, the captain greeted him. "Hello sir, welcome aboard," he said with a smile.

Joshua grinned as he held out his hand and extended a warm greeting. "Hello Bill, it's been a long time. How are Valerie and the kids?"

"They're doing fine, sir. Elizabeth starts Northwestern in the fall."

"Little Beth?" Joshua said genuinely surprised.

"She's not so little anymore, and she prefers to go by her full name now," he said with a little scoffing.

Joshua just laughed. He remembered Beth, or Elizabeth it seemed, from the party for her 13th birthday. Of course, that was back when security wasn't as big of a deal. Joshua had tried to be a part of as many moments of those he worked with as he could. He did not want to slip away or become detached from the very thing that he was trying to save. He also needed as many reminders as possible to stay focused on his ongoing mission. Joshua greeted the rest of the flight crew present before proceeding to his state room. As he approached Kelly, she became somewhat flushed. She watched him intently. *Relax*, she thought to herself. *Everything is fine.*

As Joshua looked at her, his smile faded. It was as though he saw something and was displeased. Kelly noticed the change in his expression. Her smile widened to compensate. "Dr. Arden," she said with a nod.

He stopped. "I'm sorry; I don't believe I know your name," he said as he extended his hand.

She began to perspire a little under her collar. "Kelly Granger. Second attendant, forward cabin."

"Your first time with us?"

"Yes sir. I have been trying for months to become a part of this crew. My security access was just granted a few short weeks ago."

Joshua continued to look at her. A few seconds passed in silence. He cocked his head slightly before speaking. "Well then, I hope this experience is educational." His smile returned and he continued forward.

As the pounding in her heart began to subside, she was confused by his reply. She took a deep breath and wondered if he knew. "Thank you sir."

Kelan had noticed the slight exchange between the flight attendant and Joshua. "Everything okay?"

Under his breath, Joshua said "What can you tell me about Kelly Granger?"

Kelan raised his eyebrows and pulled out the tablet from underneath his arm. He typed in a few commands and studied the information. "Class III clearance, background checks out, cleared for active-duty three and a half weeks ago."

"Yeah," said Joshua looking back. "That's what she said too."

Kelan didn't pretend he wasn't curious about what Joshua knew. He had learned long ago, though, there was always a reason and not to question. "Look, if there are any concerns, we can have her taken off the plane right now."

Joshua thought for a moment. He couldn't judge someone because they hadn't decided. After all, they were the reason the war was continual. Still, it seemed odd that she could get this far into his camp as an Undeclared. "No, that won't be necessary." He looked back as she was carrying a drink down the aisle. "Have someone keep an eye on her, though."

Kelan nodded as Joshua stepped away. "Will do."

As he moved towards his room, Joshua looked over and saw Melina's assistant in her seat, and smiled. Upon opening the door to his state room, there sat his wife with her legs curled up on the couch. "Hey there," she said with a smile.

He smiled back as he entered and closed the door.

* * *

With the passengers secured, the aircraft was now taxiing toward the runway. Watchers and analysts were at their stations on the flight deck just behind the cockpit; all systems running and tracking surveillance, communications, and telemetry.

Their plane was state-of-the-art like no one had ever seen. It rivaled military AWAC systems and Air Force One in both sophistication and functionality. It was a testament for another unfortunate necessity every time Joshua traveled.

The two pilots and the flight engineer were awaiting the clearance for takeoff as their plane moved into position.

"Heathrow Tower, this is Jonah One papa papa eight heavy, requesting permission to take off," said Capt. Bill.

"Jonah One papa papa eight heavy, runway traffic and airspace have been cleared. You are confirmed for immediate departure. Safe travels," squawked ATC.

"Roger that, London. Thank you for your hospitality."

"It was our pleasure."

The massive engines on the Boeing 747 8 throttled up with a high-pitched whine, then began accelerating the plane down the runway.

Kelly looked nervously at her watch as the wheels left the ground. A lump began to form in her throat as if it were closing from suffocation. There was no turning back. This was it. She had to see this through now. Kelly took deep breaths trying to calm herself. Looking around to make sure the other crew members were not watching, she gently blotted away the visible perspiration. *Everything will be fine,* she thought to herself. She just had to make it through the flight.

The fact that she kept having to reassure herself that everything would be fine, should have been the first clue that it wouldn't.

* * *

"Inbound transmission from approaching aircraft," said a communication analyst.

"Confirm, four aircraft incoming rapidly from the East," said a watcher.

"Jonah One, this is Whiplash Three. Outbound escort to international airspace, vector heading 582 at 180 degrees. Flanking your position in 24 seconds, over," said the pilot.

"Whiplash Three, this is Jonah One papa papa eight heavy, copy that," replied the co-pilot.

* * *

The aircraft was in full swing with activity. The press corps worked on their puff pieces in preparation for interviews with Joshua on the trip home. Langston and Alice were in one of the smaller conference rooms discussing the media response to Sen. Joffe, while Kelan and Tim were in the executive operations' room reviewing scenarios and simulations regarding the upgrade for Joshua's security.

The purser and flight crew were making their rounds to ensure everybody's comfort and refreshment supplies. Meal preparations were already underway by a team of three chefs in the very small, but efficient kitchen on the lower level.

Kelly returned to the SPICE galley. She smiled at the other attendants and made herself look busy while waiting for them to depart. Once she was alone, she bent down and opened a storage container. Pulling a few of the items aside, she peered in to see the small package that she had placed prior to take off. Her breathing became a bit more rapid as she replaced other items on top and in front of her little surprise present. She stood up and closed the container right before another attendant rounded the corner. They politely smiled at each other as Kelly waited for them to retrieve their items and walk away.

Her eyes darted back and forth as she processed her instructions. She looked at her watch and calculated the precise time she was to make her move. Kelly then picked up an innocuous item for appearances and rounded the corner to the main cabin. As she looked out the porthole window, she saw the military aircraft flying alongside. Based on her instructions and the remaining time; they shouldn't be out there much longer. Once the escorts leave, that will be the first sign for her to proceed.

* * *

Joshua opened his eyes slowly. He was lying on the couch with his head resting in Melina's lap. She casually stroked his hair while reading a book. As he stirred, she looked down. "Well, hello," she said.

He half smiled as he stretched. "Hey." He looked at his watch. "How long have I been out?"

"A little less than two hours."

"Wow, I'm surprised they let me go this long."

She giggled. "That *is* surprising," she agreed.

He yawned as he stood up, and then made a terrible face.

"What's that look for?" Melina said in response.

He answered with one simple word. "Interviews."

"Ah, the crown weighs heavy upon the King's head," she said with a grin.

"Stop that," he said with a deadpan expression.

He stretched again looking over his shoulder and casually glanced out the porthole. He noticed that the escort was now gone. As he began to move towards his jacket, he did a double take. His expression turned serious as he approached the porthole and looked out. He turned towards Melina. "Listen, I don't want you to be alarmed, but I need you to stay in this room."

She could see the concern on his face. "Josh, what is it?"

He had to decide how he was going to phrase this. "This is going to sound a bit more ominous than it should, but I believe there's going to be some trouble. The only way I'm going to be able to deal with this is knowing that you are in here safe. I will have two agents posted outside of the door."

Trouble was a bit of an understatement. Had Joshua known the full story right then, he would have run as quickly as he could; not that it was possible on an aircraft over the Atlantic.

Her mouth was as wide as her eyes, but she nodded in acquiescence. She had learned over the years with Joshua, that his instincts were always right. That was one of the things that made him a great leader. "Okay."

Joshua forgot about his jacket and left the room.

There were already two agents standing outside the door as a matter of protocol. "Sir," they said and nodded as he passed.

"Fellas, do me a favor; stay here and keep an eye on her. She supposed to be doing something for me, which requires her not to leave the room. Under no circumstances are you to let her," he said with a misleading half grin.

Both agents smiled knowingly. "Yes sir, you can count on us."

Joshua smiled back. As he turned and walked down the hallway, the smile stopped. He found a secluded nook and ducked in. "Sentinel, get me Kelan."

* * *

Tim was going over the schedule as Kelan's personal cell rang. This surprised them both, as they were completely out of any signal range. He looked at the caller ID and saw the name. He hit the button. "What's wrong?"

"Meet me in the forward arsenal. Is anyone with you?" Joshua asked. His eyes cut over. "Tim."

"Bring him; do it quickly and quietly."

Kelan stood at the same time as he hung up." Let's go."

* * *

The purser prepared refreshments for the cockpit crew. As she was arranging the tray, Kelly happened to be standing next to her. "How's everything going?"

"Oh, not so bad. A few of the media guys have been a little rowdy, but nothing that we can't control," said the purser with a grin. "How is your first flight so far?"

"It's very exciting!" She feigned. "I can't thank you enough for helping to get me here. It has been my dream to do something like this, and not just on any airline either."

"Kelly, it was my pleasure to recommend you for this crew. Your candidacy was at the top of the selection list. You deserved it."

The galley phone rang with a specific sequence of tones indicating that it was the kitchen. The purser picked it up. "Yes?" She listened intently for about three seconds. "I'm on my way."

Kelly had a curious look on her face. The purser smiled. "The meals for the executive staff are ready." As she turned, she remembered the pilot's tray. "Oh, nuts."

This worked out perfectly. "I'll be happy to take these refreshments to the pilots," said Kelly.

The purser raised her eyebrows and spoke in an appreciative tone. "Really?"

"Absolutely!" Kelly reached for the tray.

The purser punched in the code for the elevator to the lower level. "Thank you so much!"

As the door opened and the purser entered, Kelly gave her a friendly wave and turned back towards the tray. Once the door closed and she was again alone in the SPICE galley, she bent down to her secret container to retrieve her special package.

The box was sealed in a plain brown wrapper and about the size of a small brick. The weight was very light as expected, and it contained no metal; extremely easy to conceal among her toiletries in her carry-on. She half smiled thinking about what this would do for their cause.

The injustice perpetrated by the unethical testing of animals by Jonah Labs would suffer a huge blow once she opened the box in the cockpit and dumped it.

She had asked the lady with whom she was in contact, and who also brought this testing to their attention, why Kelly's animal rights group couldn't stage a more traditional demonstration at one of the many labs globally. The contact, a woman named Inara, made a case for why this moment would be more effective. "What better way for your cause to gain global attention than on the plane of a noted celebrity full of media?" Upon thinking about this, Kelly's animal-rights activists agreed that this would be more of an effective demonstration and carry a twofold purpose. One, bringing about recognition for their group, and two, showing that the mighty puppet from Jonah International was not untouchable by their cause.

Kelly did express some concerns about being arrested for this, but Inara's assurance that her employer would handle all legal matters regarding any charges, and that her consortium was just as powerful, if not more, than Jonah International, made her feel better.

Inara's instructions were very explicit. She was to get inside of the cockpit before opening the package.

The saddest part of being a pawn in someone else's plan, is the inability to think for one's self. Kelly was a bright young lady with the possibility of a brilliant future; one that would never be fulfilled because she did not recognize the signs. She, nor her organization, at no time bothered to check out the accusations against Jonah Labs. Had they done so, they would have realized early on that animals had never been, or ever would be, part of any outlandish or experimental research sanctioned by Jonah International. For that fact, many developmental projects had to do with technology, specifically around biometric fusion. None of those initiatives involved any animals whatsoever; it was mostly computer simulations powered and constructed by Sentinel.

If Kelly had been smarter, she would have questioned why her contact wanted the fighter escort gone first.

There was no background check on their source of information, the woman called Inara. They simply took her at her word.

That was their biggest and last mistake.

The Undeclared were the easiest targets for Familiars. They could be swayed into anything with the proper motivation. In this case, playing upon the sympathies for those who care about furry little beasts.

Kelly carried the pilot's tray up the staircase to the flight deck; her surprise package hidden neatly underneath the linen napkins. Her outward expression appeared professional, but the giddy little-girl inside was bursting with anticipation of the forthcoming demonstration. She smiled at those watchers and analysts who caught her eyes as she approached the cockpit security door.

* * *

Kelan and Tim entered the forward arsenal with Joshua gazing out the porthole. Upon hearing them, Joshua turned. He motioned to the doors; Tim shut them.

"Sentinel, seal it up."

The same cascading wave of light from his meeting with Lucas, enveloped the room. "The room is secure, sir," replied the voice.

"What's wrong?" Kelan repeated.

There was no way to pull this kind of a punch. "There is a demon sitting on the starboard wing."

Kelan's eyes widened as he went to the porthole.

"Excuse me?" Tim said with a slight look of confusion.

Kelan looked out and saw nothing. That was not surprising though. Only Joshua could see angels and demons at will. That was part of his gifts as the appointed champion.

Kelan turned back. "I'm not questioning you, but—"

"Yes you are, and I don't blame you. Yes, he's still sitting there; ugly little gargoyle on top of engine four."

Kelan and Tim switched places.

"What do you think this means?" Kelan asked.

"I'm not really sure. He seems to be alone, just sitting there," said Joshua thoughtfully.

"Do you think he's preparing for an attack?" Kelan said.

Tim looked all around the outside through the porthole and saw nothing but clear blue skies. He joined the other two and listened.

"No, he wouldn't be foolish enough to do it alone; they attack in packs just like the London Eye," answered Joshua.

"Whoa, what?" Tim said.

Kelan nodded his understanding. "Safety in numbers," he agreed. He threw his thumb over his shoulder motioning. "This guy a low-level soldier?"

"Wait, the London Eye incident where a bomb almost blew you and Mrs. Arden up?" Tim asked trying to keep up.

Joshua paused to finish off that conversation. "Yes Tim, that event was orchestrated by both demons and Familiars. We'll find time to talk about that later." He returned to his discussion with Kelan. "He seems to be, yes. Only mid-level commanders are stupid enough to come at me alone. Senior ranking demons have learned the errors of their ways; they steer clear of me altogether," referring to his angelic protection.

"Do you think he saw you?" Kelan said.

Joshua shook his head. "I don't think so, no."

Being a good intelligence operative, Kelan was thinking through all the scenarios. "When did you notice him?"

"As soon as I woke up," looking at his watch," four minutes ago."

"Okay, let's find some more pieces to this puzzle," he began to pace. Kelan always thought better when he did that. Tim backed up to give him some room to walk as he attempted to process everything that he was hearing. Kelan began to rationalize starting points of events from the morning until now. He tried to find the clues like a good detective. As Joshua worked through this discussion, he wandered back to the porthole to see if his little friend was still there. He saw that the demon was looking off in the distance. Joshua looked in the same direction and saw nothing. He turned around quickly. "Sentinel, give me a graphical display within a 100-mile radius of any demon activity."

Kelan stop talking as the image manifested between the three. It showed a three-dimensional holograph of fluid motion with the plane in the center as it moved through the sky. It was like they were watching a movie of their flight. In the distance, they saw twenty or so objects closing at a moderate rate. It was as if they were keeping their distance.

"Sentinel, are those what I think they are?" Joshua asked.

"Yes sir, they are the Fallen," said the voice.

"Rate of speed? Time to intercept?" Kelan said.

Sentinel replied immediately. "480 knots, 37 seconds until contact at present velocity."

Tim checked his own weapon as the other two were talking. He then walked to the gun cabinet and punched in his security code. The heavy panel slid open revealing an assortment of weapons.

Kelan looked at him. "Those aren't going to do you any good; not against *them*."

He pulled out a very sophisticated automatic weapon, popped in a magazine, and chambered a round. "Maybe not, but it will sure make me feel better."

"You can't shoot something that you can't see," said Kelan as a matter of fact.

Tim glanced over to Joshua. "You just point me in the right direction."

"None of this makes any sense. They're obviously waiting for something. What is it?" Kelan asked.

That very question was nagging at Joshua. They are in the middle of international airspace. Nothing around them for hundreds of miles. The escort is gone; they are literally alone. Why wait to attack? If their intention was like always, and they wanted to kill Joshua, they couldn't just bring the plane down. That was against the rules. They are foolish creatures, but not that stupid. They would have to be working with a Familiar from the inside to ... The pieces started coming together like a pinball bouncing off bumpers.

Joshua spun around quickly from the porthole. "He's a scout!"

"What?" Kelan asked.

"The demon on the wing, he is an advanced scout. Those others are waiting on his signal," said Joshua.

"Signal for what?" Tim asked.

"He's here to observe something. He's waiting on something to happen within this plane before he signals them to attack," said Joshua.

"Okay, but what?" Kelan said.

Joshua's eyes became wide with realization. "The flight attendant!"

"Who?" Tim asked.

"Sentinel, locate Kelly Granger," ordered Joshua.

"Kelly Granger is on the flight deck approaching the cockpit," said the voice from nowhere.

Joshua looked at Tim. "Get some men up there now and detain her."

Tim immediately started relaying orders into his sleeve.

Joshua started for the door. "I should have kicked her off the plane when you offered."

Kelan had a worried look. "When you got on the plane, what happened? What did you see when you greeted her?"

Josh had his hand on the doorknob. "Nothing, that's just it. She had no glow."

"An Undeclared," said Kelan under his breath.

"The perfect pawns for Familiars," said Joshua as he pulled open the door.

* * *

She hit the buzzer next to a security keypad then knocked on the door. That was the protocol to let the pilots and the engineer know that it was crew. Kelly looked up to the camera snuggled in the corner and smiled, then held up the platter. Her reward was a click of the security locks. The flight engineer opened the door for her.

"Hey, I have some goodies for you guys," she said as he held the door. He latched the door behind them then sat back down at his station. With one hand carefully balancing the tray, she extracted a portable table from a hidden compartment. Once both hands were free, she began distributing the refreshments.

* * *

"Copy that, sir," said an agent as he and his partner headed up the spiral staircase. They took two steps at a time.

* * *

Kelly had just finished doling out her last snack when a loud, very persistent knock came upon the security door. A panicked look struck her face as her eyes cut down to the package. She saw the perplexed expressions the men gave each other. Then the flight engineer looked at the monitor for the security camera. Kelly could see a partial of the screen. There were two men in suits.

"It looks like agents," said the flight engineer.

"You better see what they want," said Capt. Bill.

Kelly began to visibly sweat now. There hadn't been enough time. She reached for the package underneath the linen just as the engineer opened the door.

As the door seal broke, the two agents pushed their way passed the engineer to converge on her. "Kelly Granger, don't move!"

They pushed her up against one of the instrument panels. In doing so, the tray, and the package spilled to the floor.

"Wait, —" she said gasping for air under their weight. The three pilots just looked on in astonishment.

The agents placed handcuffs on her then escorted her out of the cockpit. "Gentlemen, we apologize for any inconvenience. Should you have any questions, please contact Director Tindal."

And then it was over.

* * *

Sitting in one of the smaller conference rooms weeping, Kelly thought about how terribly wrong everything had gone. Though she knew that an arrest was possible, she imagined it would have been after landing for the security breach on a tightly controlled aircraft, or the blatant disregard for health and sanitation by dumping the dead, baby kitten that was in the package. Maybe not a kitten; it could've been any number of innocent animals that would fit inside. The point being it had to be some sort of small test subject. That would make the only sense as it would carry more weight for an effective demonstration. She imagined whatever the poor small creature was, would have chemical trace tying it back to Jonah Labs. There would surely have to be some sort of investigation regarding the findings, which would most assuredly become public with all the media aboard. It was the only theory she had with no other explanation available. Kelly's mind swirled as she moved against the uncomfortable restraints.

The package.

It would be in their possession. She guessed that didn't matter now. The key to all of this would have been discovering the poor creature. As it stands, they would know now that it was planted. It was only a matter of time before they discovered her affiliation back to her activist group.

In a soap opera-type of a way, her theories might have made sense, except where accuracy was involved. Her understanding of the true nature of Jonah Labs was incorrect. She had also been duped into believing an exposure of this level was the right course of action. Worst of all, there was no way to prove her direct tie back to this contact called Inara.

None of that mattered in the eyes of the enemy. Kelly was handpicked because of her very innocence and ignorance of the truth and situation. She was expendable and didn't even know it.

* * *

The three of them entered the room where Kelly was being held by the two agents. Kelan motioned towards the door, then they left. He took the seat directly across from her while Tim stood just to the side. Joshua stayed back by the door with his arms crossed. As much as he wanted to take the point, it was best that he remained as detached as possible and let the two experts run the questioning.

"Ms. Granger, I am Director Tindal. We don't have a lot of time, so I will get straight to the point. You were sent here to do something. I need to know what that is, *now.*"

* * *

The purser was cleaning up the mess in the cockpit. As she bent down, she noticed a box. Upon reaching for it, she said, "Captain, I found something near your seat."

The captain turned and looked with creased brow as he took possession. He turned the box around and examined it. His eyes met with his copilot and flight engineer. With returning looks and shoulder shrugs; they confirmed they had no knowledge either.

He studied the box for a few more seconds and wondered if this had any connection to the flight attendant. He tore open the brown paper wrapping to reveal a darker brown box with a full lid. As he held on to the bottom portion tightly, he maneuvered the top lid back-and-forth lifting it upward until it seemed to catch on something. As he applied more pressure, it finally separated. The lid had some sort of string with a metal pin dangling from the end. He looked at the string then to the contents of the package. He saw three cylinders. The two on either side held liquid that began to mix into the center one, apparently triggered by the removal of the pin.

"Oh my," said Capt. Bill, as the liquid binary explosive detonated.

9

Wait For It

The sound was practically inaudible in the back of the plane. The progression forward ranged from something akin to a slammed door, a loud pop, a firecracker, to a car crash. Everyone heard something different. What they all felt though was the same.

The plane immediately began to dip forward in the sky. The faint whine of the engines changed tone; it was almost as if they were losing power.

The screams from the passengers became louder as the plane's descent became more prominent.

Since Joshua, Kelan, Tim, and Kelly were in a forward conference room, they heard and felt the explosion. The room shuttered then began tilting.

Joshua's reaction was immediate; secure the passengers. "Sentinel, open ship wide communications!"

"Communications systems damaged. Non-functional from—"

"Figure it out!" Joshua shouted.

Two seconds later. "Communications online."

"Everyone, this is Joshua Arden. Find the closest seat and strap yourself in. When we have more information, I will let you know."

Joshua managed to open the door. The screaming became louder.

"Sir! Where are you going?" Tim asked.

"Flight deck," Joshua responded. "That's where she came from, so whatever happened was there!"

Kelan looked back at Kelly Granger, who was screaming as the force of the descent pulled her against her restraints. "What about her?"

"Leave her. She's not going anywhere!"

The three of them began to pull and climb their way towards the flight deck.

* * *

As they entered the top deck where the watchers and analysts sat, the three men noticed that all the stations were down. The hard-light imagery powered by the plane appeared to be dead. The team of scared technicians were all holding onto their mounted stations for support.

Joshua quickly processed what he knew. The plane was losing power; the engines were shutting down and so were surveillance and communications. He looked towards the security door to the flight deck. It looked as if it were bowed in from depressurization; he wondered if it would even open. Was there damage to the control systems? Is this problem just confined to this deck, or is it ship wide? Joshua had so many questions and no answers.

"Sentinel, restore power," he said.

Within one second, the hard-light imagery flickered back into place; not that the techs could do anything with the ship still descending.

"Jack into flight controls and level us out," said Joshua.

"Flight controls inoperable. Pitch stabilization is nonfunctional. Aileron access is severely damaged," said the non-emotional voice.

Joshua's eyes darted back-and-forth." Give me a three-dimensional view of the cockpit."

Much like the dynamic visual of the aircraft in the conference room, the hard-light image appeared, first showing the full view of the plane, then rotating around coming to a stop at the cockpit.

As everyone held on to something for balance, eyes and mouths went wide with shock. The entire left side of the flight deck was gone.

From just behind where the captain's seat used to be, to the very left of the copilot's chair; all gone.

Captain Bill.

Sparks snapped and hissed from wires violently separated from computer systems. Oil and synthetic fluid from hydraulics painted a mad man's picture over what was left of the cabin from the air pressure of the descent. The man in the right seat was not moving.

"Jim?" He asked looking at the lifeless body.

"I'm sorry sir," replied Sentinel.

Joshua closed his eyes as his head began spiraling. There was nobody else left on the flight deck.

"How much time before impact?" Kelan said.

"At present altitude, course, and velocity, three minutes and 42 seconds," replied Sentinel.

"We have to do something!" Tim shouted.

"We have to get Joshua to safety," said Kelan.

Joshua ignored the impossibility of that statement. "Sentinel, we need something that will buy us more time."

"Understood sir, but aircraft flight mechanics are no longer possible in the current state," said Sentinel.

The three of them, along with the watchers and analysts were silent.

"What does that mean?" Tim asked.

Kelan confirmed what Joshua was thinking. "This plane is a dead stick."

Joshua waved his hand, and the image of the flight deck disappeared. He looked at Kelan and Tim. "Get everyone out of here."

"What—" started Kelan.

Joshua let go of the table station and fell forward towards the flight deck.

"What are you doing?!" Kelan shouted.

Joshua looked back as he leaned against the wall next to the buckled security door. "We may not be able to do anything, but we are far from helpless."

As their eyes locked, Kelan understood. "Okay, everybody out!"

Tim started to make his way down to the flight deck. "No, Tim." Joshua said.

"Sir, it is my duty to stay with you no matter what," he said as he continued advancing.

"This is something that only I can do. You can't help me," said Joshua. A couple of seconds passed. "I need you to take care of Melina," he said looking into Tim's eyes.

Tim stopped and thought. His first priority was securing the protection of Joshua. In their present state, none of them were safe; they all shared the same fate. If Joshua had some sort of plan to save them, Tim would have to trust his bosses' instincts and judgment. He pursed his lips then began his climb back towards Kelan. He and the rest made their way out of the top deck.

Joshua turned his attention back to the seemingly hopeless situation. "Sentinel, can you seal off the breach to pressurize the flight deck?"

Three more seconds passed. "The flight cabin is now pressurized, sir."

Joshua nodded as if Sentinel was standing right there and could see. "Okay, pop the security lock."

"The door is now unlocked, sir."

Joshua steadied his nerves before opening the door. A holographic image was one thing; seeing it firsthand would be tough. He took a deep breath, and with a great amount of effort, pushed opened the door. It popped and shuttered as it scraped against the floor, allowing him enough room to slide through.

The scene was horrific; it was exactly as Sentinel had depicted. It was unsettling to see the big gaping hole; even more so knowing he was a few feet from open sky. As he peered out into the wide unknown, he saw the faint, waving lights that was Sentinel. Joshua wasn't sure how it was happening, but assumed it was something like a force field. He watched and read way too many science fiction stories. There was no time to question or ponder the mechanics of how.

He made his way towards the only remaining pilot's chair. "Time to impact?"

"One minute and 58 seconds."

The copilot was wedged in his seat. The five-point harness was still engaged, but that wasn't the problem. It seemed like the explosion shifted the flight console to the right; locking his legs between the dash and the yoke. Even with the harness undone, Joshua couldn't move him.

"Lucas!"

He shimmered into place right next to Joshua. "Stand back," he said, and with one hand under the dash, he pulled. Pieces of the plane strained and snapped under the pressure. With his other hand, he gently lifted the man out of the seat.

As soon as the copilot was clear, Joshua climbed in taking his place. He peered out the window to the right and saw the demon horde advancing on the plane.

The realization of their plan made him angry now. Disable the plane from the inside then ensure its destruction by natural and explainable causes. The attack was on the plane itself, not necessarily Joshua.

No violation of the rules.

A loophole.

The enemy was beginning to get craftier at their tactics. A scarier thought was it seemed that Familiars were working more closely with their demon counterparts. It wasn't necessarily a surprise, but more of a confirmation based on recent events.

Their use of the Undeclared bothered Joshua. Those were the ones riding the line between both sides; a precious commodity to be either nurtured and directed, or used and manipulated depending on who got to them first. The enemy's willingness to kill all of those aboard demonstrated the measure of their resolve and commitment to their misguided cause.

He looked back at Lucas. "We're not alone."

Lucas laid the lifeless body down gently next to the security door and turned back. He looked out the gaping hole. "I am aware. Fear not."

As the demon horde converged on the plane, guardians swooped in from above and attacked with ferocity. The clash of weapons flashed brilliantly against the daylight sky. The downpour of angelic protection appeared to be unexpected as Joshua noticed the surprise and shock on some of the demon's faces. Although they put up their usual fight, they were easily vanquished. That did not make sense to Joshua. He was pleased with the outcome, but it appeared that it was almost *too* easy.

His thinking was interrupted by Sentinel. "Time to impact, 54 seconds."

The guardians then surrounded the aircraft; they held on to the wings and lifted it from the bottom. The plane began to level out. As Joshua's eyes met Lucas's, there was a measure of both surprise and relief.

The screams and shouts from the passengers were replaced by applause and cheers of happiness.

However, it seemed that joy would be short-lived.

As if on instinct, Joshua looked into the distant horizon. "This is not over."

Lucas saw them too. "No, it is not."

The sky began to blacken with multitudes of demons. Joshua's assessment of the ease of the first attack, as evident by the surprise of the enemy, was correct and now made sense. They were pawns; puppets to be used to draw out the angels. Most likely, to get an estimation of the supernatural protection. They gambled Lucas' guardians would come to save their precious mortal savior. Just like in ancient human military strategy, the demons sacrificed their own to gain the advantage of enemy exposure.

"Sentinel, how many?" Joshua asked.

"I count at least two legions, sir."

Joshua did the math. "12,000 demons," he whispered to himself. Of all the attacks on him to date, this was the biggest show of supernatural force from the enemy that he had seen. His thoughts drifted back to the passengers and their safety ... his colleagues and friends.

Melina.

As the demons approached the aircraft head-on, he imagined their screeching and maniacal laughing. Some things were cliché in stories depicted throughout human history regarding evil and demons. He happened to know firsthand that the shrieking that accompanies their diabolical grins were real. He often wondered if demons were cursed with that specific characteristic because of the failed rebellion, or did their eternal plight drive them mad. It didn't matter which were true. For Joshua, it was annoying and stupid.

Lucas watched the enemy advancement, then turned to his charge. Their seemingly telepathic connection still intact, Joshua turned to him. As they looked at each other, Joshua thought he saw the slightest bit of a grin form in the corner of Lucas's mouth.

At the height of a tense situation, imagining things sometimes does happen, but for Joshua, his control under pressure did not allow for his imagination to get the best of him. Over the years, his experiences with his friend have taught him that certain facial expressions meant hope.

Joshua looked out over the horizon again; the demons were almost upon them. "I know you've got something planned."

Lucas continued to stare at the advancing blackness. "Over my time spent as a guardian, I have witnessed countless battles. Of all the strategies for victory, those that come prepared for the worst are generally the ones who should be most feared, for surprise is always on their side."

Joshua followed his gaze and looked for anything that would give his wish for hope countenance. "Lucas, I don't see anything," he finally said.

"Wait for it."

* * *

"Get ready!" Shouted Melennec, a legion commander.

One of the squadron lieutenants glided up to him. "My lord, the advanced team was defeated very quickly. Do you think it wise that we approach from the front? There is no element of surprise."

Melennec looked towards him with a sneer. "They were sacrificed to gain supremacy in numbers. They are few; we are many. It does not matter from which direction we approach; they are outmatched."

"Excuse me, my lord, but—"

"You have your orders, Suroc," he replied with a menacing look; his eyes morphed from black to a glowing red. Melennec was not accustomed to being questioned, especially by a subordinate.

The lieutenant drifted back into line with his division. He caught the eyes of one of his captains who soared into place on his right. "Ready our warriors, but be cautious," he looked towards the plane. "I have a bad feeling about this. Be prepared to fall back on my signal."

The demon captain nodded. "By your command."

* * *

Some cultures of humans have long sought a founded belief on an afterlife; an existence of something beyond the confines of their limited and fragile mortal flesh. Each society views the next stage a bit differently than it actually is. Some believe it to be transcendental, a life-altering ascension to knowledge and wisdom. Others believe life just stops after death; a nothingness. Those believing the enlightened theory sometimes claim visions of the afterlife, seeing love ones or supernatural beings, which for most, stem from a traumatic event of sorts. Of all the stories and folklore throughout time, the truth was very simple. Neither of those are correct. Enlightenment comes from the individual, not from the transition between realms; and there was most definitely something on the other side.

There was no difference between the Humani generis or Majaliant realms in dimensions or space, but only rather in time and perception. Humans cannot see angels, unless they want them to. That same rule applied to demons. This clouded perception allowed both to move among the humans, to guide or influence as necessary; in some cases, to witness unexplainable events.

Sometimes though, their age-old conflict becomes more than just about mankind. The war may have spawned from the birth of humans, but their distaste for each other reached far beyond.

The streaks of movement approached quicker than any known measurement of speed. The sound of them entering the atmosphere could have been perceived as a sonic boom; if humans were aware. Upon entering the stratosphere, their approach slowed a bit as they came in from the East. The nine objects fell in line behind the plane's flight path.

Their course was swift and hidden.

Seconds from reaching the aircraft, they drew their weapons. One of them held high, a hammer. It began to pulsate with waves of blue, followed by lightning that sparked through the sky. Dark clouds began to form and swirl into a frenzy in the wake of their trail.

* * *

"Steady yourself," said Lucas.

Trusting his friend's instincts, Joshua prepared himself. Then he saw it.

They appeared from nowhere faster than anything he had ever witnessed; coming from all around the plane. Angels, but unlike any that Joshua ever saw. He could have sworn he felt the plane vibrate from their velocity. They headed straight for the mass of demons.

* * *

As the demon charge began to pick up speed, some noticed a detachment of the Host breaking off and heading straight for them. The site of these foolish angels sparked various reactions from crazed excitement and laughter, to comments regarding the demon's impending victory.

There was only a small few from the collective who had the sense enough to be wary of this new development. Suroc was one of them.

Using sight beyond sight, he peered closer at the bold assailants. His eyes grew wide, then he began to arc away. "Retreat! Fall back!"

The division was confused, but obeyed nonetheless. His captains soared in closer as they started to break away from the pack.

"Sir, what are you doing? This offense is punishable by torment," said one of them.

Suroc glanced back; the captain caught his eye, then recoiled from the look.

He was afraid.

"Inflixi Impetus," was all that Suroc said.

His captains now shared the same scared expression as this news began reverberating through the ranks.

They all flew faster.

* * *

The nine skimmed the surface of the plane from all sides. One even reached out with his free hand to lightly touch the smooth, aerodynamic shell. As they soared passed, the one with the long black hair made an outward hand command as he pulled his weapon, a form of a Chinese Dao, tight into his chest.

"Wreak havoc on all who remain; none are to be spared." He eyed the legion commanders and a half smile began to form. "Melennec and the others are mine."

* * *

What Joshua witnessed could not be adequately described. At least not in the convention of what most would consider possible by human standards. He counted nine angels in all. They charged straight into the heart of the blackness with no pause or deviation in their course.

It was like the demon numbers did not matter. What happened next was utterly impossible to believe, and purely spectacular to watch.

10

Inflixi Impetus

The nine picked up speed just before contact, then at the last second, fanned out into individual directions. Each struck the demons like bullets splintering wood.

Even with their weapons at the ready, the demons in the direct path had no chance; their bodies instantly vaporizing into ash. The nine broke through the dark mass of demons in mere seconds leaving nothing but punched holes of sunlight where hundreds once were.

The dark thundercloud conjured by the one with the hammer surged pass the plane like a rolling tidal wave. It enveloped the mass of demons who were now beginning to understand the seriousness of their situation.

"Inflixi Impetus!" Screeched one, as a whip made of light and metal wound around a cluster of a division and himself. He screamed even more as it tightened into his skin, and began dragging him through the sky. The angel wielding the whip flexed the great muscles in his arms as he grasped the hilt with both hands and spun the cluster around in a circle. With the precision and fluidity of a martial arts master, the demons trapped at the business end smashed into their brothers who had the misfortune of remaining in the sphere of destruction. The gyroscopic dance continued until the whip was empty. Then it was time to reload.

The arm of the angel wielding the hammer was just as muscular as his angelic brother. The skillful grace with which he barreled through demon after demon was only matched by the magnificence of the lightning storm he pulled down upon the lesser fortunate. Those caught in the strikes seem to linger in agony as their bodies contorted and tore from the sheer power. It was at moments like that when the measurement of time was probably felt; a sweet ending to their misery coming when the power finally exploded them into the familiar ash of their fallen brothers.

Another angel who held something like a sickle, twirled it in his hands while slicing bits and pieces from the demons. Once screeching with delight, they now squealed in anguish as they watched their body parts, and brothers, dissolve into ash. One dropped his weapon in a show of surrender. The brown-haired angel gripped both hands around the shortened handle of the sickle as it pulsated with light. The handle seemed to magically grow as he moved his arms apart, turning it into a starker and scarier version. It resembled the familiar one portrayed in pictures of the fictional grim reaper, but on a much more ominous scale. The angel moved so fast that the demon did not realize he had been struck. The last thing he saw before his destruction was half of his body falling away through the darkened sky.

One by one, each of the nine tallied their count as the enemy numbers dissipated. As chaotic as the demon's approach was before, their ranks and chain of command rapidly fell apart as they all realized who they were up against. It quickly became a free for all to escape. Their exit was cut short by the thundercloud, as it was meant to keep them corralled. The anarchic scene was madness; like rats trying to escape a sinking ship. Considering their sealed demise, most attempted to put up a valiant fight, but to no avail. The skill level of these nine angelic warriors was legendary throughout all the realms; certain angels even had mythic tales told by humans. These demons were finished before the battle had even begun.

Eight of the angelic warriors continued their magnificent onslaught without mercy. As instructed, none were spared. The ninth warrior, their leader, contributed his proficient talents as he made his way to the legion commanders.

Melennec and other commanders were shouting orders over the top of each other trying to restore some discipline; venom dripped from his mouth in anger for the disarray before him. Hearing a scream cut short, he turned to witness the last second of existence of a fellow commander, who was split in half vertically before disintegrating. Once the ash cleared, Melennec saw the source of destruction.

A sneer formed in the corners of his mouth. "Vaago."

The angel hovered in place; his long black hair partially covering one eye. A smile creased his face. "Hello Melennec."

The other commanders, and what few demons were left around them, gave wide berth as they knew what was coming. Vaago intentionally lowered his Dao into a passive position.

A commander saw this as an opportunity and charged from behind. Vaago smiled again.

"No, you fool!" Melennec shouted.

In a fluid motion, the angelic leader brought his imposing wings up. He turned at the precise moment and used them in the cheesy, classic wrestling move of a clothesline. As the doomed commander began to spin head over heels, Vaago brought his Dao around slicing the demon in half while continuing his turn back to face Melennec. The two halves of the demon were still crumbling to ash as he looked his enemy in the eyes.

The terror that struck all the other demons who witnessed the move, was embarrassing for Melennec. He expected more from his subordinates, especially his commanders.

The treachery of these bait tactics was not surprising. Those mindless angels have used these guerrilla maneuvers since the Fall.

The acceptance of Melennec's fate was set, though internally, he was disappointed that his last command would end like this. For a moment, his thoughts drifted back to Suroc's concern regarding caution. At least, they would share the same outcome.

He had no idea that Suroc had escaped the slaughter.

Melennec's misguided thoughts were interrupted by fading and frequency of intermittent screams. As he looked through the sky, he noticed that the thousands of troops were gone. All of them, wiped out by a handful of angels. He turned his head slightly and saw that only two of his remaining commanders were left.

The other eight angelic warriors approached Vaago and his quarry forming a circle. Everyone sheathed their weapons and watched.

Melennec dropped his eyes. He looked at his useless sword, then just tossed it aside. He held his head up and puffed out his chest. "Do what you came to do."

With one eye still peeking out from his thick black hair, Vaago glided towards his adversary, coming within mere feet.

Melennec closed his black eyes, and waited.

Nothing happened.

He opened his eyes and saw that Vaago held Melennec's discarded weapon in his hand. *How fitting. He is going to destroy me with my own sword.*

Instead, Vaago flipped the sword around and extended the hilt towards him.

A look of surprise crossed Melennec's face. "What trickery is this?"

"We have known each other since the beginning. You're ending should be that of a warrior," he said.

They both looked at each other for what seemed like a long moment. Vaago did not blink or flinch as he waited. Melennec eyed his once brother carefully, then slowly reached out and took the handle. His hatred waned for a thought of appreciation at the gesture. He wondered if the situation were reversed would he have done the same. He finished the thought knowing that this was probably the closest that a demon had ever gotten to Vaago without instant decimation. As he felt the full weight of the sword in his hand, he knew he was in striking distance. He could have easily attempted to take Vaago right then, but Melennec was not a complete fool. His old brother was the best in Majaliant Linaofaè, second only to Michael himself. His skill was superior.

Vaago floated back to a battling position and drew his weapon. With lightning fast reflexes, he spun in a quick circle and threw his Dao directly at one of the other demon commanders. The blade did not lose velocity as it struck the armor plating dead center in the chest cavity, passing through to the other side. The demon recoiled with the impact and contorted in a silent scream as the ash emanated from the entry point to envelop him entirely. Vaago brought his wings down in a quick motion that propelled him towards the other commander.

A fresh terror spread across the other demon's face as he recklessly charged his assailant. As he sliced down with his axe, Vaago arced up and over his head in a flip that brought him directly behind his enemy. Before the demon could turn and face him, Vaago placed one hand on its head and the other on the neck and snapped it. The last remaining Lieut. commander went limp immediately, and dissolved in the too familiar cloud of ash.

And then there was just Melennec.

Once again, Vaago took a position facing his old brother. He held out his hand as the Dao made its way back.

* * *

Joshua watched this, and the other scenes unfold. He thought that he saw some amazing things since coming into this role, but this was the most surreal yet.

He looked to Lucas. "Why was I allowed to see this?"

The question seemed very appropriate given the circumstances. Expecting a riddle in return was not unrealistic, so he was quite surprised when he received a straight answer.

"You asked earlier for the authority to do your job." He gestured towards the sky of the battlefield. "What you have witnessed is but a small piece of the power gifted by the Chairman. Inflixi Impetus are angels like no other. Where I protect, they strike; where guardians enforce, they pursue and intercept."

Joshua looked back at the nine warriors. He saw the last remaining demon raise his sword in final combat with the black-haired warrior. Sparks clashed where metal met metal. It was a final stand for what Joshua assumed was the leader of this ill-fated mission. He saw the demon bring his sword back up one last time before the black-haired one brought his weapon around in a clean motion, and then remained still. The demon's sword fell from his hand followed by the separation of his head from his body. The last of the ash disappeared with the blowing wind.

"They will be yours to command for the foreseeable future," continued Lucas.

Joshua's eyes widened; he head jerking back toward his friend, "What?!"

Lucas half smiled. "That is what I meant by being mindful for that which you ask."

Joshua began to shake his head. "Lucas, this is insane! I am just a mortal." He pointed outside. "This is supernatural stuff and way out of my depth. I can barely handle the human element of this war."

Lucas continued to smile. "Are you calling the Chairman insane?"

If it were possible, Joshua's eyes became wider. "That's not what I meant, and you know it. Stop smiling!"

Lucas could see that his charge and friend was getting upset. "Joshua, in the coming days, you will begin a new level of leadership. One in which the boundaries between the realms will become blurred. This must happen to service the needs of our cause and protect mankind, but we are all coming to a point when just protecting is not enough. The enemy, as you say, are stepping up their game; you must also be prepared to do the same."

Joshua's eyes dropped down as Lucas spoke. He flashed back to past events in his life where the enemy had made the first move. His decisions thus far have been more reactive in response. This would mean taking the fight to them. The look of shock and realization replaced his agitation and anger. Lucas leaned over and placed his hand on his shoulder.

"You are capable of much more than you realize. Our kind are not permitted to act without cause. Under your direction, we can all work together in the best interest of cooperation."

Joshua looked up.

Lucas smiled again. "Your words."

Joshua turned to look out the gaping hole. "Why me?"

"Because it is your destiny."

Crap.

His gaze drifted back to the outside as he was deep in thought. His focus changed as he realized something else. That was put on hold as the nine approached the aircraft. They looked awesome from a distance, but the closer they came, the more formidable and imposing their appearance. Each was as unique as the weapons they wielded; all expressed individualism not synonymous with other angels that Joshua had seen over the years.

As each passed, they gave Lucaous a courtesy nod or wave then soared out of sight. The last was their leader with the black hair.

He stopped just outside the cockpit. "Greetings, brother," said Lucas.

"Lucaous," replied Vaago with curt nod.

"Many thanks for your assistance."

A half smile spread across his face. "It was our pleasure." His one visible eye drifted to Joshua; the smile faded.

Joshua stared at him with great curiosity and wonder. He was taken aback when he noticed the expression changed when their eyes met. It appeared to be a look of disdain; something Joshua had not experienced in a very long time. In an automatic response, his look of intrigue faded. They maintained their stare for what seemed like minutes; almost daring each other to look away first. Joshua did not understand why an angel he had never met would view him with such indifference.

Vaago looked back to Lucaous once more, then spread his magnificent wings in a swift downward motion. He soared off in the direction of his warriors.

Lucas followed the trail of his brother, then inhaled and exhaled in what could have been perceived as a sign of dread. He turned to face Joshua.

His eyes were already locked on Lucas. "You really expect someone like that to follow me?"

"I will admit that Vaago is less than pleased with his orders. Nonetheless, he will obey."

"I don't want anyone on my team that I can't trust."

Lucas stepped closer. "Joshua, the Inflixi Impetus are the most feared and respected warriors in all the realms. Their skills will be needed in what is to come."

Joshua still maintained an unhappy expression. "I suppose they are part of the *plan*, —" he emphasized with finger quotes, "—that I don't know about yet."

"They are one of the key elements, yes."

"Well, I imagine what makes him so successful at his job is the loyalty of his team. I would expect the same. Based on the look that I just received, I see potential issues."

Lucas raised his eyebrows. "He just needs to warm up to you."

Joshua's head snapped back. "Are you kidding me?" He wanted to get up and walk around in frustration, but the close confines of the cockpit and the gaping hole prevented that.

"I'm sure that everyone would like to have more time to get used to the situation, but that doesn't seem like it's going to happen. I need people with me that will follow directions without questions. My job is to save as many souls as possible. I can't do that effectively if there is a conflict within my camp."

Lucas wanted to argue the point on behalf of Vaago and his arrogant attitude, but his brother's first impression did not leave a lot of support. What Joshua said was sound. He was impressed with his young charge and his command of leadership and perception. It was apparent to everyone why the Chairman chose him. Inflixi Impetus was going to be crucial going forward. Joshua was not yet aware of how much, and Lucas was not permitted to discuss. He needed to come up with another approach as Joshua's mind appeared to be made up. Was it possible that bluntness could be the answer?

It was Lucas's turn to point out to the battlefield. "Would you not agree that what you just witnessed was unprecedented in all of mankind?"

Joshua did not know where Lucas was going, but his look softened at the fresh memory. "I could not have imagined what I saw, no."

"Would you also agree that the odds were greatly unfavorable?"

Joshua looked at Lucas but didn't say a word.

"It is reasonable for someone in your situation to have doubt," said Lucas, "but, I have witnessed your capacity for providing the benefit of doubt where warranted. Believe me when I tell you that without Vaago and his warriors, this war will be costlier than you could fathom. This is not an opportunity; this is an imperative. You will need this type of power going forward."

Caution and concerned now crossed Joshua's face. "Why?"

Lucas had to be careful. He must not disobey his orders. "The enemy you have encountered thus far has not been the decision-makers."

Joshua straightened up slowly as he listened.

"In the grander scheme, to quote a corporate vernacular, you have only dealt with mid-level management. Both human and demon senior leadership has been watching you. They are displeased with your accomplishments and have a plan to become more actively involved."

Joshua thought for a moment. "How involved?

"Your world will be forever changed. The structures of your governments will fall. Anarchy will ensue."

Joshua looked away with a tilt of his head. Those words burned the backs of his eyes with images of an apocalyptic future; one where all humans knew, was suffering. The faces of those closest to him began to form in the rolling waves of mankind's despair. The appearance of a tyrant sitting upon a rocky and jagged throne; burning red eyes looked over them in dominion. A wicked smile stretched from ear to ear with legions upon legions of grotesque demons hovering about like locusts devouring a harvest.

Joshua steadied himself on what remained of the console as he drew a breath; it felt as if his lungs had been deprived longer than his body could tolerate. His breathing became rapid, almost to the point of hyperventilation. He looked about, wide-eyed as if trying to get his bearings. Once the breathing steadied, he saw that Lucas's hand was resting upon his shoulder.

"I *hate* it when you do that," said Joshua.

Lucas removed his hand and looked upon him sympathetically. "Joshua, what you have just seen is a possible outcome of this war if we are not properly prepared."

Their eyes met.

Joshua relented and looked down. "Fine. I'll give what's-his-name and his super friends a chance," he looked back up to Lucas. "Tell the Chairman that I still need to know the plan."

"He is fully aware of that," said Lucas with a grin.

Joshua looked out into the sky again. "I noticed something during the massacre. Is it just me or is the plane not moving?"

"It is yet another enhancement of your new level of leadership. Your plane of perception has been altered to one where time is not a factor."

Joshua had thought long ago that the unexplainable things he has witnessed were becoming easier to accept the more time he was exposed. This one caught him off-guard as he stood up and peered outside. The aircraft seemed to hover in place with time standing still. He looked back towards the ruined security door. "The passengers?"

"They are unaware of any differences. Mere seconds will have passed."

Joshua felt a bit overwhelmed. "How often is something like this going to happen?"

"Like everything else, it will happen as necessary to meet your situation," said Lucas. He patted Joshua lightly on the shoulder. "It is time for me to go."

Joshua was going to protest, but knew it would do no good. There was still the business about the damaged aircraft though. "Lucas, how are we going to get this plane to the ground safely?"

He turned toward the outside. "You are a very capable young man. I'm sure you will figure something out." He shimmered to the outside of the plane and unfolded his wings.

Shocked, Joshua scrambled out of the copilot's chair. "Wait!"

Lucas turned and smiled.

"Was that, a joke?!" Joshua said with disbelief.

"It was a good one, yes?"

"*No!* Not even close. You have *got* to work on your delivery." Joshua said in aggravation.

Lucas held up his hands in mock surrender. "Okay, point taken. You have all the tools at your disposal for landing safely. You just need to use them."

"Lucas, this plane is inoperable. As Sentinel said, none of the aircraft mechanics are functional. We're sitting at 10,000 feet in a big metal tube."

Lucas looked at Joshua knowingly. "You still have Sentinel though. He is capable of much more than you realize."

"He?"

Lucas drifted back further from the plane and spread his wings. "Work with Sentinel. I will see you soon." With that, Lucas flew away.

Joshua looked on in astonishment as he vanished out of sight. "Super," he said as he flopped back down into the seat. He stared into the distance for a few seconds then looked around the ruined cockpit. This was the first chance he had to take a hard look at the remaining instrumentation. LED panels were flickering from intermittent power surges. The surviving plasma screen displays were rippled with puddles of fluid from underneath. Scorch marks from flash fires surrounded a few switches and knobs. He imagined what this looked like before; polished, state-of-the-art technology illuminating from every functionality and capability within the small, confined space. Now, it looked as if a visionary artist with a very expensive budget purposefully trashed an elegant sculpture in the name of his craft.

Joshua looked to the left and imagined Capt. Bill sitting there. He slowly reached out to where his seat would have been. What was he going to tell Valerie, Beth? After a few moments, he looked down and withdrew his hand. He hoped that Bill and the other crew was transitioned safely and felt no pain in the end. As if on cue with that thought, time seemed to move forward again. He didn't notice the instant it started, but imagined it would look like making a jump to light speed.

Within seconds, Joshua heard the scraping of the ruined security door being pulled.

Tim's head popped around, "Sir, are you okay?" He looked about the devastation. His eyes popped out then stopped at the gaping hole.

"I'm fine Tim."

He stepped just inside the door as Kelan squeezed through. Both looked sadly at the copilot as they carefully stepped around him. Kelan had wanted to come into the cockpit alone, but Tim had insisted on taking point to ensure Joshua's safety.

"Wow!" He said looking around. Unlike Tim, he glossed over the gaping hole and looked at the remains of the console. He knew the answer, but needed to ask for Tim's benefit. "How did you get the plane to level out?"

He knew he was putting Joshua on the spot, but was certain that his boss would have a pliable and realistic explanation.

"As it turns out, Jonah's state-of-the-art technology was made to handle situations like this. There are still some working parts," he said. He placed his feet on the pedals and grabbed the yoke to make it look more convincing. It wasn't false in the sense that the working parts were, now; the angels holding the aircraft up— and apparently, Sentinel was more than just technology. Joshua didn't want to think about that too much now; he would have a lot of questions later though.

Kelan hoped that Tim bought it. Alas, hope is not a good strategy; especially in the heat of the moment.

"That doesn't make any sense. Sentinel said the plane was not functional. *You* confirmed that yourself," said Tim to Kelan.

Kelan looked a bit panicked as he searched for an answer, but Joshua's mind was quicker. As in other situations within his leadership, Joshua's innate ability to work under stressful situations kicked into play.

"Aren't you glad that is not the case?" His focus then shifted from placating Tim's curiosity to the more immediate need of landing.

This would have been much easier if Kelan and Tim were not right next to him. He had a hunch though, and hoped that Sentinel would be aware enough to understand without literal commentary.

"Sentinel, locate the nearest Associate airport," said Joshua.

"Reykjavík, Iceland," came the reply.

"Contact them and let them know we need to make an emergency stop. We need to keep a lid on this until we figure out our next move."

They waited.

Time, once again seemed to stand still. Of course, it wasn't, because Joshua could feel Kelan's and Tim's eyes upon him, and saw the clouds sailing by. That did not mean that the perception one experienced while holding their breath in anticipation was any different.

Everyone, at some point in his or her life, has experienced a type of anxiety brought about by a situation; one where a stillness preceded a moment of an abrupt emotion of some sort. Kind of like where a game show would go to a commercial break before announcing a winner. Melina had called it waiting for the "big reveal" from one of her decoration shows on television.

Joshua was experiencing one of those moments. Now, his newfound awareness of time's ability to *actually* stand still was thrown into the mix. If he were ever in a position where he had to explain the reality that he lived in, he would be hard-pressed to find a true believer. Crazy was beginning to take on a whole new definition.

Suddenly, the radio came to life. "Keflavík International, this is Jonah One papa papa eight heavy. We are requesting clearance for a precautionary landing. Engines feel a bit sluggish and instrumentation seems to be a little off. We'd like to pull in for a bit and get our bearings. Requesting vector and heading confirmation, over."

Joshua tried not to show his shock. The voice was Capt. Bill's.

Within a couple of seconds, ATC from Keflavík joined the conversation. "Jonah One, this is Keflavík air-traffic control. We have been tracking your flight path for the last 237 nautical miles. Your course and altitude seem to be steady. Has an emergency developed, over?" The aircraft's decent from the explosion was apparently covered up by supernatural misdirection.

The anticipation of the three in the cockpit began to grow.

Sentinel let a few seconds pass before responding. "Nothing that can't be handled, tower. I'd just feel a little more comfortable getting this bird on the ground. We hit a pocket of turbulence sometime back and it spooked the passengers."

"Understood, Jonah One. How are you on fuel?"

"Plenty of juice, tower," replied Sentinel.

"Roger that, Jonah One. Standby."

A couple of minutes passed.

"Jonah One, Keflavík tower, over." This was a new voice.

"Keflavík tower, this is Jonah One," said Sentinel, still using the voice of Joshua's friend.

"What is your cargo?"

Although the three in the cockpit were slightly confused by the question, Sentinel understood. Protocols for certain considerations had been established were Joshua was concerned, and had to be followed. This too had to look like it was coming from the pilot. "Say again, tower?"

The new voice replied in a more serious tone. "Captain, what type of cargo are you carrying?"

"Precious."

The response from the new voice was excited and immediate. "Copy that, captain. Standby for immediate vector. You are cleared to land on runway two nine. All air traffic will be cleared. Do you require emergency or medical services?"

"Negative tower, but we will need alternative transport for the passengers, and a safe place to park this aircraft."

"Roger that, Jonah One. By the time you arrive, we will have hanger space cleared."

"Thank you, tower," said Sentinel. The voice then shifted back to the one Joshua had been used to all of these years. "Sir, please use the heads-up display for direction." Hard-light imagery appeared in front and around him. A tactical screen took the place of what used to be the windshield. "I will take care of altitude and thrust."

"Okay," said Joshua a little nervously. His hands gripped the yoke a bit tighter.

Sentinel sensed the apprehension in his voice. "Sir, the dotted green line is you. The red directional arrow is the flight path. Just keep both aligned and you will be fine."

Joshua began to move the yoke; the dotted line responded. In a few seconds, he had the two lined up. All three of the men in the cockpit could feel the aircraft shift in response.

"Well, this is not so bad," said Joshua under his breath.

"Just like a video game," responded Sentinel.

A slight grin cracked against the side of his face. Joshua had a feeling that he was going to like this new relationship.

* * *

Keflavík International Airport was not lavish by any means. It was a remote way station on the outskirts of Iceland's southern peninsula. In the grand scheme of things, it was almost perfect; the seclusion away from the populace allowed for tighter controls of any information that could bring about unwanted attention.

The only news media that would need to be dealt with were onboard the dying aircraft. Langston and Alice were already spinning an explanation; massive turbulence due to a shift in the air pressure system causing intermittent stalling of the engines. A highly unlikely event, but could theoretically happen with astronomical odds and alignment of many key elements. It wasn't much to work with, but could be the most plausible. They didn't need to have the whole thing sorted yet;

just enough to steer the newsies away from the truth. A truth that even they didn't completely know.

True to their promise, the Icelanders cleared one of their massive hangers. With the assistance of the angelic guardians, Jonah One could land safely and taxi directly in. Whether by happenstance or planned, the hole on the port side of the cabin went largely unnoticed. This did not come as a surprise to Joshua. He knew that nothing mechanical could explain the otherwise impossible operation of the large airliner. If he didn't know any better himself, he would have a hard time wrapping his head around something like this too.

The safe landing refocused Tim from his curiosity as well. He coordinated JPS personnel with local airport security to get passengers transferred to a safeguarded area.

Keflavík International administration was in the process of securing an aircraft large enough to convey everyone back to the States. In the meantime, passengers were made comfortable within the hanger; amenities such as seating, refreshments, tables, and televisions, were brought in by airport staff. Not once did anyone look up to the damaged flight deck. Joshua half smiled at the power of suggestion from the supernatural.

There was a manager's office located in a corner of the hanger. Both Kelan and Tim felt it would be better for Joshua and Melina to remain enclosed. All available JPS personnel were armed and surrounded the office both inside and outside of the hanger.

Jillian walked in with refreshments. "Here you go, sir."

Joshua accepted the juice. "Thank you," he said as he took a drink.

She smiled and handed Melina a drink as well.

Langston walked in with Alice. He presented his computer tablet to Joshua. "I think we've got the right message. We want you to look and tell us what *you* think."

Alice took a seat in the corner. "We polled most of the media. They're buying the turbulence story. Some are already working their perspective pieces for their rags."

"We believe our official press release will corroborate their stories. This will become no more than a freak accident due to mother nature," said Langston.

"This should blow over with no further investigation," added Alice.

Joshua skimmed through the statement with a frown. He then handed the tablet back to Langston.

"Is there something wrong with the wording?" He asked.

Joshua hesitated. "No, the statement looks fine. I'm just trying to figure out what I'm going to tell the families," he brought his hand up to his head and started to rub. "Bill, Jim, —" his hand fell to the armrest with a thump, "—the others."

Melina reached over and put her hand on her husband's shoulder. He grasped it with his own.

Joshua became embroiled in his thoughts. This whole act was senseless. In all the attempts ever made against his life since he entered this world, each and every one had failed, but all had always come with a price. Four good people died today, and for what? The demon's objectives failed once again. They continued to make play after play but never seemed to obtain their purpose; never seemed to learn from their mistakes. Innocents were always caught in the middle, and sometimes, ended up making the ultimate sacrifice. Maybe that was the whole point. Maybe that was their way of getting to Joshua.

People getting hurt or dying because of him, ate away at his soul every day. The guilt over his destiny and the effect on others was becoming very burdensome and too much to bear. To throw more fuel on this fire, the incorporation of Familiars, -people who were supposed to have souls- into their heinous plans would bring about a new age of warfare. Lucas had said that Joshua would need to become more proactive going forward. It was bad enough when Familiars, and the Undeclared, were used due to their ignorance; but to willingly participate in the destruction of humanity was something Joshua had a hard time fathoming.

Ironically, he had more sympathy for the stupid ones. He immediately looked up and outside the cloudy, scratched window of the office.

His frown deepened as he watched Kelly Granger. She sat at a lone card table with a couple of agents; her hands cuffed underneath the table with a coat draped over her lap.

Langston followed Joshua's gaze. "How do you want to handle that?" He said nodding his head towards her.

"She goes back with us. Put in a call to Chief Willis down at the one nine precinct. Tell him I need a favor. I want an interrogation team to find out what she knows." He looked over to Alice. "Coordinate with the FBI on a witness relocation. I have a feeling that Ms. Granger is no longer safe. I need her invisible; off the radar. Tell the director that I need this kept quiet."

Alice nodded. "Do you want the FBI to do the interrogation as well?"

Joshua shook his head. "No, too many unknowns. We need to compartmentalize the steps-"; looking at Langston now, "-operate as individual cells to minimize the amount and flow," he said referring to the information. Langston responded with a slight nod of understanding. "Chief Willis and Director Coleman are both Associates. I trust only them to be discreet." Looking back and forth between Alice and Langston now. "Don't be afraid to use my name with either of them."

Even with the seriousness of the situation, Alice managed a grin. "Are you kidding? I use your name all the time. It gets me to the front of the line at Starbucks."

Joshua couldn't help but grin too. Tension defused; mission accomplished.

Kelan opened the door. "The tower just contacted me. An Airbus A380 is inbound and will arrive in the next 45 minutes. Once we complete the security sweep, transfer stores and armory, we can be airborne within ninety." He looked at his watch. "I've got a cleaner and transportation team on the way to take care of our plane."

Joshua nodded. Melina saw his eyebrows furrow, then his gaze drifted into a blank stare. He always got this way when he was in another place within deep thought. These responsibilities were weighing heavy on his shoulders. She hoped things would get better for him soon.

Her optimism was one of the things that he loved most about her. There were not too many black clouds in her life. Joshua was determined to keep it that way.

If Lucas was right, and he usually was, things would not be getting any better, for any of them.

11

Harbinger

His treadmill had an impressive array of lights, buttons, and various other options that made the simplistic act of merely running look like a complicated process. The model he was using today seemed to be geared towards people who either did not have the time to set up their own workout session, or were not smart enough to. The effort to decipher a board that looked like it was built for a space shuttle seemed to contradict the very reason for it.

He reached toward the touch screen to switch from the international news to the treadmill's controls. He was pleased with this morning's progress. Adjusting the speed downward from 5.5 mph, he then leveled out the 6 percent incline. The two-minute cool down period started while reaching for his towel and water bottle. Switching back to the international news, he watched a puff piece on Melina Arden's wardrobe.

Once the treadmill stopped, he stepped off and began stretching out his muscles. The only other occupant in the room was a rather unfit gentleman two units down, who seemed to be exuding an enormous amount of sweat for the limited effort put forth. The man kept fumbling with a small machine that was apparently attached to some telematics in his sneakers.

A businessman. It had to be. They are the only type to take themselves seriously enough to purchase all those gadgets thinking that it aids in their fitness and, in this man's case, weight-loss. He wanted to smile at the absurdity, but let it go. In his mind, the recipe for fitness was quite simple; eat less, move more. Tossing his towel and water into a small duffel, he made his way out of the hotel gym.

Once back in his room, he secured the lock on his door. Dropping his workout bag on the bed, he then went to the closet, and extracted a softball-sized, circular device from the confines of a secret compartment within his suitcase. Moving to his room door, he affixed the one-inch thin apparatus directly in the center and turned it slightly clockwise until it clicked.

He then very carefully pulled sensor cords from around the device, four in all, and placed them at key points on, and around the door. When he was satisfied with the positioning, he activated it; the sensor light went from green to red. Very gently he removed his hand, careful not to disturb the motion sensors. Even the slightest vibration might trigger a detonation. Although the blast was meant to project outward, it would still do quite a bit of damage on the inside as well.

He began removing layers of his workout clothes as he walked to the hotel window. Some scars in the shapes of slices, puncture wounds, and a couple that looked like bullet holes, graced a very fit frame and torso. He opened the curtains and looked at the magnificence of Lake Geneva. After a few moments, he picked up the hotel phone to order breakfast.

"Je vous remercie pour l'appel interne à manger. Comment puis-je vous aider?" Came the voice.

He rattled off something about poached eggs, toast, and tea.

"Je vous remercie Monsieur le Président. Il sera prêt en 20 minutes," was the reply.

Returning to the window for another gaze, his expression was solemn, as if in deep remembrance of something. His regal pose was that of a general or commander about to impart a speech upon his troops before battle. The man struck this stance often; completely unaware that he even did it at times. His reputation for those that knew of him, was as a man without fear. His pose added an image to the legend. Over time, the legend grew, and was given a name.

The Harbinger.

After one last look, he turned, went into the bathroom, and started the shower.

Emerging refreshed with nothing but a towel wrapped around him, he heard a knock upon his door. Reaching into the small duffel from the gym, he removed a Ruger Mark III and chambered a round.

He cautiously peered out the peephole. "Un moment," he said satisfied that it was room service. Carefully deactivating the motion sensor cords, he then tucked the gun between the small of his back and tightly wound towel, and put on a terrycloth robe. Once the server had delivered his breakfast and left, he reactivated the door's security explosive, then retreated to the table to examine his order. No sooner had he mixed his tea; a familiar chirp came through his encrypted mobile device.

The text simply read, [WHITEHORSE].

He studied the display for a second. This was a contract request. He put the mobile down on the table then began buttering the toast. Once he had everything set and took a bite, he retrieved his mobile and replied. [DESIGNATION]

The response was immediate. [001]

He reached into the robe and removed the gun, laid it upon the table, then sat. He leaned back and crossed his legs as he took a sip of tea, then another bite.

The location was the United States.

He looked out his window savoring the bitter, sweet taste of marmalade as he pondered this request.

The money wasn't a question. He had amassed quite a bit over his career, and had no need for more. Any job that he took now was purely for sport. His curiosity was peaked though. Whitehorse was a secured death contract. That usually meant a high-profile person of interest; sometimes with possible political ramifications.

He took another sip.

The only real question was the target. He could always request more information, then opt out if the risk was too high.

He thought as he ate.

The decision was to know more before he could make that determination.

He took a few more bites and another sip of tea before replying.

[RFI DROP]. This let the sender know that he was interested but wanted more information before committing.

[LOCUS], came the response; asking where to deliver the information.

One could never be too careful in his line of work. He established specific codes and key phrases for anyone wishing to contract his services. His index of terminology was not widely distributed, so whomever the person was on the other end to this conversation would have to have the credentials and contacts to get his number.

[4], he typed stating the location.

[<48], was their final reply.

He tossed the secured mobile onto the table and continued to eat his breakfast. He'll know more after the information is dead-dropped within the next 48 hours.

* * *

Matthew just finished his last class and began walking across the quad. The wind was ridiculous that day. As he moved through Killian Court, it seemed to pick up even more. Looking around, all the lesser rabble didn't seem to mind the bluster; they wandered through campus completely oblivious.

The skies were blue; the sun was brilliant, and the only "weather" to speak of, was a light gust. To Matthew, that was enough. Unless conditions were absolutely perfect, he hated being outside. This was just one of the many quirks that distinguished him from the normal populace. His plan now was to cut back through the Maclaurin buildings to stay out of his perception of the weather as much as possible. He looked down at his watch and, based on his pace, calculated another seven minutes to Ames Street.

Midterms had occupied most of his thinking over the last couple of weeks, so he was trying to shake that off in preparation for burning the midnight oil. Matthew's mind began to recalibrate from theoretical condensates to programming code. He was so close to finishing the final string; just a few more tests.

In the back of his mind, he hoped that his roommate had already left to do whatever it was he did on Friday nights. Jimmy always partied too hard on the weekends, and gave Matthew all kinds of grief for not participating. He tried to explain to Jimmy many times that it was not why he came to MIT. If *that* was to be his secondary major, he could have gone to any school he wanted; he was here to learn, not party. Jimmy's grade-point average was not as good as his, which Matthew thought had a direct correlation. Jimmy was a big boy; in some cases, a non-evolved Homo-neanderthalensis, and it wasn't Matthew's problem. He still didn't appreciate all the comments. Especially from someone who would most likely flunk out in his second year if he didn't change his ways.

The unofficial understanding around campus was that if one worked hard, they could play hard as well. Matthew didn't get that. If he worked hard, then he could achieve more. What would be the point in "playing hard" to compensate for the level of hard work? The words 'work' and 'play' were antonyms, and as far as he was concerned, should never be in the same sentence.

Matthew was an analytical thinker. Linear algorithms danced through the portion of his brain where the communal aspect to his personality should have lived. He didn't consider himself a nerd or an egg head, but his perception of his social standing differed from those around him. He seemed to be more comfortable with his nose inside a book rather than inside a Solo Cup. From the narrow-minded thinking of those around him, he supposed that was what separated him the most.

He frowned thinking why his university life would be any better than high school. He always caught a lot of crap from his high school classmates about not fitting in, albeit on a much larger level.

That was one of the things he recognized about MIT; he was no longer in the minority. Well, not as much as he used to be.

These thoughts and more swirled through his head as he cut through Eastman Court toward East Campus. Matthew's cognitive abilities superseded most at his age. It was like he could see formulas and calculations hanging in midair as he worked. He might have been a person considered to have a "beautiful mind," and unfortunately, the personality to match.

He just didn't seem to fit in with the rest of the world.

He was okay with that, for the most part. Mainly because he knew his earning potential was going to blow everyone else out of the water. He promised his parents that he would finish college first before pursuing his dominance in the scientific field. If millions were to be made from a revolutionary idea twirling about in his large brain, his mom had told him that it could wait until after graduation. He did it to appease her, but thought that it was more of a formality than anything else. He truly felt that he was smarter than anyone there.

In one specific case, that *was* true.

Upon opening the door to 62 Hayden, he could already hear the loud music emanating from Talbot Lounge. He rolled his eyes as he moved through the small lobby.

Matthew hated living at East Campus because of its distinctive reputation as the party block at MIT, but in part, because of the distance from a girl.

That was highly irregular for Matthew. He had always been wary of the female species because the only time he was ever noticed by them, was when they wanted something. Up until high school, they were nothing but a distraction. Pretty girls, specifically cheerleaders, would use him for his brain to help pass ridiculously easy classes to maintain their status on the cheer squad; another stupid and wasteful expenditure of time. It seemed that the act of throwing arms and pom-

poms up in the air would be a diversion to the Neolithic past time known as football. What does a girl in a skimpy outfit add to the overall value of the point scoring?

The bizarre act of catering to their study request, puzzled him at times, but it boiled down to a simple fact. They were pretty, and he liked the attention; Matthew was, after all, a boy and not stupid.

It bothered him a little that he was being used, but he was also being noticed. Even smart, unattractive boys fantasized about being wanted by pretty little tartlets. Popularity was never high on his priority list, but during times like that, he could see the appeal.

Sometimes his reputation served him well as being the smartest person in school. He was always the first on everybody's pick list for knowledge. No matter what capacity though, it remained that girls were just obstacles.

And then there was Jane.

This was an unknown area to Matthew, but part of the draw could have been her awkwardness and seemingly inability to fit in; just like him. He met her in orientation a year and a half ago; Ironically, over an incident of stumbling and dropping books and papers. They struck a chord with each other's gawkiness. She had been one of his best friends since. Unfortunately, she lived in the New West housing all the way across the other side of campus. It was a hardship, but not one to keep them from spending time together. Nothing romantic had developed yet, but he was always hopeful.

Before he reached the stairs, his cell phone rang. He looked down at the display with a toothy smile. "Hey Jane!"

"So how hard was that particle physics test yesterday? I think I screwed up the theorem on large electron-positron linear colliders," she said a bit nasally.

He smiled at the statement. Matthew never had an issue or question on how smart he was on anything, but Jane was always second-guessing stuff. That was one of the things that he liked about her. Her imperfection on an emotional level gave him more confidence that he might have something to offer her in the future. It had nothing to do with him being smarter or opposites attracting; more so inadequacies complementing each other.

"I'm sure you did just fine. One of the biggest things to remember is the separation of particle measurements between leptons and hadrons. Remember, the light ones are leptons, and the heavy ones are hadrons. L and H; those are the keys. The light ones are more precise while the heavy ones are composite—"

"Sometimes I hate how smart you are," she said snidely.

He could hear the smile on the other end. "That's what makes me so adorable."

She laughed. "Have you heard from Brooks yet?"

He shouldered his sliding backpack as he looked at his watch. "Nope, but that doesn't mean anything. He's always getting lost in his experiments. He's probably still in the lab with no concept to the time."

She laughed. "You're one to talk. You spend so much time on your computer; you miss meals."

He rolled his eyes again for a completely different reason. "I've told you before that I'm working—"

"On something very important," finishing his sentence. "I know, I know. You make the rest of us nerds look like normal people in comparison," she said.

He was still smiling. Matthew loved to hear her talk. He didn't notice the nasally tone or, for that fact, the snort that sometimes came with her laugh. People falling in love tend to overlook certain things that may annoy others. In Matthew's case, love was blind, and like many, it may prove to be his undoing due to his naïveté and willingness to only see what he considered perfection. Being the genius he believed he was, he should've known that perfection, by definition, meant the highest degree of proficiency, excellence, or skill. His classification of that word meant nothing in the world of emotional attachments.

Again, love was really blind.

Bellamy Brooks was Matthew's best friend since high school. They met the first day of their freshman year in old man Dobbins' second-period history class. Brooks had just moved to town two weeks before.

It was obvious that he felt out of place, but that was typical for anyone who moved somewhere new; he had that same nervous look all the freshly transplanted shared. It was double the pain for him as he was already a member of the geek community.

Brooks preferred the term geek over a nerd. To the beautiful people and the jocks, there was no difference; but to those for whom the label applied, geek was a step above. A proud moniker that could be worn as a badge of honor, a symbol shared by some of the most brilliant minds in history. How many nerds have ever made a notable contribution to the sciences? Sure, there was a branded few that slipped through the cracks to documented stardom. But not as many as the noble social class of the geek.

Matthew remembered cutting his eyes over to Brooks' desk and seeing him doodling on a piece of paper. Western civilization being a bit of a bore, Matthew kept watching, curious as to what Brooks concentrated on so hard. As he angled for a clearer view, he noticed science fiction cartoons were the results of the furious scribbling. Semi-impressed by his taste in monsters and spacemen, what captured Matthew's attention was the calculations scrawled between the images. He had discovered during the lunch period later in the day, that Brooks had been plotting trajectories and frequencies of phasers and photon percentages required to obliterate the alien caricatures. Using his own self-proclaimed hybrid method of calculus and physics, he claimed to have developed a more effective and efficient way to achieve the same results. Brooks had explained that random shots were a waste of energy and often, a show of power to the opposing force. It was a classic play, as Brooks had described, of "mine's bigger than yours."

He stated then, as he has many times since, that if testosterone were air soluble, the power hungry, neo-fascist, non-energy efficient idiots of the world would choke on their own breath. If the stupid people in charge planned accordingly, they could still decimate their enemies while maintaining an adequate supply in reserve. Wasted energy was simply unacceptable. The two have been best friends since.

That was Brooks' thing; energy. His strange childhood obsession garnered him a scholarship at MIT for his promising theories around ColdFusion.

As they spent more time together, a healthy competition developed throughout high school on everything Scholastic. Brooks was extremely smart, but Matthew knew full well *he* was the king; or so all of those who considered themselves the best always thought. They were constantly challenging each other to brainteasers both would design in the hopes of forcing the other to yield to the true master of intelligence. Of course, everything was done in fun, but each had their own secret dream of beating the other to wear the crown.

The game was mild in high school, but seemed to step up once they both came to MIT. Jane thought the whole thing was stupid and had no problem voicing her opinion. That just egged both on further to prove who was the smartest.

Regardless of the friendly rivalry, they found that when they were both accepted to MIT, it would make for a better college experience if they could rely on each other's friendship and support. That line of thinking seemed logical to both.

Matthew's hallway on the third floor was sprinkled haphazardly with obstacles on either side; bicycles propped up against walls, textbooks stacked carelessly, even a box of clothing marked with what seemed to be a mother's handwriting. The box had been there for at least a month with no visible signs that it had been moved or even opened.

He grunted at the randomness. Matthew reminded himself that some of the most notable minds in history filled their lives with clutter. Einstein was brilliant, but his house was a mess.

He walked by a whiteboard with some rudimentary formulas on it. Every time he passed, he desperately wanted to correct the inaccuracies in the calculations; not to help the poor fool out, but more so to keep himself from always noticing that it was wrong. If they weren't going to move the board, the least they could do was have the math right.

"Hello!" Jane yelled from the phone. "Earth to Matthew!"

He snapped out of his momentary disgust for his unwanted building dwellers, and resumed his goofy smile. "Sorry about that."

"You have *got* to let that stuff go. You can't get all torqued up every time you walk down the hall," she said. Jane knew him long enough to recognize the groaning sounds and what they represented, even through the phone.

"You say that every time," he said, as his smile became wider. Regardless of the context, he loved the fact that she knew him that well. "I'll let it go when they clean it up," he said as he reached his room and began shifting as he fumbled for his keys.

She laughed. "Listen, what time do you want to head over to the Miracle of Science Grill?"

He froze completely, forgetting that he had plans with Jane and Brooks that night. He looked up and down the long corridor as if the answer to her question was hidden beneath one of the clusters of hallway debris.

He needed to finish the code. It would prove to Brooks once and for all, that Matthew was absolute in his brilliance.

"Um, Jane–"

"Are you kidding me! You are going to blow us off again for work?" Came the response; proving once again, that Jane's intuitive nature was sharp.

Matthew's current situation could be defined appropriately as a conundrum. A more apt and justifiable term would be oxymoronic, with the emphasis on moron. For someone who wanted to strike up a romantic relationship, he would first have to understand the amount of effort required to initiate and sustain it. Matthew was always good at the mechanics around the principles required to create something out of nothing. However, when it came to application, he couldn't necessarily build it. He *knew* what it was going to take to make a relationship work. His heart was not going to interfere with his mind when it came to science though. For a young genius, he was already set in his ways; again, proving that he was not as smart as he thought he was.

"This is probably going to be the last night that I need to complete this project. If I get started now, there is a good chance that I can be finished before the Grill closes. Then I can join you," he said hopefully.

A few seconds passed in silence. He waited patiently as Jane was apparently mulling over his statement.

He heard a slight muffled sigh through the phone, despite the reverberating bass beat of the music coming from the floors below.

"Fine," she said with disappointment.

"Great!" Matthew said, completely oblivious of the tone.

He took her words literally instead of how they were intended, further proving just how stupid he was.

He finished his conversation happily and told her to save him some fries. As he opened the door to his room, Matthew was still smiling, then it momentarily faded. He scanned the small, shared dwelling with only the movement of his eyes. No sign of the roommate. The crooked smile slightly returned. He quickly turned towards Jimmy's closet and looked on the top shelf. His duffel was gone.

"Yes!" he said with a fist pump. Matthew slammed the heavy wooden door to his room and took a few steps over to his desk. He then dropped his backpack rather roughly on the seat. He bent over to start the boot up sequence to the process servers stacked all around his desk. While they were warming up, he extracted his laptop from his backpack, powered it up, then checked network relays. As his computer equipment was coming to life, he walked over to his small fridge and extracted two cans of Mountain Dew. On his way back to his desk, he stopped at his dresser, opened his sock and underwear drawer, and thrust his hand through the neatly folded items. Within seconds, he pulled out two giant Slim Jim's and smiled again.

Placing his snack choices on the edge of the desk, he snatched the backpack out of his seat, dropped it to the side, and plopped down into the newly vacated chair.

With his fingers clasped together, Matthew pushed outward popping his knuckles, then stretched as signs of electronic life came to his system. By the time he had finished loosening his arms and body, the laptop was waiting for its master. Making sure his machine was connected to his wireless network, he typed a security command, and was rewarded with a file that simply read 'Trojan'.

He mentally patted himself on the back for that name. While it was an accurate description of his project, it wasn't as easy as hiding in a horse. The principles were the same though. And tonight, he was going to prove once and for all that he was the best and smartest.

12

The Hydra

Three and a half hours passed. Matthew burned through the cans of soda and meat products in the first 30 minutes, but they were more so to placate any pending urges for nutrition. While he could have gotten more snacks that were scattered about, he was in the zone. His focus and attention were so in tune with his tasks; for him, time became meaningless. Any bodily signals that he was running on fat reserves were unconsciously ignored. He was a skinny little runt to begin with, so there wasn't much stored for use. His mind had a way of shutting out any autonomic cues such as hunger or waste expulsion when he was working. It was like a central core processor and his body was the spaceship. If need be, he could shut down life-support in the nonessential parts.

Matthew made another adjustment to the hydra code to allow for wider and longer aperture. He needed to have more time in the outer firewall to simultaneously deactivate the redundancies in a second and possibly third-tier shell. He had heard that some governments and companies were tripling their firewall protection, making it virtually impossible to penetrate that third barrier. Those that used phased shell sequencing would be tough. If their system detected a firewall breach on the outer shell, the second-tier firewall would begin defensive measures based on the attack, with the sole purpose of stopping any penetration to the protected mainframe or private information.

Matthew knew though, that the first and second firewalls were merely sophisticated decoys. They weren't meant to stop the hack, but stall it. The main problem was the third firewall. That was usually the one powered by artificial intelligence. It was the new game changer in cyber protection; a type of defensive barrier that would turn the tables on most hackers.

Conceptually, it was beautiful. Once the breach was detected in the first firewall, the third firewall went on the offensive. Unknown to the hackers, as the first and second firewalls slowed the attack, the third firewall gathered intelligence *about* the attack, then waited.

Hackers generally reroute network and signal IPs, use back door accesses through unprotected gateways, and sometimes, use authorized access protocols obtained by illicit and undetectable means. Of course, these were only a few of the tricks used to secure illegal entry. The pranksters were so quick in their attack though, it was generally known as impossible to detect, unless caught in the act precisely at the right time, or by another smarter-than-average hacker. By the time they could be traced, the hack had been completed, and the loop was closed.

Third firewall protocol changed that. As soon as the breach in the first firewall happened, a detection signal initiated the protocol. Once the second barrier was breached, the firewall's version of a hydra latched onto the signal at the point of entry and traveled the pathways back to the origin. The firewall's hydra simply waited for the attacker's hydra to penetrate the second barrier, letting the attacker do all the work.

The veracity and viciousness with which the third firewall's hydra responded was impressive. True to its namesake, it reached through the breach with its tentacles and did not let go. It used sophisticated technology to track the breadcrumbs from the outside and also attack from within; a military technique of a frontal assault with flanking troops on either side of the enemy. The cyber criminals never saw it coming.

Hackers were never bold enough, and in some cases, smart enough to get through the second barrier. Crackers, on the other hand, saw everything as a challenge. They were the super geniuses of cyberattacks. Some of the most notorious computerized crimes of the technology age were done by crackers. Penetrate the impenetrable; a badge worn by only a small few.

Until now.

Matthew rubbed his tired and weary eyes as he waited for his new adjustment to consolidate. It was going to take a bit longer than normal; he wanted to make sure that the change was going to populate properly so he could follow up with a string test. He was okay with waiting.

It was almost comical how his tolerance and patience wasn't an issue while code was compiling. Probably because he understood the mechanics, the elegance of the process. It was like an assembly line of activities that moved from one point to the next. No deviation, just a natural sequence of flow. The order hummed to him like a sweet lullaby. It was nothing like dealing with people. They were too erratic, unpredictable; human.

Perhaps that was why he felt more comfortable with science. It held more of a reference in his life than people. There was no emotion or gray area; everything was always black and white. There was never any debate or rationalization when it came to researching or findings; at least not for him. There was never an up without a down, or a left without a right. With Matthew, science was absolute with no free will of its own. Unless of course, the perception of free will was programmed into the technology, such as an artificial intelligence. But even then, it wasn't necessarily classified as true free will. That was something only humans possessed, or was it? A philosophical conundrum to some, but not him.

It didn't matter. He waited.

He blinked after pulling his hands from his eyes. The rendering percentage was half completed so he knew he had a few more minutes. He shifted his attention to his testing scenarios.

Over the last few weeks, he had researched various security appli-cations and protocols that were most commonly used by high-level corporations and governments.

The latest innovations in cyber technology were toted as the best-of-breed in their fields. Hotshot marketing and sales accountants in expensive suits peddled these be-all/end-all suites of applications as a front-runner in systems and information security protection. Gullible commercial corporations would spend millions as they clamored like groupies to rock stars for the latest in Department of Defense grade programs. Unwitting governments would spend millions of taxpayer dollars changing the commercial cyber code to fit their ridiculous reg-ulations; all the while funding multiple year contracts for disastrous implementations. Regardless of their approach, corporations and gov-ernments alike would demonstrate their faith in the brand-new cyber protection by placing all their information at the mercy of this new technology.

As fond as he was of the advancements in technology, Matthew knew nothing was infallible. He and Brooks had some spirited de-bates about disproving the myths of the true protection of informa-tion. There were a few occasions where Jane rolled her eyes in disgust and walked away as both boys became too involved and animated in who was right and who was wrong. Brooks had argued that security technology was okay, but only for specific things such as encrypting mobile phones or laptops.

Matthew agreed with Brooks, but stated that if it was done correctly, it could change the face of everything from information sharing, com-merce, and banking information, to even safeguarding nuclear launch codes for ICBMs. All facets of everything could be secured behind the right makeup of protection. Brooks said that was impossible, and so ensued the great debate. During one such heated conversation weeks ago, Brooks told Matthew to prove it. Thus, was born the next chal-lenge.

As the synapses of Matthew's brain popped with plans, he knew the first step in designing foolproof cyber protection, was to tear apart the latest and greatest. So, he began creating his hydra to penetrate the most sophisticated protection firewalls in existence. Of course, he would never test this on actual companies or government systems, so he developed a set of highly advanced scenarios emulating some of the toughest cyber protected systems on the planet. Those were the tests that he was loading now.

Matthew was so busy shifting back and forth between programs on his laptop; he didn't hear the knock at the door. Only when the glare caught his computer screen as the hallway light spilled into the darkened room did he notice. It was followed by a looming figure.

Matthew turned with a startled look. "Oh! Jane," he said somewhat relieved. He could barely make out her features, but the small smirk cresting her lip was unmistakable.

She stepped inside and hit the wall switch, flooding the room with brightness. "It figures."

Matthew brought his hands up shielding his squinting eyes. "What are you talking about?" He blinked widely as his eyes began to adjust.

She let the heavy door close with its own weight then plodded across the room; her steps very deliberate as if making a point. He watched and waited as she gently lowered her oversized backpack then plopped down on his bed beside the desk. She seemed miffed as she looked to the other side of the room. "Do you have any idea what time it is?"

Matthew's eyes narrowed a bit as he searched for his clock.

"Of course you don't," said Jane as she rolled her head towards him. "You never do unless it's important to you."

Matthew found the clock, but was emotionally unmoved about the concern. "Again, what are you talking about?"

"How can someone so smart be so stupid?" Jane said.

"Excuse me?" He said with eyebrows raised.

"You didn't even call, Matthew. You completely blew Brooks and me off tonight!"

His expression did not waver at the accusation. In thinking for a second, it morphed into a look of misunderstanding; but not about the lack of consideration for the plans he had with his two best friends. "You both knew that I had project work," turning his attention back to his laptop screen. "I told you how close I was to completing it."

Jane became exasperated. "Both Brooks and I *understand*," she said using finger quotes, "how important your work is. We were under no illusion that you would skip tonight, but at the very least show a little consideration and respect by calling."

He looked at her in a lecturing fashion. She was all too aware of this visage and was not in the mood to hear any of his logical excuses. That's all they were now to her, excuses; and Matthew could tell by the way she looked back. In the brief instant it took for him to answer, he thought of all the potential outcomes of his rebuttal. Each word soliciting a response where the possible results could either condemn him to further ridicule and admonishment, or smooth things over to the point of forgiveness.

This was once again, a failing in the intellect of Matthew Decker. Logic and rationale were not the only answers to life's problems, especially around the emotional construct of the female species. He couldn't understand why she was so upset. He had told her earlier in the day, that he had to get some work done after class. That simple statement implied that he would be focused on his project. Time to completion became inconsequential. That was universally understood, or so he thought. Every great scientist accepted the sacrifices that had to be made.

What Matthew's inability to comprehend was that Jane was more than just a scientist. She was a woman who became the object of his desire, and by default, the emotional entanglement in their would-be relationship. Deep down, he understood that he did not understand. The scientist in him pushed those feelings as far back as possible. The man/boy part of him, however, wanted to fan the spark of what could be; but try as he might, he continued to make one bad decision after another. This further served to confirm Jane's declaration of stupidity over smartness.

He remembered throughout his pursuing an interpretation of a relationship; that part of the bonding process was to exhibit a show of concern and consideration for a female's feelings. Of course, it was too late for that, but there were certain steps he needed to take to make amends.

He concentrated very hard to change his expression from indifference to remorse; the purpose was to outwardly show that Matthew understood her feelings, even when he had no clue. He figured that he had time to sort through the entire process later and need only to *display* his understanding.

He was wrong on both counts, but again, had no clue.

If he believed in a higher being, that would have been an excellent time to pray for guidance. Matthew was an Undeclared though; of all the decisions throughout his life, *that* should have been his first to consider. Especially now.

To show her that he was wrong, he tried to place a hint of sorrow on his face, but it came across as more of a painful look. This prompted a raised eyebrow from Jane.

"What's wrong with you?" she said.

Matthew knew he was failing. He became flustered at the onslaught of his unknown feelings while trying to placate hers and complete his project. The latter was the only one that was important to him.

He shook his head. "Look, Jane … I know that I messed up. I also know that I'm not the best boyfriend material—"

"Boyfriend?" Jane said surprised.

Matthew backpedaled. "Boyfriend, is that what I said? That is *not* what I meant."

"Then what did you mean?" She asked suspiciously.

He shook his head with even more ferocity. "Please, I'm just trying to get you to understand—"

"Understand what?" A coy smile began to spread.

Matthew's head snapped back in surprise. She was enjoying this. A few more seconds passed in what seemed like a lifetime. He began to mouth words, but nothing was coming out.

"Ha!" Jane said loudly.

Matthew's face still held shock. In a matter of seconds, Jane appeared to have gone from angry to amused to the point of sheer joy. He was confounded, and she seemed to be loving it. He did not understand the rapid movement between these uncharted emotions. What was worse was that his line of thinking was disrupted to the point where he forgot what he was going to say.

Was this how women worked?

If so, he would have to give careful consideration to beginning a relationship. If that was even possible now because of his slip of the tongue.

Jane leaned forward; a more measured smile on her face. "I am not angry anymore. Catching you off guard more than makes up for your bad boyfriend manners."

His expression became more confused. "Boyfriend?" He returned.

She looked down and blushed. "Well, that's what we both want, right?" Jane looked up and caught his eye. He leaned back as if in slow-motion; the realization of her innuendo becoming more apparent as he moved. His toothy smile spread across his face.

"So, are you going to show me why you couldn't spend time with me tonight?" She smiled.

His smile mixed with suspicion. "I thought you hated this stuff?" Meaning his competitive nature.

Jane shrugged. "I guess this is something I need to get used to," she said continuing to smile.

"Well, all right!" He said turning back to his laptop. He began rapidly switching back and forth between his test scenarios and code as she stood up and moved behind him to peer over his shoulder.

"Now, you remember the nature of what I was trying to accomplish—"

"Just get to the chase. I don't need to know how the clock is made, just the time."

Funny, she seemed annoyed again. He glanced at her with a surprised look. She returned the look with her typical Jane smirk. He half grinned. Something didn't sit right between how she responded and the smirk he had grown to love. He shrugged internally and chocked it up to his lack of understanding relationships.

Matthew's fingers danced across the keyboard with precision. As soon as he was finished, he calmly moved his hands to his lap.

A bit confused, Jane asked, "Did I miss something? Did you do your thing?"

"Not yet, I thought that you would like to press the Enter key," he said with a nod towards his computer.

"Seriously?" Jane said with anticipation.

"Yep."

She reached around him as she approached the keyboard, gently grazing his shoulder with her arm. He felt tingly from the proximity as she pressed Enter.

Numbers and codes flashed on the screen. Bar graphs showing bandwidth, measured frequencies of network tracks and IP routers, and what looked like a depiction of a virtual wall crumbling then cascading to the next, dynamically moved across the screen. Once the third-tier wall fell, Matthew sat up straight intently watching the aperture adjustment and the internal chronometer. His head bobbed as the seconds ticked. As it passed the point of failure from the last test, his smile returned. Now, it was just a matter of his code fending off the simulated company's own hydra attack. He quickly flipped between two open programs checking the progress of his code and the status of his defense against the attempted penetration. Matthew's smile broadened as his calculated time of entry increased and the competitors' hydra attack diminished. "Yes!" He said as he raised his arms in victory.

Jane straightened up. "What does this mean? Did you, do it?"

He turned facing her. "Yes, I was able to crack three levels of the toughest firewall protection available, *and* keep them from attacking me."

"What company did you test this on?"

"What do you mean what company?"

"I mean, what company did you pick to test your code on?"

He laughed. "This is just a simulation; a test scenario. I didn't pick an actual company."

She folded her arms as she looked at him skeptically. "Then how can you be sure that it works?"

His smile stopped. "Trust me, it works. My calculations are never wrong."

Arms still folded; she turned around and leaned on the desk. "Well, who created these simulations?"

"I did."

"Do you think you're being very objective with the results since you created both the testing environment, *and* the code to penetrate it?"

Matthew did not like being challenged, especially from someone he cared about. "Look, what are you getting at? I've proven that this works!"

She held her hands up in a surrendering fashion. "All I'm saying is it might be a little suspect when Brooks looks at this. Unless he's going to spend time examining the scenarios that *you* created, he is most likely going to ask the same questions. It would be like pharmaceutical companies saying they did clinical trials without any actual test subjects."

Matthew's expression softened just a bit. She unfolded her arms and placed her hand upon his. "I'm not challenging your brilliance. I'm just saying that you might want to ensure your victory with unequivocal proof."

He looked down slowly as he processed this information. Jane's expression went from understanding and sympathetic, to a hardened look of determination as she watched him ponder her suggestion.

Would he fall for it? That was the question.

Without another thought, Matthew swiveled back to his keyboard and began typing. Jane resumed her position over his shoulder and peered at the screen once again; a small unseen grin crossed her face.

He pulled up the public domain of a well-known computer brand; he needed to start with an initial IP address.

"No."

"Excuse me?" Matthew said as he snapped his head towards her.

Her look softened. Jane had to make this look like it was his idea. "Everyday hackers always target companies like this," she said nodding towards the screen. "It's too cliché; Brooks would be unimpressed."

He broke eye contact then looked at nothing particular as he tried to think of a replacement. She waited for a few seconds, then provided him a bit more focus.

"There's got to be something a little more challenging. Commercial companies just seem so average," she cut her eyes to the back of his head. "Government databases seem too untouchable and the danger too great..."

She waited.

Even though she could not see it, she knew his eyes were darting from side to side. The hook had been set.

Matthew began typing furiously on his keyboard. He opened the DOS prompt and began typing a string, casually flipping back and forth between that, the Internet, and his code. She was far from stupid, but Jane had to admit his genius seemed to be unparalleled. It would be a shame to waste that talent.

It took him a few minutes to ensure that multiple IP addresses were masked and his home-grown algorithm for misdirecting their signal lock was in place.

When everything was done, he raised his hands from the keyboard letting them hover in place. It was like he was mentally commanding it to levitate.

Jane needed to play along. "Looks like you found a worthy target?"

His head turned slowly to her. This time *he* had the smirk. He reached over with his left hand, and without looking, toggled the key to bring up a screen.

Her eyes widened as she bent down to make sure it was authentic. There, in big bold letters, was the insignia of the United States Securities and Exchange Commission. This was not the public page either. From where she stood, it looked like the logon page to something much greater.

She had to make Matthew think she was impressed. That was somewhat true. "You're going to hack into the SEC? Matthew, I wanted you to pick a harder target, but something like this..." she trailed off.

He raised a cocky eyebrow and tried to emulate her signature smirk. "The SEC is just a shell. I'm going to use it to break into the EDGAR database."

The Electronic Data Gathering, Analysis, and Retrieval system was an automated system that companies used to file the required forms that spanned everything related to securities markets for investors and corporations, both foreign and domestic. The idea was to increase the efficiency of information exchange between them and the United States. Most of the filed documents were a matter of public record and could be downloaded. However, Matthew was interested in the electronic connections behind the scenes between EDGAR and the filing entities.

Although the filing process was encrypted, the linkage for accepting the market forms, once established, always remained. Matthew was going to attempt to piggyback through the database and touch one of these companies. Of course, he would do no damage and leave no trace.

He explained this to Jane. She nodded thoughtfully, then admitted to herself that she *was* impressed.

Matthew looked directly at the screen. "Are you ready?"

Without waiting for a response, he initiated the procedure. The figures on the computer danced much like they did in his test simulation. Firewalls fell; bar graphs moved back and forth, and the internal chronometer kept counting. Matthew sat back a bit from the desk with his arms folded, and legs crossed. He tapped his foot slightly in either agitation, or nervousness. It could have been a combination of both.

Jane stood behind him watching the screen just as intently. Her motivations for the success of this was quite different from his.

Although it was not noticeable to his outward appearance, the anticipation of the outcome was almost maddening to the degree of an anxiety breakdown. This was a new emotion for Matthew as well; one of the many, he thought, that he would have to come to terms within this unfamiliar, unexplored frontier in which he was embarking. He continued looking at the screen, but the swirl of the things he had not yet mastered such as love, shifted wildly in his mind. His eyes lazily adjusted to the cloudy reflection on his screen. He saw the silhouette of Jane behind him.

She wanted more than just friendship.

Passed the exterior of his conceit and over-inflated ego of self-confidence, Matthew honestly didn't think something like that would ever happen, not for him. It was obvious from how the events of the day had unfolded that he would need to bone up on relationship etiquette if this were ever to work.

There will be time enough for that another day, or so he thought. He noticed a change in the screen as his eyes readjusted to the content. Jane stiffened; he sat up straight as a directory of file structures to one of the world's largest banking and investment companies waited patiently for a command.

"Matthew," she said softly.

He nodded involuntarily as he moved to open a few of the directories. He saw routing numbers, account codes, dollar amounts, and options for transferring funds. There at Matthew's fingertips, he could bring this company to its knees.

Jane leaned forward. She placed one of her hands on his shoulder as the other reached behind her. "You did it, lover," she whispered in his ear.

What neither of them would have noticed was the presence of another within the room.

13

No Loose Ends

He entered Matthew's residence with Jane; the guardian angel called Airowyn stood to the side with a solemn look observing the events unfolding. He became saddened by the moments that had not yet appeared. Moments which would further the cause of the enemy, and bring about tragedy for the unwitting.

A growing anger filled him at the idiocy of both demons and humans. The great Fall of his once cherished brothers spurned no remorse on their part, not that it would have any impact on their sealed fate, but it seemed to further their madness to support the doomed plan of their misguided leader; the demon the humans would come to know as Matthias. Controlling them by fear and manipulation, he continued his quest in vengeance and recognition as greater than the Most High. The Fallen had learned nothing from their actions, and saw no fault on their part. Even when the creator removed the Spirit after the casting down, they continued their cursing and blame. All this rebellion that caused warring simply because he wanted to rise above the one now known as the Chairman. A more fitting word could not be found.

Idiot.

Humans were no better. Based on the evidence and what Airowyn had witnessed over the centuries, they could just as easily be manipulated if their hearts and minds were in the wrong place. What he saw now before him was an example. There were cases, such as his last charge, where compassion and concern overruled any thoughts of evil and selfish gain. He could see no rhyme or reason to each individual; just differences based on innermost desires. Human behavior had always perplexed the guardian angel.

Although freewill was not a right of his creation, it was an option. Airowyn, along with his fellow guardians and warriors, chose obedience over separation. The fate that awaited both demon and Familiar alike was one of unimaginable agony, and after all these millennia, he was still surprised by the indecisiveness and blatant ignorance of their actions. His fallen brothers were doomed from the beginning. Humans continued to misuse the most precious gift ever created; choice. The wrong one casting them the same dismal judgment.

He continued to watch Jane and Matthew.

Airowyn's postings and responsibilities had changed somewhat from his previous assignment. Airowyn had been the guardian of Kevin Huang; a human with a very special purpose in the plan to come. Whereas most angels from the Elodine house of the Majaliant held a watchful eye over their assigned charges, Airowyn was now to chronicle specific key happenings of the human chain of events and report them to his commander, Lucaous; the protector of the chosen one, Joshua Arden.

Throughout history since the birth of everything, all matters were documented in the Great Hall of Records; an endless sanctum located in the Majaliant Genanōsys of all knowledge for both human and the angelic host. Airowyn's new appointment had granted him access to the Great Hall to ensure that all he witnessed was also properly cataloged. His travels of late provided quite the collection of information.

As with all angels, his assignments permitted him only the knowledge necessary to fulfill his duties. His was not to question, only to serve. He was brought to this place now to bear witness. And watch closely he did.

* * *

Matthew, once again, felt tingly from the closeness of Jane. Her hot sticky breath smelled of chili cheese fries, but he didn't care.

She had just called him lover. He felt a warm flush as he turned to face her; thinking that their first kiss was imminent.

She looked at him and smiled; he smiled back, then it slowly faded.

He tried to speak, but nothing came out. The tingling was replaced by dizziness and a sudden wave of nausea. His whole body seemed to feel as if on fire. He felt a wetness on his right side and reached over.

Matthew pulled his hand back. It was covered in blood. Confused, he looked at his shoulder and saw her hand still touching him. He turned his head back to look at her, then his body jerked violently as Jane pushed the knife further into his rib cage.

She had to make sure that his lung was punctured to prevent any screaming. A quick twist of the blade ensured that the wound was enough to keep him quiet. She pulled the knife out quickly getting little to no blood on herself in the process. Matthew seemed to still be conscious but could not move as the weight of his body began to slump. Jane pulled her hand from his shoulder and grabbed the back of his chair; using the forward momentum, she catapulted him out and onto the floor. She wasn't overly concerned with the sound of him landing as she could still hear the muffled bass beats of the Friday night partying.

Airowyn watched with sadness as Matthew hit the floor, eyes still open. Although it was not necessary, the angel scanned the room for a transition emissary; what humans sometimes referred to as the angel of death. His sadness seemed to grow as no one appeared.

Jane quickly took the unoccupied seat, feeling the heat from Matthew's body still radiating within. She reached into one of her pockets and pulled out a secured flash drive. Placing the unit into an open USB port, she began typing commands to copy the hydra code.

A knock came to Matthew's door. Jane jerked her head sharply at the sound, but before she could react, the door opened.

"Hey man, you missed a really good meal," said Brooks trailing off. He looked surprised to see Jane sitting at Matthew's desk. He never allowed anyone to do that, not even Brooks.

Jane's hands left the keyboard as she turned the chair to face him. Her expression was stern. The bloody knife was right next to the keyboard, but she made no move towards it. Instead, she just stared.

Brooks' surprised look faded as he looked from Jane down to what appeared to be Matthew. He was just lying there in an expanding pool of blood. Brooks set his jaw. "Is he dead?" He said in almost a whisper.

Jane's eyes widened as she pointed sharply to the door. Brooks leaned back and looked both ways down the hall. He then stepped inside the room and shut the big door. After it clicked, he stood there, not moving. "Did he finish it?"

"What do you think?" Jane said sarcastically, but not with her usual quirky, nerdy mannerism. Her voice seemed polished; her annunciation and diction changed. It had a hint of a European accent. She turned back to the computer to check the progress of the copy.

Brooks walked over, passing Airowyn without the slightest awareness. He leaned down in front of Matthew who's eyes were still open; they were fluttering slightly. Brooks swallowed hard as he watched. With the amount of blood upon the floor, he knew there wasn't much time. "Matthew, I am so sorry." Whether he could hear Brooks or not, wasn't important. The confession was more so for his need for absolution.

Jane just rolled her eyes. He was so weak. That's why she was brought in by her employer. She worked for an organization called Ministry.

Brooks was contracted to perform the deep cover assignment of becoming friends with Matthew Decker. His background and paper trail was fabricated in such a way as to insert him into Matthew's life without any cause for questions. His appearance and real age were close enough to pass as a fellow high-school student who was just different enough to be an outcast, like Matthew.

After a wide canvas of candidates with the proper aptitude, tenacity, sheer drive for perfection, and most importantly, someone not famous enough to be missed, young Matthew was chosen. The objective was to exploit Matthew's knowledge and brilliance to ultimately get him to create a computer virus for purposes unknown. This hydra code exceeded their expectations.

Everything leading up to this moment had been going per plan, but over the years, Brooks had genuinely grown to care about Matthew as a friend. That was becoming problematic for the organization. Ministry had invested a lot of time, money, and effort into this initiative and felt that Brooks was not completely committed due to his developing attachment. He could not be removed without arousing suspicions from Matthew. Inserting someone else in place of Brooks would take more time than they were willing to devote, so the decision was made to incorporate one of their own to support the effort. Ministry orchestrated the boys' entry into MIT. Jane's plan was to literally run into Matthew posing as a nerdy college girl. The fact that Matthew began falling for her was a plus.

"You have to believe me that I never wanted this," he said gesturing to his dying friend. Matthew's eyes flickered. Anguish over his part of the plan was becoming apparent. Sensing the end was near, Brooks' voice became more hurried. "We just needed you to create a computer program. I argued with them and said that we could have just asked, and you would have done it. They kept telling me that there was no other way." He started to sob. Brooks placed his shaking hand on Matthew's head and began stroking his hair. "I am so, so very sorry."

Jane finished typing a command and removed the flash drive. She placed the protective cap on the end then secured it in a zippered pocket of her jacket. In a casual fluid motion, she scooted the rolling chair back and grabbed the knife from the desk. "Brooks?"

The chair was stopped by Matthew's unmoving legs.

"Yes?" He said as she began to swing around to face him.

He looked up just in time for her to plunge the knife deep into his neck. He stared at her wide-eyed and stunned; a choking sound emanating from his mouth. She glanced at him for a couple of second before yanking the knife out. Brooks grabbed his throat as blood spewed everywhere.

Jane casually tossed the knife on Matthew's back as Brooks struggled to keep the blood in his neck. His last thoughts were that this was a fitting end for what he had done. He fell on top of Matthew as a terminal breath left his body.

Jane moved a few steps to open her backpack. She fiddled around with something inside, retrieved her belongings, and a burner phone. She stood up and walked towards the door, leaving her pack. Jane left the room without even a look back at the two men who had been her best friends over the last year and a half.

Airowyn watched expressionless as the door clicked shut. He looked to the right and saw the two souls of the dead boys; standing there beside their bodies, confused. They looked at each other as if they had never met. Neither spoke as they viewed their surroundings.

On the far side of the room, a blackness began to swirl; much like a tornado on its side. The vortex grew and increased in ferocity. Airowyn unfolded his wings and lifted into the air. He did not wish to see the despair or hear the screams yet to come.

He flew into the sky then hovered in place, knowing sadly that his mission was still not complete. Airowyn saw transition emissaries appearing one at a time; his frown deepening at the small count. He held pity for the humans who had not yet made their choice.

A scowl of contempt appeared as he watched Jane emerge from the dormitory. He was supposed to remain impartial and impassive to all that he witnessed, but found it very difficult with her blatant disregard for human life.

Jane pulled the burner phone from her pocket as she hurried across the courtyard; she dialed a number from memory.

"Dobrý den sestru. To sem já." Jane said in Czech.

"Je dobré slyšet tvůj hlas," said Inara. "It is completed; I take it?" She continued in English.

"Almost." Jane pulled out a remote-control trigger, flipped the protective cover, and depressed the red button.

The concussive explosion that radiated from the C-4 in her backpack decimated any evidence in Matthew's room. It was on the third floor, so the adjacent compartments in a forty to fifty-foot radius were destroyed or damaged within varying degrees. Due to the room's position, the structural integrity of the building gave way in sections and collapsed. When it was finished and all that remained was fire, a third of the building was gone, while parts of the remainder burned. An unfortunate, but acceptable byproduct in her mind.

Airowyn watched the emissaries collect those who had chosen wisely. He then left to make his report.

Jane nuzzled the phone into her jacket to buffer the booming sound. Once it had died down, she placed it back to her ear.

"No loose ends?" Inara said.

"No loose ends," confirmed Jane.

"I will see you soon, sister," said Inara with a smile and hung up.

Jane flipped her disposable phone shut, slid it back into her pocket, and continued walking away from the destruction. She could no longer hear the bass beat of the music.

* * *

In the few weeks that Joshua had been back, the main headquarters of Jonah International was buzzing with activity; more so than usual. News of the fake turbulence-inducing minor mechanical failure of the flight from England was still making headlines across the world. Much to Joshua's dismay, that did not blow over as quickly as Langston and Alice had predicted. Was the world so starved for information on him, that even an everyday occurrence, which happened to aircraft several times daily, still ranked as a top story of major media outlets? Granted, the truth was much more than that, but for all that the rest of the world knew, it was just turbulence.

Joshua sat behind a desk in his newly renovated and spacious office nestled nicely on the top floor within the New York City building. He pointed the remote in his hand at a ridiculously large, and most likely expensive, LED flat-screen television that was fitted perfectly within a recessed wall.

Shaking his head at the absurdity, he scrolled through the major news feeds looking for something other than his own face. Joshua finally settled on a channel talking about candidate bids for the up-coming presidential election. He turned up the sound.

"... *as President Masters has still not commented on his reelection bid. Senator Humboldt has called for a press conference later this week where he is expected to announce his candidacy for President of the United States.*

Coming up, an eyewitness account of the frightening events aboard Jonah One, the aircraft that was carrying the first family of the business world and their entourage across the Atlantic. US-CBN's own correspondent, Judith Mankiewicz, recounts the horrific—"

Joshua shut the TV off and dropped the remote down on his desk in disgust. *First family?* He thought.

He wished again, for what seemed like the millionth time, that he could just have a normal life. It was a wish he knew would not be granted, even though the power that be could give him precisely that, if it was something he truly wanted. For a quick second, Joshua thought about what would happen if he weren't, so to speak, in charge. He frowned at the thought. Not because he couldn't bear thinking of someone else taking all the prominence of the position or the power, but that he would have a hard time trusting that right intentions would be the focus of the position. This whole thing had never been about Joshua; it was about the justice and fairness to the people of the world and the freedom of their choice. A choice that must be made, one way or another.

He sighed as he slumped in his overly stuffed desk chair. Joshua made a commitment long ago, of which his own choice and pride in his work would not allow him to break. Even if he could be normal, because of his character qualities, *those stupid goody, goody qualities*, he thought; he would not be able to leave knowing that humanity might not be left in good hands.

He waved his hand and hard-light imagery flashed before him courtesy of Sentinel. The touchable light fragments danced in what look like a dashboard setting like a computer console from Star Trek.

The imagery adapted to whatever Joshua needed when called upon. In this case, it was a message board of pending memos, a calendar of events in his day, and a very sophisticated keypad resembling a phone. He wasn't exactly sure how Sentinel knew what he needed every single time he swiped his hand, but he had learned long ago to stop questioning things that would keep him up thinking at night. That usually resulted in a headache the next day.

His desk was mostly barren sans the few items that he insisted on keeping to make it appear that he had a regular job. Along with pictures of his family he had innocuous things like a pen and pad of paper; he needed something close to a normal life, but Kelan drew the line when it came to an office phone. There were too many security risks with a simple line in and out of Joshua's office. With the latest technological innovations across the world, bugging devices did not have to be physical to be effective. Kelan's argument was technical to the point where Joshua's eyes rolled back into his head. He was smart enough to know that the argument was sound though. Joshua questioned when his life became so scripted that even using a simple phone became dangerous.

Joshua had sent her on some errands earlier so he punched up the mobile phone number of his assistant, Jillian Arthur, and dialed the virtual phone. Of course, he could have just asked Sentinel to do this for him without lifting a finger, but he still wanted to feel that he had some semblance of control over what he did and when. If he became too complacent and reliant on the power given to him, then that would take away the very essence of what he was trying to preserve; his humanity, and the humility that went with it.

Part of his continuing worry was that the prophecy of his destiny would force him to change who he was; the simple boy from Wisconsin. He was determined not to let that happen, so resolved himself to perform meaningless and mundane activities like dialing a phone, even if it was a perfunctory action and looked ridiculous using a technology such as Sentinel to do it. Things like this were done in private, and mostly for Joshua's appeasement. He believed the expectation was to use the showier things of his position when around others. *We must keep up the appearance*; he would think to himself in a Julia Child-type like voice.

"Yes, sir," said Jillian picking up on the first ring.

Joshua wondered how the caller ID displayed on her side when he used the hard-light phone. A slight shake of his head dismissed the thought chalking it up to something else he just needed to accept but didn't have to understand.

"Jillian, when you get back to your desk can you get me a passenger manifest from our return flight from England?" Again, he realized that this too was a futile, human activity that Sentinel could perform in mere seconds. He was determined to do as many things himself as possible. By default, that included his staff as well. Humans needed to have a purpose.

"Yes, sir," she said without any questions.

His surprise at her immediate obedience to his instructions was waning over time. Alice would never have let a simple request like this go without badgering him for more information as to why he wanted it. She always had an insatiable desire to gather as much as possible to understand Joshua's needs, then invariably, over deliver on his expectations. That is one of the many things that made her an excellent Chief of Staff now. He smiled at the thought that Jillian and Alice were so different.

"Thank you," he said as he 'hung up' his magical phone.

A couple of knocks came upon his office door. Joshua's head cocked a little to the side thinking that was a pretty fast turnaround by Jillian, then smiled as Kelan walked in, trailed by Langston and Alice.

He leaned back in his chair and crossed his legs. "What's up?" He asked casually.

Langston held up the dossier in his hand as all three moved towards Joshua's desk. "Preliminary investigation findings on Kelly Granger."

Joshua straightened up a bit. He had been waiting for this information since they returned to the states with her in custody.

The meeting that he was supposed to have with President Masters upon his return had been postponed due to some state business; it would now most likely be extended due to probable re-election preparation of the pending Humboldt announcement. The Granger stuff had been the only other topic of interest on his agenda. Everything else that he had been doing in the last few weeks was part of the dog and pony position of his unwanted celebrity.

Joshua wanted the Granger case done right, so he bided his time for the process to run its course. Langston had multiple papers, and what looked like copies for each of them as he approached Joshua's desk. He handed the top copy over. Joshua skimmed over the first few pages as his staff waited.

Joshua flipped back-and-forth between the pages. "This is it? Nothing else?"

Langston nodded slightly. "Yeah."

Joshua stood up and motioned toward the couch and chairs on the other side of the office. "Sentinel, clear my schedule for the next hour," he said leading them over and taking a seat.

"Yes sir."

The other three sat down. Langston handed Alice and Kelan their individual copies. Alice set her notebook, agenda, and tablet on the coffee table in front of her. The three men could never recall any time that those items weren't with her. They sometimes joked about her sleeping and showering with them.

Joshua immediately began filing through the rest of the pages. Once he finished, he cut his eyes towards Langston. "Who is Inara?"

Kelan settled into the comfortable sofa. "We don't know."

Joshua's head dipped a bit in surprise. "We don't know?" He repeated.

"There are no records in any known database, in any country, of this person's existence by that name. Chief Willis did as much as he could. His report was less than informative" said Langston.

"I reached out to a trusted contact in Interpol to run a search of aliases by that name," followed Kelan. He shook his head. "Nothing."

"Sentinel?" said Joshua. Langston, Kelan, and even Alice, already knew the answer.

"Sir, I have no one by that name within the confines of my parameters."

"You know everything," said Joshua matter-of-fact.

"Not this time," came Sentinel's reply.

The other three looked shocked, not at the fact that they had already checked with Sentinel and came up with nothing, but at the informality of the last response and the way it was stated. It was almost as if there was a human element that contradicted the infallibility that had never wavered in all their time dealing with the intelligence.

Joshua looked nonplussed, practically exasperated. "Is it that you really don't know, or you're not allowed to tell us?"

Sentinel did not reply. That was the first time since Joshua had been aware of the intelligence that a response did not come.

"Figures," he mumbled.

The other three looked at Joshua expectantly. They knew that he had more answers about what was going on with Sentinel than he was letting on.

He rolled his eyes a little. "I can't get into this right now. Can we just concentrate on the Granger case?" He said shaking the papers in his hands.

Sentinel was incapable of lying, which is why nothing was said. The information around Inara did, in fact, exist. Just like Lucas, and the other angels, Sentinel was only given the information needed at the appropriate time. This protected Joshua from truths that he was not yet ready to embrace. What Joshua also did not know, was his time for the plan to be revealed was near.

Jillian knocked on the door twice, opened it, then walked over to Joshua with a folder in her hand.

"Thank you," he said, taking the folder.

As Jillian departed, Alice said, "What's that?"

"Passenger manifest from the trip back," said Joshua casually flipping through it. "We need to do some culling on the media access," he said tossing the folder onto the table. He stared at both Langston and Alice. "Some nitwit is doing a live discussion on the *harrowing* experience—" he said using finger quotes, "—of our flight."

Alice looked sorrowful. "Sorry, boss."

Joshua sighed. "I'm not mad at you or Langston, Alice; it's not your fault that they have nothing better to do. That is precisely why I want to go through the list and only choose the reputable outlets, preferably Associates, who can benefit the cause. Those people that are looking for rag material, can stick to Hollywood; I don't have room in my life for all this other stuff," he said waving to the television.

Alice took some notes. "That may have some negative ramifications along the lines of political and reporting profiling."

"In the grand scheme of things, is it really that important?" Joshua replied.

Alice just shrugged.

"Now, where were we?" He said.

Joshua began exploring what he *did* know. "Were the other members of this," he looked down at the name, "Animals Equality questioned?" He was referring to the animal rights activist group in which Kelly Granger claimed to be a member.

Alice flipped through the pages of the report until she got to the one that listed the findings. "All of the names Granger listed in her deposition did not check out. We cross matched with multiple animal welfare groups, as well as, past registrants from the annual Animal Rights National Conference," she looked up at Joshua, "none of them had ever heard of the group claiming to be Animals Equality."

Joshua was looking at the same page as Alice. He couldn't say that he was surprised to hear this. This type of situation was all-too-familiar to him. He continued piecing through the documentation.

Per Kelly's testimony, she was involved with this animal activists' organization for the last eighteen months. For anyone else looking at this, it would seem like the woman was lying. The odds and the evidence were completely against her. She had no people, documentation, or even phone records to corroborate any of her story. The evidence that Chief Willis *did* uncover pointed back to careful planning of the attack done by her, and her alone.

Joshua had previously watched some of the recorded interrogation over the last couple of weeks. He wasn't so much interested in what she was saying, but how she was saying it. The *what* could always be verified; it was the *how* that was harder to hide. Her mannerisms were frantic and erratic; she was clinging to specific details that would take even the most skilled liar time to memorize and practice.

Over the course of the last two weeks, she was subjected to many types of techniques geared to draw out the truth from many different angles. As her stories were analyzed, they continually told the same tale.

The best lie is the one that is the closest to the truth. It becomes harder to disprove when the similarities can be backed up; especially when the liar can use the truth to perpetuate their lie. If done properly, elements of the truth can sustain the lie without help from the liar. Kelly wasn't that smart, and fortunately for her; Joshua's experience with a 'long con' worked in her favor.

Someone or some organization had gone to a lot of trouble to fabricate a completely fictional background around this woman; to place her in an intricate and elaborate world of deception; one where the objective, where Joshua was involved, was always the same.

When he was satisfied with the information he had reviewed, he folded his copy of the investigation and tossed it on the table in front of them.

He looked at Langston. "Where is she now?"

"She's still down at the one nine," referring to the precinct, "awaiting transport by the FBI."

Joshua turned to Kelan. "Get a JPS team down there and bring her back here."

Langston furrowed his brow.

Alice asked, "Why? I thought we were going to get her to a safe house?"

If the situation weren't as dire, Joshua would have smiled at Alice's questioning nature. "She's not lying."

Alice looked skeptical. Langston raised his eyebrows a little more. While they could all appreciate Joshua's uncanny ability to separate the truth from fiction, the evidence before them, plus everything that they had witnessed on the plane trip, pointed to the contrary.

Kelan with his hands clasped, leaned forward on his knees. "Joshua, with all due respect, we don't have anything besides her word to back up your belief."

It was Joshua's turn to raise his eyebrows. "Have you forgotten the demon that was sitting on the wing before the explosion?"

They all looked less convinced that she was innocent as Joshua continued. "Look, I know how hard it is for the three of you to understand my reasoning and where I'm going, but what is *not* in this report is just as important," he said pointing to the copy on the table. "It wasn't a co-incidence that the demon appeared mere minutes before. Why didn't they just attack?"

"It's against the rules for them to come directly after you," said Kelan.

"Well, yes ... but that's not the point," continued Joshua. He paused to see if anyone picked up on his line of thinking.

All the sudden, Langston had a quizzical look. "How did Granger pass our security process?"

Alice looked confused. "We vetted her through the same clearance procedures that we do with all other Jonah employees."

Kelan started to look a bit defensive. "Are you saying that there is a flaw in our process?"

Langston shook his head. "No, not at all, that's not what I meant. Jonah's methods for employment, especially for our group," he said with a circular gesture to everyone, "go above and beyond standard protocol. Not only are there full-scale background checks from birth forward, but there are several psychological tests that the applicants must pass to even be considered for positions near you," he said pointing to Joshua.

Joshua looked passive, but inwardly was pleased that Langston was starting to get it.

Langston gestured with his palms up. "How did she get passed our process?"

Kelan thought for a minute then began to shake his head slowly. "There's no possible way based on the procedures I have designed. Unless … there was no deception to begin with."

Joshua leaned back and crossed his legs. "Exactly."

Alice began to nod slowly. "She actually passed."

"Her being a part of this animals activist group would not have been flag, if it actually did check out," said Kelan.

"But it doesn't exist now," Alice said.

"There would be no need to continue the charade if the plan worked. If it didn't, they couldn't afford to be caught. Either way, it would need to disappear," followed Langston.

Joshua prodded them further. "Okay, so she passed the interviewing process and security procedures to get a position on our plane. What was her end game?"

"Well, obviously to get to you," said Alice.

The gears in Langston's head were beginning to smoke. "That doesn't make any sense. She was *on* the plane with us."

Joshua smiled.

Kelan picked up the rest of the thought. "She would have died too."

Alice was still unconvinced. "Now *that* doesn't make any sense. Why would she deliberately set off a bomb knowing that she would die as well? Basic self-preservation would have prevented that. That is ingrained in every human's fundamental animal survival instinct."

Langston began shuffling through his papers from the investigation finding the one he needed. "She didn't know what was in the package. She didn't know it contained a bomb!" He dropped his papers back on the table. "You can't be afraid of something you do not know."

Alice's face creased with concern. "Okay, so let's assume, for the moment, that she was unaware of what she had brought onto the plane. She still knew that it contained something that would bring about attention to this animal cause of hers."

Langston smiled at this thought. Although the situation was very serious, he always became excited over the prospect of figuring out a mystery; he had not had one in some time, so this was thrilling to say the least. "That outcome is nonessential, the cause, I mean; for her true purpose."

Now Kelan seemed like he was lost. "I don't understand. So, she didn't know the package had a bomb, and regardless of the motivation for this cause, her intention was the same; to stage some type of attention-getting demonstration."

"That's not the point either." said Langston. He looked over to Joshua.

Almost at the same time, both said, "She wasn't supposed to survive."

Kelan's head snapped sideways at this revelation. He was now falling into their line of thinking. "If she wasn't supposed to survive–"

Joshua finished his thought, happy that all were at present caught up. "–then she is a liability they cannot afford to let live."

"Why? It's not like she can give us any more information than she already has," said Alice holding up her report.

Kelan pulled out his phone and began relaying orders to have Kelly Granger picked up and brought to the office.

"She gave us more than she was supposed to," said Joshua.

Alice looked puzzled.

"She gave us a name. Inara."

14

Liquid Sickness

Samuel Krukowski sat at the break room table, tapping his foot impatiently. It was lightly enough not to be seen by others, but just steady enough to be an involuntary annoyance when he realized he was doing it. He was alternating his glances between the clock on the cafeteria wall, and the latest volume of Emerging Infectious Diseases. The latter was slightly vibrating as he nervously shifted between pages.

Today was the day.

He just needed to get through the next ninety minutes, then it would be over; well, after the delivery of course. Samuel would finally be free of the blackmail that had been haunting him for the last two months.

The wondering of how she found out had decreased somewhat over the past few weeks; only because he now needed to focus his time on the blackmailer's request. He had recently wasted additional time contemplating the difference between the words 'request' and 'demand'.

The woman who approached him all those weeks ago at Chandler Park Station was very polite, and to the point. She began walking with him as the crowd exited onto the street. She spoke to him as if it was a teacher to a student discussion; very matter-of-fact. When she presented the evidence of what he had committed, facts about his life, his family, even his son's Boy Scout troop number, he knew the seriousness of the situation. She knew things about his position at work that the normal populace could never have known. When she had finished with her rendition of 'This is Your Life,' she told him what she wanted in return for her silence. She then provided instructions on when and where to deliver, thanked him for his time while handing him a burner phone and a small scrap of paper, then disappeared among the crowd. When the impromptu meeting was over, he stood still on the bustling sidewalk just staring at the mobile phone as people obliviously moved about him.

Samuel supposed that the amount of time given to plan this was generous on her part; considering what was being asked. He spent many nights running different scenarios and various outcomes through his mind. Questions swam through like a flood. What if he just went to the police? Surely they would be able to help. What if he just took his family and left? Surely he could find a place where the blackmailer would not find him.

No, he decided.

If they were smart enough to know all this information about his life, then they would most certainly be able to track him down.

He cursed himself repeatedly for dragging his feet, or not putting more thought into finding another way. The implications of what the blackmailer wanted were staggering. Wrapping his mind around all possible outcomes and contingencies presented a moral dilemma that slowly ate away at him; adding to the acid already within. It wasn't until the deadline to deliver had run out that it became no choice at all. He had to comply. She contacted him and threatened his family. Now, completing her request was the only way he could save them.

He took a chance and looked at his watch as inconspicuously as he could; checking to see if the time on the wall clock matched. He was starting to become concerned as his break period neared its end.

Where was Dr. Malfront?

Samuel was careful to map out the schedule; ensuring that the doctor's daily routine did not fluctuate. Over the last six days, the doctor always took his break precisely at 10:20 AM; there was never a deviation. Samuel assumed that this time was either predetermined by the virology lab, or part of Dr. Malfront's obsessive-compulsive personality to maintain the rigid structure in his life.

Samuel's eyes began shifting back-and-forth nervously. He promised her that he would have the delivery before the end of this week.

It was now Thursday.

He had to get this done today. He couldn't stand another night of tortuous thoughts about what would happen to his family if he did not deliver.

His breathing became rapid, almost to the point of hyperventilation. He needed to calm himself before he drew attention and unwanted questions from other staffers.

Just as he was about to head to the restroom, so he could get a grip on his pending breakdown, in walked Dr. Malfront; six minutes behind his normal schedule.

Samuel immediately looked down and set the timer on his watch. He had twenty minutes to make his move. Unless, the doctor decided to cut his break short to stick to his timeline. Was something like that possible? Would Dr. Malfront end his break early to return to his lab by 10:40 AM?

Almost involuntarily, Samuel shook his head to stop the onslaught of questions. Worried that he would now most definitely draw attention, his breathing began to return to normal.

As he was already headed to the restroom when the doctor entered, he casually exited the semi-crowded room and turned left towards his own department.

Samuel picked up his pace akin to speed walking, careful not to look like he was running. Six minutes behind schedule would jeopardize his chances of meeting Maxine, unless she was running late too.

Maxine, one of his department colleagues, always took her break at the same time as Samuel. Instead of pumping herself with horrible vending machine coffee, she was making attempts to get into better shape. He rounded the corner and let out a small sigh of relief as she exited the fitness room; glistening slightly from her moderate walk on a treadmill. He was not a praying man by any means, so there was no deity to thank for the coincidence in timing.

She smiled. "Hey, Sam."

Looking as calm as possible, he replied. "Hey Max."

They continued down the hall together in silence. Once they reached their department door for Epidemiology, he allowed her to swipe her badge first. She smiled again appreciating his chivalry, not knowing that he wanted to ensure that she did not tailgate *him*. As soon as she passed through, he swiped his badge to confirm his entry as well. Building security always tracked their employees based on entry and exit points. Due to the nature of their organization, this provided logs of where people were at all times.

As Maxine approached her station, she casually waved to Samuel, but before she turned the corner, he purposefully tripped and bumped her slightly.

"I am *so* sorry," he said with a small laugh.

"Are you okay?" Maxine said with slight surprise.

"Yeah, yeah… I'm just clumsy," he said with a laugh.

She grinned. "Be careful on your way to your station," she said jokingly.

He laughed as he turned to go to his area. Once Maxine was out of sight, he turned, and walked back towards the department entrance. He casually looked at her ID that he took during the small collision.

When he reached the Epidemiology entrance, he used the newly acquired ID from Maxine to exit the department. Looking both ways up and down the corridor, he began walking towards Virology. Samuel checked his watch to make sure he still had enough time.

Fifteen minutes; that would be cutting it close.

As he approached the main door to Virology, he slowed his pace; scanning the area for anyone he knew. There were a few other lab techs that he had seen on and off throughout the halls, but did he not know them well enough to be noticed. In his mind, that was a good thing. He most certainly did not want to explain why he was in a different department. Virology and Epidemiology resources had the need to commonly interact across numerous cases, but he still didn't 'belong' as one of them. If he didn't have a good reason for being there, it would be a red flag and draw unwanted attention. Once satisfied that he was not being watched, he used Maxine's ID to open the door.

Samuel had never been in the virology department before, but he knew that Max had; another reason why using her ID was his best chance.

He was somewhat familiar with the layout based on departmental diagrams that he had reviewed over the last couple of weeks.

He suddenly began to feel a flushing in his face. The nervousness in which he thought he was doing a good job of containing, began to heat him all over. All at once, the collar around his neck seemed too tight. He began to perspire. Samuel felt a small trickle of sweat run down his temple. He casually brought his hand up to wipe it away; willing himself to slow his heart rate and respiratory functions. He didn't care if he couldn't breathe, or if his heart sped up to the point of exploding; he needed to appear as if nothing was out of the ordinary. He garnered a few glances from people here and there, but no one seemed to outright recognize him, or his slightly odd behavior. Again, if he believed in a deity, he would have thanked them for that.

He made great attempts to look like he knew where he was going; finally arriving to the security vault that held all the infectious diseases. It was a clean, white room lined with rows of shelving and a table in the center; the design was much like a library. The top half of the outer wall was all glass, which made him even more nervous that he could still be caught. And for the next, he looked at his watch, thirteen minutes, it was unmanned.

Doctor Edwin Malfront, one of the department leads and, at present, containment and storage chief for virology samples at the Centers for Disease Control and Prevention, was currently taking his break.

For a moment, Samuel found it quite odd that security was not tighter; especially due to the sensitivity of some of the deadliest pathogens in existence. It looked like all the vials and trays were stored openly in specified lots and bins within the shelves. As he peered through the thick glass window, he quickly dismissed the notion of lax security at realizing where he was and the organization where he worked; the whole building was its own security box.

He didn't anticipate that it would take long to find what he needed. The woman blackmailing him was very specific; she knew exactly where to find what she wanted. The question was how the pathogens were labeled and stored. Suddenly, his eyes became wide with panic as he looked to the door leading to the vault. There was a keypad next to the badge reader.

He didn't have the code.

In the split-second realization of what this meant, all he could think about was the safety of his family. He had just doomed them. He thought he had planned everything carefully; Malfront's schedule, the review of the laboratory layout, his exit strategy of the building. Samuel stared at the key pad, almost as if to will it not to be there. He cursed himself again at his own stupidity. How could he have not known about this? On the flip side, how would he? This was not his department. He knew no one who worked in this section, on this shift, or any other shift for that fact. He didn't even know Dr. Malfront. Even if he did, what difference would that have made? It's not like Samuel could have approached his imaginary colleague and asked if he had the code to the room that held the most lethal biohazard materials in existence; and by the way, would he mind telling him so he could break in and take some?

Samuel now began to full-on sweat; and this time, it seemed to run down his face like a waterfall. The ever-growing panic seemed to accelerate beyond his control. His wide eyes began to look about frantically, almost to the point of hysteria. What was he going to do? He could abort. No. That wasn't an option now.

His family.

Thought after thought began to bombard his mind and bleed out through his senses; his vision became blurred, a metallic taste washed through his mouth on the wave of extra saliva that the panic produced. He thought he smelled sulfur; an impossibility given the clean environment of the department, but the mind had a way of altering perception and reality when pushed beyond the levels capable of containing stress.

* * *

Airowyn stood a mere five feet from him and watched as Samuel seemed to have a crisis of conscience. He did not know that Samuel's conscience was, not at present, the reason behind the delay in performing the next step in humanity's downfall; but rather Samuel's lack of knowledge around the code he needed to enter the chamber.

As with the other chronicled acts that he was charged with witnessing, Airowyn was not to interfere. Although sympathy rose for the man before him, he, Airowyn, could not lay a comforting hand upon him. Samuel was undeclared, and therefore, not sensed enough to feel the angel's presence.

Airowyn looked upon the man disappointingly, and wondered what trickery befouled him into committing this destructive act. He received a partial answer to his curiosity as he peered into the chamber.

* * *

Samuel reached out to grab the handle of the door to the vault, not so much to see if it was locked, but more to steady himself due to the wave of nausea and dizziness resulting from what could be considered a panic attack. His mind was still buzzing with the onslaught of thoughts and questions; questions that did him no good to ask because he had no answers. The only thought he knew to be certain as a way out of his predicament, was to get into the vault.

Silly notions about how to fix this began popping into his rapidly tiring mind. He could find a chair to see if the glass might break. A stupid idea, he knew, but he was becoming desperate at the thought of anything that might work. A couple of more ridiculous ideas popped from his head, such as pulling the fire alarm to see if that would unlock the door; or walking up to someone he did not know, and asking them if they minded opening the vault for him. He had one stupid thought after another that was taking more and more time for him to think through, but got him no closer to his objective of getting inside.

Samuel had one more fleeting idea with the lowest possible odds against him. Of course, he knew it wouldn't work, but of all the utterly useless ideas that have flowed through his mind so far, it was the one that required the least amount of effort. Samuel looked at the badge he had lifted from Maxine. His eyes then drifted towards the keypad, finally resting upon the badge reader. Having absolutely nothing left to lose, he swiped the card.

To his profound amazement, he heard a familiar clicking of a lock disengaging. Pulling his hand backward quickly, as if the sound had harmed him in the process, he looked from the badge reader to the keypad, and back again. With his other hand that was still resting on the door's handle, he turned it as naturally as his nerves would allow, and the door opened.

* * *

Airowyn watched intently as a gnarled hand slowly moved from the wall within the chamber and opposite the external keypad. It slid down to its owner's side with little fanfare or excitement.

A wispy little demon known as Blurr glanced at the human named Samuel's astonished expression as the door clicked open. But instead of the glee that most demons shared in their contribution to the master's futile cause, Blurr displayed a measure of sadness at his role in this event; he even pitied the human that he was forced to help.

He looked over and noticed Airowyn, who made no attempt to interfere in Blurr's assignment; then it occurred to him that the angel must be there to chronicle the deeds of this human for the Great Hall of Records. What was happening must be of significance for a scribe to be present he thought. Blurr did not know, and was told nothing when he was sent to ensure this human's mission was successful. It was only for him to carry out his duty. None of his surly commanders ever involved him in matters of importance; this time should not have been any different. Yet, here was a scribe.

He continued observing the actions of the human with expression-less eyes as Samuel entered the chamber. Even thoughts around the significance of the angel's proximity didn't seem to excite the demon.

When their eyes finally met, it was as if they shared the same understanding of what was to transpire because of this event, and the senselessness of it all. Blurr's black eyes continued to stare into the deep green of Airowyn's. The demon gave the angel a courtesy nod. It was not in any way meant as condescending or malicious, as most of the exchanges between angels and demons go. It was merely an acknowledgment of the angel's presence; as if they were old colleagues and saw each other in a coffee shop.

Airowyn, in turn, nodded back. He found the acknowledgment from the demon strange, but harmless. He could see conflicted mannerisms about the demon; a mix of apathy and remorse. The demon was obviously an underling for their cause. He was of lessor size than a warring demon, no taller than five feet. He had no ranking to speak of that could be seen, and did not possess the familiar arrogance that Airowyn and other angels had grown accustom to over the centuries of war. It was like the little demon were weary and mentally beaten down. If it were possible, Airowyn almost felt sympathy for him, for he knew that the demon probably accepted that his kind was doomed to ultimately lose.

But it was not only that. The demon seemed genuinely melancholy. Could it be that he was feeling misgivings over his part, or possibly some sort of compassion over this human's doomed path? Perplexed with these thoughts, but not betraying his look of discernment, Airowyn continued to watch.

* * *

Samuel tried to contain his excitement at the luck he was experiencing. First, with still being able to meet Maxine in the hallway even though Malfront was significantly late, then getting into the vault without the code. Maybe Maxine's ID had the extra authorization that permitted passing? –a question that formed as he moved through the door. He didn't know, and at this point– he looked at his watch, there was nine minutes left on Malfront's break; he didn't care.

He needed to move quickly, but not too fast. He didn't want to appear frantic should anyone pass by the vault's windows. Samuel pulled a slip of paper with the row and bin number of the pathogen he needed from the inside of his pants pocket; the same slip of paper handed to him by the blackmailer along with the burner phone. He scanned it quickly then began his search.

* * *

Blurr watched as the human fumbled with some sort of paper. The man stared wide-eyed at whatever was on it, then began moving back and forth looking at the markings that were inscribed on each end of the large shelves. Blurr saw that the markings were written in the human's language, which the man silently mouthed as he fluttered about like a school child looking for the correct classroom.

Blurr was not well-educated in this human's dialect; the scribblings were as foreign to him as he imagined angelic Gaelic would be to them. He knew enough about it though to mutter through his mundane assignments as they were given. The demon's mouth turned into a crooked sneer as he continued to watch the human, knowing what was on that piece of paper, came from *him*.

The sneer grew into a scowl as Blurr recounted the sequence of events of how his first assignment in this mission was to gather the specific location of the human liquid sickness, and bring that information to his commanders. He assumed, in turn, that they gave it over to the mortal agents working for their cause. He began smiling maniacally at the genius of the plan, then stopped abruptly as the horror of realization washed over him.

The curse! He shook his head to the side violently to repel the thoughts from his head. *That stupid curse!* Blurr thought. He became horrified at the evil drifting through his corrupted mind; he could not let the Fallen's Curse ravage him.

The curse was all-consuming for most of his demonic brothers, but he tried very hard to resist the temptation that had driven most of his brothers mad over the millennia. Where the angels were peaceful before the fall, the torment of their disobedience and rebellion caused them unrest and insanity at every turn. Not knowing for sure, but Blurr believed this to be by design. A fitting punishment until the end came.

Unlike most of the other Fallen, Blurr came to terms with his mistakes, and accepted the responsibility as his own. He knew forgiveness was not possible, nor ever would be, but had decided long ago even though his fate were cast, he would resist the hatred that spawned psychopathic rage and not let it overwhelm him.

He inwardly smiled, bemused by the lack of accountability or fault that was not registered by his fellow offenders, and how the insanity was accepted as something other than a punishment. It's sometimes confounded him that some of his other fallen brethren had not figured out how to control it. If they did, it was never revealed; that would cause inquiries into the loyalties to the cause. Some of the demons were stupid, but smart enough to keep their mouths shut. They most likely kept it hidden from their masters; as to reveal their thoughts would be a show of independence. An irony not lost on Blurr, but would most likely fan an already raging flame.

The insanity caused by the curse was very powerful. He knew that some of his demon brothers *did* understand what it was, but did not want to control it. They let it control them. In most cases, it played well into their master's domination and his ultimate plan. In any event, if it helped to wreak havoc and caused a high amount of chaos, that was always preferable, at least that's what was advocated.

The more Blurr controlled his ability to be affected by the curse, the easier it was to understand the consequences of his disastrous and ill-fated choice. The control also enabled him to remember what it was like before the fall.

He liked those memories.

Blurr eyed Airowyn for a moment to see if the angel had registered the change in his behavior. He wasn't sure why, but it seemed to matter to him what the angel thought. While most of the other insanity-induced demons floundered about out of control, and for the most part, not caring who was watching, the perception mattered to Blurr. It was as if he was still trying to impress the angels, and did not want them to think badly of him. He had often wondered if any angels that he encountered took notice of the difference; that he, Blurr, was not like the others. Without engaging them directly, he was like a little brother trying to get the attention and approval from an older sibling.

He was careful never to let his fellow demons see, what he imagined they would think were weakness and betrayal of their evil cause, but Blurr longed to be a part of the angelic brotherhood once more. He dreamed of his long blonde hair; lavender colored eyes, even his flowing Sirvent robes as Keeper of the Eternal Flame for the Majaliant Obelisk of the Six Realms; a job that he had taken for granted before the Fall. He was ashamed of his weak mindedness during the rebellion, and the gullibility to those who convinced him that he deserved better. He knew now that he had once had it good. A whole lot better than his present condition.

He momentarily broke his gaze from the angel and looked down at the tattered strappings that was an excuse for clothing. His hands drifted to his patchy and tangled hair, no longer blonde and beautiful, but gray and perpetually matted with dirt and grease. He lifted his eyes to the reflection in the chamber's windows; his skin was blotched like a dirty, pitted rock. Crevices and creases marked his blackened and leathery body where the rags did not cover. His angelic features were now misshapen with crooked, fanged teeth framed by a much too large mouth. Blurr's gnarled and crooked hands moved to his eyes, which were no longer lavender, but were now coal black orbs.

He turned away from his reflection in disgust. Blurr dared not look towards the angel fearing his gaze of repulsion at the sight of the pitiful demon. It is what it is, and Blurr could do nothing to take it back. Instead, he turned his attention back to the human, who seemed to be having difficulty locating the liquid sickness, even though the instructions were right in front of him on the small slip of paper.

* * *

I don't understand, thought Samuel. He walked up and down the same aisle of the number that was written on the piece of paper. His pace increased along with his panic. He glanced at his watch for what seemed like the hundredth time. He now had three minutes left.

The air seemed to be sucking out of his lungs as if he were in a vacuum. Samuel was experiencing the onset of another panic attack. He had never had those before, so he was unaware of the symptoms. He was smart enough to know that it would not do him, nor his family, any good if he freaked out or was caught.

His family.

At the thought of their suffering, the panic attack began to accelerate. He stopped pacing and braced himself on the shelf. A flood of thoughts began to race through his mind on the possible ways that the blackmailer would make his family suffer. He no longer cared for himself, but he had to ensure their safety. *He was doing all of this for them*, he thought with his eyes wildly erratic. A valiant thought for someone who might not be at fault for their current predicament, but in the back of his mind, he felt completely guilty for he knew this entire thing was, in fact, his fault. If he had not done something stupid, the blackmailer would not have anything over him. Of course, if he knew who the blackmailer was and who she worked for, he might have understood that his crime of tax evasion would not have made a difference. He was chosen because of his lower profile within the CDC and his access to what they needed.

He would not be missed as much when he disappeared.

* * *

Blurr saw the human stop moving, and lean against the large shelf. He looked as if he was ill. Why was he stopping? What was taking the man so long to find the liquid? The little demon did not understand. The information was *right there* on that piece of paper. All the human had to do was locate it. Blurr sneered at the stupidity of this mewling creature, then abruptly stopped, again remembering the curse.

He tried not to be seen, but glanced at a reflective surface towards Airowyn to see if he was still watching. Of course, he was, as that was his job as an official scribe.

Blurr did not understand the feeling he was experiencing as embarrassment. He knew that he didn't want the angel to judge him. A funny thought as no one could judge except for the Most High. Maybe it was more so not wanting to disappoint. Blurr did not understand these feelings either. This must be what it is like for humans; no wonder they struggle in their meager existence. Maybe that is what is happening to the pitiful man before him. So many things to ponder, but those must wait for another moment.

Blurr knew not the concept of time, as angels and demons existed outside of it. He knew though, that the human was running out of it. His commander was very explicit in his mission. He must ensure the completion, and the human must leave this dwelling with the liquid sickness.

Not knowing why, but almost as a reflex, he once again glanced towards the angel. Feeling the angel's eyes upon him, Blurr moved towards the human.

Samuel had composed himself and moved away from the shelf to examine the information on the slip of paper again. The demon appeared next to his shoulder and viewed the paper as well. Blurr saw the symbols of the human's language as he remembered conveying to his commanders. He could not remember if the symbols had been correct though. The human's language was very rudimentary. Fearing the torment of not fulfilling his assignment, Blurr quickly made his way to the liquid sickness in which the human was seeking. It was part of the demon's first assignment to locate it, as it was conveyed by the humans as to what they specifically required to fulfill the prophecy. Demons could not remove it though, as that would be a violation to the interaction laws established by the Host, by which they were still bound. Just like their angel counterparts, they were only to influence, and not directly intervene. The demons agreed to provide the information, while the humans agreed to provide the pitiful creature before him.

Blurr located the spot where the human needed to be. On the shelf within the tray was a hermetically sealed small metal box containing three vials of the Group V, Risk Group 4, Class A Bioterrorism Agent known as the Marburg virus.

15

Percival the Meek

The demon looked back towards the human known as Samuel, who was still staring at the piece of paper. Blurr rolled his eyes in frustration, which would not have been obvious to anyone watching since they were completely black, then shook the tray slightly that held the deadly pathogen.

Samuel did not readily see or hear the movement as he was still reading the slip of paper, as if any of the numbers or letters had changed during the many times of scanning back and forth between it and the shelves.

Blurr continued to move the tray gently in the hopes that the human would spot it. He was unfamiliar with the volatility of the sickness, and wondered if the jostling might disturb the contents. This was never something demons had to concern themselves with as they were not as frail as humans, nor susceptible to their diseases. Still, it would not bode well for him, nor the human, if the contents were damaged or spilled.

The little demon was rewarded with recognition at last.

Samuel blinked twice. Did something just move? Given his current emotional state, he played it off as a panic-induced imagination. Then it moved again. He slowly walked toward the spot where he thought he saw a tray slide back and forth. Upon examination, he looked over the label contents, then became excited. He found it! This was what he needed. He verified the numbers and letters against what was on his little slip of paper. M14J – 26a (G4). Then his excitement waned when he saw the rest of the classification. Family: Filoviridae (MARV).

"No," he said to himself softly. "This can't be right."

He slowly reached out to touch the small silver box. His fingers grazed the seal.

The Marburg virus.

What could they possibly want with the Marburg virus? He checked the paper one last time to make sure that this was exactly what was marked. Both the tray contents and the slip of paper matched. Questions and thoughts began flooding through his mind again, but this time; it wasn't just about his family's safety. This was about the world.

He dropped his hands to his side. Samuel stared at nothing, transfixed on what he was being asked of him.

Blurr saw the hesitation in the human's face. A measure of sadness filled him at seeing the realization of the human's awareness of his quest. Samuel, Blurr had decided, was not enlightened to his role in the prophecy. He supposed that it did not make any difference. The human was being used, just like Blurr. His commanders and their human agents would not see any value in keeping this human beyond this assignment. He was sure that Samuel did not know, and wondered what leverage their superiors had over him to elicit his participation.

Samuel's eyes were glazed; deep in thought over the consequences of his next act. Where only moments ago, time was a factor in his mission; it was now inconsequential compared to what he considered, the fate of the entire human race.

The Marburg virus was the deadliest known pathogen in existence. The mortality rate per total population was between 40 and 50 percent, meaning that 2 out of five people that contracted the virus would die a horrible death. Anyone who came in contact with it would carry and spread it exponentially. It could not be controlled or contained. It could very well cause an extinction-level pandemic.

What could they possibly want with this virus? They couldn't just release this into the populous without having some type of a management defense. The impact upon the world at large would be devastating. What would be the cost to him personally? Was his family worth the price to preserve mankind? His thoughts drifted to the 15 years of marriage to his wife Deirdre, and their nine-year-old son Thomas. He wished he was with them right now. What was he going to do?

As quickly as the panic faded when he found his prize, it now returned in force thinking about the repercussions of his next move. He could just stand there and wait for Malfront to come back and simply catch him in an unauthorized area with the Marburg virus in his hands. He would go to jail, but the virus would remain safe. Or would it? Would the blackmailer simply find another fool with a criminal past to pick up where Samuel had failed? Should he take the container, but deliver something else inside other than the virus? No, that would not be possible because he couldn't hermetically seal the container with the fake contents, which if the blackmailer knew what she was asking for, would know what to expect. Samuel started to develop a headache.

Deirdre? Thomas?

Were their lives worth the price?

What makes us human are the emotional relationships we build with each other; the longer the connection, the deeper the bond. The most powerful relationship is built on a foundation of love. An intoxicating emotion, love can push a human to unimaginable limits that can be both good and bad. The ability to care for something, or someone so deeply can influence or completely dismiss other emotions that make us who we are today; the caring, nurturing, morally responsible dominant species of this planet.

Another essential element that is a key to our survival is being able to think logically and rationally. Love almost always cancels those out. In Samuel's current predicament, he was not immune to this selfishness that is called love.

Samuel carefully placed the tray back in its proper spot on the shelf, not understanding the obsessiveness of the move, but more so to make sure that a casual glance from no one would spark further investigation because the tray seemed out of place. Although he didn't know

Malfront personally, he knew of his meticulousness when it came to the order of his vault. If he were to look close enough, he would obviously see the virus missing. Immediate protocol would be to contact security, who in turn, would lock down the facility within seconds. That would be problematic for his escape. He didn't have a plan passed getting the virus out of the vault, so he needed to be quick without attracting attention.

He looked at his watch again; two minutes. The metal container was too big to carry inside his lab coat pocket, so he tucked it within the coat just under his left arm and held it tight to his chest. As casually as he could, left the vault.

* * *

Blurr followed the human out of the chamber. As Samuel turned to leave the department, the demon stopped short to where Airowyn was still watching. Airowyn's eyes drifted from Samuel to Blurr, and just stared. This made the little demon uncomfortable as he did not know if he should say something, or maybe sneer at the angel's presence, which would most likely be the first option of his fellow demons.

He decided to take a chance and speak. "Beannachtaí deartháir," he said in their native Gaelic to greet his brother.

Airowyn's expression was stoic and unmoving. "We are no longer brothers."

Blurr broke eye contact and looked down sheepishly. "I am sorry—"

"What is your name, little one?" Interrupted Airowyn, who now looked at the demon with curiosity.

"I am called Blurr," came the reply with surprise. Never since the fall, had he been able to converse with an angel. His lowly station was no more than that of a house servant, a messenger between commanders, a simple gopher. This was his first real mission of significance; that truth was evident by the angel's presence. Happenstance notwithstanding, he now had the fortune of talking *with* one rather than running *from* one like demons were accustomed.

Airowyn's expression softened a little. "What *was* your name?" He asked meaning before the rebellion.

The demon's eyes widened at the question. No one ever asked this of him. There had never been any interest in him by angels or his demonic clan other than conflict.

He was not at all surprised that he was not known. He was an insignificant nothing, or so he thought before the rebellion; not acknowledged or revered for any contributions. All he did was keep the flame. Blurr once again wished he had not made the wrong choice, and desperately wished he still had that flame to keep. He wondered who the keeper was now.

Again, he reflected on his life before the fall; the splendor of the Majaliant Nexus of the Six Realms, and the Orchestra of Anthemusa with their angel's magnificent songs. What Blurr missed the most was the great Rainbow Falls beyond Mount Rakvere, and how the multiple colors illuminated the Valley of Socasanice. It was not like the seven translucent colors they had in this realm. The miraculous and vibrant colors of the falls were many variations and glistened off the Sea of Persephone as they cascaded downward. They rolled with the waves; each bringing about a different color as they rippled outward and disappeared. The beauty was glorious and everlasting. How he had taken that wondrous realm for granted.

"My name," he said looking down, "was Percival." He couldn't look the angel in his eyes; the shame was overpowering.

Airowyn's curiosity peaked. He had never witnessed remorse from a demon. He saw that the little one felt sincerity with his disgrace. This intrigued him.

"Well, Percival," said Airowyn, "it looks like your charge," he said nodding towards Samuel, "is getting away from you."

Blurr looked at him with astonishment. Not since the Fall had he ever been referred to by his given name.

"He is not my charge," said Blurr excitingly. "I am only to aid the human in his mission."

Airowyn raised an eyebrow. "And what might that mission be?"

If the demon was forthcoming, what harm would it be for the angel to probe for additional information? It might prove useful for the cause as well as clarification in his report to Lucaous.

Blurr became more animated at the thought of engaging in a conversation with the angel. "I was commissioned by Commander Wyck himself to identify and ensure that the liquid sickness was delivered to the human agents for dispersal."

The angel remained passive in his response; clearly not as excited as Blurr. "Dispersal for what?"

The demon was acting like a girl gossiping in a high school hallway between classes. "You know; I am not sure, but if I had to take a guess based on what I already know, I think it will be included in the plan of the imminent rise of Blà Tàl."

Blurr was referring to the pagan god who promised to return and sweep away the Christian threat. It was boasted the false god would lead a vast army of warriors wielding the one true weapon of their destruction, the Tor Embla.

"How would this liquid sickness play a part in his rise?" asked the angel.

Blurr moved closer to the angel as if he were about to reveal a deeper and darker secret. He shifted his eyes from side to side looking for anyone of a supernatural presence that might hear.

He spoke in barely a whisper. "We both know that although his power is supreme over demons, the dark lord is limited on true control of humans. Just like you, we are to only influence and manipulate as necessity permits." He looked into Airowyn's eyes to ensure comprehension. The angel simply nodded his acknowledgment.

"There are cases; however, where we can do more to direct the humans if we are asked," continued Blurr.

It was not uncommon knowledge to Airowyn, or the other angels, in the direct relationships of demons and misguided, disillusioned humans seeking to serve the side of evil. Satanic worshipers will sometimes present various sacrifices, or offerings to their imaginary pagan gods, and openly ask for control and dominion over their lives. These sad little people chose their side, with what some might call, gusto. Those types of humans wanted to be used, and could not be saved. It was a sadness bore by the host collective.

"I believe," continued Blurr, "that this liquid sickness is but one of the components that will be used to exercise that control." If it were possible, Blurr attempted to move even closer to Airowyn. Then he stopped abruptly. His black eyes widened at the realization of what he perceived as treachery.

"You tricked me," said Blurr barely above a whisper.

Airowyn's expression did not change except for another raised eyebrow.

The demon began to back away as if witnessing an incomprehensible horror. "You used me for information," he said a bit louder.

"I merely asked you a simple question; you continued to speak of your own volition," said Airowyn calmly.

He looked around in disbelief. "I thought that you and I could strike a relationship of sorts."

"Make no mistake, little one, I view you not as a threat, but as one of the misfortunate effects of betrayal," said the angel referring to that rebellion of long ago. "While a possibility of a truce between you and me individually, you are still on the wrong side of this war," said the angel a bit more sternly. "It is my belief that you comprehend this," said Airowyn a little softer.

The demon now had an expression of mixed sorrow and surprise. His grief openly shown as he knew the angel was correct. Not knowing what else to say, Blurr began to trail after the human.

Airowyn watched the demon disappear, then began to shimmer as he, himself, vanished.

* * *

Edward Marseilles of the Jonah Protective Services, and three other agents, walked up the small steps leading to the main doors of the one-nine precinct just off East 67th. As police stations went, this was a very nondescript, four-story brownstone. It stuck out just a bit with the blue window and door trimmings, but nonetheless, seemed to fit in well with the surroundings.

He walked and talked the part of a man comfortable in his position as a tactical team lead, but even more intimidating was his looks. A weather-worn man with hundreds of miles of fieldwork, a few scars from previous skirmishes as he would like to call them; Marseilles was considered an experienced veteran agent. He was a trusted colleague of Kelan's from back in the old Alastar-McGlocklin days as part of the ground team that had surveilled Joshua's best friend, the late Harry Gibson.

Immediately following the fall of Alastar-McGlocklin, he found himself, with no pun intended, a free agent. After a few odd jobs here and there; beefing up corporate security, or protecting the occasional self-important celebrity, he received a call from Kelan asking him if he would like something a little more permanent. He has since worked himself up to a position of command and respect within the JPS.

When Kelan contacted him about the retrieval of a high-level asset, he hand-picked his best agents for the escort and set out to accomplish his directive.

He strolled up to the main desk with a purpose. "Excuse me, I'm—"

"Just hang on a second," said the duty sergeant annoyed; not looking up while he continued to jot something down in some sort of ledger.

The other agents behind Marseilles shot each other some glances, clearly indicating that this poor slob behind the desk had no idea who he was dealing with.

Without even a second thought, Marseilles' swift hands came up and over the desk; one yanking the pen out of the sloppy desk jockey's hand, while the other slammed his credentials down on the mess of papers before him.

The desk sergeant had a mixed expression of shock and anger as he looked up. He saw four very well-dressed men in business suits; all unmoving and stone-faced. The sergeant looked down at the credentials to see who would have the nerve to—. The blood momentarily drained from his face as he looked back up to the man pictured within the internationally and federally sanctioned document.

Marseille's very calmly said, "I have a badge too if you need to see it."

The overweight sergeant shook his head as his jowls vibrated downward.

"I believe we are expected by Chief Willis," finished Marseille's.

The desk sergeant changed the direction of his massive head to a nod as he reached out to pick up the handset of the dirty thirty-year-old phone.

Within forty-five seconds, a gentleman with a gun and badge strapped to his belt walked out from a hallway to the right of the overly large sergeant's desk; his hand outstretched as he approached.

"Agent Marseilles, Brian Ackerman," he said as they shook hands. The man looked to be very fit and in his mid-30s. Marseilles noticed the firm handshake. "The chief sent me down to assist. What is it that I can do for you?"

Marseilles' expression remained passive, even though he was a bit confused. "We are here to pick up Kelly Granger for transport."

Ackerman's brow furrowed. "Excuse me, who?"

Marseilles' expression did not change in the note of Ackerman's question. "Kelly Granger," he said more clearly as he enunciated each word.

"And who would that be?" Ackerman asked.

Marseilles' was still passive, but the lack of knowledge around why he and his team were there coupled to the fact that this man did not seem to know who Granger was, prompted a red flag.

As a matter of field protocol and training as operatives, all four men were well skilled in the art of passive signaling. The other three agents knew the drill and had worked with Marseilles many times before. They all randomly glanced down at Marseille's side and saw the slight hand signal for caution. One by one they casually unbuttoned their suit jackets.

This did not go unnoticed by Ackerman. His quizzical look turned into one of suspicion.

Marseilles caught the change of facial expression. "I would like to speak directly with Chief Willis."

Ackerman smiled. "As I said, the chief sent me down to help, so that's what I want to do." He slid to the side and gestured to the hallway from which he came. "If you gentlemen will follow me; I will be happy to escort you to the chief, so we can sort this out."

"If it's all the same to you, we will wait here," said Marseilles. "I'm sure the chief won't mind taking a few minutes to meet us in the lobby with Miss Granger."

Ackerman looked cautiously at Marseilles as neither broke eye contact. After what seemed like an eternity, but was three-seconds, Ackerman smiled again. "Alright, you boys wait here, and I will be right back with the chief." As Ackerman departed, his eyes caught the desk sergeant's, who gave an ever so slightly nod.

Marseilles watched Ackerman around the corner, then turned into the small circle of his agents. One of them asked a bit louder than normal, "What do you think is going on?"

Normally, Marseilles might have been upset about the volume to the question, but that agent knew what he was doing. Marseilles' response was just as audible; not for his men but for anyone else that might be listening. "Nothing, I think it's just a mix up. I'm sure that we'll be back in time for coffee and donuts."

The other agents smiled, but understood. Each mission, of which this one was, had protocols and code phrases depending on the situations. Sometimes standard audible commands could not be given, hence the hand signal of caution. The key phrase of 'coffee and donuts' meant they were in trouble and needed backup.

Marseilles smiled back and caught the eye of his second in command, who raised his hands and arched his back in a stretching motion. He clasped his hands behind his head as he turned it first to the right, then to the left. Upon turning to the left, he spoke just above a whisper into the cuff of his jacket as his fellow agents began talking loud enough to mask the sound.

"Jack rabbit."

16

Omicron Seven

Kelan was down in the lower levels of Jonah International in what used to be known as the Artifact Acquisitions Retrieval Team Hub. It was where all missions' operations, artifacts retrieval teams' analysts, and watchers were stationed when supporting field operatives on artifact missions. Artifacts were a thing of the past after the fall of Alastar-McGlocklin, but the level was still used for JPS operations. Kelan couldn't think of anything better to call the support level, so the nickname 'rHub' stuck.

He had long since come to terms with the ghost of the office he occupied many years ago. Kelan did not know Ulysses Quaden personally, but from the stories he had heard from all who did, he was honored to occupy that room, and humbled to continue his work in the position that was abruptly vacated by his death. It was in this office where he received the forthcoming news.

The walls were made of glass, so he had complete visibility to the watcher running to his door. The pleasantries of a courteous knock were forgotten as the woman opened it. "Sir, we have received a request for backup from Marseilles' team."

Kelan said a swear word under his breath as he rose from behind his desk. He followed the young woman out of his office. "Code?"

Out of the many call codes that could be used, certain ones meant specific levels of threat. Kelan wanted to temper his reaction until he determined how bad it was.

"The call sign used came in from Agent Ingram. It was Jack rabbit," she said as she took her place at the workstation.

It was bad.

Jack rabbit was a duress call for backup. It meant that the team was in a situation where eyes and ears of the enemy were present and conflict was imminent.

"TAC team deployed?" Kelan asked standing over her shoulder.

"Yes, sir, ETA is seven minutes."

Kelan swore under his breath again. "This thing could be over by then." He paced behind her for a few seconds. "Send out a message to the Associates within the precinct."

"I've already tried that, sir," she said. "Jamming of microwave signals started right before I came to you."

That meant that the enemy was already aware of the team's mission to retrieve Granger. They were jamming communications. It also meant that any Associates within the immediate area could not be contacted. Or so the enemy thought.

"Sentinel," said Kelan.

"Yes, sir."

"Cut through the jamming and send the following message to each Associate's cell."

* * *

Officer Lincoln McDowell was processing paperwork on the third floor of the one-nine precinct. He heard the officer at the desk next to him curse. "What the—?" He started banging his mobile phone against his hand. "Stupid phone!" He glanced at McDowell. "I'm not getting a signal." McDowell didn't think anything of it, but casually pulled his cell off his belt clip and looked at the display. Funny, he didn't have a signal either. Suddenly, his phone vibrated with a text message.

[CODE 668. JPS AGENTS IN LOBBY IN NEED OF ASSISTANCE. IDENTIFICATION: STARFISH]

McDowell looked up with concern. He scanned the bullpen of desks looking for any other officers who might have received the same message. One by one, a few Associates caught each other's eyes and stood. McDowell nodded to the closest one, then they began to make their way out of the bullpen. Although they didn't communicate with each other, all of them were thinking the same thing. Code 668 meant an imminent threat. Lethal measures were authorized.

As McDowell made his way down the staircase, he looked one of his fellow officers in the eyes and simply said, "Starfish."

The officer nodded and replied with the same.

* * *

Marseilles' team continued to talk about nothing as they all waited for the chief and Granger. Each of the agents casually surveyed their surroundings as they spoke.

Ingram, Marseilles' second, noticed that the desk sergeant continued to look at them. The over-weight police officer tried to be nonchalant, but shifted his eyes every time an agent peered in his direction. Another agent noticed the desk sergeant glancing towards other police officers milling about; some had paperwork in their hands; others were walking with a purpose from one room to another along the halls on either side of the sergeant's desk. Everyone stared at the four agents as they moved about. Marseilles became uneasy when he noticed the increase in traffic. Suddenly, all four agents' earpieces came to life.

"Redeye, this is Watchdog. Jack rabbit confirmed. TAC team ETA, six minutes. Be advised, Associates on premise. Identification is Starfish."

Marseilles looked at the others to confirm that they understood. He was rewarded with slight nods. Unable to verbally respond his confirmation, he causally brought his hands together and tapped twice on the cuff of his jacket where the hidden microphone was attached.

* * *

"Signal acknowledged and received by Marseilles' team, sir," said the female watcher, as her hands danced across the hard-light imagery.

Kelan nodded, not that she could see him. "Associates?"

"Code 668 has been successfully transmitted. It is hard to know if it's been seen, and if they're responding."

Kelan paced a bit more as he nodded again, deep in thought. The retrieval team is getting pushback on the pick-up. So far, there aren't any eyes on Granger. He doesn't know her status. The enemy, whoever that may be in this case, wanted Granger, dead or alive; either way, they wanted her.

It was no big surprise that Joshua was right; he usually was. They were faced with two problems now; the safety of his retrieval team, and the condition of Granger. Joshua needed to be brought in on this. Kelan pulled out his cell phone and dialed.

* * *

As McDowell and a few other Associates rounded the corner on the first-floor stairwell, one bumped his arm and nodded towards the armory. McDowell nodded his acknowledgment and followed suit with the rest and moved towards the secured cage of weapons. As the group of uniforms approached, the watch guard spoke. "Hey Peterson. What can I—"

"Starfish," said the man identified as Peterson.

The watch guard slightly laughed. "What?"

With a quickness, Peterson pulled his service weapon and pointed it at the watch guard.

Visibly shaken, the watch guard grabbed his desk with both hands and recoiled at the action. "What are you doing?!"

"I need you to open the cage, Sal."

"Son, you know I can't—"

Peterson pushed the barrel of his Glock to the cage, gripping it with both hands. "Now."

Wincing at the sound of the gun connecting with the cage, he began nodding. The watch guard's hands were shaking as he reached under and tripped the buzzer for the lock on the door. McDowell and three others entered as quickly as they could, and started pulling flak jackets and SWAT gear. Peterson walked through the cage entrance with his weapon still pointed at Sal. Sympathy creased his face. "Sal, if you're not part of this or one of them, I am truly sorry. If we both survive this, I will try to explain why after this is over." He lifted his gun and swung it heavily against the watch guard's head. Sal hit the floor with a sickening thump.

After thirty-seconds, all five officers were dressed in a hodgepodge of tactical protection, then started pulling multiple weapons such as M4 carbines and pump action Remington 870s. They loaded all the weapons as quickly as they could, grabbed additional ammunition, and exited the cage. The entire process took less than ninety-seconds. When they were done, all moved toward the lobby.

* * *

Joshua was reviewing the media protocol and access privileges with Alice and Langston when the call came through.

"Sir, a priority call from Mr. Tindal," said Sentinel.

Before Joshua could say anything, Kelan's voice filled the room. "Joshua, the pick-up with Granger is going south."

Jumping three steps ahead of the conversation, Joshua said, "Does Inara have her, yet?"

"We don't know. We don't have eyes on her," said Kelan.

Joshua stood up. "Sentinel, give me a live tactical feed of the precinct; wire-frame reference. Relay these images down to Kelan." Hard-light imagery displayed a three-dimensional digital wire frame.

The octagonal table within the situation room in rHub came to life as the wire frame of the precinct and occupants swirled into view.

Kelan, the female watcher, and two other analysts ran to the table. As Joshua manipulated the image from his office, the same rotation happened in the situation room.

Joshua began moving the images to identify key targets. As he manipulated, he spoke to Sentinel. "Highlight the retrieval team." An image of four wire-framed men appeared in yellow. They stood in a circle in a large outer room next to the front doors.

"Your team is in the lobby," said Joshua as his hands moved around the image.

"I see them," said Kelan from rHub.

"Our target is Granger. Sentinel, highlight her in blue," said Joshua.

Her image appeared in a small room on the fourth floor towards the back left. She appeared to be seated with her hands cuffed behind her. Joshua had a grizzly thought as he looked at her slumped wire frame. "Locate Chief Willis."

The prone body of a gray digital figure appeared in the corner of what should have been his office. The wire outline looked crumpled, as if it was contorted from an unnatural fall. "Sir, Chief Willis is dead," said Sentinel in its ever-even tone.

Langston closed his eyes and lowered his head; Alice gasped with her hand on her mouth. A barely audible swear word came from Kelan.

Joshua's expression was one of anger. The sadness would come in time, but now he was just mad. "Kelan, how far out is the TAC team?"

"ETA is a little over five minutes," came the female watcher's voice.

"Associates?" Joshua asked.

He knew the drill all too well from his time as a watcher. The strategy and tactical operations' scenarios that he ran with Lucas, Langston, and when he was alive, Ulysses, had been ingrained in him for months during his training as an agent. He knew that Kelan was following the same protocol for support. Contingencies were the lifeblood of the JPS agents.

"Contact support was sent via text messaging. It's unclear whether they are reacting," replied Kelan.

"Well, let's find out." Joshua cocked his head, although the only people that could see were Langston and Alice. "They knocked out communications?" He asked knowing the answer.

"First thing they did, sir," said the female watcher.

"Sentinel, show me the responding Associates," said Joshua.

Five green wire-framed figures were walking with a quickness down a stairwell at the back of the building. Joshua manipulated the wire frame to zoom in on their position. They watched the five figures approach a small room. In a matter of a few seconds, one of the figures looked like he pulled a gun and was pointing it.

"What is this room?" Joshua asked.

"If I were a betting man, I would think the gun cage," replied Kelan.

"How so?" Langston said.

"We transmitted a 668 code to the Associates. Imminent threat; lethal measures authorized. If I were them, I would be arming up," said Kelan.

Langston and Alice looked at Joshua. They, as well as Kelan, knew he did not want any situation that would result in the loss of life; even a Familiars'.

Joshua stared at the images for a few seconds. Multiple scenarios and outcomes played through his head. Before him, was a story that could end in many ways. How could he prevent bloodshed and still secure Granger? He needed to know the enemies' players.

He was apprehensive in his next command, because he had a sinking feeling, but needed confirmation nonetheless. "Sentinel, light up all the Familiars."

It looked like a plague of walking dead. Figures highlighted in red milled about on every floor. A quick estimate would be four or five Familiars to every green figure in the building. Joshua knew that not all the Familiars belonged. They were placed there to secure Granger, one way or another. He couldn't understand why they had not already killed her though. Upon reviewing the position of all players, he saw that they placed Granger on the top floor the farthest away from the main point of entry. Other building exits, if breached, could reach her just as easily. Why weren't they guarded? Then he saw it.

"Kelan, does your team have audio?" Joshua asked. He knew the answer, and was unsure why he even asked the question. Habit he supposed.

"Yes, but they're not free to speak," said Kelan.

"That's okay. I just need them to listen."

* * *

Marseilles' team was doing their best to contain the anxiety that was building. A few of the precinct's officers were now slowing a bit while continuing to stare. Intimidation was not something in which Marseilles, or his men, was accustomed, so when it was blatantly obvious that the stares were meant as more than casual curiosity, he and his team began to stare back. He knew that they were heavily outmatched as the situation stood, but was hoping that would be rectified quickly. No sooner than that thought crossed his mind, his earpiece came alive.

"Redeye, this is Joshua Arden."

All four agents looked at each other, some with raised eyebrows. They did not expect to hear *his* voice.

"The TAC team is still a little over three minutes out," continued Joshua. "Five heavily armed officers will be approaching your position from the hall on your immediate left; they are Associates. Confirm identity, then prepare to execute omicron seven on my command. The prize is secured on the fourth floor at the back of the building. Use the right hallway for ingress; Sentinel will guide you from there."

Kelan was impressed with Joshua's plan. The omicron seven scenario was a bold play. It combined a rapid advance with three or more men interweaving along the route using a modified Greek phalanx formation to ensure a complete 360° radius of coverage. There would be no defined lead as the rotation would take agents from the point position to the rear as each man moved. This scenario was only possible under the guidance of an external source, like a watcher, with complete visibility of the situation; in this case, Sentinel would be the lead. The continual movement and rotation of the advancing team would provide a harder target for the enemy. It was very aggressive and would not be anywhere near a diplomatic approach. Joshua meant to retrieve Granger by force now.

Joshua hesitated on his next comment. He realized there was no way everyone was going to make it out in one piece, unless he sanctioned what he believed was his only option.

"Gentlemen, there will be multiple Familiars between you and Ms. Granger. Sentinel will identify those targets. You are weapons free at your own discretion. Deadly force is authorized."

Langston and Alice looked at him.

"Sir," said Alice surprised at his decision.

"They're Familiars, Alice. They've made their choice." He looked back at the digital wire frame display. "I can't help them now."

Kelan and the others stood frozen down in rHub at what Joshua had just decreed. Although he completely agreed with the order, Kelan was concerned about what this decision would do to Joshua. He had discussions with him in the past regarding a time when force would be an unfortunate, but necessary measure to tip the balance in the fight. Kelan was, of course, speaking to the human element; Familiars and such.

Joshua's inner circle, including Lucas, could see the writing on the wall from both human and supernatural perspectives. They knew Joshua could too, but respected his wish for a passive solution. The times were changing, and Joshua, although reluctantly, realized that he must consider other alternatives as well. Although he was prepared to accept the outcome of today's event, the days to come would test the weight of his responsibility, and the decisions that he must make, not just for his team and Jonah International, but for the world.

Joshua talked directly with the agents at one nine again. "Gentlemen, once the five Associates have joined you, have them switch their transceivers to channel 26. Please confirm."

Marseilles nodded to Ingram, who double tapped his jacket cuff microphone.

"Joshua, I'm not questioning your plan," said Langston.

"Yes, you are," replied Joshua with a dismal attempt at a grin, "but go ahead. What's on your mind?"

"I am not a tactical expert, nothing like you or Kelan, but the odds are not exactly in our favor," he said looking at the Familiar to Associate ratio on the digital image. "It looks like you have a plan for getting *to* Granger, but what about getting her out? Once they realize what we are trying to do, what's to keep them from just killing her?"

"Oh, they're not going to kill her," said Joshua matter-of-fact.

A quizzical look crossed Langston's face. "How can you be so sure?"

Joshua crossed his arms and turned slightly to face him. "Because they want her alive. They don't know how much she has told us, if anything. They need to know before disposing of her. My guess is they were planning some sort of ambush during the FBI transfer. Chief Willis is dead. I believe they were trying to get the time of the transfer out of him since he was the only one that knew. They wanted the extraction to happen either before or during the transfer to maximize confusion and misdirection. They also don't have any coverage along this back stairwell," he said pointing from the top floor to the bottom. "That leads me to believe that it was going to be their exit point. They didn't count on us to show up; which is why the Familiars are scattered about," he said pointing to the various red images.

Joshua's gestures were conveyed to the image in rHub for Kelan and his team in the form of a floating dot like a laser pointer.

Kelan nodded at the theory. "So our exit plan will be the same stairwell?"

"Exactly," said Joshua. "Have our TAC team secure all exits with the expectation of Marseilles' team and Granger to exit from the back. They are only to enter the building on Marseilles' command. He has a better vantage point and sense for the situation; I don't want any of our people caught in a crossfire."

Looking back at Langston, Joshua said, "…and as far as getting them out, I'm going to call for some additional assurances."

Joshua's inner circle understood what that meant. Without a command, Sentinel muted communications out of Joshua's office.

Joshua turned to the center of the room. "Vaago."

No one appeared.

Joshua might have found this strange if it had been Lucas he had called for, but this was the first time that he was calling upon the leader of the angelic warriors he had seen in action from the plane trip back from England. The long-haired leader didn't seem to take well to the news of Joshua's command.

He waited a few seconds, then called again. "Vaago!"

At that moment, a powerful angel shimmered into view. His broad chest was bigger than that of Lucas; his arms solid and muscular. He had large chestnut brown eyes to match his long, thick, below the shoulder hair. His garb was a cross between warrior and rock star; a bronze breastplate that pulsated with waves of light, forearm and shin guards that extended the pulsing light, and an amazing battle sword at his side that seemed to glow. There was what looked like a sash and skirt combined that was cut out in the front that just hung around his waist; it seemed to flutter in a nonexistent wind. He stood there expectantly; not saying anything.

Joshua frowned at his presence, because this was not who he expected. "Where is Vaago?"

Alice and Langston just stood there, star struck. They saw Lucas in his true form a few times, but never any other supernatural being. They stared, transfixed at the angel's glow. They both broke their eyes away when they saw Joshua step around the conference table and walk towards the being. He did not look happy.

"I asked you a question," he said stopping mere feet from the immense warrior.

Anyone not aware of the current crisis, would think the scene comical; the angel towered a good two feet over Joshua.

The angel was slightly taken aback by the human's boldness in his approach. His fearlessness of the warrior's presence was both admirable and curious.

"Vaago is otherwise occupied," said the olive-skinned warrior in a soft, but powerful voice. "He sent me in his stead. I am his lieutenant and second in command of the Inflixi Impetus. My name is Sebastian."

This explanation or excuse did not sit well with Joshua. The scowl on his face deepened as his anger grew. He spoke in an even and calm voice. "I asked for Vaago, and that is who I expected," he said taking one step closer to the angel. "The next time he feels so inclined to ignore my request, please remind him that the Chairman has seen fit to put *me* in command. If he has a problem with that, I suggest he talk it out with Him." He continued to look up into the angel's eyes; not wavering in the slightest. Joshua's anger did not allow him to break his stare. This had become a supernatural game of chicken.

Finally, Sebastian spoke. "I will inform him of your displeasure."

Joshua sized him up for another moment. "You *do* that," he paused for a second. "Are you prepared to take over the assignment that I had intended for him?"

"I am."

It was as if a light switch had been flipped. Joshua's anger subsided as he turned and walked back to Alice, Langston, and the hard-light imagery. "Good. Follow me."

The angel looked after the young human as he walked away. He was intrigued by his commanding presence, the lack of intimidation, and the leadership of this man. These were some of the same qualities of Vaago. He also noticed a touch of arrogance; a smattering of what exuded through his commander as well. The warrior could only imagine the conflict Vaago and this human will have as their relationship moved forward.

Sebastian followed Joshua.

17

Do Not Test Me

Samuel Krukowski had managed, what he felt in his mind, the impossible, at least the first part. A plan that he had thrown together in the last week, actually worked. Whatever the odds may have been; he was too afraid to calculate prior as that would have increased his self-doubt, he managed to escape with the pathogen known as the Marburg virus.

As he sat in his car, he panted as if he had run a marathon; the now recognizable symptoms of yet another panic attack was at present, washing over him. This was an all too familiar feeling he had been experiencing in waves over the last hour. He gripped the steering wheel until the whites of his knuckles were accentuated by the red creases of his stretched skin. Samuel tried in vain to slow his breathing. In through the nose, out through the mouth.

The decade-old Pathfinder was still in the parking lot; engine not started. He stared at nothing while deep in thought; each fighting against the other. Samuel needed to get away from the CDC before they realized what had happened. He needed to rest, take some time to reflect on what he did.

What he was about to do.

How did he get out of there? He thought he was pinched for sure as he passed through security to exit the facility. They didn't question him on anything that was in his bag. Why? That never happened to him. How could they have not seen it? It was right there; wrapped in his ugly gold and maroon winter scarf. They didn't even touch it. How was any of that possible? He reflected on the sequence of events after retrieving the virus.

* * *

Samuel had just enough time after leaving the virology department to make his way back to his locker and gather his things. He would send an email to his supervisor later feigning sickness and take a half-day of vacation. Blocking the locker with his body, he removed the small metal container hidden in his lab coat and shoved it into his messenger bag. He removed his coat and grabbed his jacket, shut the door, then made his way towards the exit.

Another wave of panic hit him as he rounded the corner toward the employee's entrance and saw the security screening staff and their machines. He wanted to smack himself in the head for being so thoughtless. He had been coming through that entrance for the last four years; he knew they were there and knew the routine. His mind and soul had been so cluttered with grief over his family's well-being and the flimsy excuse of a plan for his theft, that it did not occur to him that it could be just as difficult getting out of the building as it was trying to get into the vault.

No one was coming or going through the entrance as it was mid-morning. The security personnel, and the hallway that held them, served no purpose other than screening employees entering or leaving. The only other door visible was next to the scanning machine. Although Samuel didn't know for sure, he assumed it led to a room used by security personnel for whatever reason. Aiming for that room was not an alternative to distract from his true purpose of getting away.

There were three very large security personnel at the gate; larger than him at least. All three had turned expectantly as he rounded the corner.

Unknown to Samuel, the security cameras stationed along and around the hallway entrances provided gate personnel with complete visibility. These were the same types of cameras installed throughout the building, including the virology lab, specifically the vault. Unfortunately for Samuel, he was not aware of those either.

Having no other choice, he moved forward. Anything else would rouse more suspicions on top of his already jittery behavior. He closed his eyes briefly in hopes that he could slow down his racing heart.

As he approached the security station, he exchanged the usual pleasantries as any other employee would, and fell into the routine of dropping his bag on the belt and passing through the human portion of the detector. He watched the belt move his precious cargo through. The gentleman behind the monitor stopped the machine and peered at the screen intently.

Samuel began to noticeably sweat.

He knew in his heart that he had been caught. All of them would pull out their weapons and aim at him within a matter of seconds. The guard looked at the monitor with widening eyes, and then suddenly, as if a sedative had kicked in, dialed back down to normal. He started the belt, and Samuel's bag exited the machine. The flap of the bag was somewhat open due to the clumsy way that Samuel had set it on the conveyor. Anyone who looked into it would have an unobstructed view to most of the contents. Another security guard picked it up and peered inside; probably as a matter of habit. He turned, looked Samuel straight in the eye, then handed it to him. Samuel thanked the guard and took the bag as calmly as possible. He wished he had a mirror to see if his surprise had registered across his face.

He calmly walked down the steps and out the building, not believing the luck he had today. What Samuel did not know was that luck had nothing to do with retrieving the liquid sickness from the chamber, nor getting him through the human guards.

It was all Blurr.

The little demon was lost in his thoughts with the strange encounter of the angel when he caught up to Samuel. Blurr saw the human guards examining him and his satchel which; he assumed, carried the sickness. His black eyes drifted to their weapons. It could be a problem if they detained him, or worst yet, harmed or killed him before his time. His instructions were very clear. *Get the human to the rendezvous with the virus.*

He drifted behind the guard who was watching the bag through the machine's computer window, and placed his pitiful excuse for a hand upon his shoulder. His influence told the guard to ignore what he saw, and pass the bag through. Blurr then traveled over to the guard who picked up the bag, and planted the same suggestive thought. Once the human mule retrieved his prize, he made his way out of the edifice.

* * *

Blurr had followed his human just as Samuel had gotten into his vehicle. Peering around suspiciously with a feeling of being observed, Blurr's fear worsened as they were spotted by a group of demons flying over.

There were five in all, and howled with delight as they swooped down upon the defenseless little demon. They were larger in size than Blurr; most likely mid-level soldiers on their way somewhere to do who knew what.

A demon landed between Samuel and Blurr; a low-level lackey like himself, he was outfitted in a rude excuse for battle garb, but didn't have the usual decorations of rank. "Why are you by yourself, creature?" He appeared to be the one in command.

"That is none of your concern," said Blurr attempting to sidestep around him.

The burly commander became enraged and pushed Blurr to the ground. "I am making it my concern!"

The other demons danced and laughed as their commander circled the smaller one. Blurr looked a bit incensed at this act of aggression. He owed no one any explanation of his activities; much less these mindless ogres which were clearly under the influence of the curse. He looked at the large sword dangling from his aggressor's waist and thought better of antagonizing him. He needed to find a way to end this quickly and complete his mission.

"If you must know," he said, acquiescing to the larger demon's curiosity, "I am on a mission of vital importance."

The other demons laughed and danced even more. "Mission?" They mocked one after another.

The larger demon who hovered over Blurr, straightened his back with a slight smirk on his face. "You, on a mission? I highly doubt that."

"It is true!" Blurr said in his defense. "I must see that human to his destination," he said pointing at Samuel in the car. Blurr's regret was apparent as soon as he finished his statement; the oppressing demon's eyes grew wide with curiosity. The other dancing morons made their way to Samuel's vehicle. One jumped on top of the roof directly over the human. He glanced at his commander, who smiled and nodded with an approving look. The demon then thrust his hand through the roof and directly into Samuel's head.

"No!" Blurr said in an attempt to reach Samuel. He was thrown back and immediately pinned by the larger demon's foot. "You don't understand; I have explicit orders from Commander Wyck," he said as he continued to struggle under the weight.

The larger demon looked down with a smile. The name of Wyck apparently had no impact.

Blurr looked towards Samuel with his widened black orbs. "What you are doing; that is a direct violation of the rules! That human has not prayed to us for dominion!"

"He is correct," came a voice from behind them. Standing four or five car lengths away, was Airowyn.

Blurr's head snapped towards the direction of the voice. The shock of discovering the angel's presence was only overshadowed by his embarrassment of being restrained in an unflattering position. His weakness, ever apparent, made Blurr feel even more remorse for all his bad decisions.

The other demons ceased their screeching and dancing upon noticing the angel. They all frantically searched the grounds and skies for an expected attack. The larger one discontinued his confinement of Blurr and faced the angel; his confidence waning a bit. The little demon scrambled to his feet to avoid further disgrace in front of the angel, but cowered a little in the face of an impending conflict.

After a few seconds of sizing the angel up, the commanding demon puffed out his chest, his confidence returning at the thought that the angel was alone. "What business is this of yours?"

Airowyn just stood there, not answering; continuing to observe the events.

In a bold move, the commanding demon took one step forward. "I asked you a question!"

"I could ask the same of you," replied the angel in a calm voice.

That response further enraged the large demon. "What my force and I do regarding our business, is none of yours!"

The exchange of comments back and forth over the last minute between all parties was ironic. The demon and his team demanded to know everyone else's business, but refused to give their own. A typical trait for the cursed who could not readily think for themselves.

Blurr watched the angel with admiration, for he was outmatched and appeared to have no weapon, but remained confident in his resolute.

The larger demon pulled his sword and pointed it at Airowyn. Blurr thought it a cowardly act as he knew the commander had noticed no weapon on the angel as well. He was also sure this was for a show with his group; a prideful attempt at demonstrating his Alpha status. Another benefit of the curse.

"You have a choice, servant," the demon said to Airowyn. "State your business and the right to know, and I may let you limp away from here only slightly harmed," his fellow demons began to snicker and sneer, "or foolishly continue your arrogant stand and win the right to be dispatched." His demons laughed maniacally at the thought of seeing an angel vaporized.

Airowyn and the demon commander stared at each other for a few seconds. Blurr and the other demons waited in anticipation.

"It would be unwise for you to interfere with Percival and the human's purpose," said the angel, "for the events that are about to unfold must happen as presaged."

The black orbs of the commanding demon widened with rage. "You dare to threaten us!" At that, his group readied their weapons. The demon manipulating Samuel ripped his ethereal hand from his head and grabbed his axe.

The commander looked towards Blurr. "You are working with the enemy?!"

"No!" The little demon said shielding himself with his hands as he backed away. "We only met a few—"

"This will be your only warning," said Airowyn interrupting. He attempted to take the focus away from the little demon. "Be on your way."

The demons snarled and crouched; screams and horrid battle cries emerged from their mouths. It looked as if their jaws were elongated and disjointed to amplify the sound. Again, a grotesque visual courtesy of the curse. The demon in command brought his sword arm up in a striking position as he moved towards Airowyn.

The angel looked up right before a magnificent light streaked downward. A whip of bluish light and silver medal wrapped itself around the wrist of the demon's sword hand. With a forceful pull, the demon's arm was ripped away at the shoulder. The shock of what had just happened registered across the demon commander's face as he looked to where his arm used to be. Before he had a chance to look at his attacker, the whip twirled in a magnificent circle. It danced in a spectacular swirl of movement before the supersonic force of the tip cracked against the demon's back with a thunderclap as if struck by lightning. The demon commander disintegrated into a volley of volcanic ash.

The remaining demon invaders screamed at the sight and looked up to the source. Floating in midair with magnificent wings of white was one of the Inflixi Impetus known as Maven. He had long flowing hair of an auburn color, emerald green eyes, and a lean muscular build. Just as unique as his other eight brothers of the strike force, his clothing reflected his personality. He wore a banded military jacket, much like conventional marching bands, but vastly enhanced. The jacket itself was a long coat buttoned from the neck down, opened from the waist to his feet; it flowed with an ethereal breeze. It was dark cobalt with shimmering pockets of gray when reflected with light. The bands, buttons, and ornamental braiding on the sleeves and cuffs had the same rolling waves of blue light like his other brothers of the Inflixi Impetus. His pants and boots were that of a Gothic pirate.

A unique style, indeed, but was magnificent and glorious up close as Blurr witnessed his descent. He cowered a bit more in the presence of this new angel, especially one so famous among the Host. As with all his demonic brethren, Blurr knew of the famed elite that was the Inflixi Impetus. He also knew that no demon lived long enough to tell tales of successful encounters.

The four demon intruders knew they were no match for the powerful warrior, so they began to scramble in multiple directions to get away; tripping over each other and dropping weapons as they moved. Maven's quickness was too much for them to anticipate, and he dispatched them one by one in the same brutal fashion as their commander.

The last demon existing thought he had escaped the massacre as the sacrificial slaughter of his demonic horde played out behind him. He flew towards a nearby tree line when the quickness of Maven's whip wrapped itself around his ankle. Before his next blink, the unlucky demon was thrashed back to the ground so fiercely that it seemed to shake upon impact. Blurr watched in horror as his fellow demon melted into the pavement like a bug splattering on a windshield. What remained, disintegrated into the familiar ash.

Maven's whip automatically coiled into his hand as he touched down next to Airowyn; his wings folded back into themselves and disappeared.

The scrivener greeted him warmly. "My brother," he said as they embraced each other's forearms, "many thanks for your intervention."

Maven grinned. "I would have done it, even if I wasn't on call for chaperone enforcement. It is good to see you, friend Airowyn."

The powerful warrior noticed movement from the corner of his eye. He turned his head and saw a wispy little demon trembling behind a human conveyance. He unfurled the end of his whip; letting it fall to the ground. It began to pulsate in anticipation.

Blurr backed up wide eyed; his mouth opened in a frozen precursor to a scream. His hands were in front of him in a protective and pleading posture.

At that moment, Airowyn placed his own hand upon Maven's shoulder. "Hold, brother. This little one poses no threat."

The mighty angel cocked an eyebrow. "They *all* pose a threat. He is a fallen disgrace and disappointment deserving of no mercy or reprieve."

The meek and timid demon once known as Percival, previous keeper of the Eternal Flame of the Majaliant Obelisk, had never felt, and most assuredly never looked, more pitiful and weak in his entire existence than he did at that precise moment. He continued to cower and move backwards hitting the side of another vehicle, then tripping over the sidewalk curb. He was so frightened by the pain of eternal dispatching that he could not control his ability to shift in and out of a corporeal state. Deep down, under the fear, he was also humiliated that he was showing cowardice in front of the scribe, and now of all angels, a powerful member of the Inflixi Impetus.

Airowyn eyed Blurr carefully. "Not this one."

Blurr could hardly believe what he had heard. He blinked twice and looked between the two angels in astonishment. What did this mean? Would he survive this? He was afraid to even speak for fear of making his situation more perilous. He picked himself up off the ground but maintained a submissive stance, hoping to convey no signs of the classic demonic behavior so typical of the Fallen. It was a dauntless maneuver with no intention other than to show his willingness to accept their judgment and mercy. Blurr knew that he could be dispatched at any moment, and had nothing left to lose.

Maven eyed the little demon for a moment longer. Unwilling to trust any demon no matter what the situation, he *did* trust the judgment of his good friend. His whip recoiled back into his hand.

"You should count yourself lucky to have an advocate such as this," he said motioning to Airowyn. Maven's look then became stern. "For he is the only reason that you stand."

"Y-yes," said Blurr in agreement. He tried to nod as steadily as he could, but the movements came out jerkily and erratic.

Maven turned his attention to his friend. "I understand your mission and its purpose; what does this one's further existence add?"

With a bit of sadness in his tale, Airowyn explained. He informed his powerful friend that the little demon needed to fulfill his objective to deliver the human and the package he was holding to its destination. Although he, Airowyn, did not agree with the outcome of the demon's mission, its success was a key element of fulfilling the prophecy of Harvest.

Maven now understood the sadness with which his friend told his story.

Most angels, warrior and guardian alike, only held information needed to complete their assignments. Full knowledge was only divulged depending on the situation and their need to know. The Most High always had a purpose to his plan.

Only those closely associated knew of the coming event known as Harvest. It would be a time of great sorrow for both human and angel kind. The division among the humans would cause considerable unrest across the Humàledin Generis realm. The savagery and malcontent for those remaining, would test the human frailty and endurance to the very end of its limits. Mankind had not experienced anything of this nature ever before. Not since the time of Moses or Noah had humanity been judged as harshly; nor would they be until the very end.

Maven gave a slight shudder thinking of all ramifications. The shiver was unseen by his angelic friend, but if Airowyn had noticed, he would have understood. The coming Harvest was but one event of this everlasting war in which they all participated.

It would be most unpleasant, and the Undeclared and Familiars would never see it coming.

The Eclipse would be worse.

* * *

Samuel's blinks were long; it took all his strength to keep from falling asleep. He continued to grip the steering wheel as his head began to bob and sway in slow motion. Samuel's thoughts were jumbled; incoherent. He knew he had run out of time, both to get away before they found out what he had done, and to protect his family, but he couldn't seem to get his body to respond to his mental commands. His will just didn't seem to work. Samuel was confused and didn't understand. Why was he still just sitting there? The anxiety he felt before was now beginning to give way to madness and spiral out of his control. Medical professionals with less faith in the supernatural would most likely determine the cause of fatigue as stress related, or possibly some sort of seasonal bug floating around. It was anything but.

In the small amount of time that he sat there, the conflict between the demons and the mighty angel known as Maven had played out in mere seconds. Unaware to everything that had transpired around him, Samuel's head finally became clearer. He turned the engine over as he checked his mirrors to ensure that no one had followed him. As calmly as he could, he maneuvered his car out of the space and began to exit the parking lot for the Centers for Disease Control for the last time.

Blurr trailed after him. He looked back cautiously at the two mighty angels; they embraced forearms once again. The powerful one with the light whip unfurled his beautiful wings and shot straight upward, disappearing in a blink. The other angel who saved Blurr's life, watched as he and his human disappeared through the facilities' gates.

* * *

Joshua approached the conference table with Sebastian in tow. Alice and Langston looked on with excitement as the angelic warrior neared. Through the hard-light imagery, Joshua saw the giddiness build with his two friends. He sometimes forgets their limited exposure to the burden of a reality that he has known for years.

As if introducing a college friend, Joshua said, "Alice, Langston, this is Sebastian." He pointed his thumb over his shoulder towards the powerful angel.

The giant warrior stopped at the table's edge. "Greetings," he said with a courteous nod to each.

Each returned their salutations with different levels of weirdness and shyness. It was not exactly the most professional of introductions that either had made. Alice even attempted a wave as she said hello.

Joshua half smiled making a mental note to tease them both later. It would be a refreshing change from him always being the target.

"Kelan, where are we?" Joshua said getting back to the task at hand.

"Marseille has just briefed the Associates. Awaiting your instructions," he said responding from down below.

"All right," said Joshua with a cross between apprehension and excitement. "Let's do this."

* * *

Officers Gregory Peterson, Lincoln McDowell, Martin Callahan, Jimmy Brixton, and Sasha Flannery, approached who they believed were the JPS agents in the lobby. It was hard to miss them as they were standing in a cluster and wearing very nice suits; a different kind of wardrobe than they were used to seeing on their in-house detectives. These were polished, and made the agents look more official and federal. The men also appeared to carry a certain air about them. One that would dissuade a sane person from messing with them.

The Associates received some odd looks as they passed. Although they didn't verbally communicate, they knew they needed to act fast before those affiliated with the enemy became wise to their true allegiance.

McDowell reached the agents first. Quickly making eye contact with each, he simply said, "Starfish."

"Starfish," replied Marseille.

Before either group made any moves, Marseille quickly relayed the mission and instructions. "Our objective is a woman on the fourth floor. We *will* be taking her by force. Turn your radio transceivers to channel 26. It will be isolated with further instructions relayed from our base. We are going to be moving fast. Follow the lead of our agents," he said nodding to the other three suits, "and do exactly what they do. Listen to the instructions that come from your radios. Stay sharp, move fast, don't hesitate."

Peterson and the others nodded as they handed the extra weapons and ammo to the agents. They tuned their transceivers as instructed. Each officer was outfitted with the latest model; a bone conduction earpiece with a built-in microphone tethered to a portable unit attached to each of their duty belts.

The desk sergeant's eyes grew wide, as he looked to the other officers who were clearly not in the know. Those that were, figured out a half a second too late what was going on. An officer, who had walked by three times previously, dropped his paperwork and pulled his service revolver. Others began following suit.

Marseille and his newly expanded team quickly cocked their weapons and formed a circle facing outward; each pointing their weapons at a target.

Before anyone could speak, the PA system came alive.

"Ladies and gentlemen of Precinct One Nine, my name is Joshua Arden."

His voice didn't come across the building-wide public announcement system any louder than what would be considered normal for its infrequent use. But to those who knew of the celebrity behind the voice, the name alone was enough to make every officer, detective, administration, even janitorial and maintenance staff, pause within earshot regardless of the volume.

Back at Jonah International, Joshua was thoughtful about what he was going to say. He needed this to go smoothly, but knew that it wouldn't. The enemy was obviously prepared for more than just talking.

He knew this was the only way.

The questions that kept bumping into the back of his mind like bugs against a window, was how many lives were going to be lost in the next 10 minutes? What was going to be the absolute cost in the end for the salvation of mankind?

Associates had a guaranteed future should they pass from this world, but Familiars…they already made their choice; picked their side. Joshua was about to inform them that they might die during this exchange. That there was no turning back. He needed to make one last plea to give them the option to walk away. He also needed to be honest with those who were about to be affected by this pending conflict.

"There is a young lady being held within your building. She was brought there for interrogation as a favor to me by Chief Willis. The information she possesses has placed her in great danger, so I am going to transfer her to a more secured location. There are enemies among you known as Familiars, who are going to try to stop me. Friends, partners, people you know and care about, may be one of them. They could be standing or sitting next to you right now. They will not hesitate to hurt or kill anyone who stands in their way." Joshua paused for a moment. "They have already killed Chief Willis. I wish no further harm to anyone else in your building, so I am asking you to stand down and let my team pass. If you pose no threat, you will not be harmed."

Joshua's look became stern. Alice and Langston were seeing a glimpse of the man yet to come. Sebastian watched this young man as his presage unfolded.

"I'm speaking directly to the Familiars now. Your cause is lost. You *will* fail. If you stand against my team, you *will* die. Do not test me."

Joshua reached up on the hard-light imagery dashboard and muted the feed to the precinct. He looked at Sebastian. "Go to the precinct and find Kelly Granger. Protect her at all cost until the TAC team has her safely in custody outside of the building." Sebastian nodded.

"Go," said Joshua softly.

"By your command." Sebastian's magnificent wings unfolded and spread wide. Alice and Langston took a step back; the wings spanning every bit of twelve feet. It seemed to them that it took up more of Joshua's office than it actually did.

With the grace and elegance of a swan, Sebastian soared directly through the wall made of window into the bright sky. Within a blink, he disappeared.

* * *

Marseille, his team, and the Associates remained frozen in their stance; targets still acquired, waiting for the order to move. With the eyes of their opposition shifting with uncertainty, Marseille sized up the situation as the tactical leader. There were nine of them, and what looked like twelve to fifteen enemy personnel within the kill box. That included the rude fat one behind the desk. He had no visual of how many more may be in either hallway, so statistically he rounded the threat assessment to at least twenty immediate targets.

Sentinel went active in everyone's earpiece. "This is Command. Prepare to move on my mark."

The sentient intelligence assessed the situation from every vantage point and possibility of threats. This included the vitals of everyone in the building; gauging and measuring elevated anxiety levels, heart rates, body temperature, and even secretion levels of perspiration. Based on the known factors of psychological and physical calculations, Sentinel could predict, with remarkable accuracy, the intention of the enemy.

The overweight desk sergeant became agitated. Agent Ingram was closest, and had acquired him as an initial target. Speaking to him alone, Sentinel said, "Agent Ingram, the desk sergeant will fire upon you within 2.3 seconds."

Sure enough, the sergeant cocked the hammer on his service revolver. Ingram fired his Remington 870. The blast caught the desk sergeant directly in the chest and threw him back against the wall.

Ingram had no time to think about what he had just done; he just did it without hesitation. From a documentation of events perspective, his after-action report would list this as a good and justifiable shoot. He always wondered why they called it a "good" shoot. There was nothing ever good or positive about taking someone's life. This was just something else that he, and his team members, would have to deal with when everything was said and done.

"Officer Peterson, the target at your two o'clock will fire upon you in 1.6 seconds," said Sentinel.

Peterson shifted his weapon and immediately fired. He aimed for center mass, then shifted slightly to catch his assailant's trigger arm. He knew the officer would be wearing his protective vest, and did not have the stomach for a head shot. The opposing officer fell back with a scream of pain, dropping his weapon in the process.

The two indirectly related shootings happened within mere seconds; Sentinel directed both men simultaneously.

"Proceed to the right corridor, now," said Sentinel in everyone's ear pieces.

"Move," said Marseille in a smooth manner; almost too calm for the situation. Panicking would do no one any good, especially not him as the tactical lead.

Marseille's extended team began to move and weave their way out of the lobby and into the right hallway.

Officer Lincoln McDowell looked down behind the lobby desk as he passed and saw the limp desk sergeant, wide-eyed and unmoving. Sadness loomed in the back of his mind at his brother in arm's death, as he briefly wondered how many more, including himself, would be a casualty of this fight.

Sentinel was buzzing commands and instructions through each person's earpiece specific to them. It was as if each person had their own watcher. Once bullets started flying, the team picked up their pace.

18

If it is a fight you WANT; I will be happy to oblige

Joshua and his team watched as the battle commenced. The imagery flickered before each group in real time; the little colored cartoon figures began running about like animated characters in a video game. Everyone at headquarters knew this was anything but. It seemed very surreal as they saw a Familiar fall, then another, and another. Each red target that dropped, turned to a dismal shade of gray. *What better way to show the end of someone's life,* thought Joshua morosely. He knew full well that they were Familiars, and that they could not be saved.

He watched on in sadness; nausea building in his stomach. A life is a life. Regardless of their decision, all of it was precious to him.

Joshua backed away from the table slowly, his leg catching on one of the conference room chairs. He stumbled a bit; stopping his fall by grabbing onto another chair.

Langston's attention was drawn away from the action when he realized what had happened. He rushed over to Joshua. "Are you all right?"

"I'm fine; I'm fine," he said nodding his head in embarrassment. He briefly looked back to the imagery and saw two more red figures turn gray. Joshua turned his head, this time stifling a gag; his knees buckled.

"That's funny. You don't look like you're fine," said Langston as he hoisted Joshua back to his feet.

Alice came over to help. "Come on, let's get him in the chair."

"I told you, I'm fine," said Joshua with a bit more confidence, but clearly not feeling it.

Alice was a little annoyed at the lie. She dropped him harder in the chair than necessary.

"Ow!" Joshua said looking stunned.

"Don't be a baby, that didn't hurt." Alice crossed her arms. "When was the last time you had something to eat?"

"Lunchtime. I had it with *you*, remember?" Joshua said.

"You haven't had your afternoon juice," she said, walking over to his pantry. Upon pulling the cooler door open, she grabbed one of Joshua's favorites from the fully stocked shelves. She hurried back to his side, shaking it in the process. Alice popped the top and handed it to him. "Your blood sugar is clearly out of balance."

He was too nauseated to argue. He took the juice willingly and drank; his eyes cutting to hers in an annoyed manner as it washed down his throat. Of everyone who worked with him over the years, Alice truly knew him the best; sometimes better than he did himself. Sometimes, it ticked him off.

"You're welcome," she said sarcastically.

Already feeling a bit better, he said, "Thank you."

However, the blood sugar was only a small part of the issue. He was disgusted with himself at the thought of sitting in a cushy chair, drinking a juice, while his people were fighting for their lives. He had no right to lounge in the safety and comfort of his well-protected office like an armchair general.

Joshua felt as if he wasn't allowed to do anything; that everyone considered his life much too important to be involved in dangerous tasks. He never thought himself better than anyone, but that didn't prevent the hundreds of people, to include his executive staff, from placing several layers of various security measures around him at all times. Further isolation of himself from the real world and real people problems detached him from what he believed was his true self.

All of this began with him as a regular person, who had grown up, lived, and walked in the very shoes of the people he was trying to help. How did things become so far out of whack that he now just orchestrated missions from his office, wearing an expensive suit, and not even breaking a sweat?

He had to get out there, to take some more risks. Joshua needed to show his people, the world, that he would not ask someone to do something that he was not willing to do himself. As with many other things throughout his life, that would be easier said than done. The army of people, technology, angels, and the very power that be, might disagree with this proposed new course of action. Only time would tell if his will would win out.

First thing was first; he needed to get his people out safely. Handing the juice to Alice, Joshua straightened up in his seat and adjusted his jacket. He gave both her and Langston a look that satisfied their worry and concerns.

The dance of the battling lights continued on his conference table. The team was now working their way from the second to the third floor. Joshua stood with new resolve and walked back to the scene.

His fresh attitude bolstered a confidence that was evident in his stride. It was much needed for the current situation, and would be paramount in the events to come. His wish for being more involved, would not only be accepted by the Chairman, but encouraged by Jonah International's Board of Directors as the Chairman's proxy.

That one decision to embrace the dangers of the unknown would set Joshua on a new course. The plan he had sought for so long was coming. His newfound self-reliance would be the catalyst, the final sign in which the supernatural realms had been preparing since his birth. There was an anticipation for the next level of leadership that it would take to defeat the enemy. Or at the very least, show them that some humans were not the easily manipulated weak willed creatures the demons thought they were.

Joshua didn't yet know it, but he would bring about a new age of warfare between good and evil. Angels and humans would do the unthinkable; and the demons would never see it coming.

There would be one, though, who would stand against him; and the plan. An evil unlike any other.

* * *

Samuel's Pathfinder crossed over I-20 heading south. He had just finished talking with the blackmailer on the burner phone that she gave him at the beginning of this nightmare. He was very surprised that she picked up on the first ring; even more bewildered that everything for the drop off had already been arranged. He told her that it would be this week, but Samuel didn't say anything about taking the virus today. A brief thought that should hold more meaning than it did, but Samuel was too preoccupied with other things.

She told him that it was a straight shot down route 42, and that she was waiting for him less than 10 miles away at a secluded location.

He found that part quizzical; another red flag that should have meant something.

Where in the urban sprawl of the city would there be a place private enough to make the transfer? The CDC was practically in downtown Atlanta. The meeting place might be just outside the city limits, but not by much. He couldn't think of where this mysterious location was, and didn't recognize the address she had given him.

Atlanta traffic was light, which he found unusual, until he remembered the time of day. The traffic signal turned green and he crossed Custer Avenue passing a pharmacy on the corner.

Samuel's thoughts drifted to his wife and son as he drove.

After this mess was over, he was going to try to spend more time with them. Thomas was getting older; too fast for his father's taste. He remembered holding his son right after he was born. His baby boy was so small and frail. Samuel made a vow right then and there to always love and protect his beautiful little bundle.

Shame curled his mouth down knowing how he had failed in the protection part. The thought of that lady threatening his son made him shiver with disgust. He couldn't decide what was more sickening; the blackmailer's threat, or this entire thing being his fault for putting his family in danger from the beginning.

He passed a supermarket and an auto parts store.

Deirdre, his wife, had beautiful blue eyes. He longed to look into them, and shook with the anticipation of knowing he would soon. Pangs of guilt hit him, almost as bad as the anxiety earlier, thinking that those eyes could also see him for who he truly was; a fraud, a cheat, and now; a thief. He couldn't tell her the truth about what he had done to get into this mess. He *sure* couldn't say anything about what he was doing now. There was no way she would understand that this was to protect her and Thomas.

He put on his blinker to turn left on Key Road. The landscape of buildings and businesses morphed into residential homes; which became fewer the further he drove. He tried to calm himself as he approached his destination. Samuel just wanted to get this done. Over with. Get back to his life.

He slowed the Pathfinder as the GPS informed him that he had arrived. Samuel stopped in the middle of the road and looked around. Nothing but field and deserted highway was in sight. There was a decayed turn off through the overgrown brush and foliage to the right. An old couch was turned up on its side, and what looked like concrete barriers that had long been moved so people could disobey the clearly marked "no trespassing" sign at the entrance. Trash and debris was strewn about as if on purpose; warding off any unwanted visitors. It was dirty and uninviting.

Samuel looked up and down the highway road. There were no signs of anything. No people. No cars. Nothing. A country setting right in the middle of the city. Samuel found it funny that something so drastic and immediate was this close to civilization.

Turning back to the decrepit passage, he decided this had to be it. He threw the Pathfinder into drive, then carefully navigated around the concrete blocks onto the narrow, forgotten path. High trees of about 15 feet or so shaded the excuse for a road as he moved. It curved in a wide arc to the right that eventually emptied into an equally forgotten clearing.

Ahead, he spotted a ruin of sorts. Aged concrete walls in the shape of what used to be a large building. Weeds and bushes made this place their home now. What sections of the walls that were visible, was covered in graffiti. He slowly pulled to the front of the dilapidated, burned-out structure. As he stopped, the squeal of his brakes cut the horror movie silence that hung in the air. The creepy scene cast a grayish gloom that seemed to replace the clear sunny morning. Samuel felt as if he had stepped into an Alfred Hitchcock film. It didn't help that the air was also crisp that fall day. It only accentuated the setting like frosting did for a cake. He grabbed his satchel as he exited the truck, and slowly moved towards the broken building.

* * *

The little demon known as Blurr followed Samuel as he made his way to the derelict structure. He had barely to continue after his close encounter with both the powerful angels, and his demented and unfortunate demonic brothers, to be more cautious than ever before. He had flown low to his human's vehicle, and looked over his shoulder continuously, perpetually wary that he was being watched or followed.

Unlike Samuel's observation of his quiet surroundings, Blurr's account of activity was drastically different.

It was complete madness.

Demons of various ranks and factions, screeched and howled all around him. There must have been hundreds of them; and all were there to bear witness to an important event that would shape the human's world.

Forever.

Blurr winced as he was taunted by some shrieking demons as he passed. They seemed obstinate and more unruly than usual; like a bunch of drunken bikers outside of a bar looking for a fight.

He peered into the sky and saw swirling rows of them in packs; some patterns were perfect circles, while others were scattered about. For this fall day, they appeared like birds on the landscape. They pecked at each other in a chaotic manner. Mindless minions. Uncontrollable and dangerous.

Oblivious to the reality around him, Samuel continued to walk in a straight line towards the broken building. As he followed his human around the corner, Blurr saw three powerful demons standing amid the debris of a toppled wall at the far end of the large enclosure. Their weapons sheathed, all stood stoic as they turned seeing Samuel, and Blurr.

The little demon became nervous over this new attention. Although certain the focus was specific to the human, Blurr couldn't help but sense their gaze drifting through the creature, and falling directly upon himself. He made a pitiful attempt to use Samuel as a shield to block their vision. Like a child in trouble, he peeped around Samuel every so often as they both moved closer to the trio.

A figure suddenly came into view; she appeared from behind a pile of decayed rubble to stand directly in front of the three large demons.

Samuel stopped abruptly at the sight of the woman. Blurr was so close, that he passed right through. Had he been corporeal, he would have knocked Samuel down.

The sudden exposure without the cover of the human, made Blurr even more nervous. As a matter of reflex, he stared to the three demons. Now that he was paying more attention, he could see they were high-ranking commanders. His black eyes widened as they fell upon the demon at the end. It was Commander Wyck himself.

He didn't believe it possible, but the nervousness at present reached an epic high. Open and exposed, he now sensed all eyes upon him. The little demon felt even smaller believing he was currently the center of everyone's attention. With his eyes closed, Blurr desperately wished for a distraction to remove the stares.

The screeching and howling lessened, then became quiet altogether. Opening his eyes slowly, he noticed the three commanders looking beyond him. When Blurr followed their gaze, his jaw fell gaping.

There, in the open field just outside the ruins, stood Airowyn. He was unmoving and emotionless, exactly like he was at his human, Samuel's, place of work. The angel appeared unfazed by the numerous demons who began to encircle him.

One by one, each demon of various ranks and size looked towards one or all three commanders; their hands began to fall upon their weapons. None of the commanders made a move to either indicate or prevent an unprovoked attack.

Blurr wanted badly to shout to the angel to flee, but knew better to tip his hand that he had conversed with this one before. Instead, he reacted on another instinct as he saw a demon draw his blade.

"Stop!" He shouted.

All demons turned to Blurr. The three commanders provided stares suggesting that this outburst had better have good cause.

The little one, although shivering inside, straightened up as much as his crooked, broken form would allow, and addressed the three powerful demons, specifically Commander Wyck. "I encountered this one," gesturing towards Airowyn, "at the place that houses the liquid sickness, this human," said Blur shifting his arm to Samuel, "has successfully retrieved." He threw that in for good measure to let his commander know that he had completed his own mission. "The angel spy is a scribe sent by the enemy. Although not armed, he is well-protected," he finished with outward confidence. He tried not to shake as violently as he felt.

Wyck looked down to the little demon with a raised eyebrow. "And how would you know this?" His voice was deep and booming; it matched his immense size perfectly.

Normally, Blurr would take time to craft a specific response, giving the appropriate amount of information for fulfilling his mission; but mostly to ensure self-preservation. He was flying off the cuff this time though. In a split second of the human time measurement, the little demon formerly known as Percival decided that his best approach, was to simply tell the truth.

He bowed his head to his commander in reverence. "My lord, I witnessed the eternal dispatching of a squad of our brothers by one of the Inflixi Impetus."

Mouths gaped; eyes widened. Sounds of gasps echoed throughout the demon ranks. Some demons hunkered as they looked skyward for any signs of an impending attack.

"Impossible," snarled one of the other commanders. "How could a lowly creature like yourself survive such an encounter?"

"Because I allowed it," came the response from Airowyn.

The demons surrounding the angel jumped back at the sound of his voice, as if startled by the appearance of a poisonous snake.

As the circle around the lone angel widened, the commanders continued their stare. It was hard to read their expressions as they maintained their stoic stance to match the angel. The demons watching knew not to make any sudden moves, for their very lives depended on absolute stillness; both from an obedient posture, and now, with the threat of the angelic strike force raining down upon them.

It was uncertain of the thoughts that ran through the evil minds of the commanders, but the fact that pause was given showed consideration for this angel's position.

Of the three commanders, it seemed that Wyck was the one in charge. "Why?" He said addressing the angel.

Airowyn's expression did not change. "This little demon was sent on a mission of escort. He was unarmed and posed no threat to me or my mission, unlike the aforementioned squad."

"He lies. It has always been the way of their kind to punish without provocation," said the second commander; his expression dripping with animosity towards the angel.

The regal angel remained unmoving and unfazed by the comment.

Commander Wyck thought briefly for a moment, then raised his hand in restraint of his subordinate's agitation. "What are you doing here?"

"Fulfilling my assignment," said Airowyn.

"Which is?" Wyck responded.

"To observe."

"So you are going to allow this transaction to take place?" The third commander said warily.

"I will not interfere," said the angel.

"He lies!" The agitated second commander said, partially drawing his sword.

Commander Wyck turned his head, his eyes morphing from black to red with the growing anger of the disobedience. "You are one of my most trusted lieutenants." His eyes grew brighter. "But your continued outbursts will no longer be tolerated."

The boisterous commander met Wyck's eyes, then deflated his ego appropriately. "My apologies, my lord." He returned his eyes to the angel, and sneered.

Wyck shifted his attention back to Airowyn and pondered his last statement. It made no sense to walk into the den of a heavily armed enemy, unless there were just cause and safety assurances that he would walk out. The angel was alone and unarmed, which would indicate that backup would not be far away; if he was not foolhardy. No hostile movements were made or alluded to since his appearance. All the angel had done to this point was simply watch. It would seem that he was, indeed, a scribe sent by the Most High. Blurr was telling the truth; a rarity for any low-level demon who wished to climb the chain of command.

Looking at Blurr, Commander Wyck said, "Do you trust him?" He gestured towards Airowyn.

Almost as if scripted, the little demon replied, "I trust no angel, my lord." He looked back and met Airowyn's eyes. "But this one *did* stop my destruction by the Inflixi Impetus for reasons unknown." He paused. "If trust were matched by truth, then this angel poses no threat, unless provoked." He bowed obediently to his commander.

Wyck looked at the little demon carefully. After a moment, he said, "Very well." His eyes then moved back to the angel. "Remain where you are and observe without hindrance."

The second commander's eyes began to blaze crimson. "No, my lord! This is a trap!"

Without even looking, Wyck's hand came up and grabbed his lieutenant around the throat. "Fine, then you will be the one to dispatch him!" He threw the commander forward.

The unruly commander stumbled, then stood straight up. An evil smile began to form around the edge of his gnarled lips. His tattered wings unfurled at lightning speed as he charged towards Airowyn. All the demons scrambled to get out of the way. He drew his massive sword when he was halfway to the angel.

Airowyn remained unfazed and did not move.

At twenty feet out, the enraged demon raised the sword.

In the blink of an eye, a bolt of brilliant light streaked downward and hit the unaware commander. He disintegrated into ash without so much as a chance to grimace from the excruciating pain.

The ripple of the bolt fanned outward, knocking most of the demons over as the sonic thunderclap that usually followed, hit them like a tidal wave.

Blurr brought his hands up shielding his eyes as he hit the ground. Commander Wyck swayed, but managed to stay on his feet. He turned his head slightly and squinted from the light, but made no move to show weakness.

The two demons noticed the lone angel had not been affected by the lightning strike nor the sonic wave. It was like both passed right through him.

As all the demons slowly began to recover from the attack, their eyes automatically gaped skyward.

There, in the distance, floating high above, was yet another member of the Inflixi Impetus. The one known as Mace; the thunder god as some humans throughout their history were known to call him.

His blond hair flowed down to his black armored chest plate. The armor encased four circular disks, each pulsating with blue waves of light. In his hand, he held a massive silver hammer; blunt at both ends with intricate designs and angelic Gaelic inscriptions that glowed with the same white light it had just emitted. His imposing white wings were spread wide like that of an eagle as he glided down and landed softly next to his brother. His wings folded in slightly, but then morphed into a long, flowing dark-blue cape.

He nodded towards Airowyn, who returned his gesture. "Do we have a problem here, brother?" He said in a voice booming just as loudly as his thunder clap.

Airowyn's gaze shifted back to Wyck. Knowing this was a teachable moment, he said, "I believe that we are fine."

Not wanting to lose face, Wyck then bellowed in his own deep and carrying voice, "The object lesson for disobedience is concluded. If any still choose to question or defy me, now is your opportunity," he said with a gesture towards the two angels. Why not let them do his dirty work?

Sensing the demon commander's plan, Mace turned facing him. "It is not my position to enforce punishment due to your lack of leadership and control, but if it is a fight you seek, I will be happy to oblige." With one fluid move, he flipped his hammer in midair then attached the leather handle to his magnificent gold belt.

The snickering at the humiliation was barely audible, and only so to those closest to the culprits, but it was clearly apparent that Wyck ruled by fear rather than respect. Given the opportunity, most under his command would watch his demise with glee. Seeing him taunted by an obviously superior being, and one of the Inflixi Impetus no less, was the second-best thing.

Wyck sneered at the remark. "The fight will come soon enough, slave. Witness the ignorance of the All Father's creature."

Everyone's eyes then shifted to the human called Samuel.

* * *

Samuel stared at the woman for what seemed like an eternity. She stood there, very still; hands tucked firmly into the pockets of a full body trench coat. Her dark-brown hair was pulled back into a tight ponytail that wavered slightly with the arpeggio of the breeze. She was just as he remembered; cold with no emotion.

This location, the odd change in the weather, and her seemingly morbid fascination with the macabre, took its final toll. He was tired and wanted this over. This was plain creepy, and he had just about enough.

"I have what you want," he said with a contempt that surprised him. "Let's get this over with."

After a few more moments, she smiled. "Very good, Mr. Krukowski. Well done."

She began to walk towards him. Belted, knee-high chunky heeled boots moved rhythmically through the slit of the coat as she stepped across the uneven terrain. She finally stopped fifteen feet away, then waited.

The illusion of control made him even more agitated. Her smile was in a condescending, expecting sort of way. Her calm and relaxed façade was in deep contrast with his jerky and nervous demeanor; a carefree cat watching a shaking Chihuahua. It was like they had all the time in the world as she waited for him to make the next move.

His nerves finally snapped. In a rapid motion, he reached into his satchel and grabbed the virus container. She had no reaction to this other than a wider smile.

Her eyes glanced towards the container as she removed her left hand from her pocket and held it out. With some distance still between them, it looked like the expectation was for him to bring it to her. A scowl began to form on his face as he stepped forward. The combination of the anxiety and nervousness caused an adrenaline surge in which he was not prepared; so his advance was almost like a charge.

Her smile faded somewhat as she motioned for him to stop. "Mr. Krukowski, you need to calm down."

His reaction was borderline hysterical mixed with a bit of surprise. "Calm down?! You can't be serious! Do you have any idea what you have put me through over the last two months? You put my job in jeopardy, threatened my family! You–"

"Samuel," she said sternly. "I suggest you stop now before *I* have to stop you."

At four feet away from her, he froze. With her open hand, she pointed to his chest. Lowering his head, Samuel's eyes slowly drifted down to find a bright-red dot fixed to the center of his sternum, right above his heart. It was unwavering and unaffected by the winter wind.

Once again, he began to gulp large amounts of air. It was an inopportune time for another anxiety attack, but just like the others; he could not control it.

"You need to breathe, slowly," she said. A couple of seconds passed. "Samuel, breathe," she continued. A few more passed. "Look at me, Samuel" she said calmly. He looked up. "That's right, look at me. You need to hand me the package, very carefully." It was like a parent talking to a five-year-old child. She held out her hand, palm up, and waited.

Wide-eyed, the comprehension began to sink in. Samuel began to move the silver box containing the deadly pathogen closer to her hand. Just before she was about to take it, he stopped. "Do you know what this is?" Samuel said softly.

"Yes, Samuel, I do," she replied, her eyes never leaving his.

"What are you going to do with it?" He said fearful of the answer.

"Change the world."

With his eyes still wide, he looked down to the container. "My family."

"Samuel, if your family conforms, they will not be harmed," she said.

"Conforms? What does that mean?"

"The package," she said matter-of-fact, as she held her hand up closer.

He felt lost; empty inside. A betrayal of his family, his employer, and now humanity, he handed her the container.

Blurr had a look of sadness as he removed his hand from the human's shoulder. Commander Wyck grinned as the other demons began to screech and dance. Airowyn and Mace stood stoic and watched.

The glaze from Samuel's eyes began to clear as the supernatural influence wore off; he blinked. She was walking anyway. "What happens now?"

She stopped about twenty feet and turned facing him. "We tie up loose ends."

"What?"

Samuel's head then snapped sharply as a bullet ripped through his right temple and exploded out of the left. His body dropped to the ground soundlessly as the wind whipped harder.

She turned to walk around the ruined wall from which she came. Inara pulled out her cell phone and said something in Czech. Moments later, a helicopter landed in the clearing just beyond the ruins. A man with a sniper rifle joined her as she boarded the aircraft. The chop chop of the rotors faded away leaving nothing but the wind and Samuel's body behind.

With the humans gone, Commander Wyck turned a defiant and satisfactory look towards the two angels. They stared back, emotionless and unmoving. Wyck unfolded his large leathery wings to take the news of his victory to his superiors. Most of the demonic horde left with him, but thirty or so remained to see the consumption of the human's soul. They danced at the anticipation; like waiting for a delicious desert after dinner.

* * *

Most humans that begin the transition from their earthly life are somewhat disoriented; in some cases, blissfully unaware of where they are and what has happened. For those who have chosen the side of light, a peaceful feeling of serenity and happiness accompanies them, along with their emissaries, to their next destination. All their cares, and concerns from their previous life are left behind.

Those who have chosen darkness, or have not chosen at all, are met with the beginnings of a nightmare from which they cannot wake. Their experiences will vary depending on the circumstances of how they died, and in this case, the supernatural torment inflicted by those present.

Samuel's indecision placed him in the very heart of the demon mob. He screamed with terror at the sight of the unholy ones, and recoiled as they took turns shoving him and ripping at his clothing. As he was pushed to his knees, he saw his body, and the shattered remains of his head. He knew it was him, and screamed louder.

The sound stoked the fire of the frenzied madness of the demons, and they danced even more wildly than before. Then, some began to clap as the black vortex began to appear.

For the first time, Airowyn showed sadness. It was only matched by Blurr's, who stood on the opposite side of the wild crowd and watched the cruelty along with the two angels.

As the vortex approached its apogee, it began to draw the soul of Samuel Krukowski toward it. However, as he approached the edge, the demons pulled him back to continue their mistreatment. Over again, they laughed wildly at his cries.

Angels had never been permitted to interfere with the consumption of those who had chosen wrongly. Nevertheless, some could bend the rules as needed.

With his anger now at a level of no tolerance, Mace pulled his hammer swiftly. Both the hammer and his armor began to pulsate. Upon lifting the mighty weapon towards the sky, he brought it down quickly and struck the ground. Shock waves of oscillating lightning sped across the surface to each of the dancing demons hitting them individually at various forces. The crack of thunder accompanied each strike. Their demise was not instant as was the commanders before, but purposefully tempered to inflict agony. They screeched and screamed, and contorted their grotesque bodies as they all dissipated in assorted ways. Some slowly exploded losing first their arms and legs, then the rest; while others began to melt and fuse to the ground. Some simply burst into flames and burned into nothing as they ran. All were dispatched within an acceptable amount of administered pain. And afterwards, just as suddenly as the area was filled with their laughter then screams, it became eerily still with all visible signs of their presence gone. All that was left to be seen and heard, was Samuel.

Mace's anger subsided as he looked around; his eyes finally resting upon the little demon.

Blurr still stood at a distance, but this time, did not cower at the magnificent display of power. Instead, with a confidence he knew not, he gave both angels an approving nod; a signal that he agreed with the justice dispensed. A scream from Samuel drew their attention back to the consumption.

The vortex was at full force now; having increased its speed and ferocity to claim its rightful due. Bits of rock and dirt swirled with the blackness. It was a violent tornado of terror with the suction of a black hole. Samuel's legs were on the event horizon. As his feet began to crest, the material of his shoes withered and flaked away; followed by his socks, then bits of his skin. The flesh left began to pucker as if the moisture had been drawn out; replaced by leathery, brittle patches of raw hide. The further in he moved, the more of his soul began to rip away and decay.

In all that Airowyn had witnessed on this assignment, the worst part was the human souls lost, and that grieved him. There would be no end to their suffering. What Samuel was experiencing was just the beginning. As he did many times before, Airowyn pitied the foolish humans that took so many things for granted. The most precious of these was thinking there was always more time.

"Help me!" Samuel screamed as he clawed against the ground; his nails pulling away from his fingers as he dug into the dirt. He was now waist deep into the vortex. Samuel managed to grab onto a jagged rock embedded within the earth and slowed his descent. His screams of agony from the pain of being ripped apart from the waist down were coming in waves. Just then, a guttural growl emanated from the vortex followed by a bloodied claw. The nails on the grotesque hand ripped into the tattered remains of his coat, leaving deep gouges in what would have been his back. He let out an agonizing moan and let go of the rock. Another claw reached out and grabbed his arm. The decay advanced quickly through the rest of his soul now. His hair and skin melted into his skull leaving nothing but a tongue between rotten teeth and bulging bloodshot eyes rolling in their sockets.

"Nnnooooo!!"

The last thing he saw before being swallowed was the pair of angels lifting into the air, and a demon with his head bowed.

19

Sitting Ducks

"Sasha, watch out!" Brixton yelled as a Familiar lined her up in the sights of his revolver. She ducked just in time as the bullet smashed into the glass wall pane above her head.

"Quiet!" Yelled one of the JPS agents as he passed her to take another position. "Listen to the instructions on your earpiece! Do not deviate from the plan!"

Brixton looked a bit annoyed as he moved to take a flanking position. "Hey pal, I just saved her life!"

"Command has this covered. All you have to do is advance," said another JPS agent as he moved with the quickness around the next corner.

All team members moved quickly through the building. The elegance of omicron seven had all agents and police officers in a synchronized pattern of spins and weapons' fire. The chaotic patterns to which the Familiars were advancing and firing were a direct result of their inability to track and isolate the team's movements. By the time they drew a bead on an Associate or agent, both had moved on to a new position directed by Sentinel.

The orchestrated dance was executed perfectly as long as they listened to their instructions and acted immediately. The only one that appeared to be out of sync was Brixton. There was a slight hesitation in his responses as he questioned his orders with a visual inspection of the area. He continually looked before he leapt; a good practice when left to his own devices, but in a synchronized unit, led by Sentinel, it posed both a hindrance and risk to the lives of his teammates.

The team had just cleared the tertiary floor and began to corner near a stairwell. Brixton was third in position at the end, then Sasha, followed up by a JPS agent. The agent made his move based on Sentinel's orders, and advanced to his next position, spinning and firing his weapon as necessary.

Not all the team's shots were meant to be deadly. Some were purposefully executed on Sentinel's orders to detour the Familiars and throw them off balance; buying the team enough time to move on and out of the immediate way of harm. The smart intelligence knew that Joshua wanted to preserve as many lives on both sides as possible. Sentinel's calculations of the remaining ammo plus the number of threats until reaching the target, allowed for diversionary shots to increase the team's chances for reaching their objective and exiting the building safely.

"Officer Flannery, move six feet to your 10 o'clock and cover the South hallway," said Sentinel.

Her instincts had fought against everything this person from Jonah's command had said since the lobby; but she quickly learned to adapt as this mystery person seemed to know exactly where she was at all times, and guided her through the barrage of bullets and enemies. Whoever this was, had to be watching them through the in-house cameras. A simple explanation, but couldn't be farther from the truth. She reached her destination and spun around to cover the hallway.

Brixton yelled just as she raised her weapon. "Sasha, behind you!"

Instincts taking over for a split second, she looked back. There, in the corner of a room off the hallway, was a Familiar with a gun pointing straight at her. She turned around as quickly as she could. Just then, a person appeared down the South hallway. They flung themselves between rooms on either side, firing as they passed through the hallway. A lucky shot struck officer Sasha Flannery in the base of her skull propelling her forward. Her black hair was still pulled into a loose bun as it became damp with her blood. She fell face first to the floor with a sickening thud. Sasha lay with the side of her face on the cold white and green checkered tile as the redness spread wider. Her eyes were half open and fixed on nothing.

Brixton became wide-eyed and froze. He stared at Sasha's body in disbelief. Rage replaced instinct, which was ignoring the voice in his ear piece. He flung his weapon around the corner and shot randomly down the hall; a primal scream accompanied each round. The Familiar in the room behind Sasha's body fired a shot that caught Brixton in his right shoulder. He screamed in pain as his arm dropped slightly. He whirled around to face his assailant; bringing his good arm up and swapping the weapon over. The movement of his spin shifted him somewhat from the cover of the corner, exposing part of his body in the hallway. He used his left leg to center his balance, bringing him further into the open. The Familiar from down the South hall, fired a shot that caught Brixton in the thigh just above the protective armor. He fell on one knee screaming, dropping his good arm in a natural reflex to maintain his balance. The other Familiar in the room capitalized on this unfortunate opportunity, and squeezed off a shot. The bullet hit Brixton directly between the eyes and exploded out of the back of his head. His body fell two feet from Sasha's splattering in her ever-widening pool of blood.

Had Sasha ignored Brixton's outburst, or for that fact, had he waited and acted upon Sentinel's orders, both would still be alive and advancing. Brixton was meant to eliminate the target in the room behind Sasha; whose focus would have been down the South hallway. Had both followed direction and not hesitated, each would have taken care of their own respective targets.

Two decisions with deadly consequences.

Sentinel reconfigured the team's calculations minus the two fallen Associates in 1.4 seconds. Marseilles, who had point when the team approached the corner, was now on the six.

"Agent Marseilles, tango in room will look around the corner in five...four...three," said Sentinel.

Marseilles leveled off his weapon at five feet above the floor and waited for the countdown. When it reached one, the Familiar darted his head out for a quick assessment; Marseilles compensated vertically for the height and squeezed the trigger. The bullet went through the side of the tango's head splattering blood all over the door frame and the opposite wall. His body fell between Sasha and Brixton. Marseilles paused briefly to look at the two dead Associates, then quickly fell into rotation.

* * *

Deep in the bowels of rHub, Kelan swore out loud this time when he saw the two green animated figures depicting Associates fall in succession and dim to gray. He made no attempt to hide his anger at the loss.

Joshua fared no better forty-eight levels above, as he grabbed the back of an empty conference chair and flung it across the room. It crashed into a credenza with a force that caused drawers and doors to pop open and spill some of the contents.

He turned in a slow circle with one hand on his hip and the other on his forehead smoothing his hair back. Even with a tactically superior plan such as omicron seven, they still suffered casualties. His team had the strategic advantage with Sentinel even though they were drastically outnumbered. What happened? Why did the two police officers die?

Joshua could only see what was happening, so was hampered by no first-person account and couldn't hear anything. He didn't request the audio of the action as he knew it would be a jumbled mess with Sentinel's voice overlapping as instructions were doled out. There would obviously be audio playback after everything was said and done, so they could figure out the breakdown, but that didn't help the situation now.

There had to be a better way.

He walked back to the conference table where the action continued to unfold. The margin between Associate and Familiar was decreasing dramatically with several the enemy either dead or backing down to avoid a similar fate. There were still a large number of them between his team and Granger; and from the looks of it, were closing in on her fast. Joshua studied the little blue figure cuffed and apparently struggling. She was most likely responding in fear at the sounds of chaos and gunfire.

Scared.

Alone.

In rHub, an analyst turned to Kelan. "Sir, the TAC team has arrived."

"Get them into position and have them hold," he said. "Joshua...,"

"I heard, thank you," came his response through Sentinel.

Upstairs Joshua leaned in placing both hands on the conference table and spoke in barely a whisper. "Sebastian, where are you?"

* * *

"Here they come!" Yelled one of the Familiars relaying the Intel backwards. He had just pulled back from the stairwell entrance to the fourth floor where he heard the Jonah team coming from below. The old door on four creaked as it shut with the hardware making a weak clicking sound as it latched. The Familiar cursed as he backed up knowing it would be no barrier to slow them down.

The one nine precinct was an old building built in the late 1800s. Even though much of the structure had been converted to meet New York City's fire safety standards, there were still elements of the aged construction present; this included the heavy wooden door standing between the remaining Familiars and the advancing team from Jonah. It wasn't even a solid piece of wood; the top panel held a dated frosted window that only allowed a shadowed outline of anything on the immediate other side.

"Throw me those rolling chairs!" shouted someone. The men and women left to defend the floor began pulling chairs from offices and open bullpen desks and tossing them down the walkways like a water chain from a bucket brigade. As the chairs made it to the end, a couple of the men began shoving and stacking them against the door. Their hopes were to make some sort of makeshift blockade.

After Joshua Arden had finished speaking, those not loyal to the cause vacated as quickly as they could. The Familiars couldn't necessarily blame them; those people were not enlightened to the way of the new order of things to come.

The New Order was touted as a fresh and idealistic purpose for how the world should be run; a rebirth of sorts. Some of the law-enforcement community had been following this false doctrine for some time, and truly believed this new way of thinking would bring the world back to the perceived core values of capitalism and social standing. The world, specifically this country, had become much too liberal in their views and acceptance of equality among all genders, races, religions, etc. It was time to make things right.

This same strategy, or way of thinking, would be varied from commercial and corporate organizations, to military services and government agencies. Regardless of who, all would be subject to the same misinformation to further the cause of the unknown puppet master.

The enemy used whatever methods necessary to reach their goals; in the case of right now, even if it meant the falsehood of duty and honor smeared with propaganda and lies.

None of the Familiars defending the precinct knew that Granger was a simple patsy in another indirectly related scheme of the enemy; they were told she was detained on suspicion of terroristic activity planned against the Federal Stock Exchange. Given the level of terrorism against the United States over the last couple of decades, this story was not that far-fetched. It was also pointed out that Jonah International was tied to this conspiracy and might try to extract her under a separate and unrecognized authority, whereby claiming jurisdiction and protecting the accused.

A claim of purview was a pretty sensitive subject for tight-knit law-enforcement communities such as the NYPD. It wasn't hard to convince the Familiars embedded in the one nine that Jonah would most likely make a play for her as soon as the federal government's transfer orders came through. They were sent reinforcements, and told that Chief Willis was a traitor to the cause and would have to be dealt with accordingly. All this had been backed up with fabricated documentation and evidence that would have convinced even the keenest of eyes.

Sure enough, all the predictions came true, which solidified the story as believable. They had no idea they were being used.

All of those remaining on the fourth floor were now working in the moment. They weren't necessarily thinking about a way out if they managed to stop the Jonah team, or if any of the other exits down to street-level were free and clear. All communications to their superiors were cut; an unfortunate byproduct of ensuring that the Jonah team couldn't call for back up. They were on their own and beginning to panic.

The one in command started to sweat. He was the farthest from the room that held Granger.

"LT, are you okay?" Officer Marcus James said. He saw that Lieutenant Brian McClement seemed nervous, and for a good reason. It didn't appear that things were going their way. The Familiars left holding the fourth floor tried not to react to the approaching gunfire; but like a speeding eighteen-wheeler heading towards them, it was inevitably going to hit. All of them were a bit jumpy from the events of the last 10 minutes. When the screams of the dying accompanied the gunshots, fear began to creep in like a rolling fog.

McClement shook off his dread. "Yeah, yeah... I'm good."

They both looked towards the stairwell where their opposition was going to try to enter. Carlito and Stein were frantically stacking the chairs as the rest of the people checked and rechecked their guns and ammo. There were fifteen of them in total; more than enough to stave off a run-of-the-mill siege, but it didn't seem quite enough now. Not based on the Jonah team's uncanny ability to penetrate their forces below.

Belinda Gleason, an office clerk, scurried over in her much too high heels and form fitting skirt. She carried a service revolver by its handle like it was a cell phone. It would have been obvious to anyone that she knew nothing about firearms, but she had to be prepared to protect herself, or so she was told. Her boyfriend, whom she was heading toward, Marcus, had given her his side arm and taken for himself one of the few shotguns from the lone rack on this level.

The main gun cage was on the first floor; none of remaining NYPD officers thought that they would need the extra weapons this soon, so they didn't stockpile. They wouldn't have been able to retrieve that many weapons without arousing suspicion anyway. They were quickly realizing this decision as one of the many mistakes made this day; better to be under suspicion and prepared.

Belinda decided to stay and fight because Marcus refused to leave after the announcement. He didn't have much of a choice, but she still had a little time left.

He was a Familiar; she was an Undeclared.

If he really cared about her, he would have sent her away with the others when there was a chance. His feelings for her, though, were not based on affection or necessarily love, but more like a flavor of the day. Belinda was fun, for the moment, and that was enough for him. Good enough for a good time, but not for the long haul. He was a typical player.

She was a New York brunette with rock hard hair and heavy makeup who never thought more than 15 minutes ahead into her future. If someone had told her this morning that she would most likely be dead before the end of the day, she probably would have gone back to her magazine to criticize those awful dresses worn by the starlets on the red carpet.

"Sweetie," she said in the horribly cliché nasally New York accent. "Whadda ya want me to do?"

With a scowl on his face, he snatched the gun out of her hand. "Baby, you're not holdin' it right!" He checked the clip, slapped it back in place, and pulled the chamber. "Aim between these two sights here, keep your finger off the trigger unless you're going to fire, here's the safety," he said pointing to make sure she saw it, "red means it's ready to fire."

Handing the gun back to her, he spun her around and pointed. "I want you behind this desk. The enemy is going to come through that door," he shifted his pointing finger to the stairwell. "We'll handle all the hard stuff. You just point the gun at anyone you don't know and pull the trigger, got it?" She nodded her head nervously and waddled behind the desk. She squatted down in her tight skirt careful not to lean her knees on the floor. She didn't want to get a run in her hose.

* * *

The Jonah team reached the door leading out of the stairwell to the fourth floor. Agent Ingram had point as they approached; he held up his fist signaling them to stop. The glass pane in the old door showed odd silhouettes from various angles on the other side. Ingram could not make out the shadows. He doubted that the enemy would be that stupid and hide directly in front of a frosted window. But then again, they weren't making the best choices today.

He looked down the staircase to his boss, Agent Marseilles, who was covering the rear flank below with Officer Callahan. Marseilles' instincts told him to look up, and their eyes met. He gave his fellow agent and friend a confirming nod indicating it was Ingram's call.

Ingram took a step back from the door and raised the cuff of his sleeve to speak. "Command, request Intel and tactical assessment of our position and access," he whispered.

Sentinel spoke in everyone's ear piece. "Fifteen tangos in various positions. Closest is four feet behind west corner of stairway exit. Nine rolling office chairs have been stacked haphazardly at the stairwell exit. They are wedged between the opposing wall and your entry door."

"That's not going to be a problem. The stairwell door opens inward, not out," said Officer Peterson.

McDowell shook his head. "It won't make a difference. Even if they shift, the chairs will still be in the way."

A JPS agent nodded in agreement. "It will make it hard to get position. Chances are that all guns are pointed to those chairs. We'll be sitting ducks."

Marseilles' listen to the conversation as he covered the rear; flashes of Brixton and Flannery flickered in his mind. They didn't listen, and they got dead. That wouldn't be the case this time, but his team didn't possess the tactical advantage. The enemy had the proverbial higher ground. He wasn't going to risk any more of his team, unless he had the upper hand.

"McDowell, take my place," he said.

Officer McDowell nodded and switched places leveling off his M4 carbine down the staircase.

Marseilles walked up the staircase gently as Ingram and the others gathered close. "I need some options," he said looking at them.

They all had concerned looks, but no one spoke.

After a few seconds, Officer Peterson said, "I don't have a plan, but I know eventually they're going to figure out we have stopped moving and where we are. The ones down below that aren't dead are going to be ticked off and start coming up those stairs," he said with a head gesture, "with more guns and ammo than us." He looked Marseilles in the eyes. "Either way, we're sitting ducks."

The team leader pulled his sleeve to his mouth and whispered. "Command, I haven't heard anything that gives me confidence we can enter without losing more people," he looked at Peterson, "and we are not going to be able to stay where we are for long." Marseilles then glanced over to the stairwell door. "Even if those chairs weren't there, it would still be a choke point with no cover. Please advise."

* * *

Kelan looked at his analyst and watchers. During the last ten minutes, all of those in rHub were now observing the current operation.

His on-site team was in trouble, and they needed a plan. Before he could even utter the order, his on-duty mission teams scurried back to their workstations and started running scenarios and simulations. He was just about to provide a little more focused direction when Joshua came through on his COM.

"Kelan, I've got an idea, but it's for executive team ears only."

He looked at the two other analysts still in the situation room. "Head back to your stations. Let me know if you come up with any viable options," he ordered.

As soon as they left, he sealed the room. "We're clear."

Joshua quickly explained his idea to Alice, Langston, and Kelan. It was a bit unorthodox, but as they have learned over the last several years, stranger things have happened.

Knowing time was short, Kelan spoke first. "Why not? Given how our world really operates, this doesn't seem odd at all."

Langston nodded, while Alice slowly grinned. "Well," she said. "I'll bet they won't see *this* coming."

Joshua half-smiled, then turned to the middle of the room. "Lucas."

The guardian angel shimmered into view a few feet from Joshua.

"Greetings Joshua," he said. He nodded towards Alice and Langston, who politely returned the greeting. Joshua was proud of them both, for neither of them made a show of being startled at the supernatural appearance. He wondered briefly if they both were trying hard to accept this as a normal part of the workday, or just simply tired of looking and sounding like babbling idiots in front of the angels.

"Hey," he said returning the greeting, then turned back towards the hard-light imagery. "Sentinel, is Sebastian on site?"

"Yes, sir."

"Show me."

A brilliant white glow appeared next to the small shackled and sitting blue light depicting Granger. The glow was so bright that all three humans had to squint until their eyes adjusted. Once Joshua could focus, he noticed that it was a man-shaped aura with floating tendrils in the shape of wings. He stared at the magnificence for a moment longer, then turned to Lucas.

"Question; can you communicate with Sebastian?" Joshua asked as he nodded towards the brilliant light.

Lucas smiled. "Of course."

Joshua returned the smile, as did Alice and Langston.

"Good."

* * *

Sebastian stood next to the human Kelly Granger as she struggled erratically against the metal restraints. Her efforts were admirable as evidenced by raw circles of bloody flesh around both wrists. The angel could not tell if the hysterical sobbing was from the pain, or the ruckus caused by the other humans and their pitiful weapons. Either way, the poor girl was not fit for combat or any actions by the name of self-preservation. She was a blubbering mess.

The human-made walls were not a barrier for his sight beyond sight. He had full visibility to the battlefield of those who would be the young female's rescuers and their enemy. Sebastian looked at them curiously and analyzed their tactics.

The posture was weak on the doomed Familiars; no defined line of defense or strategy gave them first-strike capability other than the obstruction they placed in front of their opponents. Even then, they would be counting on their opposition to make the first move, and were scattered about like sheep on a hillside just waiting to be picked off by wolves. With the exception, Sebastian noted, of these heavily armed humans closest to the girl. They seemed different from the others.

This would have driven Vaago mad, thought Sebastian. He knew his commander well having served with him for over a millennia. Vaago would wait for no one. Had this been his battle, he would have been on the offensive; this attack would have been on his terms alone, and most assuredly swift and complete. Not something that Sebastian necessarily agreed with all the time, but still, very effective and yielded the desired results.

Sebastian's thoughts drifted to Joshua. The Most High's young master was strong-willed, but appeared to have skill and reason to match his motives. That was something he felt that Vaago lacked; not the skill part, but the reason. He was mostly reactionary, and blunt to a fault. A large battering ram in lieu of a simple knock against a door.

He then looked to the cramped stairwell where the Jonah team huddled. They were obviously awaiting further instructions; most likely from young Joshua's Command and Control.

It was hard for Sebastian to tell who the commander was from the group gathered and conversing. He also found it strange that whomever was the field leader, sought counsel among his warriors. Sebastian could count on one hand how many times throughout his existence he was asked for his opinion by Vaago. Although he most assuredly had one, it was never out right requested; and when it was, never in front of his seven other brothers within the Inflixi Impetus.

It was good to see though, that the Jonah team had the sense enough to cover their rear flank from the approaching enemy, whom Sebastian could see, was mustering their forces a few floors below. The enemy pursuit was only a matter of human time.

The obstruction was going to be problematic as the doorway was the most accessible means of entrance, for a human that is. He thought it sad that humans were limited to a corporeal state. Angelic beings were so much more versatile when it came to–

Sebastian's thoughts paused as contact was made. He raised his head slightly as he responded to Lucaous. Sebastian questioned whether the Most High would sanction such a maneuver as it conflicted with the terms of interference, then tilted his head to the other side and received his authorization from the Host.

Well, now, this should be interesting, he thought, and drew his massive sword.

* * *

"Starfish, this is Command," said Sentinel.

The Jonah team did not have to wait long for the plan, but wasn't expecting what they heard. When Sentinel had finished with instructions, the Associates were stunned; the JPS agents were somewhat surprised, but given the rumors that circulated over the years about the amazing situations involving Joshua; they were more curious than shocked.

"Please confirm," followed Sentinel.

Everything seemed to become eerily quiet in the stairwell. It was more the perception of stillness than anything else; like the air, sound, and even light, were sucked away. The seven remaining members of the Kelly Granger liberation force stared at one another; each comprehending what they were told, and the seemingly impossible obstacle that lay before them.

What this boiled down to was a matter of trust. Could they trust this plan? Did they have the faith to literally step into a barrage of gunfire? Would they be forever known as the lunatics who embraced a fool's errand? Each one examined their individual willingness to accept the unknown.

That only lasted for a moment; then, without a word, they moved in unison.

Ingram took a position at the bottom of the door bracing his shoulder firmly against the wood. He swapped out his Remington with Peterson's M4, and positioned it where he could fire immediately when the door gave way. Peterson, in turn, held Ingram's tactical harness to steady him from the blast of the door; the force of the suction would throw him off balance when the door disappeared. They needed to respond quickly during the enemy's confusion, and Ingram was selected as the point man.

The rest of the team reloaded their weapons as fast as they could, then arranged themselves into the positions as directed by Sentinel.

Marseilles looked at each person to make sure they understood and were ready. Each nodded in turn as eyes met. When he was satisfied they were good, he raised his cuff and spoke. "Command, we are a go; say again, we are a go."

* * *

Sebastian's wings sprang from his body with unbridled splendor. With the force of hurricane winds, he brought them forward propelling himself instantly backwards through the mortal structure and out into the open space, leaving Kelly Granger behind.

He grasped his two-handed sword in an inverted position with the handle to his chest and the blade to his feet. Sebastian pulled it in tightly as he picked up speed and spiraled through the air. The powerful angel made a graceful arc that spanned ten square city blocks, then headed back toward the police station. Approaching a trajectory that would lead him directly to the makeshift obstruction parallel with the Jonah team, his speed continued to increase.

Sebastian's flight stance shifted quickly like that of an advancing bird of prey about to make its kill. As he moved through the corporeal structure toward the gathering of chairs, he swung his battle sword in an upward motion sending the flimsy objects hurtling forward like projectiles being shot from a cannon. In a fluid follow-through from the swing, he sheathed his sword and twirled toward the stairwell door. Grabbing it with both hands, he ripped it from the wall and sent it flying into the fray of the unsuspecting Familiars. Sebastian then landed as an unseen barrier between the shocked enemy and the stairwell.

* * *

Even with a solid door as a buffer, the impact of whatever hit those chairs was deafening to Ingram. As he winced, Ingram thought he felt the shockwave of the redistribution of pressure from the other side.

Marseilles stood just behind Peterson, who was still holding onto Ingram's belt, and saw the shadows shift behind the frosted glass; within a blink, they were gone.

Then, without any forewarning, the door ripped away along with part of the frame; it was like a tornado pulling a roof from a house. The jagged remains of the frame sucked outward from the stairwell along with a change in pressure as anticipated. Peterson and Ingram ducked their heads instinctively as it seemed like the building was coming apart around them. The rest of the team was ambushed by the sudden rush of wind barreling up the stairwell.

Only two seconds passed before their COMs became active. Each person was now receiving their individual instructions like before, but only after a one-word collective broadcast from Sentinel.

"Go."

* * *

Lieutenant McClement barely had enough time to issue a command to reinforce the protection of the supposed suspected terrorist, when his world was literally shattered. "Daniels, Penske! Make sure you cover—"

A loud thunder crack permeated the air. For the split second that McClement could comprehend what had happened, he turned towards the stairwell to see the chairs exploding outward. One came at him with an unrealistic speed; like it wasn't even touching the floor. It was just slow enough, though, that he could deflect and sidestep it by a couple of feet. Since his focus was on the chair, he did not see the heavily constructed door from the stairwell barreling towards him.

The door shattered as it impacted the wall, sending it splintering in all directions; however, not before snapping Lieutenant Brian McClement's neck between the two solid objects. His body fell in a slump down the side of the wall; his head rolling unnaturally on his shoulders.

Belinda screamed as she fell from her precarious perch atop her high heels; not from the sight of McClement's dead body, but from a shard of wood that had ripped through her leg, and the pantyhose she had desperately wanted to preserve.

Her would-be boyfriend, Marcus James, was heading for the holding room of Kelly Granger when the chair explosion and Belinda's scream spun him around reflexively. He brought his shotgun up and fired in the direction of the chairs without fixing upon a single target. That was his last mistake. A bullet from Ingram's M4 carbine caught him in the left eye and exploded out of the back of his head.

Still screaming from the pain, Belinda dropped the handgun that her late boyfriend had thrust upon her earlier. That one unintentional act saved her life. The other Familiars were not as smart.

Or lucky.

* * *

Sentinel's instructions were systematic and timed down to the millisecond. The four JPS agents had worked many field simulations over the years, so they were accustomed to having another voice inside their head. The tactical training and exercises covering multiple scenarios and situations were common core requirements within basic and advanced field operations, and having to share their brains with their watchers was as normal to them as their badges and weapons.

Out of the four, only Marseilles had been in live combat situations such as this. The other three, although they were good agents, seemed like children in his eyes; twenty something, snot-nosed, still wet behind the ears kids with simulation experience, but never put to the test until today. So far, they had been performing admirably and following their instructions to the letter without question. He now saw them as men; not the boys he had walked with into the station. Marseilles was proud to lead them, and hoped they were equally proud of their own actions. If he made it out of this, he would make sure his team was recognized for their valor and commitment.

Up to this point, that was a big *if.* The team lead had his own misgivings about this op when things rapidly turned south. Everything about it screamed un-winnable.

After receiving his initial instructions in the lobby, he quickly employed a little approach he had learned from field combat many years ago. Let the enemy worry about him; *he* was the threat. It was a practiced technique, but he always assumed that the enemy was more scared of him and the damage he could inflict rather than the other way around. Thinking something other than that would give the enemy the upper hand. That was leverage he was not willing to relinquish without a fight.

However, as he currently sized up the odds, his opponents, the close quarters of combat, and his team's lack of matching firepower, he began to doubt their chances. Even with the help of the officers, Jonah, and any other mysterious forces that seem to always follow Dr. Arden wherever he was, things still did not look good.

He was a combat veteran. He knew his training well, and tried to live each day as his last. Today would not be any different.

By concentrating on his mission at hand, Marseilles would not give into second-guessing his actions or thoughts. He refused to compromise. In his mind, today's exercise was just a big game of laser tag. The Familiars were only targets, nothing more.

He looked down at his teammates after they had all received orders from Command. Peterson released the tactical harness as Ingram moved around the corner. Ingram subsequently pointed to where he was instructed and fired. Peterson, then Marseille, moved through the jagged archway where the door was once attached. The rest of the team then advanced in the order received by Sentinel.

Marseilles' shotgun came up and drew a bead on a woman screaming next to a dead body, but before he pulled the trigger was ordered to stand down by Command. He was quickly informed that the woman was not a threat.

Fine by him. He had a feeling that the body count was high enough, but knew that this was still not over.

* * *

The two men called Penske and Daniels, half looked over their shoulders as the room exploded with activity. Penske was a few feet away from the door to the room holding Kelly Granger when blood and gray matter from Marcus James hit the wall and speckled the right side of his face. He swore as he spun around bringing up his HK MP5-N.

The semiautomatic was mostly compact for a sub machine gun, and easily maneuverable for him whereby making it his weapon of choice. It was, however, not part of NYPD's standard cache of approved weaponry. This was a tactical firearm used by special forces; specifically, the United States Navy SEALs.

Both Penske and Daniels, as well as the other six individuals closest to the room, were part of the fortification called in by Ministry, a secret organization and soon to be thorn in Jonah International's side. None of those eight were NYPD; each came from a special ops team loyal to the cause. Everyone were trained and deadly; and they were Familiars, through and through.

Their mission was different from those who thought they were doing good by protecting a suspected terrorist awaiting trial. The eight specialized soldiers all knew their true purpose for being there. Granger was not to fall into the hands of anybody other than their superiors. They were soldiers, and took their orders seriously. Just like their day jobs, they staked their lives on this mission. Collateral damage for this operation, no matter which side, didn't matter. Their determination showed on their faces; they didn't know the meaning of failure.

And as soon as Marseilles saw them, he knew that as well.

* * *

As each one of the Jonah agents came out of the stairwell, they scrambled to the nearest cover as directed by Sentinel and braced for the inevitable onslaught of bullets they were told was coming. All except for Marseilles. His gaze shifted from the screaming woman to the cluster of men standing between him and the objective, and he saw it.

His eyes met theirs, and he knew. The steel determination was unmistakable for anyone, but it was the body language that confirmed it. Combat stance, two by two pairings, and their formation in relation to the target.

"Duck and cover!" He yelled as a fire of bullets rained down upon them.

The Jonah team and officers cringed at the deafening sound of multiple automatic gunfire; some with their eyes closed, while others gritted their teeth. It was a cacophony of thunder cracks from gunpowder, expended shell casings falling on the floor, and the muted cries from the nonmilitary Familiars hit by the ricochet of bullets.

Peterson was the first to notice that it was only sound that hit them. Then the others began looking at each other in confusion. It didn't appear that the bullets were making contact. In fact, nothing aside from the symphony of the noise seemed to be attacking them.

* * *

Sebastian stood in the middle of the room facing the aggressors. The weak and cowardly weapons were gripped tightly in their small meager hands. Their intentions were clear; they meant harm to the humans emerging from the stairwell.

As time was not a factor in Sebastian's presence, he communicated to Joshua through Lucaous. Sebastian found it fascinating that the Most High would grant a human angelic abilities reserved for only those who served the Light. The demon enemy did not even possess these enhanced capabilities. This human must indeed be favored, and very special.

Joshua had requested that Sebastian shield his human team from enemy fire until they were positioned to strike. As the volley from the Familiars streaked towards the frail rescuers, Sebastian spread his wings wide. The bullets bounced harmlessly off him and his wings like rocks skipping across water.

* * *

"Thunder two two, engage," said Penske through his tactical throat mic to his team, then he began firing three shot bursts from his HK MP5-N. The remaining members of his squad held their position as they tracked their individual targets and fired. There was no synchronicity or cadence to their shots; they simply fired as they saw fit to achieve their goal of rapid elimination of the enemy.

A few seconds passed, and Penske saw that nothing was happening. "Hold!"

The gunfire ceased.

"What the—" said Daniels.

"Compton, pineapple," said Penske.

The soldier called Compton lowered his MP5K for a moment as he simultaneously grabbed a grenade from his flak vest. He popped the pin, released the lever, and lobbed it towards the Jonah team. "Fire in the hole!"

The special forces Familiars braced for the explosion.

* * *

Marseilles held his position during what he thought was a barrage of incoming bullets. He was a half a second behind Peterson in the realization that nothing was hitting them, when he decided to take a chance and grab a better tactical vantage of the enemy. It was at that precise moment that he saw the grenade casually floating through the air. He pulled his head in tight under his arms. With his cuff near his mouth, he screamed, "Incoming!"

* * *

Joshua and company gasped; Kelan swore out loud, as they all watched the scene unfold. Joshua looked toward Lucas with a pleading request. The guardian angel's head was already cocked at an angle as Joshua realized he was in communication with Sebastian.

* * *

Sebastian watched the small device float slowly through the air. He studied it with great curiosity. He saw variations of these things throughout human history. It seemed with each iteration, that the humans were learning to increase the damage and radius of such while making the objects of their destruction smaller and smaller. He supposed that the weapons they used, regardless of how barbaric and lacking of honor, were of no different purpose than those chosen by angels and demons. He, and his fellow Inflixi, preferred facing their enemy in battle, something which seemed that the humans avoided at all costs.

His curiosity continued as Lucaous reached out with yet another request from the young master.

As the mortal perception of time continued to move slowly, the powerful warrior looked around to the other human would-be combatants who were left alive after surviving the deflected bullets. All wounded, some had the look of horror as their eyes were fixed upon the last visage of their destruction. Sebastian's gaze then drifted through the corporeal structure along the path of human corpses, and he watched the process of consumption rip the souls away from those who were not of the Light.

He and the other angelic warriors had never wept for those lost in battle; for their deaths were an inevitable choice when faced with the ultimate truth. He supposed it was no different for the humans. Their screams were commonplace now, and that caused Sebastian a small amount of sadness. But alas, the humans should have made better choices; just as the demons.

Sebastian sent his acknowledgment to Lucaous and again, spread his wings and arms wide.

* * *

The grenade exploded upon contact with something unseen. The remaining Familiars that were not part of the special forces team caught the brunt of the fragmentation, ending their lives in what could be considered a pitiful waste. To Sebastian's earlier thought, they should have made better choices.

Sadly, choices or not, the destruction was vicious. The detonation, in what should have been disbursed throughout a wider area based on the floor's dimensions, was confined to little less than half that as Sebastian's presence separated the two parties. The blowback of the force was almost double the yield back upon the special forces and regular Familiars.

The special forces' unit had been trained for situations such as this, and prepared for the impact by taking positions along the room holding Granger, and shielding themselves with sturdy furniture and metal filing cabinets. Other unsuspecting Familiars were at ground zero with Sebastian when the explosion occurred. Their lives ended in an instant.

The whole event lasted less than ten-seconds, but seemed like an eternity.

One by one, the special forces Familiars recovered from their protective positions. Each lowered their weapons as they stared in disbelief once again.

Office furniture was scorched and scattered about. Heavy-duty wooden desks were splintered at the edges, but held together amid the shrapnel that was once computer components. Inboxes, some made of metal mesh and others' plastic, were melted and deformed, while their contents were set ablaze floating about like feathers in the wind.

And then there were the bodies. All the other Familiars; crushed and skewered by the flying furniture and objects, or simply caught in the explosion itself. Some of them unrecognizable due to the contortions of their mangled forms that were either on fire, or missing parts. The only one that survived was Belinda; and only because she was behind Sebastian.

This type of damage was to be expected, and was not why the special forces' unit was surprised. It was the clear line of destruction that stopped where Sebastian was standing that gave them pause. For the humans that did not know the truth, the unseen barrier left the other half of the wide area completely untouched. It was like an invisible wall separated the room. Even the scorch marks on the walls were in sharp contrast; like only half the walls were painted.

Unimaginable outcomes were par for the course in their field of work, but even this had defied their mortal logic.

Penske snapped out of it first. His disbelief quickly turned into anger. He didn't understand why this happened, or how they could have possibly survived, and didn't care. He noticed minor movement from the enemy behind their own barricades, so he knew that beyond whatever belief or comprehension of the current situation, the grenade had failed, and the enemy was still a threat.

He clicked on his throat mic. "Thunder two two, fall back." Then he began firing his weapon at the Jonah team.

In a practiced formation, the other men began firing as well, and one by one; they backed into the room holding Kelly Granger.

20

Contribute, Or Shut Up

Joshua watched the digital image in the center of his conference room table on the top floor of Jonah International as all unfolded. The flurry of activity made the multicolored figures weave in and out causing him difficulty in separating details other than colors identifying friend versus foe. He asked Sentinel to switch to real-time imaging; something he had never used before because the cartoon figures of the digital wire frames made the ending of lives much more palatable. For a brief second, he supposed that was something he was going to need to get used to; people dying that is. The foreboding cloud over the future was spreading quickly, and he had a sinking, gut-churning feeling that death would be riding across the land; a reaper on a black horse claiming its victims at every turn. He wasn't sure whether his role would permit him to prevent that, or at the very least, make sure those who died transitioned instead of being consumed.

He didn't have all the answers, and never pretended to. As with what played out in front of him, he too knew that his own involvement was just a means to an end; part of a broader plan for which he was still unaware. His lack of knowledge would soon be remedied though; much quicker than he anticipated.

Joshua did a visual headcount of his team. All JPS agents were still intact, and alive. The three remaining NYPD officers were mobile and looked unharmed. Joshua noticed that they appeared visibly shaken.

That was completely understandable given their first exposure to what they probably thought was madness and impossibility. In the back of his mind, Joshua mused that every human thrust into this world had to go through some type of ritual, a psychedelic indoctrination of sorts, and have a reality that they have known their entire lives, shatter like broken glass. To have fellow officers though, turn on them for reasons unknown, was a bit much for an initiation process. Should they survive, Joshua would make sure they had a place with Jonah. He believed that they had earned it.

Both he and Kelan watched the sequence of events play out from the explosion. Once the eight highly trained Familiars began entering the room with Granger, both men raised a series of red flags. Something wasn't right.

"Joshua, are you seeing this?" Kelan said.

"Yes, they're entering Granger's room," replied Joshua.

"That will put them at a tactical disadvantage. The room has only one exit, and they just went through it."

Joshua thought for a second. "If they did their homework, they would have to know that the back staircase here, —" he said pointing, "—is the only other exit available to the left, and just behind the room that they're in."

"You think they would use an explosive to blow through the back wall to that staircase?" Langston added.

Unseen, Kelan shrugged. "I don't know, maybe." He traced his finger down along the path from the top floor to the bottom. "There's minimal opposition along that back stairwell. It would have made more sense for them to retreat that way; around the room."

Alice watched. "What about our TAC team at the bottom?"

"A strategic transition; close the loop on one threat, and refocus on another," said Kelan.

Alice nodded her head as if understanding, but didn't.

Kelan couldn't see it, but knew Alice well enough that her lack of response and quips, probably meant that she didn't process what he had said. "They don't have to beat the enemy if that's not the mission.

In this case, leave Granger and the Jonah team behind, and focus their efforts on the team below. A different set of opposition, and it gets them one step closer to safety."

"But that's just it; the mission was not to retreat, but to prevent our team from getting Granger," said Langston. "They've essentially backed themselves into a corner by entering that room. What do they have to gain by doing that?"

"Maybe the plan is to use Granger as some type of human shield then follow the pathway down those back stairs," said Alice.

Joshua raised an eyebrow. "One hostage to protect eight tactically outfitted and trained soldiers? She then becomes a liability; something that refocuses at least one soldier's attention away from the group. The odds are that some of their men would get clipped by our team as well. A more plausible option would be to use her as a bargaining chip; a high valued asset they know that we want in exchange for their safe passage."

"So far, their precision and formations have been near perfect," said Kelan.

"Agreed," he said thinking. "Do they seem like the type that would not have a plan B ready?" Joshua continued with skepticism.

Before anyone answered, something changed on the image.

"Look!" Alice said pointing. "They appear to be arguing."

* * *

Smith, one of the larger soldiers, ripped his ear piece out of his ear and aggressively approached Penske. "What the hell are we supposed to do now?! You've backed us into a room with no way out!"

"Back off, Smith!" Daniels said laying his hand on the larger man's shoulder.

Smith refocused his aggression towards Daniels by first looking at his hand, then the smaller man. "If you want to keep that, you'll get it off me now," he said softly.

Daniels immediately removed his hand.

Penske reached into his vest to retrieve a fresh clip. "Our objective is to protect this asset."

Smith puffed up his chest and raised his voice. "That objective has changed! Did you see what just happened out there?" He pointed his MP5K toward the door. "We unloaded half of our ammo and tossed a frag! It didn't even make a dent! They only fired one shot and took out that useless sack of—"

"Smith, you are damaging my calm," said Johnson; another soldier. He was part of Delta Force. "We all saw what happened. Contribute, or shut up."

Smith was normally considered a hot head. Not a good trait for someone of his size and specialized training. He was also Delta Force, and had worked with Johnson on a previous mission. Smith respected the man's opinion, which was something he didn't do lightly.

Smith took a deep breath but retained the intense demeanor. "All I'm saying is that something or someone is working with them. There is *no way* that four suits and a hand full of would-be cops could navigate through all that firepower to here, blow out all those chairs the idiots stacked, rip a door off its hinge at the same time, *and* survive a high-yield grenade without even a scratch."

Penske looked into the man's eyes for a couple of seconds. He turned to look at Daniels, then Johnson.

Johnson shrugged. "Man has a point; that's messed up."

"I'm okay with not knowing how all of that was possible; I'm *not* OK with the odds switching. I say we lick our wounds and call it a day. We use thermals to detect their heat signature and come out blazing," said Smith, thankful that someone seemed to see his point of view.

Penske looked at the other soldiers. "Once again, our mission objective has not changed. We are to protect this asset."

Smith practically exploded. "Are you freaking kidding me?!" He cocked the slide on his weapon to chamber a round from the fresh magazine. "There is no more mission if I ice this broad."

* * *

Kelly Granger was practically crazed. She screamed when the door opened and the soldiers poured through; along with gunfire immediately succeeding a booming explosion. The boom was so loud that it shook the room and slightly slid the chair to which she was cuffed. When the noise had died down, she tried with all her might to quell the agonizing and hysterical shrieks welling up inside of her. A wishful maneuver in hopes that her new roommates wouldn't even realize she was there. It was an optimistic ploy and seemed to work for a moment. Then the crazy man pointed his gun right at her head. The screams and sobs came blurting out even louder.

* * *

"I can't allow that," said Penske as he raised his own weapon and lined its sites with Smith's head. This movement took a few other soldiers by surprise; they raised their weapons reflexively not recognizing who they were aiming at, but simply responding out of habit.

Johnson thought Smith was a jerk, but instinctively covered his Delta Force brother. He leveled his weapon off at Penske. Likewise, Daniels was Navy SEALs and loyal to his lead, so targeted Johnson. Things were quickly becoming out of hand.

* * *

Joshua tensed as he saw all the weapons raise and turn on each other. The enemy soldiers looked like they were on the edge, and obviously conflicted about their next move.

So much happened in the last fifteen minutes. The carnage in the wake of the war to rescue this woman seemed endless. Joshua wasn't even sure if she possessed any useful information at all, but this now became a moral imperative. He was convinced that she had no idea what she had done, and simply thought she was supporting her animal cause. For everything he didn't know about Kelly Granger, he knew that she was a pawn being used by the enemy; and he knew how that felt. She didn't deserve this.

Putting himself in the place of these soldiers, he would wonder how all that had happened was possible. From their perspective, how could a lesser force penetrate deep into their territory and deflect that kind of firepower? At this point, in their mission, he would begin to wonder how they could make it out of this situation alive.

It was quite apparent that they were beginning to turn on each other, and there would be no upside for anyone in that room. What if there was a pause in the battle? What if they could be given one more chance to stand down and walk away? Maybe he could appeal to their understanding one last time.

"Lucas," he said turning towards his guardian angel and friend, "please ask Sebastian to protect Kelly now."

Lucas nodded and relayed the request.

Focusing on the image again, Joshua said, "Sentinel, patch me through to the men in that room, and make sure our team can hear as well."

"Yes, sir."

Langston and Alice looked at each other quizzically, then glanced towards Joshua. He gave them a reassuring look to indicate he had everything under control. The truth of the matter was that he didn't have the slightest clue as to whether this was going to work or not; he was playing this one strictly by instinct.

"I'm speaking to the gentlemen currently in the room with Kelly Granger. Can everyone please relax a moment and listen to what I have to say?"

* * *

The soldiers in the room stiffened at Joshua's voice. Weapons remained pointed at their targets, but no one made a move. Joshua wasn't sure whether that was a good or a bad sign. At least, they weren't killing each other; or the girl.

Penske's eyes did not leave Smith's head; his weapon still waiting for him to put his finger on the trigger. He slowly released his support hand to push his PTT button. "Thunder two two. Identify yourself."

"My name is Joshua Arden. I was the one who spoke over the PA system earlier. May I ask who I am speaking with?"

Penske's eyes cut to Daniels, who shook his head indicating it was not a good idea to reveal anything to the enemy.

Joshua and Company were watching the exchange unbeknownst to anyone else in the room. The man pointing his weapon at the soldier who was threatening Granger was the one that spoke. The others stood about with their weapons ready and watched. That told Joshua and Kelan that the man speaking was in command. This was good. The fact that he even answered was a small gesture that he was willing to discuss options.

He waited a few seconds for the person to reply before speaking. When nothing came, Joshua thought that reassurance might help. "Sir, I want to make sure that no harm comes to you or your men. No more lives have to be lost. I just want to know who I'm talking to; that's all."

A sneer crossed Smith's face. "Yeah, right," he said softly. "How's *this* working into your mission objective?" The sarcasm was dripping from each syllable.

Insubordinate attitude and defiance of direct orders were becoming a pattern here in which Penske was trying to ignore; for the moment. Thinking about this for a few more seconds, he looked over to Johnson, who was still pointing his weapon at him. "Do you want to make it out of this alive?"

Without wavering, Johnson said, "That would be nice."

"This girl needs to stay alive, do you understand?" Penske said.

Their eyes didn't leave each other's for a solid ten-seconds. The unspoken communication conveyed what needed to happen.

Johnson shifted his eyes back-and-forth between Smith and his mission commander. "Copy that," he finally said. "Smith, stand down."

"Not gonna happen," he responded to Johnson.

"Smith—" started Johnson.

"No! This chick is not worth dying over. She is a liability that needs to be dealt with." Smith tightened his grip on his weapon.

Johnson's eyes relaxed with sadness. In some weird way, he was going to miss Smith. With the precision of a trained soldier, Johnson fired one round directly into the left side of Smith's temple. The larger man toppled to the left of Kelly Granger, but not before his finger reflexively squeezed off a three-shot burst. At four feet from his target, there was no way that Smith could have missed.

Kelly continued to scream with the intensity of a woman gone mad.

Back at Jonah International, Alice gasped as she saw the big man fall. Langston stiffened while Joshua just stood there. He didn't seem worried at all; neither did Lucas.

Penske swore as the shots rang out, then froze again in disbelief. She was completely unharmed; still unseen, Sebastian protected her as instructed. His wings were wrapped around her like a mother holding her child. This time the bullets didn't deflect; they just simply vanished upon contact. He then laid his hands upon Kelly Granger, and her sobbing immediately subsided. She had a look of confusion and misunderstanding.

Penske dropped to one knee and gently put his hands close to her while examining every inch. Without touching her, his hands hovered as if feeling for the wounds that weren't there. "I don't believe it," he said in barely whisper.

"You don't have to believe it for it to be true, Captain Penske," said Joshua directly to him.

Eyes wide and still stunned, Penske looked at the back of his hands; he never reached to push his talk button. How did he hear him? He never gave him his name. How did he know who he was?

Joshua didn't leave anything to chance. Once the imagery switched to real time, Sentinel ran facial recognition and identified each of the soldiers within seconds. Their dossiers appeared and disappeared as Joshua manipulated the hard-light in search for useful information. Then he had a thought and looked towards Lucas. "He's on the edge. Have Sebastian show himself."

Lucas raised an eyebrow. "Everyone?" Referring to the whole special forces' unit.

"No," he said casually gesturing to the image. "Just him. He can make all this go away if he believes. The troublemaker is down. The rest should follow if we can get the leader to commit."

Lucas half smiled. His charge was thinking outside of the scenarios that separate the standard conventional warfare tactics between mankind and angelic beings.

Joshua was merging the two in order to reach beyond the limitations of humans. The council would be very pleased at his progress. He was beginning to expand his way of thinking; learning how to achieve more with his available resources. That would be needed to outsmart the next level of the enemy command.

* * *

In all his existence, Sebastian probably saw more than the average creature. The fall of his once brothers, man-made and natural disasters, the birth of this and other new realms, and even the creation of the humans; the Inflixi Impetus had been there for almost everything that required enforcement of a specialized nature. This was the first time; however, that he had been asked to put on a "show" for a human. There were other angels whose responsibilities were more in line with appearance requests; that could do far more to persuade a human to change his ways. As it stands though, he was the only one available, and more importantly, the one asked by the Most High's young master.

He was unskilled in this area and therefore, was not sure how to convey what young Joshua wanted. He *did* know that had Vaago come as requested and been standing here right now, he would not have dignified the young master's instructions with so much as an impertinent snort at the very thought. That, of course, would have caused more issues for the present situation, and most likely increased the ever-widening chasm between his current commander, and what was looking to be his new commander going forward. It was Sebastian's turn to half smile at what he knew was going to be a war of epic proportions between the two.

* * *

Penske's mind was still trying to grapple with how she could have survived a close-range kill shot, and now this voice in his head, when a brilliant light hit him. Backpedaling away from Granger, he saw that it began to take shape. A man was beginning to form ... with... were those wings?!

Sebastian unfurled his wings in a slow and dramatic fashion.

Penske continued stumbling backwards until he hit the wall. He watched stupefied as the being's wingspan filled the room. His eyes shot to Daniels, then Johnson wondering why they were not reacting in kind. It didn't make any sense, unless ... they couldn't see it. Wait! No one was moving.

What's happening? He thought as he looked at each of his squad. They appeared to be statues; still pointing their guns at each other in various positions, not moving an inch. *I'm going insane.*

After what seemed like an eternity, Penske finally composed himself and stood. He tentatively watched the winged man as he moved to examine and confirm what he knew was impossible, but was happening anyway. Daniels, Johnson, and the others were frozen. He steadied himself for the inevitable, then turned to face the being.

* * *

Sebastian expressed his concerns to Lucas about not knowing what to do. Joshua smiled and asked Lucas to inform Sebastian that he would walk him through each step. For this to work though, Joshua, Sebastian, Lucas, and Penske, would need to be removed from the time continuum. Joshua had become accustomed to the odd sensation of slipping between seconds, but he would bet that this effect would bolster

Penske's belief. Seeing is believing for most humans; he didn't think that this soldier was any different.

* * *

Sebastian brought his wings down slowly, and the glow softened. Penske saw that the man was huge; at least seven or eight feet tall. The man's piercing brown eyes tracked him as Penske moved to face him. He looked down at Kelly Granger whose perpetual expression of sorrow was also stock-still.

"Jeremy Penske," said Sebastian in his angelic tone.

Penske stiffened at the mention of his name. Although he shouldn't have been surprised based on everything that had happened in the last five minutes, he was.

"I am the face of those, you and your team oppose in your quest to hurt this woman," continued Sebastian.

Penske furrowed his brow in confusion. "My orders are to protect her from capture and deliver her to safety, not hurt her."

"Your orders are a ruse to *prevent* her from safety."

"I— I don't understand."

A wind that was not felt seemed to blow the being's hair and clothes ever so slightly. "The humans that commissioned your services are dishonest and seek a different outcome. They in turn, are foolishly led by beings not of your realm."

Penske looked a bit skeptical, but asked, "Humans? Are you from outer-space? An alien?"

Joshua found the comment comical. He remembered thinking the same thing all those years ago in the home of Malcolm Holden, Jonah International's global CEO, right before he found out the truth, and met Lucas for the first time.

Sebastian tried not to show his disgust at the stupid questions, but did not hide his disappointment. "No, we are not aliens. They do not exist."

"Then who are you?" Penske said almost challenging Sebastian.

"I am not the evil that leads mankind to ruin; nor am I tolerant of those who serve it." Sebastian's voice grew louder with each word. His glow began to manifest and shift in a manner where all light except him disappeared, and it rippled as his anger grew. "I am the representation of your absolution! I am a protector of the Light!" A thunderclap echoed with the last word, shaking the room, and leaving a jagged crack through part of a wall and the ceiling.

* * *

Sebastian's rage at the provocation unleashed in a display that surprised Joshua, and enforced the purpose for exposing the angel in the first place.

Penske had his hands up shielding him from the brilliance and the words. Joshua could see genuine fear; he could not have scripted it better.

It was time to end this. He looked over to Lucas, who conveyed one last request to warrior angel.

* * *

"Gaze upon me, human," said Sebastian.

Penske dropped his hands slightly in obedience. The being's eyes were no longer brown; they were glowing white. Penske's hands now began to shake.

"You would do well to listen to Joshua Arden, for he is your only salvation from this misguided crusade. Heed his warning, or suffer the fate of those unfortunate souls damned for eternity." Sebastian stepped aside to show Penske the final moments of Smith's consumption. He barely recognized the once big man as he clawed at the floor with withered, brittle hands trying to escape the black vortex. His screams were unmistakable though. Penske turned away, not wanting to see or hear anymore.

With another thunderclap, the darkness disappeared. Penske found himself pressed against the side wall to the far left of Granger with Daniels kneeling beside him. "Cap, what's going on? You were over there a second ago," he pointed toward the front of the room.

The disorientation started to leave as he stood to get his bearings. All his men were moving, weapons ready to address whatever came next. They no longer seemed to be divided now that Smith was gone.

Smith.

He looked down at his body. A memory flash of the bulging eyes and gnashing teeth being pulled through a swirling blackness rocked him, and he staggered.

Daniels grabbed hold of his arm. "Jeremy, are you okay?" He said softly.

"I'm fine. I'm good," he said shaking his head to clear the cobwebs.

Penske placed his hand on the wall to steady himself and felt a crack. He turned to look, and tracked the jagged scar of the wall up and across the ceiling. It ended right about where the man with the wings stood. That was real? How could that be? So, it wasn't a dream. How could so much time have passed for him, but not even a second for his men? Nothing made sense, but it happened, and he remembered.

Penske stood still; deep in thought about the line between reality and imagination. How he once understood that the simplicity of his pragmatic thinking would always be the familiar tether grounding him; keeping him in check when his chosen profession put him and his men in situations that would rip the minds of normal people to shreds. He wasn't so sure anymore; about that line. What just happened changed all of that. The crack was the proof that he wasn't going crazy, but coming to his senses.

He took a deep breath, then walked calmly to Kelly Granger; he knelt in front of her and placed his hands on her knees. "Ma'am, I am sorry for the harm that has come to you. I know that you're scared, but this is over now." He stood up and walked around behind her and started to remove her handcuffs.

Daniels grabbed his arm. "Cap, what are you doing?"

"I'm going to release her, Jim. What we're doing here is wrong. I believe she would be safer with the Jonah team."

Daniels' grip tightened. "That's not the mission. You said as much yourself when you had him executed," nodding toward Smith's unmoving body.

"I didn't *have* him executed; I planted a suggestion that his agenda was not the best choice, and gave Johnson a reason to see that. Smith's objective was to kill her. I do not have to explain myself to you!"

Penske tried to pull away, but the grip was like a vice holding him in place. "Daniels!" Penske yelled in pain. "Release me now, soldier!"

"Can't do that, captain," he said as he twisted his hand slightly.

There was an audible snap as Penske's arm bent sideways in an unnatural position. He screamed as Daniels picked him up by his mangled arm, and slammed him into the floor, leaving a splintered crater from the impact.

The other soldiers were shocked and readied their weapons. Daniels turned to square off against them, and they fired. The bullets had no effect, bouncing off as he moved towards them.

"Now fellas, is that any way to treat a friend?" He grinned in an abnormally contorted way. His features and shape began to morph; the eyes became black as coal. Daniels wasn't human, and the rest of the unit figured that out a little too late.

21

The Shape Master

Alice turned her head not understanding what she was seeing. Langston had a good idea though, and became horrified at the sight, and what he thought was coming.

"Kelan! Pull back Marseilles' team now!" Joshua shouted as he began to manipulate the real-time image.

"Starfish! Pull back to the stairwell and hold." Kelan said. The adrenaline was pumping through his system like a fuel-injected engine.

"Copy that," came the radio reply.

Kelan then began operating his own controls on the hard-light imagery. "Sanders! Send in the TAC team. Have them secure the first three floors then hold for further instructions." He hoped that he could contain or prevent any advancement on his teams' flank from the stairs. He didn't want to lose anyone else, and it looked like his guys would have enough to worry about with that ... he didn't even know what to call it.

Back on the top floor of Jonah International, Joshua zoomed in on the thing that used to be Daniels. It was transforming in mid stride; like something out of one of those cheesy, B-rated werewolf movies. It grabbed the barrel of one of the guns as the soldier fired point blank into the monster's chest. This time the bullets didn't bounce off but rather slammed into its target, ripping away clothes and chewing up flesh. It did not affect the monster's momentum, and it even seemed to be laughing as it jerked the weapon to one side. It then took its free claw-like hand and shoved it into the chest of the gun's owner. Alice screamed as the bloody claw emerged from the helpless Familiar's back.

What is this thing? Joshua had never seen a demon like this before. He quickly turned to Lucas, who had a cross look on his face as he watched the carnage. "Do you know what that is?"

"Máistir cruth," said Lucas in his native angelic Gaelic, muttering it as an aftermath of realization.

Joshua was still learning the dialect of the angels, so he partially understood the translation of one word. "Can you be a little more specific?"

"He is a shape master; a lower form of a demon, a brute with the ability to possess and control corporeal creatures, and not easily detectable," he said with disgust dripping off his tongue.

Of all the sad curses inflicted by the Chairman as punishment for their rebellion, the shape masters, as they are called, were stripped of the essence of who they once were. Mindless automatons with no will or memory. Bound to their demon leaders as slaves; and when necessary, expendable pawns.

It was not known to Lucas or his brothers for certain, why specific Fallen were chosen to exist in this state; only that these demons must have been selected for a reason. It was never theirs to question. After all, the punishments were always just. Though, some in the angelic realms had their suspicions based purely on their fallen brother's prior professions.

In the beginning, the demon leadership saw the mindless mishaps more as a nuisance rather than worthy of acceptance. All that changed when they realized the lowly demons could not be seen by their former brothers of the Light.

It appeared that a byproduct of removing their angelic essence was the ability to be indistinguishable from the form they possessed; virtually invisible to the supernatural realm. Which is why this one slipped passed both angels.

As with everything else in Joshua's ever dynamic role, he would have more questions for his guardian; that, like always, would have to wait for another time. His more immediate concern was the woman. "Lucas?"

"I have already called to him," he said, upset with himself for not anticipating the demon enforcer.

* * *

The shape master demon laughed with glee as it tore into its former comrades. The process of dismantling the soldiers in various ways amused it. Euphoric pleasure grew as it took its time with a few as they realized there was no way to kill it. The Daniels demon taunted them by allowing the now frightened men to attempt escaping through the sole door; only to pull them back and bat them around the room like a cat with a ball.

One by one, the demon killed its human prey with no evidence of remorse. As doing such, it could hear the screams of the mewling woman from the middle of the room, which broadened its already maniacal and contorted smile.

With the focus split between the soldiers, the demon was not paying as much attention when the screaming from behind had stopped.

* * *

Joshua watched the eerie stillness that was left once the screaming had finally died down. The three-dimensional scene played out as one would expect from a gore-filled horror film. The camera would pan towards the human remains, lingering just long enough for the nausea to reach the top of the throat; then focus on the monster as it came down off its rage-induced killing binge. It's breathing would slow as it turned to seek out its final victim. The camera would then zoom in on its face as the inhuman grin would start to form at the anticipation of its last kill. However, as with most slasher films, it is never as easy as the bad guy thought.

* * *

Had this been a typical psychopathic killer, it might have paused for a brief second wondering why the woman was no longer sitting shackled to the chair. Acting as an animal based on pure instinct though, the Daniels demon advanced towards its prey.

Kelly Granger was standing on the opposite end of the room facing the corner like a child in time out. Her head was slightly lobbed to one side in a relaxed position. She made no attempt to move at the sound of the thumping footsteps belonging to the approaching, growling monster.

As the Daniels demon came upon her, it raised its clawed hand and brought it down with all its might, only to be stopped inches from her body. Sebastian's powerful hand had grabbed the wrist of the dim-witted shape master with the speed of a striking black mamba.

The demon turned its coal-black eyes upon the warrior angel; not with the fear that normally accompanied those demons when confronted with the Inflixi Impetus, but rather outrage. This reaction showed its ignorance and the simple basic comprehension of its situation.

It growled as it attempted to pull its arm away from its aggressor, but to no avail. Sebastian yanked its arm to one side, then with a powerful thrust, punched the Daniels demon in the chest sending it hurtling at an unrealistic speed against the opposite wall.

Drywall and wood splintered as it struck with a force that would kill a normal human being; but the demon just pulled itself out of the partial imprint left from the impact, unscathed and angrier. It screamed and acted like a territorial gorilla, then charged the angel with reckless abandon.

* * *

Joshua watched this play out like another scene from an even worse movie. The seriousness of the events was starting to be overshadowed by all, what he thought, were theatrics. He had a pretty good idea that the mortal part of Daniels was unrecoverable. This would later be confirmed by Lucas and explained that as once a possession by a máistir cruth was complete, the human body of the possessed would be nothing more than a puppet. The soul already departed the stricken, as they are called by the angelic realm.

When Joshua had pulled up the dossiers of the paramilitary soldiers, Daniels background looked just like the others. There was no evidence that he was acting any different from normal prior to this mission. At what point did the possession take place? His former teammates, who now laid in pieces all around the room, obviously had no indication that this thing was not the person they knew.

As a human, Joshua expected not to be able to distinguish the difference, but was shaken that neither Lucas nor Sebastian could either. How could this thing walk, talk, and act like the human it took if the soul was gone? The flickering thought of zombie-type characteristics entered Joshua's mind, but he quickly dismissed that as ridiculous fiction. Although, what was happening right now, at one time could have been considered fiction as well. Angels and Demons; who would believe something like that exist?

But it did.

Supposing the zombie thing was a reality; the transformation is distinctive with little to no residual human characteristics. For all appearances, intents and purposes, this thing *was* Daniels.

How was he going to fight something like this?

His head started to hurt like it always did when confronted with these types of thoughts.

* * *

Sebastian stood his ground, not wavering in the face of the approaching monster. His sword remained at his side. Once the Daniels imposter reached him, Sebastian sidestepped the charging tackle, and used its weight against it to force its face into the wall.

The powerful angel wasted no time yanking the demon from its wall imprint into a choke hold. Struggling under the force of the hold, the demon lashed out in pitiful attempts to release itself. It sputtered as if gasping for breath, but Sebastian was not fooled. The human known as Daniels was no longer present, and this demon had no need for breathing. It was nothing more than an animal now that needed to be put out of its misery.

By the originating decree from the Most High, the permanent dispatching of all Fallen must be done with the holy objects given to each of the warriors within the Inflixi Impetus. As much as Sebastian's anger warranted choking the remaining life from this brute, it would not be permanently sealed in Infernotous to await judgment if he merely snapped its neck.

In one swift motion, he released the brute with a twirl, sending it crashing back into the wall. The warrior then pulled a dagger from a sheath behind his back. As he flipped it in his hand to the desired position, the blade began to pulsate in the familiar glow of blue. The Daniels demon snarled one last time before Sebastian plunged the dagger into its forehead.

The monster immediately stopped moving. It seemed to deflate like a balloon as residue of ash poured off the human shape and vaporized. The husk of what was left of Daniels fell to the floor; a stark representation of a dehydrated, shriveled up form. Those who might examine it would liken it to mummified remains.

"Abomination," said Sebastian looking down. He held out his hand, and the dagger flew into it. He replaced it in the sheath and turned towards Kelly Granger, who was still motionless in the corner. He lifted his head in communication and placed his hand upon her.

* * *

"Starfish, this is Command. The threat has been neutralized. You may retrieve the package in preparation for transport," cracked their radio receivers.

Marseilles and Ingram looked at each other with caution. It had been more than twenty-seconds since anything had been heard from the room.

When the screaming had first started, all Starfish team members could clearly hear the terror through their COMs. Some of them opted quickly to change frequency as their stomachs began to turn at the gurgling and snapping. Thankfully, Command saw fit to disconnect the link shortly thereafter.

Marseilles felt helpless in the face of his opposition's horrific situation. Compassion was an emotion that was not frequently used in his line of work, but hearing the mercenaries call out for help, even when the COMs were not active, was hard for him and his team. Especially the police officers; something like this tested the boundaries of their motto to 'protect and serve'. Those soldiers were the enemy, but no one should have to go through *that* nightmare.

He waited a few extra seconds to make sure that no sound or radio chatter was coming out of the room. "Let's move."

Ingram nodded. Using hand signals, he motioned on the team from the stairwell towards the room where Kelly Granger was located. Everyone approached with caution, wading through the debris and organic matter from the explosion. Once at the door, Peterson pressed his ear against it listening for any sounds of movement or activity on the other side. Satisfied with radio confirmation and audio and visual cues, Marseilles took the lead, and slowly opened the heavy, wooden barrier.

He swallowed slightly as he surveyed the room and what was left of the soldiers. His eyes then stopped on the young lady standing in the far corner. She was facing them. She appeared to have abrasions on her forearms, and what looked like blood splattered in various places across her clothing. Given what she had witnessed, the catatonic look on her face was understandable.

He approached her slowly and spoke softly. "Miss Granger, my name is Richard Marseilles. I am with Jonah Protective Services. We were sent here by Dr. Joshua Arden to take you to safety."

He handed his weapons to Officer Callahan, then calmly reached for his credentials for verification. He wasn't sure if she registered who he was, or even saw him, as he shifted his badge into her line of sight.

He was four to five feet from her as he replaced his credentials back into his jacket. Afterwards, he held out his arms as a father would to his daughter. She slowly lifted her gaze to meet his eyes, then started to weep as she fell into his arms.

He held her up, supporting her as she gripped him tightly and sobbed. "It's okay now," he said softly. He turned his head slightly. "Get the TAC team and medical up here ASAP."

"Copy that," said Ingram as he lifted his sleeve.

In less than a minute, various first responders from JPS and Associates were swarming over the floor.

The young lady was triaged and treated, then carefully placed on a gurney for transport. Marseilles did not leave Granger's side the entire time as she gripped his hand like a scared little girl. Once they started to move her, he tried to pull away, but she tightened her grip. "Please, don't leave me."

He looked down at her thinking his own daughter was about her age. "Okay. I'll stay with you," he said gently; seeing the face of his little girl in her pleading eyes.

On the way passed other agents, he saw Ingram, who came over to walk with them. "How're they holding up?" Marseilles said gesturing to the three officers from their team. They were all huddled together, giving statements to JPS agents, and getting once-overs by first responders.

"Oh, they're shaken up." Ingram responded.

"Understandably," came Marseilles' deadpan reply. Without so much as a glance his way, he told Ingram to make sure they signed the non-disclosure agreement to prevent any information leakage, and get them scheduled for a full debriefing. "Make sure they understand that they now work for JPS. Inform them that they will be on administrative leave until the mission assessment and background investigations are complete."

Ingram smiled as his boss continued to issue orders. Marseilles caught the expression out of the corner of his eye. "What?"

"You act like this is my first day working with you. I know your routine."

"It's not *my* routine; it's standard protocol, and I'll thank you to keep your opinions to yourself," he replied in a calm military fashion. He looked down at the young woman still holding his hand. "I will be accompanying Miss Granger to the hospital, so I am leaving you in command. I will not be able to provide my lead assessment to Director Tindal."

Marseilles motioned for the medics to stop, then turned facing Ingram. "You will need to make the report," he said in a look that Ingram understood meant he should pay close attention to the next words out of his bosses' mouth. "By my count, the collateral damage assessment is total," meaning the structure and human casualties. "The director will ask for your appraisal." That meant that the director will be asking for on-site disposition recommendations, which was a technical phrase for the level of effort for clean-up.

Marseilles paused for a second to make sure Ingram understood his next sentence. "Tell the director that a Level Six sanitization is my recommendation. He will ask you for a confirmation, and you will repeat that my recommendation is for a Level Six sanitization."

Ingram's semi-serious demeanor changed to all business. He knew the protocols for after-action containment, just like Marseilles. Their line of work, and the sensitivity of security, warranted many possibilities, all of which could only be answered with varied levels of cover-ups and clean-ups requiring any number of resources from media to military enforcement. Each category was assigned a level and a number. A Level Six sanitization meant an unrecoverable site. No clean up would be possible.

"Copy that," replied Ingram.

Marseilles nodded. "Tell the director that it needs to happen sooner than later."

"Understood."

His boss softened a bit. "You did good work here today, Bill; all of you. I will make sure the director knows that."

Ingram half-smiled. "Thank you, sir."

Marseilles' no-nonsense attitude returned. "Get this wrapped up quickly, and get our people out. The director will most likely have a team here ASAP."

With that, Marseilles, Granger, and the medics moved one way while Ingram went toward the other.

* * *

Joshua's office was cleared out; his previous business before the harrowing event was forgotten.

Langston and Alice politely excused themselves after Granger was confirmed to be in transit to the nearest Jonah-friendly hospital. Lucas had even made his exit after stating he was called to another matter.

Joshua had just finished a discussion with Kelan regarding the cleanup strategy for the precinct debacle from this morning. Kelan explained that the assessment concluded the site, and situation was a total loss. The best way to contain the damage, and bring any media attention to a swift close, was to stage an accidental explosion. It would take care of the bodies and minimizing any external investigations of the structure, which was riddled with bullets.

His demolitions team was already placing the appropriate charges to simulate a gas main explosion. The package would come complete with controlled gas fires along the principal lines around the precinct to make the story more plausible. His team would work with the city Associates to control the burn to ensure that the fire destroyed the structure and its contents.

All officers who perished that day would receive the full benefits of their positions from the city, just as if they died in the line of duty.

The other officers whom either left before the shootings began, or happen to make it out during the assault, would be dealt with like any other Familiar or Undeclared; a paid stipend to keep their mouths shut, complete with contractual documents and a clause to deal with any violators. Monitoring and enforcement of the arrangements would not be an issue: Jonah had a lot of resources.

Joshua's head was already hurting from the stress of the morning, so he readily agreed to Kelan's plan. He was now left alone staring out the all-too-familiar window of his high-rise office.

He had done a lot of that lately; lost in his thoughts of so many situations and happenings, that he pondered writing them down to keep them all straight. With a slight smirk, he thought why even bother. A mere wave of his hand, or a simple request to Sentinel, could easily project everything in his head into spectacular swirling images. All, of course, would be categorized and indexed, with probability statistics, threat assessments, and whatever else metric was appropriate. Everything floating in an orderly fashion before him awaiting his next command. He shook his head at the absurdity and overkill of technology. Whatever happened to simple paper in a manila folder? A pen or pencil to jot down notes?

For a moment, he wondered if Sentinel *could* read his mind. Joshua knew there was more to *him*, as Lucas had referred to the super intelligence, rather than just processing computer algorithms. If it wasn't a computer, what else could it be? Joshua had his ideas, although he was concerned that it might be a bit more far-fetched than anything else within his reality. To be honest though, what would be considered *too* unbelievable at this point? Anyone looking in from the outside would think his life was a complete circus anyway. Why not throw another flaming hoop act in on it?

Frustrated, he began to turn in his swivel chair like a child; again, something he had done a lot lately.

Who would he even ask? He had plagued Lucas with so many questions over the last few years, and received vague, and sometimes nonsensical responses in return, that he was no longer sure it was worth the effort. If every answer to his questions were always going to be like some sort of a quiz, again— why bother. His growing responsibilities were wearing heavier every day; he simply did not need to be tested anymore. He felt after all these years, that he had put in his time; paid his dues. The questions and answers sessions began to feel like a game that was no longer fun.

How much would he have to endure before he just got simple answers to his simple questions?

He sat up a bit in his chair. Joshua needed something more concrete. For the first time, he was determined to get the answers without butting his head up against a supernatural wall.

The question was, how would he go about it? Sentinel still responded to his commands and requests, although as of late, it felt like there was a bit more resistance to the probing. He figured Sentinel's loyalty would always be to the Chairman; who rightly doled out information as needed. He was the only player in this game who knew everything. Joshua understood that, and it was as it should be. But that still didn't mean Sentinel couldn't be used in the normal analytical sense.

Joshua swiveled one last time then faced his desk. "Sentinel."

"Yes, sir," came the voice of ever-present, and now sentient intelligence.

"Please display the statistics of transitions and consumptions."

A multicolored file in various hues of green and red swirled in front of him. Joshua immediately rolled his eyes at the tech. "Could you please display on my desktop monitor?"

The three-dimensional hard-light images quickly slid into the inlay of his flat, shiny desk. "Thank you," he said in a polite tone.

He began making swirly motions on his desk as he manipulated files and images. For anyone who might come in the office, it would simply appear that he was making elaborate drawings with his fingers across the surface.

Joshua continued to review, opening and closing documents, and typing notes as necessary based on his analysis. Then, in an uncharacteristic move, Sentinel asked, "Is there anything I can help you with sir?"

Joshua raised an eyebrow at this. He sat back in his chair slightly. "You know; I believe that is the first time that you have offered to help me unsolicited."

"I am capable of sensing your every need."

Joshua laughed. "I find that hard to believe as when I have asked for your help before, you have either chosen not to respond, or told me that it; what were the words that you used, —" said Joshua tapping his chin "—oh yeah, 'wasn't within the confines of your parameters.'"

There were a few seconds of silence.

"Joshua, I am only allowed to give you the information that is necessary at *that* moment in time. Much like Lucaous, my directives bind me. I am truly sorry that is hard for you."

The casualness of the response by Sentinel took him aback. It was talking to him like a conflicted human.

For the first time in months of feeling in command, and as the leader of the "earthly" resistance, he was speechless, befuddled at the tenderness within Sentinel's voice. Joshua could truly sense the sorrow of not being able to assist him. This was a new thing, and made Joshua think about how he might not have given the intelligence the credit that it deserved. All the sudden he felt he could no longer call it an 'it'. Sentinel was not just a computer program. Joshua didn't believe that it was a sophisticated artificial intelligence either. If the Chairman created this, there had to be more to it than just software and lights. Joshua decided right there and then that he was going to treat him as such.

"Sentinel, I'm not mad at you. I'm sorry if I hurt your feelings with my remark. I am simply frustrated at not being able to get the information I need, or at least, I *think* I need, to effectively perform and complete what the Chairman has tasked me to do."

"It's okay, sir, no apology necessary."

Joshua could hear the softness in Sentinel's voice. He almost sensed the forgiving smile behind it. "Can you do me a favor?"

"I will try," replied Sentinel.

"Now that our relationship is taking on a different dynamic, can you please stop calling me sir?"

Sentinel chuckled. "I think I can arrange that."

Joshua's eyes widened at yet another new emotion. He smiled, thinking that Sentinel could probably see it. "That's all I can ask for; well ... apart from everything else."

Sentinel laughed.

Joshua was going to like this relationship.

"Now, is there something I can help you with?" His new friend asked.

"Yes; can you please give me the data on any activity, criminal or otherwise, with spikes in supernatural events?"

As Joshua was going through the transitions and consumptions files, he was looking at specific differences in the geographical pockets of data where activity was higher or lower than normal. The clusters of death, and in some cases, the lack of, interested him.

As he reviewed these files over the years to see the Associates and the Familiars ratios, the margins of activity, whether the Undeclared had made a choice, or standard mortal life had come to term, had always presented a predictable pattern. If this pattern fell within, what he was told, acceptable limits, there was no need for concern. Over the last few months though, Joshua had noticed swells in activity. He wanted to know why.

Joshua was pleasantly rewarded with one file after another from Sentinel. As per usual, Sentinel catalogued and organized files in the preferred way that Joshua was used to preforming his analysis. His initial grin at finally being able to retrieve information that he didn't think he would get, began to fade as he thumbed through the documents. The geographical locations from this new information was odd. In certain instances, where one human died, a cluster of supernatural activity spiked. He expected to see something like mass human casualties in situations like that, such as the police precinct earlier. More mortal deaths equaled more supernatural activity, or so was the logical progression of thought. That was not the case at all here.

There were too many files for him to go through one by one to see all the anomalies. "Sentinel, please cross reference transition and consumption activity with both supernatural spikes and anomalous events."

"Query parameters?" Sentinel asked.

"Out of the ordinary criminal activity, unexplained deaths, unusual thefts, and background oddities." What Joshua meant by the last one, was any situation or person with a background that might be of interest. Of course, Sentinel did not need any explanation; he knew what the young master wanted.

The computational sorting only took a few seconds, then Joshua's desk cleared. One by one, certain files came into view. As Joshua opened them, the alarm with the blinking red light in the back of his head began to sound. Individually, these events meant nothing, but looking at all of them together …

"Sentinel, I need these printed out." He had always been better at analysis if he had something in his hand with which he could jot down notes.

"Joshua, I recommend a different course of action."

For the third time today, Joshua was surprised by his new friend. "Can you tell me why?" He said with concern.

"The only way to maintain a secret is to ensure that no one else knows. If you print these files, someone *will* surely find out."

Joshua thought for a moment. Why would he call this data, a secret? "I'm right; there *is* something to this information," he said. "Something that will change everything?"

"Yes, but you must be careful."

Normally, in this information technology age, keeping data on a server, or in the cloud, would provide a point of reference for anyone who wanted to gather intelligence. Hackers today could always find a way to get information if they knew where to look. Sometimes, old-school tactics such as pen and paper were the best. No one could ever breach Sentinel's security. For him to state that printing these files would be a bad idea, meant something. That also meant that Sentinel *knew* something.

"Are we in danger?" He said as an afterthought. Fighting the enemy when he didn't have to worry about his team and family was one thing; it didn't seem fair to have to deal with something like that too.

Sentinel's ease with his responses brought a more comforting feeling, but didn't take away from the seriousness. "You could be if it becomes known that you possess this data."

"I will need to access this for further analysis at any time." Once it came out, Joshua knew it was a stupid thing to say.

"It will remain safe with me," finished Sentinel.

"Do you know what's going on here?" Joshua asked with trepidation.

"I believe the answers you seek will get here quicker than you think."

"That sounded like it was straight from a fortune cookie," said Joshua.

Just then, Lucas appeared. Joshua thought it strange that Sentinel did not forewarn him. But as he would soon find out, the warning would not have prepared him anyway.

"Joshua," said Lucas. His look was stoic and unemotional. Joshua almost felt like he was going to get reprimanded for something in which he was not aware.

"Yes?" He stood slowly.

"Your presence has been requested by the Council of 12."

"The board of directors?" Joshua said slowly; clearly stunned at the statement.

Jonah International's Board of Directors was, in every sense, the governing body of the publicly traded stock for JOI. As far as the world of corporations and businesses knew, the Jonah International representatives established corporate management and policies on behalf of their shareholders, just like any other industry. What the world did not know, was that the mist that veiled their perception of Jonah's corporate structure, held 12 members who were the Chairman's right-hand. To Joshua's knowledge, and discussions with Malcolm Holden, Jonah's CEO; no one has ever met, or been invited to meet with the Board of Directors.

Until now.

They have asked for Joshua personally.

He continued looking at Lucas for any sign of what this may be concerning, but was getting nothing. He nodded his head in acceptance of this information. "Okay, when?"

"Now."

22

Not you, Silly Man

In a backlit lot on Otto Reuchlinweg St., workers had just finished transferring dock shifts, or were heading home for the evening. It was foggy, dank, and not the kind of weather that promoted a pleasant walk. The chill was only slight, but held a specific crispness that caused those unfortunate few to walk swiftly to their destinations. The rising sea level was not the only global warming affect in Western Europe touching Rotterdam, Netherlands.

A smart choice of location on their part; a semi-secluded area that was sparsely populated in an unpopular part of town, where unwanted attention from prying eyes, both human and electronic, would be hard given the dismal atmosphere.

This meeting location had finally been agreed upon after weeks of delay due to one issue or another. The thieves said that the high pro-filed theft had garnered them status on Interpol's most wanted; that they couldn't afford to leave Taipei until things had cooled down a bit. They managed to keep pushing out the delivery date due to a perceived threat that they were being followed. The last part was probably true, but that was due to their own foolishness documented on camera.

She shook her head again reviewing the surveillance video showing the Englishman's poor attempt at stealth during the robbery. At one point near the end, just before he shot the guard, it looked like he had stared straight into the camera.

Idiot.

During the initial negotiations to secure the two thieves' specialized services, the man seemed more boastful and condescending; the woman had dutifully kept her mouth shut and just listened. By observation, it appeared the that his partner had opinions that would most likely be ignored, so simply watched the man as he talked up how great they were at what they did. He was a cocky self-righteous prat that thought more of himself than he was worth. *No matter*, she thought. He would be taken care of accordingly.

The woman put the tablet down in the seat beside her and stared out the back window of her comfortably warm black limousine. She had been waiting 10 minutes; which was too long for a person in her position. Inara studied her watch. The conference call was in 15 minutes. She preferred to acquire the fusion device beforehand to make her report complete.

There were three men in the car with her, including the driver. One was wearing dark sunglasses, a black suit, and sitting opposite of her when his cell phone rang. He flipped it open and listened, then simply responded with "Děkuji". Upon hanging up the phone he nodded towards his boss.

"Buďte připraveni přejít na můj signál," she said in Czech telling him to be ready when she signaled, then grudgingly exited the car.

The weather was unacceptable, as Inara pulled the collar of her coat up around her cashmere scarf. Her pristine classic demure was in direct contrast with her favorite knee-high chunky heeled boots. Fashion that was usually important, was now, not a great deal of concern as she was meeting with no one of significance. She hated the patent pumps required of her other job, so the boots were an easy choice.

She casually strolled to the middle of the abandoned lot and waited. Even with dismal visibility, she could see the two British thieves talking in their van less than one hundred feet away.

* * *

"All I'm saying is don't hack her off!" Victoria said, exasperated at Nigel's attitude.

"My dear," he replied in genuine surprise. "Do you really think that I would jeopardize our nest egg this close to the finish?"

"A bit, yeah," she said with the side look as she scanned out the windshield.

Nigel played it off as he lifted his leg, placing his foot on the middle console of their stolen 1977 Dodge b200 van. "Look love, all's *I'm* saying is that they're willing to pay 1.4 million for this little device." He flipped it in his hand like a ball. "It might be worth a bit more if we ask."

"Nigel, we took this job in agreement for the 1.4. I don't think these people are to be trifled with," she said with a fearful look, remembering the lady and her no-nonsense job offer. "I would like to make it out of this alive," she said more softly.

His flippant attitude softened a bit as he noticed the visual cue. His gaze drifted from her eyes down to the purplish-blue bruise on the side of her face. For a split second, he felt bad that he retaliated. Nevertheless, she shouldn't have hit him. She got what she deserved.

Not that he was one to admit it, Nigel *did* have a bit more understanding of her cautious attitude based on what they've endured over the last few weeks. It would most definitely be a challenge to enjoy the fortunes that they had amassed during their careers while looking over their shoulders everywhere they went. He couldn't deny that they both were a little on edge.

He grabbed her hand. "Don't worry, love. We will."

After their robbery of Advanced IntelliCorp, the two thieves couldn't risk using any of their aliases trying to leave Taipei; due mostly in part, to Nigel's sloppy work during the heist.

In less than twenty minutes after gathering him from the dramatic parachute escape from the 56th floor of the corporate and commercial monolith known as Taipei 101, facial recognition of the company's intelligence system had matched him, and the local authorities put out the international equivalent of an all-points bulletin.

As part of her surveillance tactics while Nigel did the job, Victoria had set up a communications array to cover all police band activity. When they were pulling away from the corporate district, his name came across an audio frequency. Victoria slammed on the brakes of her service van converted to a surveillance post, and made her way back to her computer systems. After punching in a few keystrokes, there on her screen, was Nigel's face, plain as day on Interpol's most wanted. One click to open the details showed two shots; a smug self-confident picture from a previous arrest, and the other one of him looking directly into a security camera no more than thirty minutes previously.

She knew it was only a matter of time before they connected her to him.

The fury had built up in her at the sight and sound of his name so rapidly, that as she made her way back to the driver seat, she punched him square in the face.

The hit that she took in return was only now slightly visible.

Now, they both sat in their stolen van with the motor idling about to make the exchange of their lives; but neither understood the magnitude of their situation, or for that fact, their part in changing the face of humanity.

The little device that Nigel so casually tossed around, was a biometric fusion accelerator. It allowed re-atomization of molecules, whether organic or technical in nature. The mechanism was quite literally the key to creating a new viable and sustainable particle element. It was but a small component in a much larger system that would produce a hybrid between two or more of those, or any other particles.

A small group of people outside of Inara's employer, Ministry, knew the applications of this capability. Only the sane ones could see the devastating global impact if used incorrectly.

If Nigel were as smart as he thought, he could parlay his asking price up to three or four times the original contract amount. Not that it would matter in the end; some sort of working civilization involving monetary trade would have to be around for him to spend it.

* * *

The walk from his office into the hallway felt surreal. Like he was almost floating on air, and his legs were nonexistent. Joshua knew he was standing though because his legs were shaking slightly within his pants. He was certain if he stopped for any reason, he would collapse as they would not be able to carry the weight; not his mass, but that of the world.

As he and Lucas passed the double doors, the guardian angel's wardrobe transformed in the blink of an eye. He was now in a very sharp gray business suit posing as the clean-cut Lucas Aldridge, liaison to the Chairman of the Board of Jonah International. Joshua, still transfixed by this request for the board meeting, didn't even notice the change or Lucas's presence. His assistant Jillian, on the other hand, did.

"Mr. Aldridge?! I was not aware that you were meeting with Dr. Arden today." She stood up from her desk awkwardly, then began shuffling through her papers and Joshua's calendar to see if the meeting were registered, and she forgot.

Lucas smiled as he shut the office door behind him. "It's okay, Jillian. It was an impromptu visit."

She smiled back slightly confused. "I didn't even see you go in."

"Well, you must have been away from your desk. I did not see you when I came in either." Not a lie, but a convergence of two separate truths.

Jillian continued to smile as both, he and Joshua, headed down the hall.

Lucas looked over to Joshua when they were out of earshot, "Breathe."

"Huh, what?"

"Joshua, it is okay. This meeting was inevitable."

Somewhat embarrassed, he said, "I know; it's just ... There was no warning. I mean, how long have you known that it was going to be today, I mean right now?"

Lucas guided him towards the elevator banks. "Oh, about thirty of your human seconds before I told you."

Joshua's eyes blew up as round as a ball, "Are you kidding me?!"

"Have you ever known me to kid, as you say?"

"Sometimes; and most of those, I don't think you know that you're doing it."

Lucas rolled his eyes slightly. "I have been in existence since the beginning of all time, and I still fail to understand some of the human idiosyncrasies." An elevator door opened as they approached.

Both stopped short and faced each other. It was very quiet where they stood. No one was seen or heard in the intersections of the corridors or office space. It was as if both Lucas and Joshua were the only ones on the floor. Normally, a situation like that would provide a sort of eerie feeling, but Joshua's experience over the years made this a normal part of his day.

He started fidgeting with his coat and tie. It was reminiscent of his interview day in that horrible suit when he met his future bride, Melina, for the very first time.

"Joshua, you must calm down. This is what you have been awaiting. The plan is about to be revealed." Lucas reached up and placed his hand on his young master's shoulder. The calming effect that was intended began coursing through his body. Joshua's knees were no longer shaking. His cool demeanor began to return; the nervousness abated.

He looked at his friend, "Thank you."

Lucas smiled and slightly nodded. "You are most welcome."

"Okay," said Joshua clapping his hands together. "Shall we?" He entered the elevator, but Lucas remained in the hallway. Joshua stared at his escort expectantly.

"This meeting is for you alone."

The nervousness began to return as Joshua opened his mouth to protest.

Lucas held up a hand. "Joshua, what needs to be said is between you and the Council. Each of us has our role. Mine is not involved here."

Joshua thought for a moment, then closed his mouth and stood straight. "Can you at least tell me where I am going?"

Lucas smiled. "Sentinel knows."

"Of course he does," said Joshua as the elevator doors closed.

* * *

While Nigel was making his way to meet Inara, he casually brought his hand up and scratched the back of his head. The movement held a twofold purpose; one to check the communications ear bud, and the other to see if he was targeted.

"Anything?" He said into this earpiece.

"There are no little red dots, if that's what you mean," said Victoria a bit annoyed at his narrow-minded thinking.

Nigel thought he was slick in making a demand for this location on this night. He had studied the weather patterns for quite some time in hopes that the murky atmosphere was something that could be used to his advantage. The rationale was that it would be easier to spot laser-guided weapons, and much harder to see through a scope site for long-range sniper shots; if their benefactor was so inclined to resort to those tactics. The middle of the semi secluded parking lot allowed him full 360° visibility to any approaching threats on foot.

Victoria sneered at the resentful thoughts. Of all the things that he had considered, what if one of those actually happened? It's not like he could keep anyone from shooting him whether he was spotted with a scope or a laser. What was she supposed to do? Jump out and wave at the sniper? *Oh, please don't shoot this poor idiot.*

As far as seeing anyone approaching from any direction, he wasn't the biggest or strongest, or most athletic person she had ever known. He talked a pretty good game, but would not be able to back up anything should a larger, or for that fact, and average size man threatened him physically. He had a gun, sure, but would have to be quicker than his adversary, who most assuredly would have a weapon as well.

He had it all figured out, mused Victoria. She watched him strut closer to the scary lady; ever cocky and full of self-confidence. *A complete sham*, she thought. All that pontification on the outside, when she knew very well that he was a scared, paranoid, little child too afraid to show any type of rational emotion, on the inside. She often thought of the external shell just breaking away, and a little baby in a soggy diaper, sucking his thumb, curled in a fetal position rolling out, kind of like that icky goo inside of a Cadbury chocolate egg.

Victoria slightly smiled at the thought of—

A sharp pain hit the inside of her head; she grabbed it out of reflex.

Not again! She thought, knowing what was coming next.

The face.

"No," she moaned, as she began rocking back-and-forth.

The guard from the Taipei building began flashing like lightning in her mind. "No, no, no ..."

She tried to open her eyes to get a fix on Nigel; giving her focus to remain on mission and watch, but she couldn't stop the headache.

That poor guard's face continued to pound at her from every angle. Each time was slightly different. A view from the monitor as she watched Nigel shoot him. Another like she was standing next to them both, and the worst of all; one where she pulled the trigger herself, and his head snapping backwards.

Victoria felt the guilt of the poor man's death as if she was the one who killed him. She *was* responsible though. Her actions lead to the murder of this innocent man.

Nigel was a wild card, uncontrollable in his urges and snap decisions. If not the poor guard, it would've happened to someone else. Regardless, she was as much to blame as he was. Had they not taken this job, that guard would still be alive. Had they planned the theft on another night, that guard would still be alive. Had there been a sixty-second difference in timing, that guard would still be alive. Had Nigel not taken a gun against Victoria's wishes, that guard would still be alive.

The remorse for what had happened became so overwhelming for her that it was now unbearable; not only over the poor guard, but lately for everything she had ever done that was wrong. For weeks, she had been experiencing a lethal combination of guilt, headaches, and sadness over the waste of life that she, herself, had become. She found herself spiraling so quickly, the flood of emotions drove her to think dark thoughts.

In the last couple of days, Victoria seriously contemplated suicide. She had no way of knowing that those thoughts were not of her own making, but heavily influenced by the evil surrounding her.

Snapping at another surge of pain inside her head, she reached for the Smith and Wesson revolver tucked neatly between the old console and her tattered bucket seat.

* * *

The less than perfect weather conditions did not distract from the gathering of demons. Airowyn arrived a few moments earlier; not surprised at the growing turnout. In fact, it appeared that the dismal setting added to their warped sense of joy over what was about to happen.

Each of these significant events in which the celestial scribe had witnessed, were all part of an elaborate plan of the enemy; a plan not readily known by angelic or human forces, but understood as a coming plot to further the enemy's own evil cause. They worked cleverly with their human agents to orchestrate all in service to their masters with little or no interference from the Light. The only signs of interest in their activities came in the form of the lone angel, Airowyn, who simply observed; nothing more, nothing less. The angelic guardian posed no threat unless otherwise provoked; and even then, his actions of defense came in a mighty show of power from the Inflixi Impetus.

In each instance, curiosity from the demon ranks was always about what the angel wanted or whether the angel would attempt to meddle in their affairs. What they failed to understand in all their inquisitions was *why* the angel was there.

Airowyn proceeded to watch the skies as the demons continued to amass. They kept filing in as if it were a sporting event at a large venue.

* * *

Nigel heard the moaning in his earpiece. *What is she prattling on about?* Within talking distance of the mysterious benefactor, he couldn't afford to let the woman in front of him see any weakness within his team, so Nigel decided to ignore Victoria.

As he came to a stop, both, he and Inara stared at each other expectantly. He watched her intently, putting on a show of bravado waiting for her to make the first move. Under the exterior of the false courage, he eagerly hoped that her move would be a simple exchange of product and payment.

He was trying to figure out how he could negotiate for a higher price when she spoke.

"Did you bring it?" She said in her European accent.

Nigel hesitated. "It's close."

She was unmoving; stoic in her stance. He couldn't seem to get any kind of an emotional read on her.

"By close, I hope you mean in that van."

He casually glanced over his shoulder then looked back to her.

"Otherwise," she continued, "you will have wasted my time."

The implied result of 'wasting her time' hung in the air like the dense, murky fog surrounding them. He got a read on her now.

"Of course, love, that is what I meant," he smarmed charmingly.

Inara's detest for this man was growing exponentially the more he talked. Although she had an appreciation for an English accent, his specific cockney spin made it sound like fingernails on a chalkboard.

Her hands thrust deeply into her coat pockets; she was still unmoving. "I am on a schedule."

For someone as dense as Nigel when it came to grasping meaning from a woman, he again understood the implication. But it was now or never.

"Our contract was for a pretty hefty sum," he said. "Why is that little thing so important to you?"

Inara tried not to smile as she had expected this.

When Ministry contracted for the theft of the accelerator, the fee for services was debated among the syndicate members. Some argued that the price should reflect the expertise, while others contended that if the payment were too high, it would provoke curiosity and questions, both of which could not be afforded in the long-term plan. The fact that the stupid man in front of her was probably going to attempt to negotiate a higher fee, only confirmed the latter.

"The contract also stipulated that there were no questions," she responded.

It looked to Nigel like she had a slight hesitation in trying to find the right words. *This may actually work,* he thought.

Of course, like everything else he thought he understood, he was mistaken. "Fair enough, but it seems that it may be worth a bit more seeing as you've waited this long," he gestured around with open palms, "and you agreed to meet here after weeks of delay."

"The delay was not on our part."

"Exactly," he said in an 'aha' exclamation. "My partner and I were holding all the proverbial cards, and yet you were still willing to wait until we could extradite ourselves from the local inquest."

"More like an international manhunt."

"You say 'potato'..." he said in a gesture of charm. "The point being, that whatever that little device is, you cannot proceed forward with your *nefarious* plan." He finished in finger quotes. Nigel puffed his chest a bit and paced as he now thought himself the alpha with the upper-hand.

The irony of his motivation for more money, was overshadowed by lack of understanding the bigger picture. Inara didn't doubt for a second that this man's intellect did not extend beyond petty thievery, but he had to have surely considered that the ultimate outcome might be less than he expected. Even if she was going to pay him, he wouldn't be able to do anything with it.

Her gaze was intense. "I would tread carefully going forward."

His cockiness seemed to die down a bit; stopping at her words.

"Your hand is not as good as you think," she finished in a card game vernacular.

Nigel turned and faced her as his eyes began moving from side to side. He was smart enough to recognize a threat when he heard it. The intimidation of her saying it, only intensified in his mind as it reeled with all the wrong outcomes. Suddenly, his selection for this eerie meeting place took on a whole new meaning. Where only a few moments ago, it gave him the security of cover and mission completion; it now served as a backdrop for what could be, the last moments of his life. Victoria's assessment of the diapered baby in icky goo started to surface.

"My partner and I have been under quite a bit of stress over the last few weeks due to the," he paused for a moment, "results of the job."

"You went in ill-prepared, and underestimated the company's surveillance capabilities," she said matter-of-fact.

Nigel sort of bobbed his head as a sign of agreement. "Possibly."

"You looked straight into the security camera as if it were the May Ball," she said, referring to the closest thing to a British version of an American prom.

Inara saw the hesitation and discomfort in Nigel's posture at the accusation. She proceeded to provide just a bit more information outside of his pay grade. After all, it wouldn't matter what he knew in the end.

"What you took will change the face of the world."

He froze. "How do you mean?"

"Mr. Mandeville, you and Miss Yeatts are providing us a key component to genetic manipulation; an ability to create a permanent construct that will redefine humanity forever."

Nigel stared at Inara in bewilderment. He wasn't sure how to react against the thought of his participation in global change, or how this woman knew his and Victoria's real last names.

For the first time in their meeting, Inara shifted her weight then walked two steps forward. "My employer has no patience for inept performance, unwanted attention, or theatrics of those who fail to deliver." She stared deeply into his eyes. "I have even less."

Inara took one more step forward. "We will have the device, with or without the agreed payment. The choice is yours."

Casually pulling her hand out of her coat pocket, she checked her watch. "You have about sixty-seconds to decide."

* * *

The angelic scribe known as Airowyn, commissioned by the Chairman to witness these significant events, took notice and count of the ranks and demonic attendees for what would be the last transaction on his ethereal list.

During these times, he had thought about how he would record each sequence of happenings. It occurred to him that they were no more than simple transactions as General Wyck's lieutenant had stated during their last encounter. These objects, whether intended for good or ill, belonged to an original owner or creator, and was subsequently stolen by, or given to, another party. The death of humans or demons notwithstanding, the objects moved from one hand to another; a transaction. Therefore, his observations would be in a linear, chronological format that culminated with the completion of said transaction.

Of all the exchanges that he had witnessed thus far, none had come without a sacrifice or a trail of tears for those who served the Light. Of course, tears and screams of repentance came for the humans, both Familiar and Undeclared alike, after their demise, but as it has been foretold; decisions must be made by everyone. There are no exceptions.

Airowyn noticed Wyck alongside the human woman as she and the man talked. The demon commander was one short in his entourage due to a lieutenant demon's immediate and decisive demise at the hand of the mighty warrior known as Mace.

The angelic historian took no joy or comfort in one less bothersome enemy, but the resulting impact and impression left by the last two encounters with his brothers from the Inflixi Impetus now placed him in a celebrity status. The understanding was now widespread that this humble angel was to be given a wide berth with no provocation of any kind.

Wyck's remaining lieutenant looked around with a wary eye. He seemed to be less than thrilled to be exposed in the open; most likely due to his memory of his comrade's ignorance and disobedience. Although he did not appear as stupid as his colleague, it brought no comfort to the demon's confidence that this exchange would be as easy as his superior thought.

Off to the side, cowering at the cackling and screeching, was the little wispy demon called Blurr. Airowyn was not surprised, but intrigued at the insignificant demon's presence. He wondered if Wyck had taken favor of his boldness and somewhat bravery from their last encounter, and let him attend, what the demonic clan would probably deem, a significant victory over the Host.

Knowing what the angel knew about the demon commander's methods, he would expect some type of underlying strategy or purpose. There was never anything straightforward when it came to the enemy's version of kindness or reward. It was always a plus to show off in front of underlings as well.

The angel stood right at the forefront with the blackness swirling around him as the humans continued their dialogue.

* * *

Nigel's panic at the countdown made him shift into a slight crouch. To his amazement at both the lack of warning from Victoria, and the visibility conditions, he found an intense beam of green light aimed directly at his chest; most likely prompted by his sudden movement. His eyes followed the beam back to its point of origin, but it seemed to drift from his chest upward into nothingness. The dense fog both shielded his would-be aggressor, and provided spiraling ringlets around the beam. It was obviously a visual effect made more realistic by the surroundings, but it looked like a ray gun from outer space.

He appeared to have 'stepped in it' by doing exactly what Victoria had warned him not to do; ticking her off. He raised his hands in surrender to his current predicament when he noticed the woman cocking her head ever so slightly.

Inara was receiving reports in her own earpiece. She looked straight into her victim's eyes. "Mr. Mandeville, you were told that no weapons were to be present during the exchange."

"I could say the same for you," he said slightly above a whisper. He wondered for a split second how she knew he was packing, then thought it best to immediately come clean. After all, he was at a slight disadvantage. "All right, all right … apologies for the misunderstanding." He reached very gingerly into his breast coat pocket and pulled out the skimpy revolver with two fingers.

Inara raised one eyebrow. "Not you, silly man; I expected that." She motioned towards the van with a head nod. "Her."

* * *

A demon was protruding from the back of the van; his clawed hand deep into the young woman's red curly hair. Airowyn stared in disgust at the blatant disregard for the rules.

To sway or manipulate a human beyond their ability to make a choice was to torment them; push them into a direction that, in their mind, gave them no other alternatives except a desire to free themselves from their anguish. This type of supernatural manipulation from the enemy was the number-one cause for human suicides.

For centuries, it was thought by humans that mental illness or some type of traumatic event was the catalyst that propelled them down this afflicted path. It was somewhat true as it is a seed initially planted, but is then exploited by the enemy, pushing the human beyond rational thought to an unjustifiable end.

Those not keenly in tune with their spiritual side simply accepted the Darwinistic approach of a chemical imbalance or insurmountable despair. This was the one bane of existence that would make mankind feel truly alone in the universe.

Without hope, there is nothing.

The angelic record keeper, as well as his many brethren, felt sadness in this type of profiteering on human souls, as the taking of one's own life was one of the few unforgivable sins. His sadness quickly turned to anger in remembrance of the purpose in which he was created. He was a guardian angel; and his job was to protect those with no defense against these unseen agents of evil.

Knowing he was vastly outnumbered, with powerful allies standing by, he started towards the gleeful demon as it howled with laughter at the young woman's torment.

None of them took notice as his scrivener robes began to shift to battle-ready armor, but in mid-transition he froze; as did the demons in proximity of the young lady. For she did something completely unexpected.

* * *

Victoria continued to rock back and forth; the pain at the apex of her tolerance. Her hands moved desperately around her head with the gun in her left. Above it all, her vision blurred as she strained to watch Nigel. It was amazing to her that through the sheer agony of which her head felt like it was going to explode, she still felt loyalty to the buffoon who had been her partner for so many years.

She managed to get an eye on Nigel not comprehending the change in his stance, or the strange green light emanating from him? To him?

Victoria didn't know as she felt her sanity slipping away. Everything seemed like a dream. Barely having time to register what was happening, a surge of pain rattled her body. She jerked so violently, that she dropped the gun and squeezed her head.

The manipulating demon cackled with elation at the reward of his puppeteering of the stupid human woman.

Having nowhere else to turn, she prayed. "Dear God, please forgive me for what happened to that poor man. I have been so stupid with my life. Please help me!"

It has been known throughout the existence of mankind that during a time of crisis, those who have not been close to a deity of their choosing, tend to reach out reflexively in a last-ditch effort to deliver them from whatever is torturing or placing them in danger. For those that have discounted, defied, or even renounced a supernatural existence, the inane humanistic instinct to call out to that which they deny is as spontaneous as scratching a simple itch. Most humans don't even realize they have done it.

In Victoria's case, she had been struggling with the development of faith over the last few weeks due to the loss of that man's life, and her part in his end. She had always been an Undeclared with no clear path either way. All of that changed now with those few words as a cry for help.

She had just made a decision.

When someone chooses the path of the Light, many miraculous things happen in an instant. For a human, the burden of their torment is lifted. The clarity of their thinking and their mind changed; a new force protecting them from hopelessness is present. It's as if taking a deep breath of crisp clear air for the very first time through lungs unhampered by compression or sickness. The cool part though, happens on the supernatural side.

A bright burst of light emanated from the woman like her human form had changed into a million tiny stars. The transformation effect emitted a supernatural explosion.

The demons who appeared to be frozen in shock, were suspended by the paralysis inflicted from the human's prayer. The unfortunate little gargoyle manipulating Victoria was at ground zero. His expression unchanged, his grotesque hands began to dissolve within her mind. The rest of his body then dissipated into ash with no fanfare, drama, or howling. However, that did not mean that the anguish of his eternal dispatching was any less painful.

The bubble of the collateral circle of light had a lesser effect the further it went out, but the brilliance drew every demon's attention. All quickly looked from the human man to the woman in the vehicle.

General Wyck turned in rage at what had just happened. He knew that everything his master was working towards was to prevent this very thing from occurring. The loss of a soul was a loss of the most valuable commodity in existence.

His master would blame him for letting this happen, regardless of whether Wyck could control it.

His gaze drifted ten feet away and caught the angel sent to observe by the Host. For a moment, he thought he saw the angel with battle armament. His eyes widened in realization. This was not a scribe from the Majaliant Genanōsys; the realm of knowledge and education within the Host. He was a guardian at best, or at worst, a warrior. They were the only ones who would be sanctioned for battle or defending.

This deception further enraged the demon commander; although he should not have been surprised. Sneering at the thought, Wyck could not have expected more from his once-brother. They were all mindless creations that could not think for themselves, which was one of the main reasons for Wyck to follow Lucifer, before they were so unjustly cast down.

His master's forward thinking taught him of the unfairness of providing the mewling humans more free will and choices than what should have been given. After all, angels were His *first* creations.

Wyck's rage began to control his emotions and actions. The surrounding demons took notice like they had caught the pheromone scent of a wild animal.

The demon commander crouched as he drew his sword and pointed straight at Airowyn. "You!"

The angel looked away from the miracle of choice to face the demon.

"This is of your doing!" Drops of spittle slipped from his mouth like a bulldog. "You said you were here just to observe!"

"And I am," said the angel calmly. "What you see before you is of her choice, and hers alone."

"Liar!"

"You cannot be that far gone of sanity not to remember the process of humàledin selection; mankind's birth right to choose the path of their souls. For neither of us, angel nor demon, decide their course. It must come solely from them."

Wyck began to shake with greater rage. Further back behind the angel, was Blurr, who seemed to be the only demon to maintain his wits. He watched as the other demons began to whip into a frenzy at their commander's loss of control. If ever the curse of their rebellion was present, it was now. He was afraid of standing out as he was not affected nor caught up in the demonic energy building around him. To his surprise though, his presence was oblivious. All the other demons were in a frenetic trance and could not turn away from their commander.

"I should never have allowed you to watch," slithered Wyck. The black orbs of his eyes began to emanate a crimson hue. One by one, all the other demon's eyes began to transfer as well. The scene looked like the eerie reflective glow of hundreds of cat's eyes in darkness. The uncharacteristic quietness that spawned from the absence of screeching and howling added to the horror movie setting. All the evil surrounding the angel was now transfixed on him.

Airowyn was in a bad spot, and he knew it.

Wyck started toward him slowly, his hand squeezing the sword held tightly with his leathery muscular arm. As he picked up his pace, the surrounding demons began to unsheathe their weapons.

Airowyn, faced by the inevitable, shouted in an angelic voice. "Stop!" His scrivener robes now shifted into full battle gear; material swirled and changed density with form-fitting armor. It was much like those fictional automotive vehicles that transformed into robots.

Wyck laughed. "Your flimsy armor will not save you," drool still running from his lips. His pace quickened more. "What can you do, but die?"

A magnificent battle sword extended much like the transformation of his armor. In a swirl of fluid motion, the angel's stance ended with a Gar-tak sword form. Had Wyck not been so consumed with hatred, he might have been impressed.

"You are foolish in many ways, but mostly in the belief that I am alone," said Airowyn.

The demons were too focused on their prey to notice the change to the atmosphere. The already murky skies began to fill with rolling clouds and smattering sparks of lightning.

Wyck spread his tattered, leathery wings as he accelerated his approach to the guardian angel; not so much as to take flight, but to intimidate. The angel's attack posture remained unchanged.

A sonic crack from the sky drew the demon general to a sudden stop. With his rage abating, the demon commander finally comprehended what the lone angel said. He looked up and around but took notice of nothing other than the thunder clouds and lightning.

As the tiny demon Blurr watched, he saw the realization cross the general's face then flow rapidly through the ranks. The screeching and howling returned in waves of fear at what this meant. The unimportant demon who was once known as Percival lowered his head, for he knew that his end was now near. He reflected on how far lost he had become since the rebellion. No amount of remorse or good deeds could ever take back the worst decision of his existence.

Without forewarning, a streak of black with pulsating blue light landed feet first square between the wings of General Wyck. The impact was so powerful that it snapped Wyck's body face-first into the pavement; chunks flying and rippling up like that of a crater. The speed with which the assailant collided pushed the general across the surface for another seventy-five to one hundred feet. It looked like he was using the demon as a surfboard, with more pieces of pavement flying like waves over the bow of a boat. The aggressor was on one knee with the fingertips of one hand on the demon's head. With his black wings extended behind him, the angel looked very regal.

When the demonic ride came to a stop, the area became deathly quiet. The warrior commander remained in his surfing pose for a few additional seconds; most likely for an effect. The demons froze as if movement would draw the angelic warrior's attention. They held their breath for fear that the slightest sound would provoke him.

Of all the Inflixi Impetus, this was the one all demons feared the most.

The angelic warrior of destruction looked up with one gray eye visible beneath the lengthy black hair. He then stood slowly as his immense black wings folded back behind his long black gothic rock coat.

The Inflixi Impetus leader known as Vaago was slightly smaller than his eight brothers, but the most intimidating. His wardrobe was cast all in black; a mixture of leather and suede. A belt with ornate buckles and hanging chains pulsated with rhythmic blue waves of light. Black calf-length boots with the same buckles down the outside of each held a similar pattern of light. There was one silver spur attached to his left boot.

As a high-ranking angel within the Majaliant Linaofaè, he, like his brothers, had been gifted with powers that enabled them to intercept and defend against the enemy as needed or instructed. Imbued with the strength of all the Majaliant in the form of the blue waving light, they called upon their endowments during times of need. As of late, he and his brothers were very busy.

Vaago adjusted his coat and took a step down off the broken form of Wyck; his spur jangled. His raven-black hair covered his right eye as it fell to beneath his shoulders. He walked slowly scanning the demon crowd with the other. No one moved. It was as if all were statues.

Finally stopping, he turned his head slightly towards Airowyn. "How goes it, brother?"

Airowyn straightened up and sheathed his sword. He looked around the demon horde, all appearing fearful of the answer. His gaze finally landed upon Blurr. The little demon did not cower like the rest, but held his head up ready to look his punishment in the eye. He seemed resigned to his fate.

The guardian angel noticed a sharp contrast in the wincing of the stronger demons, and the courage of the weakest. It was a pity that he chose the wrong side. Airowyn thought he would have been a good servant for the Light.

"Fairly well." He looked around the silent gargoyle statues again. "We have a miracle of transformation, brother."

"So I see."

Airowyn continued to scan the crowd. "Praise be to the Highest."

"Indeed." Vaago continued his stroll along the pavement. "Why do we have a disturbance?"

"It seems that the transformation is not agreeable with our counterparts."

Vaago raised his eyebrow in mock surprise. "Really?" He looked down upon the pavement as he continued his walk. "Do you think our adversaries understand the process of humàledin selection?"

"It was explained prior to the upheaval." Airowyn glanced towards the disfigured general. "The reception was still unwelcomed."

Vaago nodded as he processed this information. "Was the human manipulated prior?"

"She was."

"By our opponents?"

"Of course."

"Well then, that is a clear violation within the Rebellion Accords."

"Yes, it is."

"And to whom is this accountable?"

"That would be the large demon laying before you."

Vaago had known this, as he had known everything that had transpired. He was not in the business of being misinformed or unprepared.

He walked over to Wyck and nudged him with his boot. "Do you have any defense against these accusations?"

"Hmff. Tifgguffg," he slurred. The large demon commander moved slightly as he tried to upright himself.

"Come now, face me like a warrior, so we may discuss this."

Vaago casually reached out and grabbed one of the leathery, tattered wings. With what seemed like minimal effort, he separated the large demon from his asphalt imprint and jerked him to his feet.

For the first time since the angel warrior's arrival, the demons gasped at what they saw. The demon leader was a mesh of mutilated skin and asphalt. Since supernatural creatures did not bleed, bits of ash fell from his wounds. Fingers on a disfigured hand twisted back unnaturally on the left side of his body, which appeared to have taken most the impact skid. A demonic equivalent of jutting bones and road rash made the creature look like the result of a horrible car crash. Even Airowyn gave a disgusted look at what was before him.

Vaago reached over and brushed some asphalt from the wounded general's shoulder. "You were saying?"

Wyck's left eye was missing; the side of his face bruised and swollen. He spat out some loosened teeth. "Stop toying with me and get on with it."

Everything happening now was just for show. The fate of those in attendance was sealed. The breach of the Accords saw to that. For it to be effective though, a few must survive to spread the tale.

"Now where's the fun in that? Tell you what, you verbally declare your misconduct and accept full responsibility for these shameless acts of unjust manipulation, and I will make your eternal dispatchment painless. I will also guarantee the survival of some of those under your command. Decide now."

With what was left of the demon commander's mouth, he sneered. "I will give you nothing!"

Airowyn knew how this was going to end. The fact that Vaago was the one who came in his time of need for this transaction spoke volumes. He glanced upward to see brothers of the Inflixi Impetus appear one at a time. His gaze then drifted over to the little wispy demon who was now visibly shaking. The angel imagined that he too knew what was coming.

Blurr looked over to the angel one last time. Their eyes met as regret for the demon's decisions throughout his existence came to fruition.

Airowyn spoke with what seemed to be only for him. "Run."

The little demon's shock lasted for but a moment before he turned and quickly slithered his way through his doomed brothers. He must move hastily before they figured out what he already knew.

The taunting now over, Vaago cut loose a small smile. "Very well."

Blurr flew as fast as his little wings would carry him through the streets and away from the docks. Even with his hands covering his ears, he could still hear the screaming.

* * *

As most humans are intentionally shielded from celestial activity, Inara, Nigel, and Victoria were completely unaware of the supernatural battle surrounding them. All that existed were the three of them and the dismal weather conditions; except for Inara's strategically placed colleagues, who now, also had a bead on the unsuspecting woman in the van.

Victoria's head began to clear after reaching out for the unknown help to find Nigel spinning towards her with a panicked look.

"Victoria! Put the bloody gun d–"

The strange green light that she thought she saw emanating from Nigel, was now aimed through the windshield at her. With her head still clearing, she caught on just a little too late.

A powerful crack echoed through the atmosphere as the windshield shattered; a spider web of cracks surrounded a golf ball sized hole. Victoria jerked back violently from the impact; her head slumping immediately, with blood trickling down all around her.

Nigel fell to his knees in disbelief. "Victoria?" He said quietly.

She did not move or respond. All he saw was her beautiful cascading red hair hanging in front of her immobile body.

An unknown man dressed in black walked to her side of the van and opened the door. As he reached through, Nigel snapped out of his shock and scrambled to his feet. He ran toward the van in desperation. "Don't you touch her! Get away from her!"

Inara held up her hand signaling her sniper in the sky not to shoot. The man in black reached over to the console after a few seconds of searching and found the fusion accelerator.

As Nigel reached the side door, he boldly pushed the man out of the way. His eyes widened in further shock, as his hands hovered over her bloody body. Nigel stared at the hole in her chest.

He gently cradled her head towards him and began to weep. "I am so sorry, love. I should have listened to you. I should have listened to everything you have ever said to me. This is all my fault." He stroked her hair softly.

The man in black seemed annoyed at being pushed, but before he reacted, he looked towards Inara and nodded as he held the device up for her to see.

She smiled slightly and nodded back, then gave a hand signal to wrap things up. She turned back towards the car and looked at her watch. *No loose ends, and in time to make the call.*

Nigel closed his eyes as he heard the round chamber in the Glock. The echo of the shot hung in the air as Inara entered the car.

* * *

He blinked in a confused state, still standing in the same spot. Nigel did not know how he managed to survive the shot. He quickly felt over his body, then his head for any signs of damage or wounds; there was none. He turned around and was surprised to see someone watching. Someone with long hair in strange clothes stood four or five meters away, just staring. Nigel did not recognize the angel known as

Airowyn. Where did he come from? He wasn't the man whom he pulled away from Victoria.

Victoria!

He turned back around and froze. She was still sitting in her seat with her head slumped forward. There was blood everywhere. He didn't understand, but then remembered.

She was dead, and it was his fault.

He stepped away from the van in anguish and fell, tripping upon something large and soft. Looking at the object of his fall, he realized it was a body. Awkwardly scrambling to his feet, he took a closer look.

"Impossible!" He gasped. "This can't be."

The body was his own. The face was completely gone, but Nigel recognized his clothes. "What is happening!"

"Nigel," came the soft voice.

He jumped at the sound. There, standing in front of him, was Victoria. She was dressed in something completely different; her hair flowed in beautiful red ringlets down past her shoulders. Her skin was radiant. There were no visible signs of the stress they had experienced over the past few weeks.

The bruise where he had struck her was gone. He was immediately ashamed, and briefly wondered why he never noticed how beautiful she was.

"Victoria! Thank g–" as he reached for her, his hand passed right through. Nigel stepped back, aghast at what had just happened. As he looked her up-and-down with wide eyes, her expression was very serene and calm.

He then stared at his hands, not believing what had just occurred. "What is this!"

"Nigel, I want you to know that I forgive you."

"Forgive me?! For what?"

She smiled at him. "I am so sorry."

"I don't understand!" Nigel screamed.

"You didn't make a choice," said a voice from behind, deadpan and unfeeling.

Nigel jumped like a jittery Chihuahua. He turned to find what appeared to be a punk rocker with long hair in solid black clothing. He was casually leaning against the side of the van with his arms crossed.

"Not making a decision is just as bad as making the wrong one," continued Vaago.

Still facing the dark-haired stranger, Nigel said, "Victoria, I still don't–"

"I have to go now," she said; a sincere smile crossed her face.

A transition emissary stood right next to her.

Nigel jumped again noticing this new person for the first time. *Where are these people coming from?*

Victoria turned to look at the new arrival, and her smile widen. The angelic emissary returned her smile and held out his hand.

In an attempt to walk to her, Nigel found himself unwilling or unable to move. The man with the long black hair trailed after Victoria and the other man. With his only visible eye, he looked at Nigel with dispassion as he passed.

Vaago saw a lot human suffering throughout mankind's existence. Some were victims of persecution and oppression; mostly inflicted by the enemy's manipulation, and almost always unjustified. He had zero tolerance for bullies, and thoroughly enjoyed making them pay for their transgressions. Those were easy calls for him and his team as most situations were black and white. The bad guy does something wrong; the little guy can't take care of it themselves, Vaago and his team intercept, fix, and dispatch.

In circumstances such as this where choices are crystal-clear and there is plenty of what humans call 'time' to make those choices, and yet still do not; Vaago had even less tolerance, if that were possible.

Apathy replaced compassion at the indecisiveness simply because these creatures continually waited. At least, Lucifer made a choice. A bad one albeit, but a choice nonetheless.

The rules were clear. Everyone must decide.

Vaago supposed his role as an angel was to care about mankind's most important decision, but he didn't. They were supposed to figure this out on their own. It wouldn't make a difference if he cared or not; and there were plenty of other brothers to do his share.

Nigel stared in amazed disbelief as the only person in the world he ever cared about walked away. He couldn't move to chase after her.

"Victoria!" He screamed reaching out.

"Goodbye Nigel." With that, she and the man who held her hand disappeared into a bright light.

After all he had witnessed in the last couple of minutes, her disappearance surprised him. Then a sudden movement caught his eye a few meters away. The man with the strange clothes suddenly sprouted large wings.

Airowyn had a solemn look on his face as he lifted into the sky.

Nigel jerked his head, terrified of what he had just seen, toward the man in black with the long hair.

With his weight upon one leg and his hands clasped casually behind him, large black wings emerged from the back of his coat. At lightning-quick speed, they came down, lifting him into the air, and Vaago disappeared into the sky.

Nigel found himself alone, frightened, and shaking. Then he heard a demonic growl as a swirling vortex opened.

23

The Council of 12

For many years, he has ridden in almost all the elevators within the huge corporate structure of Jonah International. He thought about the times he came from the cafeteria with the warm pastries; the jokes that he shared with Alice and Sally as they headed towards meetings, even the simple activities of coming into and leaving from work. Endless times of just being in the box with other Jonah employees.

This was one of the loneliest and creepiest rides Joshua had ever experienced.

It didn't even feel like the box was moving. It just existed. Even for the elevators that were controlled by Sentinel and had no buttons, there was always a floor number display showing the progress of movement.

At first he looked around with just his eyes, then he casually turned in a slow circle; there was nothing. He couldn't even see the seam of the elevator door. He was quite literally in a small box with no visible way out.

Joshua's already rising anxiety would have spiraled out of control if he was claustrophobic. "Sentinel, what's going on? Is this supposed to be normal?"

"Joshua, be patient" replied his invisible friend. "Things are as they should be. You will be there momentarily."

"Be where? Are we going up or down? We could be going sideways for all I know." Joshua was trying not to be rude with his remarks, but the culmination of knowing that everything he had always questioned, was about to be answered. Meeting the closest thing to the Chairman he would most likely get— little short of dying— was building to the point of his head exploding.

As he was about to question Sentinel again, the box jolted as if coming to a stop. He wondered if it was supposed to be that way, or if Sentinel was just placating him to ease his mind.

"We are here," said Sentinel.

Then, almost as a well-placed joke, an elevator bell ding announced their arrival. Joshua might have laughed had this been any other situation.

When the doors opened, a bright light flooded the small compartment. Joshua held up his hands as a shield. He thought he heard the faint whisper of Sentinel. "Good luck." Joshua half smiled as he knew his sentient friend *did* have a sense of humor.

With his eyes adjusted, Joshua lowered his hands. The doors opened into a plain, nondescript, unassuming conference room.

He was surprised by this; half expecting some magnificent and ornate cathedral-sized chamber with immense heavenly sculptures and priceless works of art donning the walls. He imagined twelve thrones centered in the middle of a gold and marble floor with a beautiful ceiling mural painted by Michelangelo himself.

The absurdity of the impracticality that this thought represented was not lost on him. Someone with real power had no need to flaunt it. They could see pass the need to display their prominence in compensation for other lacking characteristics.

From a pragmatic standpoint, Joshua had never seen a show of the Chairman's power; angelic battles notwithstanding. It would serve no point to show off now. After everything Joshua had seen and been through, he didn't need any pomp and circumstance to win him over. He was already there.

Joshua was sure that wherever he was, no longer resided within the mortal confines of the Jonah International building. Then again, he had no way of knowing.

He stepped into the room and looked around. A standard-size conference table was in the middle with six chairs on either side, and another at the end closest to him. There were a couple of credenzas on the wall to his right, and a floor to ceiling window on his left. Bright light was shining through closed sheer curtains. He wanted to step over and look out, but thought better of it. Truth be told, he didn't want to be surprised by what might be on the other side.

As he looked around, he was the only one in the room. Joshua furled his brow and turned around to the elevator, but was met with a blank solid wall. The elevator or anything resembling it, was gone. Once again, he found himself enclosed with no visible way out.

Turning back to the table, he jumped. Twelve men in business suits we're now sitting in the empty spaces; six to each side. The only chair left was the one at the very end.

The hot seat.

The one chair that most men dreamed of being in as the head of a corporation, but dreaded during an inquisition. Was that what this was? An inquisition? Would he be judged for the actions taken, or the lack of actions since he assumed this unwanted position?

No. That wasn't this at all. Lucas said that the Council wanted to speak with him. That they were going to share the plan. A plan that he had been asking about for what seemed like years.

Now that the time had come, he questioned whether he wanted to know.

Joshua thought about this moment for so long. He built it up in his mind to something like a pirate finding a buried treasure. He searched everywhere; traveled many seas on many different ships. Captained a crew of various people, and went on worldwide adventures; losing friends and family along the way. He was finally here to claim his rightful bounty.

Now, the fear of the unknown, the uncertainty of a plan he had thought about every day for so long, scared him.

The uncanny timing of that thought was jolted as a council member spoke. "Hello Joshua, please sit down."

A man sitting on the right gestured to the empty chair at the end. His smile was kind.

As Joshua made his way to the table, he scanned each member of the Council of 12.

All were men in various stages of their lives; older and younger. Each with creases of experience in their faces and welcoming eyes. Some had salt and pepper hair; some were completely gray. Most had neatly trimmed beards; except for the younger one who asked him to sit. He was barely older than Joshua, and like him, preferred a clean-shaven look.

All twelve were dressed very sharp, but in seemingly inexpensive suits. Then again, how would Joshua know. He never paid much attention to the status of clothing. They could've been dressed in Brooks Brothers, or ordered their suits out of a Sears catalog. Joshua was never good at that; Alice and Melina always picked out his wardrobe.

Inwardly, Joshua chastised himself yet again for assuming that the Council themselves would be pretentious in their appearance. He made a mental note to stop drawing conclusions based solely on the imaginary pictures that he had burned into his mind about this day.

As his eyes met each member, all looked back with compassion and kindness. If what they were about to impart on him held any kind of bad news, he could not tell. They all had excellent poker faces. Joshua knew all too well how game faces worked. He had used them many times throughout his life.

When Joshua took his seat, a gentleman on the left towards the end of the table spoke. "Thank you for meeting with us, Joshua. We appreciate your time."

Joshua hoped that his look did not give away the shock. "Not at all, but I must say I don't feel that my time is nearly as important as yours," he said with a head gesture around the table.

They smiled and laughed. "To the contrary, your time is much more valuable than ours," said another gentleman to the right.

Joshua smiled uneasily. "I'm afraid I don't really understand."

"Joshua, your works during your time in the company have been, at the very least, remarkable," he said.

Joshua couldn't believe what he was hearing. Sitting here in front of the most influential committee on the planet— was he even on the planet? — and *they* were praising *him* for works he didn't see, or couldn't acknowledge as anything out of the ordinary. He was just doing his job. Nothing more.

When a person does not seek or readily accept validation for their perceived accomplishments, sometimes, that goes more noticed than the act itself. At least, it did for the Council. Lucas and other humans have seen this; Joshua never has. This was one of the reasons he was chosen. In this case though, the Council was referring to all the victories against the enemy as a direct result of Joshua's leadership.

The wide-eyed look Joshua gave back made the Council laugh once again.

"Don't be so surprised, Joshua," said the same Council member on the left. "Your focus on these small events has enabled significant progress towards defeating the enemy."

Small events? Joshua thought. People have lost their lives. Captain Bill and his crew from the plane, all those officers just today at the precinct, and probably countless others as an indirect impact from choices that he has made. These were not small events; they were human beings, people with family and loved ones. Children who no longer had a mother or a father.

Mother.

He was just as much a victim of these so-called small events as anyone else. His mother was taken from him by the enemy; taken long before he was old enough to understand how sheltered and naïve he and the rest of mankind were at their very existence.

Joshua looked around the conference room. Not at the Council, but the room itself. It was the very representation of the façade that humans operated under that blinded them to understanding what was really important. Corporate status, cars, money — he frowned at that thought — all tangible things that drove people away from the truth.

Every person at other stations of his or her life had similar idols that they chased. A woman might place value on jewelry, a man on the size of his house or his golf game, or even the dreaded self-worth of his position in the workforce. Parents might place their social standing on the best schools for their children's education, and all for what? So they can have something to show for everything they've done, or their kids could someday sit in a chair much like the one he occupied? All of this was just a vicious cycle from generation to generation; passing on expectations to achieve more by works of their own.

Joshua shook his head. All of it was fake. In the end, we would leave this world as we entered it; with no status or possessions. The only thing that mattered would be the one decision that must be made.

All the positions that business people so desperately coveted, like a seat in the executive conference room, was temporary. Joshua was under the same pretense when he was sucked into this world. Now though, things were much clearer.

"Joshua, is there something on your mind?" The Council member to the left said.

This was a business meeting with the board of directors of Jonah International. Nothing more. While he had the deepest respect for the men in this room, Joshua shook off his childlike adoration for who they were and the positions they held, and decided to treat this like any other meeting.

The youngest one of the Council was sitting to Joshua's immediate right; the clean-shaven gentleman who offered the chair.

Joshua turned his head slightly to face him and held out his hand. "I'm sorry. I didn't catch your name."

A smile curved at the end of his lips as he accepted Joshua's hand. "My name is Stephen."

Joshua turned to each of the Council members, and they introduced themselves. The gentleman who spoke at the far right was called Peter.

The one who spoke to the left of the table was called Paul. None of the gentlemen gave their last names as it seemed unimportant, but each name spoken confirmed Joshua's theory. He sat in the presence of Christian history.

Joshua needed to employ his game face now because he did not want to come off like a groupie at a rock concert.

He sat back in his chair and crossed his legs. "Gentlemen, as I said earlier, I understand how valuable your time is. I appreciate you adjusting your schedules, so we could meet. I am assuming that we are here to discuss the next steps?"

"The Chairman has asked us to provide you some additional details to aid you in the strategy against the enemy," said Stephen.

"You're referring to the plan?" Joshua said, wanting him to say the words.

"Yes, the plan," smiled Stephen.

Finally, here we go, thought Joshua inwardly, but maintained his business demeanor.

Stephen reached forward and pressed an intercom button on a small box that looked to be from circa 1980s. "Elsbeth, can you please bring in the folder?"

Joshua hadn't noticed the intercom box before. A few seconds passed, then a door in the back of the room opened. Joshua hadn't noticed the door either. Did these simple things just appear out of nowhere, or were they so inconspicuous that he glanced over them when he scanned the room?

The curious thought disappeared when a striking fair-haired young lady with deep green irises entered carrying a single standard newish manila office folder. Joshua's eyes never left her as she approached and placed the folder on the table in front of him. Her beauty appeared flawless and hypnotic to the point of where she didn't look human. A faint, almost translucent glow fell about her skin making her origin appear more supernatural than anything; as if she were a specter masquerading as an executive assistant.

She stared into Joshua's eyes and smiled, then turned making her way back through the door.

"Thank you, Elsbeth," said Stephen. She simply nodded without any words and shut the door after her.

Once the sound of the clicking door faded, Joshua's trance seemed to be broken.

The realization of the blatant gawking at the young lady became apparent as Joshua's eyes met a few of the council members. His embarrassment manifested in a slight blush. "My apologies, I didn't mean to— "

"It's okay, Joshua," said Stephen.

Joshua came to a silent understanding as he tried to compose himself, for he had never seen a female angel. Was that what she was? There was never any mention of that from Lucas or his other supernatural contacts. There were no references to gender-specific angels in any of his studies. Theoretically, he supposed; anything like that was possible. As his thinking increased, he wondered why something like that *wouldn't* be possible.

Seeing the confusion, Stephen said, "She is what she needs to be."

The simplicity of the statement did not fall short on Joshua. It merely clarified how little understanding he had of the other side. In all this time, he knew nothing other than what he had read or been told about the afterlife.

He understood that the world as he knew it was a temporal plane; a means to eternal life. He had never seriously given thought to what type of life that would be. The revelation of realizing how much he did not know, washed over him. Unfortunately, there wasn't enough time to take up yet another knowledge transfer; but this was something he wanted to circle back around to understand.

Joshua internally chastised himself once again for losing focus and objectivity to this meeting. He has twice allowed his thoughts to stray; once, from his lofty perception of the council members, and now the appearance of the silent and beautiful angel, if that's truly what she was. However, at this point, it didn't matter what she was. The effort of even wondering about that was *still* a distraction that he, his team, the plan, or the mission could not afford.

His patience for receiving any answers had been thin for so long, but now he felt certain that was changing. He was on the verge for getting everything he had asked for. His only obstacle, was him. Joshua was now getting in his own way. He was becoming the bottleneck.

All of that stops now. He needed move past his expectations of how he believes things *should* be, and accept that things are the way they *must* be.

Joshua took a breath and calmly folded his hands in his lap. He looked down at the folder to compose his thoughts before speaking. He found the irony in the key for stopping the enemy, was tucked neatly inside a nondescript folder. He wasn't sure if this was the Chairman's way of compromising on the complexity of Sentinel's AI and technology overkill, with the simplicity of Joshua's wish for normalcy.

Stephen and the rest of the council waited patiently.

Closing his eyes, Joshua breathed through his nose and out of his mouth. He could feel his anxiety and heart rate lowering, but only just a little.

"Gentlemen, as I'm sure you can imagine, this meeting, as well as all the events to date, have been very surreal for me. I understand the magnitude of our mission, and the ramifications of failure. It is my belief that this plan–" he said tapping the top of the folder, "–will be the key to a unified strategy between human and supernatural-kind to stop the enemy's advance of corruption and collections." Joshua was referring to the evil influence and the taking of souls.

Although he was not expecting thunderous applause, Joshua saw what amounted to a lack of enthusiasm across most council member's faces.

After a few seconds of uncomfortable silence, Joshua spoke first. "Was it something I said?"

Some of the council shared knowing glances as Joshua awaited a response. Stephen, ever the diplomat, spoke first. "Joshua, it is not our intention to mislead you in any way, but we are not here to provide the steps towards the enemy's defeat."

Joshua made no attempt to hide his surprise. "Excuse me?"

"It seems as if there is a misunderstanding," said the one called Andrew. "Our purpose is to provide insights into the events to come."

For not the first time since Joshua had taken this position, he was at a loss for words. The look on his face seemed to say enough.

The one called Timothy spoke next. "Joshua, we understand–"

"No, I don't think that you do," interrupted Joshua; shocked more than upset. "My team ... *I* have been struggling for months–" his wild eyes jerked to the left. *Has it been more like years?* He thought, stopping in mid-sentence.

He was truly at a loss for words. Joshua didn't know how to convey what he was feeling without offending the council. He was smart enough to know that it was probably best not to say anything at all.

Timothy did not finish his sentence. He could see that Joshua was upset; as could the rest of the council. They wanted to give him a chance to collect his thoughts.

Joshua had assumed that where they were meeting, time was inconsequential. At least, he had hoped so, because he was not anywhere near a rational response. As he continued to process what was said, his emotional spectrum moved back and forth like a seismic scale.

They didn't have a plan.

Everything that Joshua had been working towards would fall apart without a plan to defeat the enemy.

The establishment of the One-World Health foundation to provide worldwide medical and professional services free of charge to those who could not afford it. The unification of Third-World countries to educate them on various things such as organic development of their agriculture and geospatial sustainability to help them thrive as independent nations. And probably what would be deemed as his most successful initiative, the JPS. Although their services had been diversified over the years, the global mission statement was always driven towards a world without tyranny and injustice.

These things were just ideas that Joshua had. A thought that turned into a reality with no hidden agendas; he only ever wanted to help people and give them opportunities that he had never had.

Over the years, Jonah International, more specifically Joshua, had been judged harshly for some, or all of these initiatives. There were always naysayers or trolls looking forward to bringing down something they either did not understand, or wanted to corrupt for their own personal agendas. These negative people towed the party line for the enemy, whose sole purpose was to inflict as much pain to the Chairman, and damage to the cause, as they could.

Joshua sat back in his chair.

They didn't have a plan.

He looked at the folder on the table in front of him. Only now did he notice that it wasn't as thick as he would have expected. He reached out his hand and hovered over it, almost as if the fear of touching it would make the fact that the Council did not have a plan even truer. He placed his palm on the folder, and began tapping his index finger. Joshua pursed his lips as he chewed on the knowledge that this folder did not contain the equivalent of the answer to the colonel's secret original recipe.

Time relative or not, he couldn't sit here and waste the Councils, or for that fact his own, refusing to accept the truth.

There was no plan.

Deal with it.

Okay, maybe not everything would fall apart, but everything that Joshua had his hand in, that was driving towards the ultimate victory of defeating the enemy was going to be affected; he didn't think he was going to have to do this alone.

Wait? Was he?

There had to be a reason that he was called here. Whether they had a plan or not, they had something.

He looked around the table. "Gentlemen, my apologies again for losing my composure. There are so many things that I built this meeting up to be," he looked down towards the table again, ashamed, "that I lost sight of the fact maybe not getting a plan, *was* the plan all along."

Joshua brought his eyes back up to meet theirs, and noticed a few smiles.

He tried not to show his annoyance, as these were the kind of games that he had experienced with Lucas over the last decade or so. His supernatural colleague seemed to invariably be one step closer than him in understanding his "path" as the chosen one; always seeming to know what was going to happen in the next chapter to his life.

He shook his head slightly. It's like they wanted him to figure this out on his own.

Joshua's head snapped up in surprise.

Wait ...

Again, there were more smiles across the council's faces, as they saw he was beginning to understand.

Now, it was starting to make sense.

"You don't have a plan to defeat the enemy. It's supposed to come from me, isn't it?"

"The Chairman chose you well, Joshua," said Timothy.

"Your reputation for problem-solving proceeds you," said Andrew.

"Why has it taken this long to figure out that I had to do it?" Said Joshua. "I mean, if that was the Chairman's plan all along, He could have just said something."

Joshua looked down answering his own question. "That's not His style now, is it?"

"We above anyone else understand the mysteries of His parables," said Peter.

Stephen leaned in. "Joshua, you needed to develop in your own time; to understand your capabilities and probable limitations based on what you know and what you haven't yet discovered."

"Based on that line of thinking, I still have a lot to learn," replied Joshua.

"You don't have as much to learn as you think," said Paul. "At this point, you are only hampered by your understanding of your limitations."

Joshua had a look of confusion at that statement.

Stephen smiled. "Your imagination."

Joshua's expression remained stoic as he processed that. He reached back into his memory for specific events where he needed to decide, or act on some Intel, but thought about it in a linear fashion.

He thought like a human.

What if anything *were* truly possible? The fresh memory of utilizing Sebastian's skill to aid the retrieval team revealed his ingenuity of co-operation across the realms. Without the angelic warrior's assistance, his team would most likely have died, along with Kelly Granger.

Self-doubt began to creep in, and he looked at Stephen. "Are you sure you have the right person for this job?"

Stephen smiled again; that's all he did was smile. "I'm afraid it's too late for that, my friend."

Joshua raised an eyebrow. Was that a joke?

Joshua remembered when he was first exposed to this world way back when at the home of Malcolm Holden, the current CEO of Jonah International. Both Holden and Lucas, his guardian angel and presently his closest friend, shared the true nature of mankind's existence. Lucas made a statement that now holds so much more clarity. *Imagine a future with unlimited resources, and the support of the Chairman.*

Joshua's look turned solemn. "What makes you think I can do what needs to come?"

"The Chairman has every confidence in you, Joshua. It only matters what *He* thinks," replied Stephen.

Out of everything that Joshua had experienced and learned since moving to New York all those years ago, his confidence level in his leadership capabilities had hung over his head like an addiction he couldn't shake.

All humans have a weakness in certain areas. Joshua did not feel like he was any different; regardless of all the encouragement he received from both the supernatural and human side.

He remembered something else from that conversation in Holden's house. Lucas told him not to have fear; that the confidence in his abilities and gifts would present themselves as they are needed.

Joshua didn't have any idea why his self-confidence was constantly getting in his way, other than the fact that maybe this was the enemy's play to prevent him from achieving his full potential. He had always been told that he was their biggest threat. It would be a good strategy on their part to shake his nerves.

But maybe, just possibly, it was time for him to fully unload and cut loose. If anything truly was possible, he was now ready to find out.

As with many other revelations since Joshua's rise, once again, a burden was now being lifted from his shoulders. No longer would self-doubt creep into his leadership capabilities. Not so much due to his realization, but because he finally decided to embrace it, and that was what the Chairman was awaiting.

Joshua's questioning nature was never about a crisis of faith around his leadership abilities, but if it could've had a label, it would be an inward journey phase; a deep, personal, and unsettling experience that questioned the very meaning of his purpose in what has become his life's mission.

The intensity of this crisis subsided, thanks in part to the completion of his self-induced lack of confidence. With this weight now gone, he took a breath of what seemed like crisp clean air.

The veil of his confidence would now be clearer than it ever had been before; and this would not bode well for the enemy.

Joshua smiled at the council. "All right gentlemen, let's talk about the additional details."

He reached for the folder, but Stephen slid his hand over to prevent him from opening. "Joshua, as we said, there are insights into the events to come that need to be shared. What is in this folder is more like guiding principles in those events."

"Are we not going to look at these now?" Joshua said with a raised eyebrow.

"We need to convey the insights before you view the principles," said Timothy.

Joshua waited patiently thinking that if what he needed to know was not in the folder, someone else would speak up, or maybe a projector with a nifty slide show would present itself. When nothing happened in what Joshua assumed was the appropriate amount of time, he wondered if Sentinel was going to throw out some images.

A couple more seconds passed before Joshua began to understand *how* they were going to give him this information. "I'm going to have a vision, aren't I?" He groaned.

Stephen smiled sympathetically. "You might want to brace yourself."

No sooner had he finished speaking, and it felt like Joshua was shot through a cannon with a gravitational force that rivaled a rocket launch; it pushed him back into his chair making his limbs practically immobile. Of course, that was just the effect upon his mind being blown, and not the physical stress that would accompany such an event in the literal sense. Nevertheless, each time Joshua experienced these "visions" the aftermath was akin to a bad hangover. It was not something he looked forward to, and one of the many reasons he hated them.

The view was like jumping to hyperspace. A vortex of swirling images and colors changed like scenes of a live-action slide show. The first scene was of a political movement sweeping first one nation, next the world. He saw government leaders, some of which he knew; their defeat at the hands of unknown opponents, then civil unrest. The next scene showed multiple media coverage around what looked like a world health crisis. A pandemic was sweeping countries; news footages and flashes of images showed a sickness like he had never seen, then row upon row of body bags. The scene after catapulted him from ground level to earth's orbit. He watched the impossible picture of all the lights flickering out across the globe; and what appeared to be mushroom clouds of fire billowing skyward in sporadic places. Joshua quickly recognized them as nuclear explosions. A horrific sight as he has only watched something like that in high budget Hollywood movies.

This can't be happening.

He thought he could feel the heat, but knew that was impossible this far above the planet. He tried to remind himself that this was only a vision, but was then thrown into the next scene. People, dirty and bloodied walking through countrysides, smoke rising in the distance. Military tanks, aircraft, and soldiers of all nations turning on each other regardless of their country. Some had faint hues of red and green as they battled each other; slaughtered and massacred.

Associates and Familiars.

That scene was like a collage on multiple video screens. Joshua's eyes danced back-and-forth to the point of nausea. As quickly as that scene had come, it was replaced with another. A charismatic man rising to prominence. Cheers and applause from humans, and what appeared to be demons, at his leadership and control that spread across the globe; country after country falling under this man's control. The image depiction in front of Joshua reminded him of an old Nazi propaganda film from the 1940s.

It felt like the chair he was sitting in was whipped around suddenly. Joshua's eyes widened at the new scene in front of him. Persecution, slavery, death, all in the name of an anti-Christian movement. Hordes of demons mixed with humans waging war on those who served the Light. A medallion, a large broadsword, a French rapier with an ornate hilt.

The Artifacts.

They circled the image and then combined in the middle to form the Tor Embla, the enemy's weapon and symbol of leadership to destroy the threat of Christianity. Joshua looked closely and noticed the charismatic man holding the Tor Embla in one hand, and what looked like an ancient scroll in the other. That scene was pulled away from him as another crashed like an ocean wave during a storm to take its place.

Of all the images he had witnessed thus far, this new one horrified him the most. There was no blood-lusting enemy, no bombs, no death nor destruction. This one held people that he knew. General acquaintances, coworkers, family and friends, and those closest to him that he trusted and loved.

One of them would betray him.

Joshua screamed. "No!"

24

Trigger

His head jerked up, and Joshua was back in the conference room. A cold compress was on his forehead as the soft, delicate hands of a woman cradled his head gently. "It's okay, be still," came the ethereal voice.

Joshua was shaking as his wide eyes tried to focus. The young lady moved the compress gently down his face and around his neck with the skill and care of a nurturing mother. He gasped for air as he fumbled to hold onto something solid; desperate to be grounded, to have his hands on anything that would anchor him in one place. He found the heavy wooden conference table in front of him and seized it with a death grip. He needed some semblance of control to counteract everything that he had just seen.

Those vivid images of things yet to be had shaken him like nothing ever before experienced.

Joshua began to take long deep breaths. He was returning now; like coming out of a deep sleep where nightmares ruled. He looked up to his caregiver. She smiled. It was Elsbeth, the pretty angel from before. She handed him a beverage and small white pill; Joshua assumed it was an aspirin. He slowly took it as he held her gaze.

"How are you feeling?" She said.

He took a drink. "Better," he responded hoarsely. "Thank you."

A few more moments passed, and Joshua began to shake off the effects of the visions. True to his predictions, a headache began to form right behind his eyes beginning what he called the hangover process.

Elsbeth removed the compress and stepped back from the table. Only when she moved did Joshua notice the council members.

"Will there be anything else?" She asked.

Joshua almost answered her, then he realized that she was talking to Stephen.

"No, thank you," said Stephen with a head nod.

With that, Elsbeth the angel left through that same door at the back of the room.

Joshua adjusted his tie and coat, as he was sure his jerky movements through the visions were quite literal in the real world. *Real world,* he thought. Once finished, he stared expectantly at the council.

"Are you okay?" Timothy said, reinforcing Elsbeth's question.

"I am fine now," said Joshua, although not quite true as his headache began moving to his temples. "That was quite a series of videos and pictures." He couldn't think of a better description, as it felt like he was immersed in a virtual reality world.

Curiously, he asked, "Is it safe to assume that you know what I just saw?"

"Yes, Joshua. We are aware of the series of events yet to transpire," said Peter.

Joshua leaned forward businesslike with his elbows on the table. "These things, these events ... It seems impossible. I've only read or seen stuff like this in fiction. How am I supposed to come up with a plan with no support from the Chairman on its development?"

"Don't misunderstand the Chairman's involvement. From the beginning, He has pledged unlimited resources to aid you. It is your responsibility to come up with how to use this assistance," said Andrew.

Joshua thought about that for a moment. "Still, a task of this magnitude will require specialized and detailed planning at all levels. With so many moving parts–" he thought, such as the health and safety of citizens, military reinforcements and coordination, political adjustments to maintain a working government, and global economy– "it seems a bit overwhelming to prevent the chaos that I just witnessed."

Joshua was deep in thought, so he did not see some of the grim expressions crossing the faces of the council.

"Joshua," said Stephen softly, "I'm afraid that you are again, misunderstanding."

"Now what?" How could there possibly be anything else on top of what he had just heard and seen in this meeting? He waited patiently for the hammer.

"You are not meant to prevent these things to come."

Joshua stared, afraid to say anything.

"You are meant to survive it."

His look said it all. Surprised, stunned, disbelief. "I've gotta tell you," he said shaking his head slightly, "this meeting is *not* what I expected."

"Joshua, the events that you witnessed are part of the plan for humanity. Just as the same in our day, our choices can only do so much, but His Will shapes mankind's very existence. You need to remember that the Chairman has a purpose to everything He does," said Timothy.

"What about the suffering of those people that I saw, the weak, injured," Joshua paused. "All that death."

"As with every human, their fate depends on their choices. Their deaths may be inevitable, but where they go from there are two separate journeys," said Peter.

Joshua looked down in thought. "I guess some things have to happen whether we understand it or not."

Council members nodded softly.

"But, also remember," added Andrew, "some of what you have just witnessed may not come to pass in the literal sense. Certain events may be figurative in nature. As a leader, you must be able to distinguish what can and cannot be changed."

Joshua thought about that last statement in reference to the events of today at the precinct. Regardless of his decisions, he may not have been able to prevent any more or any less deaths. The outcome would not have changed. The battle was inevitable; but the elements or the components, the events within the battle, *were* controllable. This gave him hope as he thought about it like controlling the flow of water. The water itself would continue to move, but Joshua could manipulate the direction. The sheer magnitude of planning just became both harder and easier based on this one key piece of information.

Joshua's eyes focused on the folder before him. Not wanting to misunderstand anything else, he asked, "Is it time to look at this information?

Stephen nodded, "But before you do, we need to set your expectations."

Sure, why not? Joshua thought. Why would anything become easier to understand now?

"These guidelines will help you form the foundation of your planning going forward. Not all of them may be used at any given time. They could be used individually or in combination depending on the circumstances presented. What is written here is meant to help you bridge the dichotomy between reality and the impossible."

Joshua nodded thoughtfully then open the file. It contained a single sheet of paper. It was not written on parchment or in a holy script like he had imagined. It was a simple white copy paper with 12 point Arial font in boldface typing. It held only six lines that were double spaced.

Mankind must have a purpose.
Impossibilities can be overcome.
Misdirection and deception are always an option.
A lie is not a lie if it contains the truth.
Beware of the obvious.
Provide opportunity where none exist.

At first, Joshua wanted to laugh. Was this a joke? These are just fragmented parables. Things some businessman might see on those stupid success posters, or a diner might get inside of a fortune cookie. These were poorly written Japanese haikus at best. How was something like this thought of as guidelines to prevent or direct the fall of mankind?

Then Joshua looked harder, and began to understand.

These were battle tactics.

A supernatural version of the Art of War. He cocked his head as he read the lines over and over.

A purpose ... humans must have something to give them hope; to feel useful.

Impossibilities ... he is no longer bound by the mortal confines of reason or realism.

Misdirection, deception ... tactics used by the enemy can also be used by him.

Not a lie if it holds the truth ... he can skirt the edge of the rules without breaking them.

Beware the obvious ... things may not always be as clear as they appear.

Provide opportunity ... there is no such thing as a no-win scenario.

Joshua blinked as he absorbed each of the lines. *Brilliant.*

These six simple lines gave his yet to be developed plan the framework for success.

Joshua Arden had entered this meeting with assumptions that couldn't have been further from the truth. He saw visions of a future with despair and lost hope. If those visions prove true, that meant the enemy has, or is working on a plan of their own.

Mankind was no longer at a crossroad. The balance between good and evil was very precarious, and at this moment in time, leaning towards the darkness more than ever before. The cliché of one man able to save the world now fell to him. Never in his wildest imagination did he think that this was what he was born to do.

But it was true.

His destiny had been decided before his mother gave birth. It was now time to embrace it.

* * *

Joshua's walk back to his office was lonely and full of thought even though the executive floor was bustling with activity.

He thanked the Council for their time; appreciating the advice imparted and their kind words of support.

Once he left the meeting though, his mind began to race. Ideas about how to begin the plans swirled through his head like van Gogh's Starry Night. He felt the overwhelming pressure of his position, and it began to crush him like a shoe on a bug.

Joshua was so lost in concentration that his body moved through the halls automatically. Muscle memory controlled his steps while it seemed an internal radar prevented him from bumping into objects and people. Those who passed him greeted him with a smile or a cordial hello, but Joshua was immune. He was not rude in any way, but flowed through the corridors like a branch in a stream; oblivious to anything else floating nearby. It wasn't until he came to the outer doors to his office that Jillian broke his trance.

"Dr. Arden," she said with a smile. "Did you forget something?"

After realizing where he was, he looked at her with a raised eyebrow. "Excuse me?"

She looked around him. "Is Mr. Aldridge with you?"

"No, why would he be?"

Her look drifted into curiosity. "Because you and Mr. Aldridge just left a couple of minutes ago."

With a puzzled expression, Joshua looked at his watch. Sure enough, barely ninety-seconds passed. A little nausea made its way up to the back of his throat. This whole time displacement thing, or temporal break, or whatever the supernatural world called it, was very unsettling. Joshua wasn't sure why it bothered him now; it's not like this was the first time. Maybe it was a combination of that, and the strong visions that he had just experienced. He had no clue, but felt like he was going to be sick.

He put his hand on his office door. "Jillian, could you have some ginger ale brought in?"

"Of course," she said, reaching for her phone.

"Also, I need you to clear my schedule."

"Umm, okay," responding in mid-dial. She rapidly reviewed his calendar on her computer screen. "You only have a 2:30 PM this afternoon. I can push that back to–" she traced her finger across the screen over the next few days "–this Friday at 10:30 AM."

"No."

Jillian put the phone back in its cradle. "Okay, I can try to rearrange your schedule next week? Maybe a Tuesday or Wednesday?"

Joshua began to open his door. "No, that won't work either. I need the rest of this week and next week completely clear."

Jillian's eyes widened. Looking at his agenda, it was completely packed with internal meetings, executive luncheons with political and corporate power brokers, even a speaking engagement at the United Nations. "Dr. Arden, that may be a bit of a challenge–"

"Better make that the next two weeks," he said. "I'm going to be doing some work, and I don't want to be disturbed." With that, he went into his office and shut the doors behind him.

Joshua walked with the quickness towards his private bathroom, taking his coat off in the process and throwing it on his couch. He loosened his tie and undid the cufflinks on his shirt. He dropped them on the side of his vanity, rapidly pulled the sleeves up, and splashed wave after wave of cold water into his face.

His hair and shirt collar became soaked from the excess flying from his hands and dripping face. As the nausea began to subside, he paused to look at himself in the mirror. All he saw were bloodshot eyes on a disheveled, pale face. His hand traced a few small creases in the corner of his eye. Were those wrinkles? How did someone who just graduated college become so … old? He reminded himself that he wasn't the small-town boy from Wisconsin anymore, and it had been nearly ten years since he graduated. Joshua was practically thirty, but felt like he was sixty. Funny how time displacement didn't prevent aging. That was irony at its finest. He grimaced at the thought of getting older before his time, but knew that may very well be the case based on his current position and responsibilities. He heard of jobs that aged people rapidly, most due to stress or constantly being subjected to difficult situations. Joshua experienced a lot of both.

Growing older was the least of his worries now. The die was cast. He was the man; the chosen one whether he liked it or not.

A knock came to the door as it slowly opened. "Dr. Arden?" Jillian had brought him the ginger ale as requested.

He came out of the bathroom; sleeves rolled up and drying himself off with a towel. He smiled; a contrast expression from a few moments ago. "Thanks, Jillian," he said, as he walked over to her and took the drink. "Listen, I'm sorry I was so curt with you earlier." His expression softened. "I have a lot on my mind, but it was no reason to be rude."

She shook her head dismissively. "I didn't take it that way at all, sir. It's my job to ensure that your requests are met. I was just trying to work with your schedule."

He placed a hand on her forearm. "I know that," he said, then paused.

Joshua's look was very sincere; almost sorry for a wrong that didn't exist, but weighed as heavily on him as his new mission. "This may not make any sense, Jillian, but things are going to be a little different for me going forward. I'm going to need somebody to protect me from the day-to-day business activities."

She cocked her head to one side indicating that more clarity might be needed.

"I have a special project that will require my undivided focus. That means I need a bulldog in front of me to clear the way."

She smiled. "You want me to pull an Alice?"

Joshua straightened up in surprise; a coy smile spread across his face. "Yes... That's exactly what I want you to do."

She didn't need clarity at all. Joshua underestimated her intuition, and that made his smile even wider.

"Not a problem, Dr. Arden. After all, I was trained by the best." Jillian was still smiling as she left the room.

Joshua nodded in agreement as an idea popped into his head. Alice *was* the best, and he had a special job in mind for her. However, that was only one small part of this; now it was time to get down to work and figure out the rest.

He walked behind his desk tossing his towel on the edge as he began to sit, but hesitated before making contact with the chair. The guidelines from the meeting ran through his mind like a Teleprompter with a speech. When it came to the one with relevance, it stopped.

Impossibilities can be overcome. That statement held more meaning than just defying the impossible. It could also be a sign of the times; a call to embrace that which he has so long refused in a futile attempt to keep his life as simple as possible. The time had finally come for him to stop clinging to an ideal that had long lost its meaning.

He stood straight and looked about the room. It became the very definition of what had been blinding *him* in the realm of the possible. If he sat behind this desk, he would continue to think like a human. There was no longer the time or the space for linear thought. It was time to figure out a way to outsmart the enemy by whatever means appropriate within the rules.

Joshua needed to start planning, and it looked like the Chairman was providing some inspiration.

He walked from around the desk to the middle of the room. "Sentinel, are you there?"

"I am always here."

"It's time we get to know each other. Are you ready to work?"

"For you, I can clear my schedule."

"I'm glad you have a sense of humor," said Joshua with a slight grin. "I have a feeling we're going to need it. Please seal the room. We need to be invisible while we work."

A blue wave of light momentarily washed over the room preventing supernatural and human detection or entry of any kind.

"Pull up the files from this morning," said Joshua.

An array of folder directories, files, dossiers of individuals, all instantly appeared in midair.

On the assumption that Sentinel knew everything, Joshua asked, "Can you please give me a visual illustration of the visions I just experienced?"

He was pleasantly surprised by Sentinel's compliance as hard-light images of the scenes began to manifest one by one. Once the visuals completed, Sentinel categorized and grouped them chronologically based on similarities, and an assumed natural progression of despair.

Joshua scanned each of the images finally resting on the Artifacts. He was hoping once he put these into hiding, he would never have to worry about them again. He should have known it wouldn't be that easy.

His eyes glanced over all the floating images in front of him. And then, another one magically appeared. It was a list of the guidelines from his meeting. Joshua smiled at the anticipation. "Thank you," he said under his breath.

"You're welcome," came the reply.

* * *

When Melina Arden called to ask her out for lunch, Alice thought it would be a corporate excursion to one of the many eateries affiliated with Jonah. It always had been in the past when they got together, *and* it was always just the two of them.

When Melina had said she wanted to take in a show before the late lunch, Alice imagined a movie. Probably that new girly flick that came out over the weekend.

Of all the venues and themes available in the wondrous metropolis of New York City, an immersive cinema and art noir exhibition at the Whitney Museum of American Art was the last place Alice ever thought that she would go on a weekday. For that fact, it wasn't exactly her cup of tea on a weekend either.

This place was not part of the cleared and safe Associate-ran establishments, and neither was the small eatery in which they currently sat called the Untitled at the Whitney. Even though she and Alice were at their own table, there were about four other tables with three to four JPS agents each "inconspicuously" eating and trying not to be noticed.

For someone who wanted to socialize, Melina was not talking much. "Hey, you okay?" Alice asked.

Melina pushed her fork through her Arctic char, mostly just moving bits of anchovy and trout around rather than eating. Each time she moved it, a malodorous fish smell wafted through the air. Alice was sure that this was pleasing to most patrons, but she was not a big fish fan.

After dabbing her mouth from a bite of her tasty burger, she reached over and grabbed Melina's hand. "Hey," she said softly. "Where are you?"

Melina looked up and saw Alice grin. "Oh, I'm sorry Alice. I'm just …" She took her napkin and dabbed her own mouth politely. "I'm afraid I'm a poor excuse for company."

Melina looked very sad as she lowered her hand. Alice saw her eyes rimmed with tears. "Aw, honey," reaching over to comfort her. She imagined that Melina's life was stressful at the moment. She had a lot going on.

Melina's head lowered as her shoulders moved rhythmically to match her sobs. As Alice rose from her seat to be near Melina, she noticed that some of their JPS bodyguards began to shift in response. Alice held up her hand to keep them at bay. The last thing she needed was for Melina to see how far from normal their lives truly were. Alice hugged her tightly as Melina buried her face into her suit jacket. Not saying a word, Alice just let her get it all out.

With the sobs subsiding, Melina took her napkin and uncharacteristically blew her nose. Had she not been feeling so sad, Alice thought that Melina would have laughed at the sound. After all, that's who she was at heart; a carefree and happy person by nature. Always quick to spot the funny side of everything.

Alice could barely remember the last time she saw Melina smile.

Melina looked up at her with a polite, quivering grin. In an attempt to regain her composure, she nodded and patted Alice's arm. "I'm fine, really."

Alice gave her one reassuring hug before taking her own seat again. "Okay, spill it," she said in true Alice fashion. "I hate seeing one of my friends, especially my boss's wife, so upset."

Melina was back now; slightly embarrassed for losing her equanimity. "It's Joshua."

Alice being Alice, took a big bite of her burger. With her cheeks packed, she said, "Is that all? I thought it was going to be something serious."

Melina looked at her surprised at the callousness, then began to laugh at the absurdity of Alice eating like a diner at a truck stop.

Alice began to cough as she tried to choke down the bite and keep from laughing herself at the same time. "Mission accomplished," she said taking a drink to wash the final piece down.

Melina shook her head. "And this is why I came to you." She knew that Alice would be able to take her ever-depressing mood and turn it around.

"Seriously," said Alice regaining her businesslike composure, at least for her. "What's got you so bummed?" Still smiling as she said it, Alice too, had growing concerns about her boss.

"He's been so ... distant lately," said Melina.

"Tell me about it," came the sarcastic reply.

"It's like when he's there, he's not!"

"At least you can see him."

"Not during the day."

"I don't even get passed Jillian. She's always intercepting and weaving; making excuses for why Joshua can't be bothered. I tell you, sometimes it ticks me off."

Melina smiled. "It ticks you off because she is just like you."

"What?"

"Oh come on Alice, you would have done the same thing."

Alice thought for a second. "Well, I wouldn't be such a b—"

"Yes, you would."

"I would've been a lot nicer."

"No, you wouldn't."

"*I* am his Chief of Staff," said Alice changing the direction.

"So?"

"That is supposed to get me in the door."

"Says who?"

"Says *me*! We have important things to go over."

"Apparently not."

Alice looked genuinely shocked. "My job is extremely important!"

"I never said it wasn't."

"Well, you're acting like it."

"Not really, I'm just saying that nobody, regardless of their position, are getting anywhere near him."

"Again, at least you get to see him."

"*Again*," countered Melina, "he's not there when he is."

They looked at each other. The two of them bantered back-and-forth like the Gilmore Girls.

They smiled. It was very cathartic for both. Each had their own pressure cooker of stress, and that little exercise helped relieve some of the tension.

"Alice, do you have any idea what he's working on?" Melina's tone held the seriousness associated with life or death.

"No, not a clue. Langston and Kelan are just as in the dark as we are. Jillian says she doesn't know either. All she will tell me is that Joshua said he didn't want to be bothered until further notice. We've even tried to ask Sentinel, who apparently knows pretty much everything."

"And what did it say?" Melina asked.

"That we do not have the clearance." Alice said annoyed.

Melina's eyes went wide. "Really?! The three of you have more clearance than anyone I know."

"Not for what's going on behind those doors." Alice paused for a second. "How are things at home?"

"Pretty much the same. I'll ask how things are going; he'll give me one or two words but no specifics. Regardless of clearance, he has always told me things. More so to share the burden of his responsibilities, I think. But never anything more that would endanger me or his mission. It's just, you know," she went on further to explain. "He needs someone to confide in." Melina looked down like she was losing her best friend. "I thought my responsibility as his wife was to support him."

"And I'm sure that is still something he wants and needs." Alice said reassuringly. "Knowing Joshua for as long as I have, my gut tells me that whatever is happening, he is purposefully keeping us at a distance to protect us."

"You don't think it's anything more than that?"

"You know he can't do any of this without us," said Alice with a smirk. "I think when the time is right, he will let us know."

"It has been weeks," said Melina.

"I know, honey. I can promise you that it won't be like this forever. Joshua has got something big brewing. You and I both know how fixated he can become when he's in the middle of a project."

"I know," replied Melina knowing her husband. "The whole building could be burning around him, and he would still be trying to figure something out on a whiteboard."

"Yep," said Alice with a grin remembering the years of working with him.

Both ladies remain silent for a bit. Alice noticed a familiar thoughtfulness coming from Melina as she stared through the table into nothing.

"Still haven't told him?"

"I can't right now," came the response in barely a whisper. "It's just not the right time."

"Honey, you need to find the right time. He's going to find out eventually."

* * *

Joshua sat alone in the empty room that was his office. It was void of any life or movement. Even the sunlight from the full-length window was masked and dulled due to the protective shield that Sentinel placed around them as they worked. It was like that by design as he didn't even want the birds to look in. The only visible illumination came from ambient objects such as the surface light over his juice bar, or the sink light from the bathroom that Joshua occasionally left on from the many trips back and forth.

A meal tray from the cafeteria sat on the coffee table in front of his couch. The food was half eaten and picked through, as was normal these days.

His only human contact besides Melina was Jillian, who left a fresh tray in replacement for the previous one. Even then, his assistant was not allowed into the office. She simply left the tray outside the door like a hotel steward. Sometimes, she would catch a brief glimpse of the door closing, but never saw him, or the tray exchange.

He came to the building before anyone else, and was the last to leave. Never deviating from his routine, he was always locked in his office. It was as if Dr. Joshua Arden had disappeared from the face of the earth.

The burden of seclusion and isolation was beginning to wear on him. He stopped shaving after the second week; what was the point? Of course, he had Sentinel, but eventually those just became lights and a voice hanging in midair. For its vast intelligence, Sentinel was only his partner in crime with whom he had any contact or conversation; even so, he was still not human.

Time had started to lose its meaning as he poured over every single detail. He rewrote, rethought, and reanalyzed each section of the intricate plan to the point of where he began to second-guess previous decisions. There was a moment where he began to understand the conflict that Ernest Hemingway had felt in rewriting *A Farewell to Arms* thirty-nine separate times. Without his team, he had no barometer or sounding board to provide rational logic to his thinking.

Unfortunately, that was by design. This had to be a secret. The only way to keep a true secret was not to share it with anyone. This was for their protection. They would understand someday.

The days passed as they began to melt into each other; until it finally appeared it was all coming to an end.

Joshua rubbed his eyes. "Plan analysis."

"Situational interpretation, considering the variables on human nature and unpredictability, have given your plan and 89.7% chance of success. Contingencies to address the remaining 10.3% for each section are sound. You have employed the Tenth Man Rule for each given stage, whereby covering all aspects to enable the desired results." Sentinel replied.

"Intelligence." Joshua said through a yawn.

"All global government, corporate, and private agencies, networked and isolated, are now connected to the Great Hall of Records. Keyword search algorithms based on known data have been cross-referenced and categorized with plan stages. Satellite, drone, and supernatural reconnaissance will be ready to provide off-grid information as directed by the plan. Once the intelligence theater is active, all information will flow to the Achilles Dome for redistribution, activity, and execution."

Joshua nodded his head thoughtfully. "Construction."

"Properties of interest, depots, storage facilities, medical units, safe houses, and waypoints have been identified to support the initial stages of the plan. Once the word is given, locations for strategic construction and development will begin. All points will be connected through the Plexus and networked on a modulated frequency through the Quantum Transmatter Gate controlled by me. Once completed, all mission facilities will be fully operational and transparent to the enemy."

"Recruitment."

"Resource selection is 73% complete. Algorithms have, and are continuing, to identify key individuals to populate each facet of mission parameters, as well as the operational staff for the Achilles Dome.

Upon completion of the Ever, recruitment will be at 100% with an additional 15% projected for Undeclared on boarding."

"Military."

"All global resources with military and government civilian experience has been identified and included within the recruitment selection process."

"Warfare."

The room came alive with hard-light images of strategic maps and plans.

"Enemy movement will be coordinated with our intelligence division. Battle simulations, active theaters of war, and predictable enemy patterns have been identified based on current technology, active conflicts, and historical wars predating 2700 B.C.E. Mesopotamia. All are catalogued and referenceable upon request by personnel with proper security clearance."

"Our forces?" Joshua asked.

"Associate civilian, government, and military forces across the globe will be retrofitted with the most advanced technology and surveillance capabilities currently in existence. Supernatural augmentation, to include tactical hand-to-hand combat, will be available by your direction as needed to support all military and clandestine operations throughout the mission."

"Cooperative employment."

"All resources nonessential to government and/or military applications will be reassigned and placed based on preferences, skill set, and contribution capacity beginning at initial transport to the Ever, and the first wave of the Harvest."

A timely segue, thought Joshua. "The Harvest."

"Off boarding will begin at your command. Strategic personnel will be in the first wave. Medical, religious, and selective government leadership will be in the second wave, followed by military assets in the third. All other nonessentials will be coordinated through disembarkation points as outlined within the plan."

Joshua walked slowly through the room. "Let me see it all."

In addition to the warfare summarization hanging in the air, every facet of the plan now floated with hard-light imagery brilliance, and filled the entire workspace. Joshua watched the steady streams of information flow through, around, and back-and-forth all the planned phases.

This was it. From his vantage point, it looked like the Plan was complete. After a few more seconds of careful consideration and thought, Joshua paused. With one more look over everything that he had been working on in the last four weeks, he asked his only confidant a single question. "Are we ready?"

"This is a good plan, Joshua. We are ready to go on your command."

The anticipation of this finally coming to a reality now hinged on Joshua's word. Once given, there was no turning back. He straightened up and walked over to his desk. He folded down and fastened his sleeves; straightened his tie and put on his suit coat. Walking back around to the front of his desk, he took one last glance at everything he had developed. "Close all files and seal classified documents. Initiate phase one of the Gathering on my mark."

One by one, as if turned off by a light switch, all components of the Plan shutdown and disappear.

Joshua stared intently into the nothingness.

"Trigger."

Epilogue

New York City on a crisp Sunday morning. Midtown Manhattan wasn't busy, but still active enough to maintain the city's reputation of one that never sleeps.

The trains at Penn Station were running on schedule, but as with everything else at 6:27 AM, not nearly as congested like normal.

The New York Knicks hosted the Washington Wizards the night before at Madison Square Garden. The venue was not at capacity, but still had a decent turnout. It was unfortunate that the home team lost by seven points.

The game was over by 10:00 PM, with facilities shutting down a little after midnight. No more events were scheduled outside of MSG's All-Access Tour, which normally began at 9:30 AM on most mornings. However, no tours were scheduled on this day. The venue would be completely vacant. Even if a tour was planned it would be much later in the morning, and only include the known areas of the arena.

No one had any idea about the subterranean levels far below the trains and sewer lines. Construction and maintenance entrances throughout New York's underground existed for many reasons; mostly to provide easy access to infrastructure utilities such as communications or electric, gas, and water conduits. Today these passages were used for something entirely different. Not even Consolidated Edison came down here.

A lone figure walked through the dark and dank tunnels; turning through stairwells and walkways like someone who knew these forgotten passages well.

After one last turn, the claustrophobic space opened into an unexpected cavernous area. Where most people would question why a large space like this was in existence in a forgotten part of Manhattan; this individual simply stopped and looked around, as if trying to locate something specific.

Seventy-five yards away, was a portico under which was a lone single door. The wandering soul headed towards it without hesitation; as if being beckoned. Once reached, a blue wave of light shimmered as it came down to allow access.

As soon as the individual opened the door, a wave of fresh light washed into the dark cavern. Once the woman passed through the entrance, an ethereal hand released from their charge upon completing the mission. The guardian angel then shimmered away to avoid any detection by enemy forces.

* * *

The chancellor from Germany entered what looked like a ballroom. It was large, but not ostentatious. There were three hanging chandeliers, ceiling to floor length drapes complementing the cherry oak walls and matching carpet. Rows of chairs sat next to each other facing what looked like a nondescript platform.

Hundreds of people milled about talking quietly with each other. She noticed the British prime minister with his Canadian counterpart. Off to one side, she saw the American president speaking with some other people, and some fellow G8 leaders talking with other notable and influential people from across the globe.

She saw that none of the heads of state had any security contingent flanking them. She thought that strange for a second, until she looked at her side and noticed that her own detachment was not present as well. It seemed to have not made a difference to her, and felt no sense of threat or danger. It was as if she was supposed to be there, in this place, at this time. Thinking nothing of it, she headed towards one of her European counterparts. They greeted her warmly with a handshake, and began chatting as if this meeting was a standard part of their political routine.

As if on a silent cue, conversations quieted and people began to find seats. The attendees of this event were made up of the Who's Who of their specialized fields.

From Jonah International, Joshua Arden's top team; Langston, Kelan, and Alice. Jonathan Sinclair, Director of International Relief sat next to Jonah's CEO, Malcolm Holden. Joshua's bodyguard and head of security detail from JPS, Tim Marshall rounded out the top Jonah officers.

Other notable top executives from Jonah sat within the corporate cluster as well. Next to Alice, was Joshua's wife, Melina. Sitting next to Melina was Joshua's guardian and closest person to a mother, Amanda Gibson. She was the global chairman for One-World Health, one of Joshua's passions to provide healthcare around the world.

A few rows back to the right, sat Albert Masters, the current President of United States. Alongside him were a couple of his cabinet members, and the chairman of the Joint Chiefs, General Raymond Mc-Cready. Government agency representatives such as the FBI, CIA, and NSA directors also sat near POTUS.

Pockets of other clusters included notable representatives and heads of state from Germany, Australia, Canada, and other influential countries, which had strong ties with Jonah. The remainder of the attendees were comprised of high-level people within the communications media, entertainment industry, religious and medical communities, corporate conglomerates, and military personnel, just to name a few. The total attendees for this event was upwards around 150 souls.

Never in the history of world events, has a more influential group of people gathered in a stripped-down, informal setting such as this. Coordination of something of this magnitude would normally take months, if not years, based on individual schedules, security requirements, and cooperation. This meeting, however, was scheduled and deployed within days, and all done by Sentinel.

The more-than-artificial intelligence worked its supernatural magic to bypass individual security requirements for heads of state, and other notable professionals as needed. Sentinel secured individual private transportation from around the globe, fabricated and cleared schedules as necessary to ensure their time away, all while not raising any suspicions. He led them all using suggestive guidance by their angelic guardians from the Majaliant Elodine. At no time, was any human technology and/or intervention used in bringing all those needed for phase one known as the Gathering. This was completely untraceable, and off the grid.

Of course, everyone initially contacted had a choice to make. None who were present was forced or coerced by their position or relationship to Joshua or Jonah International. If they decided not to participate in the plan, it would simply be a matter of employing the next-man-in method. All of this was part of Joshua's plan. Each person present chose to be there and offer their support. There wasn't one single person initially contacted that chose otherwise.

The room fell into an unexpected silence. For a gathering of over 150, not a sound could be heard. Within a matter of seconds, the single door into the room opened, and in walked Joshua Arden. He was clean-shaven now; however, not wearing a standard business suit. For that fact, most of the men and women around the room were dressed in casual attire. Joshua sported jeans, and a familiar hoodie that he used to wear in his college days. He caught the eyes of some who were in attendance as he made his way to the small stage. He grinned and nodded greetings to the ones that he could, then took his place on the elevated platform.

There was no podium or sound system; he did not need it, for his voice would carry above anything else. Joshua simply stood there and began addressing the crowd.

"Ladies and gentlemen, thank you all for coming. I know that this," he said gesturing around the room, "and the method for getting you here seems a bit unorthodox, but it is necessary to prepare for what is coming. Absolute secrecy is required.

"I brought you here because I need your help. I have been given a mission that I cannot do alone. It would be hard to explain in any other terms, but I need your help to save people."

Everyone in the room began to mumble at that statement.

"More specifically, souls," said Joshua.

The room became quiet again; all stared back at him with uncertainty or lack of understanding.

"Some of you have partnered in the past with Jonah to provide aid and hope where none existed." Joshua's eyes fell across people like Jonathan Sinclair and his international relief team. He looked at the heads of state from many of the partnering countries. He glanced at Amanda Gibson and her dedication to the One-World Health initiatives. As their eyes met, they both smiled at each other affectionately.

"Others have aided our movement to ensure that mankind remains immune to the evils of this world." Joshua looked to representatives from the clergy, communications, and entertainment media.

"While our cause has participated in many battles over many centuries, the ongoing war continues to take its toll, and fair share of casualties. I've recently discovered some disturbing trends," Joshua paused. He wasn't exactly sure how to say this based upon his findings and the visions. He looked down and to the side as if he was searching for the correct words. The last thing he wanted to do was alarm those whose help he needed the most.

"Trends that point to the end of mankind as we know it."

Horrific and terrified looks began to cross some faces. Melina and Alice both brought their hands up to their mouths. Everyone in the room that had worked with Joshua, knew he would not have made a statement like this lightly unless he had unequivocal proof to back it up. No one challenged him; they waited for him to present it.

"Enemy movement has increased in areas of theft and murder." Hard-light illumination to illustrate Joshua's words appeared. Everyone's eyes were drawn immediately to it.

The depiction showed real-life images of some of the file content that Joshua had been assembling over the last couple of months. The murder of a security guard at a Taiwanese technology company due to the theft of an unknown component. The loss of a significant biological agent from the CDC in Atlanta; the recovery of a body at an abandoned prison with a dossier showing the identity as a CDC employee. The next image was an aerial shot of a burning building on the campus of MIT, and all the bodies being recovered.

Joshua watched with the audience as other disturbing images showed the targets and activities of additional events. Each one could've been a newsreel from an evening broadcast; nevertheless, the men and women in this room knew that combined, they all meant something entirely different.

Just as quickly as the images appeared, they vanished. The lights in the ballroom came back up. "The enemy has already begun their plans to—" started Joshua.

"What plans? Are they targeting nuclear installations? Are they creating a biological weapon?" These questions came from the section of the room that held the news media and trusted Associate reporters.

"We don't know what the enemy's plans are—" began Joshua.

"Then how are we supposed to fight them?!" Said another reporter. She seemed on the edge of hysteria.

People began to murmur as they speculated. Joshua held up his hand for silence. "Ladies and gentlemen, I am not here to answer questions. I'm simply giving you some of the information that I know to solicit your help."

"How are people like us supposed to help?" Said somebody from the entertainment field. "It sounds like the military would be more qualified." He gestured towards those in uniform.

Jonathan Sinclair rose from his chair and turned to face the audience. "In all the years that we have worked together for the cause, have you ever had reason to question the purpose or direction of the Chairman of Jonah International?"

People paused to consider that statement.

Jonathan looked at those who spoke. When no response came, his eyes searched the rest of the audience.

"Now, Dr. Arden assembled us to help. There is something that each of us can contribute to ensure the success and continuity of our way of life." He nodded confidently, then turned back around to take his seat. "I'm sure that the Chairman has a plan."

That statement seemed to be pointed directly towards Joshua. All eyes fell upon him.

"No."

Confusion crossed Jonathan's face as whispering around the room began to swell.

"*I* do." Joshua's response seemed to resonate through the room. Once again, everyone fell silent.

"I have been given additional information and insight to the coming events, and know what must be done. I have a plan."

"By accepting the invitation to this meeting, you have indicated your support. All of you were given a choice, but now I'm going to give you a second chance to reconsider." He looked around patiently. No one made a move showing they wanted to leave.

Joshua tried not to show his frustration. "I am serious, people. I have worked for weeks developing a very detailed plan. There is not a single person in here that cannot be replaced." He wagged his finger around the room pointing in general directions. "You are my first choice, but if you don't want this, you are free to walk away. Once you return home, you won't remember any of this. The plan will still be intact with or without your participation."

No one said a word. No one certainly questioned whether their memory could be erased if they chose not to stay.

Joshua looked around waiting for someone to challenge him. Langston, Kelan, Alice, and even Melina, had seen that look before. They knew better than anyone, that Joshua would not tolerate any-one second-guessing him. He could do it to himself all day long, but no one else would dare.

"I am not accustomed to being questioned on my directives or orders. I never wanted this position, but I have it. The Chairman chose *me*. I committed to this because years ago *I* was given a choice, and I chose to make a difference."

He looked around and waited expectantly. Still, no one made a move to leave.

"Good."

Joshua took a couple of deep breaths to calm down. He didn't like getting his dander up over things that were inconsequential given the light of the current situation. However, he had to remember that not everyone in this room had his same level of exposure to the reality that he had been living in for so many years. They would naturally be scared, after all, they were only human.

"Look around the room, then to your left, then right. You are no longer competitors of industry. You are no longer countries at odds. You are no longer separated by positions, genders, races, or religions. Your stations in life are now equal.

"You all have a common enemy; one that doesn't care about anything except your soul. The enemy doesn't even care about that. It simply wants to hurt the Chairman. If it is in my power, I cannot allow that.

"We will all have different roles going forward. Each of you has a part in the plan, and will operate independently. None of you will know what the others are doing. It is the only way to protect you and the plan. You will not be concerned about the plan as a whole; that is my job. Your individual assignments will be given to you within the week. I will be your only contact."

Joshua looked around. He saw resilience in a few faces. The scared look in those that asked questions seemed to be gone. Everyone looked as if they were prepared to do what it took to make the plan work. Inwardly, Joshua smiled. They looked like a team.

As he was about to close the meeting, one last person spoke up. "Dr. Arden, can we really stop the enemy from doing more of the terrible things that we saw?" Referring to the images from earlier.

"I don't know, but we are sure going to try. They have made mistakes in the past," he said, remembering the failed attempts on his life, letting the woman Kelly Granger survive to provide a crucial clue, and most recently, subtle elements of events from the files that he has been researching.

"They will make more. The actual show of force is going to come from the Chairman. That is the real power behind everything that we are going to do," finished Joshua.

"What makes you think they won't be expecting a show of force?"

"Nothing at all; in fact, I am counting on it."

"Sir?"

Joshua stared with cold determination. "They won't be expecting *this.*"

Dear reader,

We hope you enjoyed reading *Plan: Chaos Rising*. Please take a moment to leave a review, even if it's a short one. Your opinion is important to us.

Discover more books by Steven Neil Moore at
https://www.nextchapter.pub/authors/steven-neil-moore

Want to know when one of our books is free or discounted? Join the newsletter at http://eepurl.com/bqqB3H

Best regards,
Steven Neil Moore and the Next Chapter Team

About the Author

Steven Neil Moore is an author of the Joshua Chronicles; an epic series about an age-old conflict and a young man caught in the middle. The first book in the nine-part series *Glorious Incorporated* sets the stage for the boy who would become a leader and change the face of the world forever. Steven's passion for character details and their expressive conflict highlight each story thread and gets the reader hooked into cheering for the good guy while hating the bad. He is continuing on with the next part of the series while also developing a standalone romance, Echo's of Ella. He lives on the East Coast of the United States with his wife and three sons.

Plan: Chaos Rising
ISBN: 978-4-82410-139-6

Published by
Next Chapter
1-60-20 Minami-Otsuka
170-0005 Toshima-Ku, Tokyo
+818035793528
26th August 2021

Lightning Source UK Ltd.
Milton Keynes UK
UKHW011849140921
390594UK00001B/113